Contessa

Ex-Libris

ROBERT G. EVERDING

Also by Richard Oliver Collin

Imbroglio
Winter of Fire

Contessa

Richard Oliver Collin

St. Martin's Press

NEW YORK

Design by Barbara Bachman

Library of Congress Cataloging-in-Publication Data

Collin, Richard.
    Contessa / Richard Oliver Collin.
        p.   cm.
    ISBN 0-312-09773-5
    1. Man-woman relationships—Italy—Fiction.   2. World War,
1939–1945—Italy—Fiction.   I. Title.
PS3553.0474694C66   1994
813'.54—dc20   *93-44049*
                                                          CIP

First Edition: May 1994
10   9   8   7   6   5   4   3   2   1

*For
Al Zuckerman*

SOUTHERN EUROPE AND THE CENTRAL MEDITERRANEAN AFTER WORLD WAR I

Book
One

1911

I.

. . . .

I am only the garden girl, she thought. Why did they send for me?

Her hands were already shaking. To avoid upsetting the Irish porcelain pot of steaming coffee, she paused upon the staircase and rested the tray against the mahogany banister.

Who is "they"? Who actually sent for me?

Was it possible that Count Leonida Leone had seen her digging potatoes in the kitchen garden and ordered her into his presence? No, surely it was more likely that His Excellency's son had ordained this horrible embarrassment.

Damn! If Achille wanted to see me, after going away for two long years, he could have come to the cottage. In the evening, perhaps. When no one was around. Instead, word comes down to the kitchen that I have two minutes to wash between my toes, find my shoes, and learn how to serve coffee to him and his father, like a serving maid instead of a garden girl.

Who does he think he is?

Who indeed? Rosaria's anger drained away, leaving only the venial fear of making a fool of herself. Achille has always known precisely who he was, she thought, climbing the last few steps to the second floor. Even when we were children, he was always Achille, and we were always just us.

Feeling small, she nudged the door open with her hip, wondering if she ought to knock. She was stunned at the enormity of the space. There were thousands of leather-bound books on shelves along the walls, and—since these May mornings were still cool—a cedar log burned slowly in the fireplace. The sun poured through a bay window to the east and in the distance Rosaria could see the foothills of the Apennines.

There was no sign of Count Leone.

"Ah, signorina!" At the distant end of the study a tall slender youth with sandy hair was sprawled on a couch. With his stocking feet on the coffee table, he was reading that morning's *Messaggero* from Rome. After two years at the Military Academy, Achille had just become a lieutenant, and Rosaria expected to find him in a uniform with ribbons and insignia, like the costume his noble father wore to visit the King.

Instead, he was in mufti, wearing faded khaki trousers and a white shirt. It was wrinkled and she wondered who would be assigned to press his cottons now that he was home.

"Buon giorno, signor . . ." Her voice trailed off as she wondered what to call this young *tenente*. When I was a little girl, I called him Achille, and he called me Rosi. Once he kissed me in the garden. Now he calls me signorina? How things have changed!

"Let me help." Bowing courteously, as if he were in the presence of a lady, Achille took the tray from her hands.

"Grazie, signore." She felt his alert brown eyes scrutinizing her. Was there something wrong? After the summons, she had raced back to the cottage and changed into her best wool skirt and put on a clean cotton blouse, not too badly worn, with a pretty frill along the neckline. And before sending her upstairs, the kitchen staff had inspected her, making sure her buttons were in place and her long auburn hair was neatly tied in back.

She felt a ripple of excitement run through her body and shyly raised her eyes to Achille. He had not changed much. He was thinner and his hair was very short. His eyes were still beautiful and he looked more like his father than ever.

What does he think of me? I was only sixteen when he went away. Is that why he sent for me today? To see how much I have changed?

"How good it is to see you. How is your brother?" Achille Leone extended his arms. For one frenzied instant she thought he was going to hug her but instead he offered his right hand for a handshake.

"My brother's looking forward to seeing you, Signor Achille." It felt silly, shaking hands like Englishmen. "Sandro never changes."

"Really? I hear he's become quite the revolutionary. Look, would you tell him to meet me at Savarino's Trattoria tomorrow for lunch? We can argue about pasta and politics."

For years now, young Sandro Lombardi had been the tallest man in Cederna, and he had now become the town's leading advocate of revolutionary socialism. This was a topic she wished to avoid, so Rosaria poured out the coffee and added a heaping spoonful of Demerara sugar and a splash of hot fresh milk. "Well, we're all glad you're home. You were gone so long."

"At the academy, we only got two furloughs," he apologized. "For the first one, Father carted me off to London to practice my English. And last year, I went to Paris with my friend Guido for a bit of soldierly hell-raising."

"And where will you be sent now?"

"Not far. I've been assigned to an infantry training battalion over in Bracciano. My wicked father pulled some strings so I could spend my weekends at home."

"That's good. Shall I . . . ah, pour His Excellency's coffee?"

"No, Father's still in bed." Achille laughed. "To celebrate my homecoming, we sat up half the night with a bottle of his Vecchia Romagna, and I think he will be sleeping late this morning."

"His coffee will get cold."

"That's your coffee." He shrugged, as if she had missed the point.

Dazed, she sat down and poured a cup of cappuccino for herself, savoring the taste of genuine coffee. Every morning in their cottage, she and her brother Sandro brewed coffee, but it was so expensive that they mixed the cheapest grind available with hickory to make it last longer, and then drank it black and bitter, since sugar cost almost as much as coffee.

"Now, Rosaria." He smiled at her. "Tell me what you know about typing machines."

"I don't know what a typing machine is." She gulped her coffee, her mind registering a blank.

"But you still remember your letters?"

"Of course. I read all the time." The question made her indignant. Back in the days when Achille and Sandro had been teenagers and she had been their collective little sister, they had taught her to read. It had been more of a lark than anything else, since girls hardly needed book-learning to secure husbands and raise babies, but Rosaria had clung to literacy.

I never forgot anything you taught me, she almost told him.

"Then this should be easy for you. Are you ready?"

Jumping to her feet, she realized that she had been summoned for more than cappuccino and chat. Oh, Achille, don't change things too fast, she pleaded with him mentally. When you made them give me a job as garden girl, I could do it because my family has always grown things. But we know nothing about machines.

Achille led her to a little alcove under the bay window. Through the glass, she could see the little tufa-brick cottage she shared with Sandro. A kilometer to the east, the red tile roof tops of Cederna gleamed vermilion in the morning sun. At this very moment, she reflected, the other girls are lining up at the well with buckets on their hips. And I'm up here with Achille Leone.

"Signorina Rosaria, I present the first Italian typewriter." His voice was jubilant as he made her sit down. "It is called the Olivetti M-1. See, it has a back-space key here, and a two-color ribbon so you can type Sandro's speeches in revolutionary red. It also has a multiple margin adjustment capability, just like an American Remington. But our Olivetti was designed by an Italian, so it is also very beautiful."

"Is it beautiful?" She felt utterly stupid. Before her was a gleaming black machine with lettered keys and a confusing array of levers and wheels. She twisted around to face him, terrified that she would reveal herself to be nothing more than a contadina, an ignorant peasant. "What does it do?"

"It gets you out of the kitchen garden and into a real profession."

Rosaria heard the intensity in his voice. "But what . . . specifically?"

"It prints words on paper. They've had machines like this in America for a long time, but a man named Olivetti has just produced an Italian model, and I bought one for my father."

"Why?"

"Father is a busy man, even though he's no longer active in the government." From a stack on the window, Achille took a sheet of paper and fed it deftly into the Olivetti. The platen made a clicking sound as he turned a little wheel on the side. "He has this whole estate to run, and our investments in England, and Prime Minister Giolitti keeps calling him back for odd jobs even though he's trying to stay retired. My brother and sister are not much help, and I'll still be away a lot. Besides . . ."

"Yes?" she asked breathlessly."

"Besides, I've convinced Father to write his memoirs. He can't seem to get started, so he needs a secretary. And you need a career."

"Signor Achille, I can't . . ." she faltered, her eyes filling with tears.

"Yes, you can. Find the *r* and we'll do your name."

Rosaria heard the tone of command in his voice. Gadgets had been Achille's passion ever since his days as an engineering student at the University of Rome. Rosaria still remembered the awful day when he had appeared in Cederna with a *trebbiatrice,* a threshing machine, ordering Sandro to bridle four horses for a trial run. Fearing that the newfangled steel contraption would cost them their jobs, the field hands called a wild-cat strike. For the first time, Sandro had defied Achille, refusing to lead out the horses until the Count himself had intervened, promising that the grain threshers would be given other jobs.

But they had been using the thresher ever since, she reminded herself, and Achille always gets his way. So calm down. Systematically, she started at the top row of buttons and scanned from left to right until she found the one marked *r.* She pounded it and a little hammer appeared from out of the bowels of the instrument, struck the paper sharply, and then vanished, leaving a tiny neat *r* printed upon the white paper.

"Not so hard," he cautioned. "It's a very sensitive mechanism. Now the *o.*"

O took more of a search, but after she had successfully hammered out "Rosaria Lombardi," Achille set her to work printing out the alphabet from beginning to end, and then gave her a letter to type. Written with a pen in Achille's neat, rectangular script, it was a short note to his army friend, Guido Rosselli, who was in Venice on leave. Thrilled at the idea of participating in Achille's social life, she was patiently printing the letter one character at a time when the door opened at the far end of the study.

She had been expecting Count Leonida Leone to emerge from his bedroom with a nobleman's hangover, but it was only Girolamo, a wizened old soldier who had followed Leonida Leone through all his wars and adventures and now served as majordomo for the Castello Leone. He was the oldest and most powerful member of the castle's hierarchy of servants, but Girolamo had always been kind to her in a gruff and grandfatherly way.

Girolamo whispered something in Achille's ear and the young man frowned. Then he sauntered over to his father's giant oak desk and found a lengthy handwritten document.

"My sister needs to see me," he said, and she could tell that he was suddenly irritated. "After you've finished my note, perhaps you could work on this for my father. If it could be done when he wakes up, it would make a great impression on him." He placed the paper next to the Olivetti and strode toward the study door.

Scanning the second letter, she found that His Excellency's handwriting was nowhere as good as Achille's. Count Leone's long letter was addressed to an Englishman with the impossibly complex name of George Macauley Trevelyan, who had apparently just written a book about Garibaldi.

"Come and see what I'm doing!" she called to Girolamo as soon as they were alone. "Achille is going to make me into a secretary."

"Girl, you watch yourself up here!" There was a frown on Girolamo's deeply lined face. "That young man has always had a soft spot for you, and Cederna is full of girls with fat bellies and no husbands."

"Don't talk to me like that!" Her fantasies about Achille had always involved hazy, romantic visions where he swept her chastely into his arms and vowed to love her forever. Getting pregnant had never occurred to her.

"Rosaria, Rosaria," he soothed her. "I know this family. My father worked for His Excellency's father, and he was a perfect devil with peasant girls. And as for Leonida Leone himself . . ." Girolamo hesitated and fell silent, since discretion forbade a recitation of his master's sins.

"His Excellency must have been a good man to become a general and a count," Rosaria objected.

"Fidelity to the Sixth Commandment was not a key factor in His Excellency's career. He got to be a general because he was good at winning battles and the Leone family got the title a thousand years ago from some medieval Pope."

"And Achille will be a count when His Excellency dies?" Rosaria wondered how Achille would treat her when he became the undisputed master of the Cederna Estate.

"As the oldest son, Achille inherits everything," Girolamo said and hobbled toward the door. "But you are never going to be a contessa, girl, even if a count gets you pregnant. So watch yourself."

I've missed her, Achille admitted to himself, pausing on the landing on his way down the central staircase to gaze out at the formal gardens.

How long has it been? I was twenty-two in 1909, when I left for the academy, and she was sixteen, with skinny legs and bright brown eyes and braids in her hair. It was a cold, rainy day in September, and she rushed up just as I was getting into the Fiat and gave me a bouquet of wildflowers. She said she was going to miss me.

We were alone, and I administered a brotherly hug and went to kiss her chastely on the forehead. Instead, at the last instant, she raised her face and I kissed her on the mouth.

Hard. I kissed her hard on the lips.

The memory evoked a rueful smile and a tingle in his groin. Then I got in the car and Rosi ran away crying. Father laughed when he saw the flowers, understanding everything in an instant. I was embarrassed. Once we got onto the main road, he dropped the bouquet out the window.

What did I promise with that kiss? Does she still remember?

"Giorgina? Girolamo said you wanted me?" In the salon, Achille found his sister, Giorgina Leone Benelli, irritably smoking her habitual Turkish cigarette. He approached her with diffidence. As the firstborn, Giorgina had always asserted her absolute primacy over her two younger brothers, and had now extended her dominion to include Bruno Benelli, her husband.

We assumed marriage would soften her, he reflected, but she's twenty-seven now, and as belligerent as ever. And being pregnant didn't seem to have cheered her up much. With a private smile, Achille tried to imagine the scene of Giorgina's being impregnated by the plump, roly-poly Bruno, but the scene was beyond his powers of imagination.

"Fratellino, what is Sandro's sister doing upstairs?" Giorgina stabbed the cigarette into an ashtray and glared at him furiously. "You can't expect to drop in here every few years and scramble my staff around to satisfy your puerile emotional attachments. I run this household, and I decide who works where!"

Achille took a deep breath to master his anger. "I asked Rosaria to try her hand at our new typing machine. She's very bright, you know, and Father does need a secretary."

"Rosaria's a contadina. Since when do peasants become secretaries? And since you've been away, that huge brother of hers has become an absolute Marxist pig. Sergeant Cirillo has been around more than once asking questions about him."

"Giorgina, the days are gone when we could sit up here in our castle and tell everyone down in Cederna what to think. Besides, Sandro's beliefs have nothing to do with his sister. Doesn't she do well as your garden girl?"

"Potatoes don't seem to mind being grown by a socialist." Giorgina puffed yellow smoke in his direction.

"I don't understand your hostility."

"I'll draw you a picture! If you want a peasant girl for a mistress, have the decency to keep her out of sight somewhere."

"Giorgina, she's not my mistress."

"She will be by midnight. The day is young."

"Listen, I'm an honorable man."

"You're your father's son," Giorgina snapped.

"I want her to learn to type."

"And I want her to peel potatoes for tonight's dinner, and that's final!"

Too angry to negotiate, Achille spun on his heel and he marched out of the *salotto,* furious that Giorgina should have focused with such precision on the heart of his problem with Rosaria.

I've never touched her, he kept repeating beneath his breath as he climbed the stairs. One foolish kiss two years ago, but nothing more.

He paused at the entrance to his father's office and looked in. Rosaria was bent over the Olivetti, chewing on her lower lip as she pounded out one letter after another, so intent upon her task that she was unaware of his presence.

Suddenly she sighed, as if losing heart. Then she glanced toward the door, catching him in the act of staring at her. They both blushed. "It's going so slowly."

"Oh, please, keep trying." He entered the room, wondering if she realized that he was in love with her.

"I'll try." She gazed at him questioningly before returning to her task with a nod.

He ran through his options for the hundredth time. Sandro is my best friend, so I can hardly have his sister as my mistress. And I could hardly offer to marry a peasant girl without destroying my family's reputation and ending my army career before it has begun.

"How do I make the big letters?"

He pointed to the shift key. He could smell the fields of home in her hair as he stood behind her, pretending to be inspecting her work, but actually looking down at the gentle rise of her breasts.

Perhaps, he speculated, perhaps after she has served for a time as Father's secretary, she could be sent to a lyceum in Rome for a proper secondary-school education. I could find her an apartment in the city—far from Giorgina's prying eyes—where we could be together from time to time, should she desire my company. And Sandro might come to accept that his sister had become my . . . not mistress but companion.

We would be companions. He savored the word. "Compagni" was what leftists like Sandro called one another, but Achille liked the word. Yes, we could become compagni, loving companions. And the world is changing quickly. There will come a day when these absurd social strictures will disappear . . . but can I wait that long? I want her now.

"I made a mistake." Her voice was trembling, and for a moment he feared that she might cry. He put his hands on her shoulders to comfort her.

"We're just practicing. Use the back space and mark it out with an *x.*"

"This is very difficult," she confessed bluntly.

"It's important for me that you learn to type." He pressed himself against the back of her chair, feeling the hardness growing in his loins.

How can I explain? Could I kiss her and put my hand on her breast and say that she needs to learn how to type so that we can be loving companions at some unspecified time in the future? That I am standing here with an erection, worrying about my honor, and hers?

"If it's important for you, then I'll do it." Her voice quivered. "Although . . ."

"Although what?"

"I like it when you touch my shoulders, but it stops me from thinking."

"I'm sorry." Quickly he pulled his hands away.

"No, I'm sorry." He could see the flame in her cheeks. "I'm just a little nervous."

"I'm sorry."

"Then we're both sorry." She giggled away the tension. "Now let me work!"

The Leone family home was a great rambling granite structure overlooking the town of Cederna, forty kilometers north of Rome on the Via Salaria.

The peasants who worked there always called it the "Castello Leone," because it had once been a medieval castle, engineered by some ancestral Leone as a defense against marauding feudal armies.

The ground floor was dominated by a spacious salotto with a fireplace and an enormous Sicilian refectory table where the family ate. To the north, there were servants' quarters; Giorgina and her husband Bruno Benelli lived in the south wing. On the second floor was the huge study where Leonida spent most of his waking hours, avoiding the cavernous bedchamber he had shared with his late wife. On the same floor were smaller apartments for Achille and his younger brother, Terenzio Leone, who lived at home but commuted daily to a lyceum in Rome to do battle with the Latin language.

That night, to celebrate Achille's homecoming, Leonida Leone hosted a gala party in the salotto. Dinner for twenty-six people meant that there were stacks of dirty dishes to be dealt with afterward. Valeria, the cook, collapsed with exhaustion after dessert and retreated to her room, leaving Rosaria to contend with the washing up.

It was dark before she was finished and she knew that her brother was waiting dinner for her. Rosaria took off her shoes and scampered barefoot out the back door of the Castello Leone along the path through the kitchen garden to the little cottage where she and Sandro had lived alone since their parents died.

"You're late, Rosaria." Sandro glanced up from their only table, where he was reading by the light of a tallow lamp and making notes with a steel-nibbed pen. It was another book by Carlo Marx, the latest in a series of translations being published in paperback by a Milanese editor. Sandro was spending an enormous portion of his meager salary to buy them one by one.

"It was Achille's homecoming," she explained cheerfully as Sandro lifted a crockery stew-pot from the fireplace to the table. "You're invited to lunch with him tomorrow at Savarino's Trattoria."

"I guess I can make time." He shrugged. "What were you doing all morning in Leonida's study?"

"Achille bought a typing machine. I'm going to be a secretary."

"A secretary? You have no qualifications to be a secretary." Sandro sat down heavily and tore off a piece of that morning's bread. It was already a little stale, and he soaked it in the stew.

"Well, I did it, qualifications or not!" In fact, the letter to Professore George Macauley Trevelyan had been protracted agony and her fingers were aching. She had worked most of the morning on it, leaving blank places where she could not read the Count's spidery script. The letter had been far from finished when they had summoned her to help in the kitchen.

"Look, you're a girl and you don't understand these things," Sandro said quickly. "Achille wants you up there as kind of an ornament. You're growing up to be pretty, and if you took a job in the Castello, people would talk."

"What are you saying?" A tear started its way down one cheek. "People talking? People always talk."

"Don't start weeping." Sandro patted her hand. "When the revolution comes, we don't want anyone saying you were a traitor to the proletariat. Come on, let's eat."

She dropped the subject. Sandro had worked all day with His Excellency's livestock and he was irritable when hungry. To improve their mood, she poured them each a glass of clear, slightly sparkling peasants' wine. After His Excellency's grapes had been pressed and the original grape juice extracted for fermentation, the peasants added sugar and water to the crushed grapes and then carried out a second pressing to produce an inferior vintage for their own consumption. It didn't taste as good as proper Cederna bianco, but it made you just as drunk.

"What's it going to be like, then, our revolution?" She watched him raise the glass to his lips. "Will we form an army and fight with the King's army? Where will we get the guns?"

"No, it will probably begin with a general strike. When we have convinced enough of our brothers that we have the real power in this country, we will simply withhold our labor and bring capitalism to its knees."

"Will there be fighting?"

"There may be some violence," Sandro confessed awkwardly. He was privately convinced that there would be a great deal of violence, but the local police only allowed him to preach revolution on the condition that he refrain from advocating actual bloodshed. "The upper classes will hardly allow a bunch of barefoot peasants to seize their wealth without a fight."

"And Achille?" She could picture Achille with a platoon of soldiers facing Sandro and a mob of angry peasants, and she fantasized dashing into the fray to prevent her two big brothers from hurting each another. "He was once your best friend."

"There was a time when we shared everything," Sandro admitted, and Rosaria remembered how the two boys had studied together as children. All the Leone offspring were educated by an Irish governess named Helen Higgens, and when it had been time for Achille to begin his lessons, Leonida had quixotically ordered Helen to teach Sandro as well.

"You were lucky," she told him. "No one ever bothered tutoring me."

"You're a girl," he reminded her. "And my private lessons ended when Achille went off to study in Rome and I stayed behind to feed the cows."

"But His Excellency was so kind when Momma and Papa died, letting us live here in the cottage and giving both of us jobs!"

"Kindness is not the issue!" Sandro snapped. "I cannot accept a social system that divides men into counts and cattle attendants on the accidental basis of birth. Why didn't Achille stay home and watch the cows while I studied engineering? I was better at math than he was."

"I was better than either one of you," she asserted quietly as she cleared away the plates. The two boys had always needed pen and ink to do long division. Rosaria could do it in her head. "Giorgina gives big parties, smokes foreign cigarettes, drinks pink gin, and shouts at her servants while I grow vegetables in the kitchen garden. What does Marx have to say about that?"

"When the revolution comes . . ."

"The revolutionaries will need a typist! And Achille's offering me the chance to learn."

"He's tempting you to sell out." Exhausted, Sandro collapsed with his book on the couch where he slept at night. "Your place is in the fields with us."

"When the revolution comes, what exactly is going to happen?"

"Oh, don't worry about it, sorellina." He shut his eyes and folded the book against his chest, sleepy after two glasses of wine. "By the time the revolution comes, you'll be married and raising a family of good little socialists for us . . ."

His voice trailed off. Within a few minutes he was asleep.

Poor Sandro, she thought, covering his broad shoulders with a wool blanket as she struggled to overcome her resentment. You're so strong and big and almost as smart as Achille and better at math, but if there isn't a revolution you will have to spend the rest of your life taking care of His Excellency's horses and cows. And you can't even look for a wife until I'm out of the house, because there wouldn't be room. You've taken such good care of me, and I do love you.

But I'm eighteen. People expect you to find me a husband and they expect me to like whomever you select. Is it going to be Emilio Lodi? You keep bringing him home for dinner. Emilio is a good socialist like you, and when we are married he will come back at night exhausted and smelling like horses.

I will feed him his dinner and then he will fall asleep on the couch with his boots on, mumbling about the revolution.

Discouraged, she picked up the flickering lamp and retreated to her tiny bedroom in the rear of the cottage. Slowly she undressed for bed, washing herself in some lukewarm water she poured from a pitcher, and then running a comb through her long hair. Then she removed the last of her clothing and gazed at herself naked in the mirror.

She wondered if that was the sort of body men liked and what Sandro had meant about becoming an ornament. Sometimes the men in Cederna stared at her in the piazza, but they were too afraid of her very big brother to be fresh. Would Achille persuade His Excellency to take her on as a secretary? If not, Sandro would find her a husband, and Father Maurizio would perform the ceremony and someone would take her to bed and make her pregnant.

The prospect depressed her. Rosaria had grown up on a farm and there were no mysteries about sex. But the animals never seemed to enjoy it much, and the older peasant women sometimes complained that it hurt. Sighing, she touched her nipples, watching them spring into life and wondering if her breasts would grow any larger and how long it would be before her body developed that lumpish quality which seemed to be the destiny of peasant women. Too much bread and not enough meat, she concluded unhappily as she pulled the nightdress over her head and crawled beneath the sheets.

I never say any prayers, she thought. Poor Momma died too soon to teach me, and Sandro thinks that God was invented by the capitalists to keep us in line.

She wondered if Sandro prayed to Carlo Marx and then fell asleep.

2.

....

I'm going to make it happen!

She awoke the following morning feeling older and stronger. I won't be a traitor to socialism or Sandro, but I want to be a secretary.

Her skin tingling with energy, she swung her legs off the narrow bed and planted her bare feet on the damp flagstone floor. It was chilly and she shivered as she stripped off her nightdress and scrubbed her body fiercely with cold water and the harsh yellow soap they used for both skin and clothing. Then she opened a bottle of Bellaria perfume, a gift from Sandro on her sixteenth birthday. Carefully she sprinkled a few drops of scent on her fingertips, touching herself under her arms and in the furrow between her breasts.

At the foot of her bed stood a cedar chest with elegant bronze hinges, once the property of Achille's mother, the late Contessa Maria Pia Leone. When the top had splintered, years ago, the chest had been handed down to Sandro, who had lovingly repaired it for Rosaria's best clothing.

Digging deeply beneath the sheets, she located a pair of silk panties, purchased for her mother's wedding a quarter century ago and never worn since. Rosaria put them on, and then pulled a fine cotton vest over her head.

I need one of those corsets that the Signora Giorgina wears, she complained to herself, since the vest was loose and barely covered her bosom. Wealthy women wore corsets to hold up their silk stockings, tuck in their stomachs, and keep their breasts from moving. But they were expensive and you needed a maid to lace up the corset for you in back, so only wealthy ladies wore them.

Rich women also owned light, gaily colored dresses of cotton and silk, but peasant girls never wore anything but ankle-length black wool skirts, winter and summer. Rosaria put on the best skirt she possessed, which was none too good, and then topped it off with a white dress shirt that had belonged to her late father. The man's garment looked strange in the mirror, but she decided that it was the sort of thing a modern secretary might wear for a day in the office pounding an Olivetti.

When she emerged, Sandro was already gone. Rosaria was glad to avoid an argument. She skipped through the vegetable garden, holding her shoes in her hand to keep them dry from the morning dew.

In the kitchen, the Leone family cook was preparing breakfast trays. Behind her back, people called Valeria a *zitella,* the contemptuous word for an old maid, but she had been a great beauty in her youth and was now a slender, dignified woman in her forties, still attractive despite her graying hair.

Valeria had made a deliberate decision to remain a *zitella,* and Rosaria admired her for it. She had never let them marry her off to anyone who wasn't good enough for her. She was a professional, and her salary gave her independence.

"I'll take a tray up to the library," Rosaria announced firmly. The *caffettiera,* a complicated steel device which forced steam through finely ground coffee powder to make espresso, was already announcing with a gurgling noise that the coffee was ready.

"If Giorgina hears about it, there'll be trouble."

"I'll tell them you'd stepped out," Rosaria proposed. "I saw that the coffee was ready, and decided to take it up without asking your permission. So if the Signora complains, you're innocent."

"Don't spill the coffee." Valeria sighed. "We're going to need all the innocence we can get."

Feeling gloomy, Leonida Leone sat in the little alcove under the east window, his fingers resting lightly on the keys of the Olivetti.

Autobiographies are what you write when you've done everything you're ever going to do, he reminded himself. Have I reached that point? Now I write a book. Then I die. They erect a statue of me in the park. And the pigeons shit on my bronze head. So much for fame and fortune.

He tried to cheer himself up by contemplating the truth that life, thus far, had been enormously good to him. A half century's consumption of brandy and cigars had left his lungs and liver intact. Despite a half dozen wars, he had escaped a serious wound or crippling injury. At seventy-one, his hair had that stark whiteness of a healthy old age. His tanned, leathery face was deeply lined, but otherwise Leonida projected the physical appearance of a man in his mid-fifties.

"Look, do you think this is the right moment for my memoirs to appear?" he asked his son just as the door at the far end of his study opened. Leonida observed that their morning coffee was being delivered by—was that Sandro Lombardi's little sister? Whoever she was, the girl seemed to be wearing an old-fashioned man's shirt.

"It's a perfect moment," Achille responded. "With the appearance of Trevelyan's book . . . ."

"Trevelyan never mentioned me by name." Leonida Leone inserted a fresh piece of paper into the Olivetti and poked experimentally at one key that did not seem to do anything. Discouraged, he hit another key, frowning as the wrong letter appeared. "Sic transit gloria mundi, eh? But with all this talk about Italy conquering colonies, perhaps people need to be reminded that

Garibaldi fought to free people from foreign domination, not the reverse. Damn, I've mucked it up again.''

''Father, I know that you were good with a sword and fair with a pistol.'' Achille chuckled as his father struggled with the new machine. ''But that sort of expertise . . .''

''I was more than fair with a pistol.'' Leonida tried to master his petulance. ''Did I ever tell you about that duel in 1867?''

''Girolamo says that you missed with the first shot and nicked your opponent on the second.'' Achille's answer was terribly prompt. With a burst of embarrassment, Leonida realized that he must have told the story about the duel on many previous occasions.

''I nicked him on the first shot and knocked him down with the second. The bastard recovered and became prime minister, of course, but . . .''

''Father, your talent with a pistol is clearly not translating itself into skill with a typing machine. Yesterday Rosaria had a go and did really very well. Why don't we let her deal with it?''

''Who?'' Leonida had forgotten Rosaria's name. The Lombardi siblings had been orphaned as children, but the girl's brother was developing into a reliable young man who looked after the livestock. Sandro could someday become general manager of the entire estate if he didn't go totally crazy over politics.

''Buon giorno, Signor Conte,'' Rosaria stammered as she curtsied. Leonida saw that she was terrified.

''Buon giorno, Rosaria.'' Count Leone left the typing table and carried his coffee to his desk. Achille was clearly stage-managing a staff promotion here and he wondered how he could refuse without offending this pretty contadina. ''Achille, don't you think that typing might be difficult for our young friend?''

''Actually, she did splendidly with this one.'' Achille was nonchalant as he displayed a neatly typed note to Guido Rosselli. ''I noticed that Trevelyan's letter to you came typed and I thought you'd want yours to go back the same way, so I put Rosaria to work on it. Signorina, how far did you get?''

''Signor Tenente, there was just a bit more to finish.'' Rosaria produced Leonida's hand-written draft and took her place before the Olivetti while Achille retreated to the couch with his coffee and the morning paper. Without waiting for anyone's permission, she bent over the Olivetti and began hammering the keys savagely.

This is impossible, Leonida thought. I can't concentrate with a nervous girl pounding that infernal machine. And she's too beautiful. When he was an old man, even Giuseppe Garibaldi made an absolute fool of himself over a pretty wench. And these are my grandfather years.

Finishing his coffee, Leonida Leone surveyed his cluttered desk and began to search through the papers and books before him, realizing that he had forgotten what he was supposed to be doing. Am I getting senile?

Restless, he rose and scanned the bookshelves as if he needed a reference for his memoirs. Near the doorway, he halted before a Leone family portrait, a fading daguerreotype taken in 1905 on the occasion of his sixty-fifth birthday. It was the day he had retired from the Royal Army at the grade of lieutenant general to become the Italian Ambassador to Great Britain. By his side was the frail figure of his late wife, Contessa Maria Pia Leone, who had died that second winter in London.

With a sigh, Leonida inspected the images of his three good-looking children: Giorgina, who would be beautiful if she didn't scowl all the time, and a blithe little Terenzio, making funny faces at the camera. And the apple of his father's eye, a smiling, confident Achille, who went off that year to tackle an engineering degree at the University of Rome with the best brain the Leone family had ever produced.

Leonida leaned closer to the daguerreotype, noticing in the background the hazy image of a girl in a straw hat playing with a puppy. Was that Rosaria? But the child's face was out of focus, as if the camera's lens had been calibrated for aristocracy alone.

I can't have her up here every day, he told himself, wandering back to his desk. If Achille wants to bundle her into bed, that's his business, but I . . .

"Oh, Signor Conte, there's a word here I can't read."

With long, graceful strides, Rosaria crossed the room and placed the handwritten document before him, her finger pointing to a smudged phrase. Leonida tried to focus on the obscure word, but Rosaria was leaning over his desk, resting on her elbows, an insouciant, innocent pose that allowed him for an instant to look down the front of the man's shirt she was wearing. Count Leone quickly redirected his gaze to the text, but not before he had caught a glimpse of her young bosom, full, lovely breasts beneath the cotton fabric of her undervest.

"The word is Calatafimi," he muttered in a choked voice, ashamed, wondering if she knew where his eyes had been. "The Battle of Calatafimi."

"Oh? Was Calatafimi a general?" Her hand fluttered defensively to the front of her shirt as she stood erect. Her face was flushed. She knows, he thought. She must think me a vile old man.

"No, our general was Giuseppe Garibaldi. Calatafimi is a town in western Sicily." Was it possible that she had lived all her life in the shadow of the castello without knowing how his career had begun? "We Italians landed at Marsala from the sea and marched to Calatafimi, where we defeated the Bourbon Army. It was a famous battle."

"I'm sorry, I don't know much about history."

"Italy wasn't always a unified country, you know." He brought gentleness into his voice and smiled to put her at ease. "When I was your age, everything from Naples to the south belonged to the Spanish Bourbons. The Pope was the dictator of central Italy, and the beastly Austrians dominated almost all of the north. It was Garibaldi who changed everything, and our first real fight was at Calatafimi. How old are you?"

"I'm eighteen, sir."

"Eighteen? I was only a year or two older than that when I fought my first battle."

We were pinned down when Garibaldi gave the order to charge, he remembered. I was so frightened that I wet my pants. When the attack began, an enemy soldier attacked me and I stuck him in the chest with my bayonet. He screamed and fell down and I ran up the hill towards the enemy, hysterical, and the others followed me, and we drove the Bourbon troops away. After the march on Palermo, Garibaldi told everyone I was a hero, and there were peasant girls all over Sicily who let me make love to them. Girls with breasts like yours. Fifty years ago.

"And you won?"

"Yes, yes, bless our hearts we won." He decided, in the writing of his memoirs, to omit the part about wetting his pants. "There were just a thousand of us, you know, all young and crazy, Garibaldi and Nino Bixio and the others." And they're almost all dead but me, he realized. There was a catch in his throat, and he stopped before his voice betrayed him. I am a tiresome old fool, he thought.

"I'm sorry I didn't know about your battle," she said. "I'd like to hear about it sometime."

"And sometime I will tell you all about it." She seemed so perfectly sincere that he touched her hand with what he hoped was a paternal gesture. She giggled, retreating to the typing table. "And I shall bore your pants off!"

"O soave fanciulla." He remembered that famous line from Puccini's *La Bohème,* the moment when the poet Rodolfo meets his flower girl, Mimi. "O soave fanciulla." Oh, gentle girl . . .

It was a knock like a policeman's. Nearly finished with the Trevelyan letter, Rosaria startled in her seat. The study door flew open, and the pregnant Giorgina rolled in with the inexorability of a locomotive.

"Buon giorno, babbo," she greeted her father. "Babbo" was baby talk for "daddy." It sounded strange in Giorgina's cold voice.

"How are you feeling, figlia?" Leonida asked solicitously. Rosaria kept her head down, dreading what was coming next.

"Father, I cannot run a household if you keep stealing my servants! This creature belongs in the kitchen garden."

There was a silence. Rosaria saw a hard expression come over Leonida's face, the look of a man who still had more battles to win.

"Not anymore. She is to be transferred up here to serve as my secretary."

"Since when do you need a secretary?"

"Since when do you tell me my business, daughter? Find someone else for the kitchen garden."

For an instant Giorgina stood at the door, trying to find the courage to defy her father, and failing. Then she shot one hateful look at Rosaria and disappeared, slamming the door.

There was another long silence. Leonida Leone inhaled sharply, and then returned to the work on his desk. Achille glanced casually up from his newspaper, nodded in approval, and then resumed reading a story on the front page about Italy's deteriorating relationship with the Ottoman Empire.

Rosaria sat in her chair, frozen before the Olivetti, looking at Achille. You did it, she thought. Oh, my God, how I love you.

3.

....

The ladder was braced against the outside wall of the Castello. Clinging to it with both hands, Sandro nodded grimly to the electrician from the telephone company who was perched twenty-five meters away atop a new telephone pole on the Cederna road. It was August and hot, and Achille was taking a long time to finish whatever he was doing inside Leonida's study.

"Can you see the line yet?" Achille appeared at the window, looking jubilant. "I've attached this end."

They had just drilled a hole through the Castello wall, twenty centimeters of solid granite, and a thick black cable suddenly poked through from inside, the bare wire showing. Sandro took it gingerly in one hand, nervous because he understood nothing about electricity beyond the fact that workers were occasionally fried to death by it.

"Got it," he said, trailing the wire behind him as he climbed down into the formal garden and towed it to the telephone pole. A moment later the lineman pulled the cable taut and the connection was made.

Achille waved triumphantly from the window of the study. "Come up," he shouted. "It's working."

Another surge into Achille's technological future, Sandro told himself irritably as he trudged back toward the Leone mansion. After he did that electricity course at the university, we couldn't rest until there was a row of ugly wooden poles running down the road so that Edison bulbs could burn in every room in the Castello. When his friend Olivetti invented that typing machine, Rosaria had to become a secretary.

And now we have a telephone. In Sandro's opinion, all this new technology was actually making the gulf between rich and poor even wider. When there was no electricity in Cederna, peasant and lord went to bed in the dark. Now the rich had electric lights while the poor still relied upon candles and oil lamps. And when Sandro's revolution came, this telephone system would permit the upper classes to stay in contact with one another and coordinate their resistance to the proletariat.

There were days when Sandro wondered whether the revolution would ever really come, Carlo Marx notwithstanding. And how would it feel to rise up against Leonida Leone and his family? Against Achille?

As always, Sandro entered the castello feeling intimidated, and he was particularly distressed at the prospect of running into the hateful Giorgina Leone Benelli. Was Rosaria up there in the study, pecking away at her infernal Olivetti? There had been a coolness between them ever since she had defied him to become the Count's secretary, and Sandro disliked the idea of encountering her on what had become her territory.

But Achille was alone in the study, leaning against his father's oak desk and talking into the telephone, a gleaming black porcelain mechanism with an earpiece on a flexible wire.

"Guido, I'll come with a staff car to meet your train tomorrow morning," Achille shouted into the mouthpiece of the telefono. "What? Good, put her on . . . hello, Cristina, yes, it's nice to talk to you. I'm looking forward to meeting you someday in person. Convince your big brother to take you on a visit to Rome. Good-bye now."

Achille put the phone down with a manic grin. "Can you believe it? My army friend Guido Rosselli is in Venice on leave and I was just talking to him and his little sister in their own home. Their voices were perfectly clear."

"How does it work?" Sandro hated to admit how little he understood. Could sound actually travel through little copper wires all the way from Rome to Venice? If I could have gone to the university, then I would comprehend all of this. It's not fair.

"I'll explain over lunch. Is that electrician still out there? I want a word with him before he leaves." Achille raced toward the door. "Call someone if you want. It's fun."

Sandro shook his head in irritation. Who the hell am I supposed to call? he thought. Achille's a good man, and he means well, but he never did get it through his head that he is a nobleman and I am a peasant. I don't know anyone with a telephone. Maybe I'll ring up the King and inform him that he will be executed as soon as we can organize a revolt.

Nervously he picked up the earpiece and listened. There was a buzzing sound, and then the clear, crystal voice of a woman. "Centralino."

"Is this the Rome switchboard? Yes? Good morning," he stammered, embarrassed.

"Good morning, signore," said the *centralinista.* "To whom did you wish to speak?"

"Can you connect me with the headquarters of the Italian Socialist Party?" Sandro answered after a moment's consideration. For years, he had been reading a socialist newspaper called *Avanti,* and over the past few months he had been fascinated by the great dispute that threatened to split the Partito socialista italiano, or PSI, as they called it. On one side, there were young radicals like Benito Mussolini and Amadeo Bordiga, who wanted a revolution. Opposing them were the great reformists of the Socialist movement like Filippo Turati, who demanded that socialists work within the existing political system.

It's time for me to get involved, he decided. There was a series of buzzes and clicks before he heard another woman's voice, this time speaking with a modified working-class accent. "Partito socialista."

Sandro was stunned. It had never occurred to him that calling the Socialist Party on the telephone could be quite this easy.

"I want to speak to someone about organizing a rural party section," he said, gathering confidence.

"If you will hold, I believe Signor Bordiga is here." There was a slight pause before a young man with Naples in his voice came on the line.

"Amadeo Bordiga."

"My name is Sandro Lombardi. I live in Cederna, just off the Via Salaria, and we don't have a farmworkers' union here or a party organization."

There was a short pause. "Is there a coach service to Cederna?"

"There's a bus that runs every day from downtown Rome to the Piazza Bixio here," Sandro reported. "It arrives at twelve o'clock."

"We need to talk," said Bordiga. "I'll be there tomorrow at noon. How will I recognize you?"

"I'm big," said Sandro, who was nearly two meters in height.

"You'd better be," laughed Bordiga, and the phone went dead.

Sandro had just replaced the earpiece when Achille bounded back into the study. "Want to catch lunch at Savarino's place?" he inquired. "What do you think of the telefono?"

"It has revolutionary potential," said Sandro dryly, and the two young men went off to the Trattoria in Cederna to talk about telephones and politics.

4.

. . . .

It was the last day of September. There was a curious formality in Girolamo's voice as he appeared at the door of the study, bearing an embossed envelope on a silver tray. "M'lord! A message from the King."

"Oh, our royal dwarf." Leonida looked up from his writing. "I wonder what His Imperial Shortness wants now."

Rosaria giggled, although it was scandalous to hear the Count talking disrespectfully about the monarch. She had seen pictures of His Majesty in the *Messaggero,* and knew that King Vittorio Emanuele III was not a man of great physical stature. Sandro said that the royal family had always been cruel to the working class, but Rosaria thrilled with the knowledge that she was secretary to a man who received letters from a king, albeit a short, bad king.

I don't want anything to change, she thought, feeling a vague apprehension. It had been the happiest summer of her life. She and Sandro had both joined the Socialist Party, and Sandro had never been so jubilant, since there were now meetings to organize and speeches to prepare.

And Leonida was beginning to trust her with personal matters, like administrative problems with the farm or Terenzio's academic difficulties. Whenever he discovered inadequacies in her education, he paused in his own work to deliver lectures on bookkeeping or eighteenth-century Italian literature or astral navigation or the tactics employed by Garibaldi during the Calabrian Campaign.

And every weekend, Achille came home to cheer them all up with funny stories about the army. He brought her books to read, and every Sunday, just before it was time for him to go back to the battalion at Bracciano, they usually managed to spend a little time alone together, although . . .

"Merda!" This common vulgarity seemed shocking on the lips of a gentleman like Leonida. Girolamo stopped smiling. "Damn! I was afraid of this. I warned them."

"M'lord?"

"The government has declared war on the Ottoman Empire and the army has been directed to undertake the invasion of Libya. The King wants to know if I have any advice."

The room suddenly went silent. Rosaria paused in her work, not sure what the Count was talking about. Where was Libya?

"The messenger is waiting, sir."

"Tell him that His Majesty will have my considered reply on Monday." There was anger in Leonida's voice. "Although he will not like what I have to say."

There was a silence in the study as the old general stalked furiously to his map case and took out a military ordnance chart. "I am the only living Italian general who has actually laid eyes on Libya," he said, securing the map on his desk with a book on each corner. "And no one bothered to ask me whether the place was worth conquering."

"I don't know where Libya is." Rosaria approached his desk, grappling with the implications of Italy declaring war. Would Achille have to go?

"It's here." Her eyes followed his finger across the map. Italy was red, a long boot of a peninsula kicking a Sicilian football toward Spain. Below that was the blue Mediterranean, and then Northern Africa, colored yellow, perhaps because it was supposed to be mostly sand. It looked a long way off. Sandro had a map in one of his books, and once showed her France, where they had once chopped the heads off all the aristocrats, and England, where Marx had written *Il Capitale,* and America, where several of their cousins lived in what was believed to be obscene capitalist opulence.

Rosaria had never traveled further from home than Rome, forty kilometers down the Via Salaria, so it was difficult to imagine how far away Libya might be.

"What's there?"

"Nothing." The Count pointed at the map. "Libya is a worthless piece of desert between Egypt and Tunisia. It belongs to the Turks, the Ottoman Empire. When the Suez Canal was finished in 1869, the army sent me out to attend the celebrations. On my way home, I traveled right across the North African coast from Cairo to Tunis, and there is nothing in Libya but sand and some half-starved Senusi bedouin."

"Why do we want to conquer it?"

"Politics!" Leonida leaned back in his chair and touched a sulfur match to the end of a toscano panatela. Dr. Beniolo had advised him against smoking, but he puffed on a cigar whenever he was agitated. "Prime Minister Giovanni Giolitti is an accountant at heart. Whenever his government does something for you socialists, Giolitti feels he has to balance the books by making a concession to the nationalists. Last year, the left got voting rights for the working class, and now our loony right-wingers want an empire, like the British and the French. Giolitti needs to keep everyone happy."

"Will Achille have to go and fight?" She finally found the courage to say what both of them were thinking.

"I don't know." Leonida's voice dropped to a whisper. "He has no combat experience, and at the moment they have him training a company which is nowhere ready for a field assignment. It might depend upon how long the war lasts. The General Staff is saying it will be a matter of weeks, but I think it could go on for decades. The Turkish Army will be tough, and those Senusi Arabs will fight to defend their sand dunes.''

''Signor Conte, can't you . . . couldn't you forbid them to do it?''

''Stop the war?'' The Count seemed astonished. ''No, they're asking my advice on how to do it, not whether it's a good idea. I knew the old King, and his father before him, but our little Vittorio Emanuele doesn't like tall men around him.''

''Then at least you could stop the army from sending Achille?'' she pleaded.

''With a telegram! But Achille would never forgive me.''

''Well, just do it and don't tell him!'' She could feel a tear starting down one cheek. She turned away to hide her crying, but the count saw and put his arms around her.

''I couldn't do that, fanciulla,'' he said, using the affectionate colloquialism for ''young girl.'' ''But thank you for caring enough to suggest it.''

When the hug was over, Leonida sat down to compose a nasty letter to King Vittorio Emanuele III. Rosaria retreated to her alcove under the east window, her emotions in a turmoil. He called me ''fanciulla,'' she thought.

5.

. . . .

"Did you hear the news?" Achille Leone called excitedly from the door. "My battalion hasn't been mobilized yet, but we're hoping we can go with the second contingent."

There was silence in the study. Leonida Leone glanced up from his work, looking pale and preoccupied. Girolamo was frowning and Rosaria's eyes were red, as if she had been crying.

What's wrong? Lieutenant Leone unbuttoned his uniform jacket and dropped casually into a chair, awaiting his father's reaction. At the headquarters of the Battaglione Lupi di Lazio, everyone was worried that the Wolves of Latium would be left out of the great Libyan adventure, since the unit had not fired a shot in anger for forty years.

Ah well, Father has enough *gloria* to last the family for several more generations, Achille reflected, but still . . . For a moment, he surrendered to a brief fantasy, seeing himself astride a prancing white palomino, leading a column of cheering troopers through an Arab city while veiled Muslim women with dark eyes stood by the side of the road shouting, "Viva il Tenente Leone!"

"I hope you will not be involved in this war." Leonida's deep voice jolted Achille out of his daydream. "And I am particularly sorry that you think imperialism is a good idea."

"Father, as a serving officer, it's hardly my job to decide whether or not it's a good idea." Ever since the newspapers had begun gossiping about a possible move against Libya, Leonida had expressed his misgivings, but Achille was stunned at the force of his father's feelings. "Besides, the Ottoman Empire has been falling apart for centuries. If Italy doesn't move quickly, Britain and France will pick up all the pieces. And Libya . . ."

"Libya does not belong to us!" Count Leone puffed dark, venomous smoke into the air. "If we were going to help the Arabs win their freedom from the Turks, it would be different, but seizing the place for ourselves is theft."

"Father, when you were ambassador in London, didn't you negotiate with the British so that we could consolidate our hold on Italian Somaliland?"

Leonida shook his head. "It was strictly a commercial deal. Italy needed a permanent station in the Gulf of Aden, and I persuaded the British that our presence there had no military implications. But a wholesale attack on sovereign Turkish territory is quite different."

"Father, Italy is a modern European nation. We can bring science and culture and medicine and good government to the bedouin."

"We will invade with field artillery and machine guns." Leonida turned on him angrily. "We will kill very large numbers of Libyans in the process of bringing the dubious benefits of the twentieth century to the survivors. And what good government? We can barely govern ourselves."

"There's a lot of arable land down there. Enough for millions of Italian peasants," Achille reasoned, hoping this argument would appeal to Rosaria's working-class sympathies. But the Lombardi girl dropped her eyes, opting out of the argument, her face white with anxiety.

"It's not good land, and it's not our land!" Leonida was suddenly shouting. "We did not free this country from the Pope and the Bourbons and the Austrians in order to steal sand from poverty-stricken Arabs."

"Father!" Stunned, Achille stood to attention. "I've got to obey orders, Signor Generale. Just the way you did."

There was a long silence.

"I'm sorry, pupo," said Leonida softly, and Achille felt a sudden surge of emotion when his father used the old Roman word for "little boy." He called me pupo when I was a child, he reflected. Now that I might have to go off and fight, I've become his little boy again.

"I understand, Papa." Achille reached across the desk and put his hand over Leonida's.

"It's just that real war is so complicated and dangerous, and most of what they taught you at the *Accademia Militare* was nonsense."

"Then teach me!" Achille reacted with sudden passion. "Teach me what I didn't learn at the academy."

"I suppose we could start after dinner. Giorgina is probably waiting."

"To hell with Giorgina! Let's start now. Signorina, bring us rolls and cheese and wine from the kitchen. My father is going to teach me how to win battles."

"To hell with winning battles," grunted Leonida Leone as he swept books and papers from the surface of his desk. "I'm going to teach you how to stay alive."

Leonida is tired, Rosaria fretted. She was sorting papers at her desk in the alcove, making work for herself between trips down to the kitchen for coffee. It's almost eleven and they've been working for hours. We need to get him to bed.

"All right," Achille said, touching the map with the tip of his pen. "Suppose I were ordered to attack along this axis, with enemy forces here and here. I would position my heavy machine guns in the south to provide grazing fire. With one platoon in reserve and another in a holding position there, I would send the third platoon in a circling maneuver, thus.''

"No."

"Why not?" There was perplexity in Achille's voice.

"Your solutions are always too complicated. Remember von Clausewitz. In this situation, you would put all your platoons into one concentrated attack along this azimuth and expect to take some casualties."

"Suppose I moved laterally?"

"Achille, this is battle, not ballet," the old general groaned. "Think in terms of thrusts, not pirouettes."

"But we're assuming that I had been ordered—"

"Then you would disobey orders, or lose your company."

"Father, you can't go around disobeying orders."

"Of course you can," Leonida dissented stubbornly. "I disobeyed stupid orders for forty years, and they made me a lieutenant general."

"Did you ever disobey Garibaldi?"

"Garibaldi didn't give stupid orders. Try this. Turn the map upside down so you look at the terrain the way your enemy sees it."

Achille obediently upended the map. Leonida stood and stretched and Rosaria noticed that his skin was gray with fatigue. I've got to take better care of him, she resolved. He's seventy-one, even if he doesn't look it. He drinks too much cognac, and today he skipped his afternoon nap and smoked four cigars.

"Rosaria, what do you think? Could we perhaps do with more coffee?" Leonida suggested.

"You look tired, sir," she told him boldly. "Perhaps you should sleep."

"What?" For a moment, she feared that he would object to being dispatched to bed by his secretary. Then he squeezed her hand and smiled. "Perhaps I should. Good night, son. And thank you for taking care of us tonight, fanciulla."

"Good night, Papa," Achille called from the desk as his father opened the door leading into his bed chamber and disappeared. Achille's eyes never left the chart, where he was protractoring an angle.

Knowing that she should leave, Rosaria approached the desk, watching the young lieutenant draw fields of fire on his map.

"Achille, do you want to go to Libya?" she asked.

"We still have no orders to go anywhere, but the idea of a trip to Africa is exciting." He flashed a quick, distracted smile in her direction, avoiding her eyes. "I know my father has some philosophical objections to the war, Rosi, but I'm a young man and I don't want to be left out of this great adventure."

"So you want to go?"

"Well, I am reluctant to leave . . . ah, all of you." He glanced up at her quickly before returning his attention to his ordnance chart. "Being a soldier means having to go away and fight once in a while."

For an instant she was tempted to scream at him. How could you? How could you want to leave us? Your father loves you, and I . . .

"Now look at that." Achille seemed oblivious to her distress. "Father was absolutely right. But he saw it immediately and I'm just getting the point now."

Rosaria came to his side, because he seemed to have invited her to observe something. She found the closeness of his body disturbing.

He must have noticed how I've grown up, she told herself as her eyes uncomprehendingly followed the lines he had sketched on the chart. I don't want him to make love to me because I know there is no future for us. But . . . but it would be nice if he would put his arm around my waist and give me a kiss.

Amazed at her own boldness, she took a deep breath and moved closer, deliberately allowing her breast to brush against his arm. I'm here, she wanted to whisper in his ear. You could be killed in this silly war and I might never see you again. You loved me when I was a little girl even though I was a contadina. Why won't you look at me now?

Achille bent closer to the map for a moment, separating their bodies, and then stood up abruptly, giving no sign that he was aware that they had touched.

"Well, I'd better be getting to bed myself," he said casually. "Father will probably start his next strategy lesson at dawn."

"Good night, Signor Tenente." She turned away from him abruptly.

"Good night, signorina." His response was so rigorously formal that for a moment she interpreted it as a joke. But when she looked back from the door, he was bending again over his map, drawing more lines with his protractor.

"Good night, then," she said again, and ran down the stairs crying.

His upper arm tingled where her breast had touched him.

Breathless, he listened to her skip down the marble steps to the *pianterreno*. Then there was silence, and he knew she was bending to remove her sandals before running barefoot through the kitchen and into the garden.

Downstairs, she's still a shoeless peasant, he mused. Is this insane, this Pygmalion project of mine, trying to change a contadina into a modern professional woman? No, it was all working according to plan. After only a few months, Rosaria was typing brilliantly. She had organized Leonida's files and begun to handle all his correspondence. The Count had come to depend utterly upon her and she tended to him like a daughter.

Anxious to see her one last time, Achille walked to the window, gazing down at the dark cottage where she lived with Sandro. It suddenly struck him that the place needed both electricity and running water.

My Rosi shall have a bathroom, he decided. How romantic! What an ass I am! But how else do I tell her how I feel? And if I have to go to Libya, what will I find upon my returning? She's eighteen, high time for a contadina to be married, and Sandro has been talking about arranging a marriage with that friend of his, Emilio Lodi. I could come home to find her fat with someone else's child.

Suddenly worried, Achille mentally assembled a rogue's gallery of men who might take Rosi away from him. There was Tommaso Savarino, the lawyer, and Junio Mosconi, the mayor's son. Christ, not Junio! But when we were kids, Junio was always following her around, trying to pinch her bottom or look under her dress. Suddenly Achille's subconscious lashed him with an uninvited fantasy, a picture of Rosaria lying naked in Junio's bed.

"Dammit," he swore to himself, clenching his fists and feeling his face go hot. There is so much injustice in the world. Had Rosi not been born into a peasant family, the sons of generals and cabinet ministers would be lining up to ask for her hand in marriage.

And I'd be first in line!

Achille watched Rosaria making her way through the tomato plants toward the cottage. If I don't stake some kind of claim, he worried, she will give her heart to someone else.

But what can I possibly say? She must have understood long since that society would never tolerate a formal marriage between us. And an offer of anything less would seem like a vulgar proposition. Sandro would break my neck.

Suddenly, she turned at the door to the cottage and looked up at the alcove where he was sitting. They stared at each other for a long time. Then Achille pressed his fingertips to his lips and blew her a kiss. She looked perplexed for a moment, and then seemed to understand, returning the gesture with an excited flutter of her hands.

Achille felt absurdly happy. Then Rosaria smiled and went inside.

6.

. . . .

"What a disaster! And the little wretch looks just like her father." Giorgina gestured irritably in the direction of her week-old daughter, sleeping peacefully in Helen's arms. Helen Higgens had come from Ireland to be governess to one whole generation of Leone children and now she had been recalled from semi-retirement to deal with Leonida's first grandchild.

Collectively deciding to treat this as a joke, the company dutifully chuckled. Everyone knew how badly Giorgina and Bruno had wanted a boy.

"What do you think, Helen?" Achille rose from his place at the far end of the refectory table and approached the old Irish nanny. "Are you ready to inflict your Irish accent on another member of this family? Here, let me hold her."

Poor little tyke, he thought as Helen surrendered the little girl. You have such a savage momma. Serene and comfortable after a session with her wet nurse, Teresa Benelli opened her pale brown eyes and regarded him solemnly. With a burst of avuncular affection, Achille kissed her on the forehead.

I want a child, he resolved. In fact, more than one. Rosaria will certainly want children someday, and she would make lovely babies. How do *compagni* bring babies into the world without complications? Perhaps we could go away to some foreign country and make our babies there.

"Oh, Helen, do take her away!" Giorgina ordered as Achille put the tiny bundle back into her pram.

"I don't see why I can't come with you." Terenzio continued the argument they had been having since the beginning of November. The insouciant Terenzio had decided that fighting Arabs would be more enjoyable than finishing his last semester at the lyceum. "I could be your aide-de-camp. Father could arrange it."

"Fratellino, I think Father would prefer that you launch one final assault upon the Latin language," Achille told him gently. "Once you finish school, we can get you a lieutenancy."

"The war will be over before I learn Latin."

"I doubt that." There was no need to upset the family with a gloomy discussion of the war, but Leonida had been correct in predicting a fierce Arab resistance. In early October, Italian troops had successfully seized both of Libya's major cities, Tripoli and Benghazi, but the push into the Libyan interior was proving difficult. The war would wait for Terenzio to learn Latin.

"Do you think your unit will be sent, Achille?" Bruno Benelli interjected from the far end of the long mahogany refectory table. Achille smiled amicably at his brother-in-law, wondering how the Benelli marriage survived. Bruno was a short, heavyset, intelligent man from a good bourgeois family who had come to work for Leonida as a business manager and accountant. The bookkeeper had stayed to become His Excellency's son-in-law, but Giorgina continued to treat him like one of the servants.

"Frankly, I don't know. The General Staff seems to be totally confused. For several weeks we've been expecting orders at any minute, but so far . . ."

Giorgina glared at him. "If you chase off to Libya, you'll leave us with this mess you've created."

"What are you talking about?"

"My wife has been worrying about the Rosaria situation." Bruno struggled to recapture the initiative. "She's an excellent employee, but we feel she is developing a hold over your father."

"Father's infatuated with her." Giorgina's voice was an angry hiss. "That peasant wench tells him what to eat and how to run his farm and when to take a nap. It's only a matter of time before he disgraces us."

"Oh, Giorgina, Father is seventy-one." Achille wondered how to prevent a major brawl during dinner.

"And now a bathroom! An absolute fortune has been spent putting pipes and water out there. Sandro used an outdoor privy all his life and now suddenly it isn't good enough for his delicate little sister."

"It was my idea and my money," Achille said. "And I also paid for the electric lights we're installing next week."

"Why do peasants need electric lights?" Giorgina shrieked.

"You know, Rosaria doesn't look like a peasant anymore." Bored with the discussion, Terenzio had wandered to the far end of the parlor, where he was running his fingers silently up and down the keyboard of the family Blütner.

"Shut up, Terenzio!" Giorgina stormed. "Listen, Achille, if Father wanted to keep a discreet widow or the usual maiden schoolteacher tucked away somewhere, it would be between him and God. But this Lombardi girl is dangerous."

"She has finely chiseled features and delicate fingers." Terenzio's tone was studiously bland, but Achille realized that his younger brother was deliberately enraging their sister. "Furthermore, she has a large bosom but a small bottom. Bruno, wouldn't you agree that these are the typical physical characteristics of a gentlewoman?"

Terenzio seemed to have observed her anatomy with some attention, Achille noticed. With sudden alarm, he studied his brother's blithe, cheerful features. He and Rosaria were almost the same age, and they had often played together as children. Should I talk to him privately? he thought. What could I possibly say?

"I'm sure Bruno has never thought about anyone's bottom." Giorgina seemed angry enough to start throwing the silverware. "And if you could pay as much attention to the Latin language as you do to girls' bosoms, Terenzio, you might graduate from the lyceum this year."

"Latin doesn't interest me," grinned Terenzio. "I want to join the army and fight the Arabs in Libya."

"Look, Giorgina, you've got the wrong end of this completely," Achille intervened. "Rosaria became the old man's secretary because I sold him the idea over his objections. Their relationship is entirely innocent, and Father has been educating her. Rosaria is very bright, you know."

"Why bother educating a woman?"

"Father believes that even women need to be taught." Achille lowered his voice. They could hear Leonida's footsteps in the hallway.

"He never bothered to teach me anything," said Giorgina, and the company fell silent as the great man came in to dine with his family.

The meal was strained. Unable to fathom the cause of Giorgina's irritation, Leonida organized his escape from the dinner table by announcing that he and Achille had planned another installment of their strategy seminar. As soon as the sherbet bowls had been cleared away, the two men retreated to the study, where Count Leone could fortify himself with cognac and cigars.

Contentedly, he lit the last panatela of the day. Concerned that he was smoking too much, Rosaria had begun a policy of placing only six cigars per day in the humidor, and hiding the rest. To preserve his dignity, Leonida pretended not to notice that he was being rationed by his eighteen-year-old secretary. Actually, he was rather charmed by the idea, partially because he enjoyed being fussed over, and partially because he had several reserve boxes of Tuscan *sigari* cached behind books in his library.

"Should we talk about retreats and strategic withdrawals tonight?" he suggested, wondering if this crash course in military science would do any good. I politely ignored everything my poor father told me, he reflected. Perhaps my brave young lieutenant here is doing the same.

"Father, Giorgina has been fussing," Achille interjected with a frown. "As I see it, the problem is—"

"M'lord!" There was an interruption from the door as Girolamo entered with the young Neapolitan trooper who served as Achille's aide-de-camp. Corporal Franco Grassi was clad in khaki combat dress and field boots. He looked terrified.

"We have our mobilization orders, Signor Tenente. The trucks are coming to get us in a few hours, and we sail from Naples tomorrow. Major Tobino sends his compliments and requests that you return immediately."

So it's happening at last, Leonida realized. Feeling momentarily faint, he steadied himself against the desk as he rose. "Well, you wanted to go to Libya. Girolamo, give Caporale Grassi some coffee in the kitchen. Have Valeria prepare a hamper for them to take on the road, sandwiches . . . yes, have her make lots of sandwiches."

There was a moment of silence. Leonida gazed at his son and observed that Achille looked preoccupied. That's good, he decided. We have always been warriors in our family, but no Leone has ever really enjoyed the prospect of war.

"I'm almost packed," Achille said. "I'll throw a few last-minute things in my bag and then say good-bye to the family."

"Take a bottle of this cognac with you, and have a drink with that young Guido Rosselli on the boat. Did you know his grandfather led a company of Venetian light infantry against Marshall Radetzky's Austrians in '49? That boy should have inherited some talent."

Agitated, Leonida produced a bottle of Vecchia Romagna and then began digging through the top drawer of his desk, looking for something else to give his son. "Do you have enough cash with you? I have some British pounds here, and you can use sterling in places where they've never heard of the lira italiana."

"I'll be all right, Papa," Achille laughed, but Leonida stuffed several hundred pounds into an envelope and thrust it into the pocket of his son's jacket.

"And here, take this with you." From the back of his desk, Leonida produced a leather-covered stainless-steel whiskey flask. He wondered briefly if he had ever explained how he and Girolamo had raided the palace of the Archbishop of Palermo in 1860 during Garibaldi's Sicilian campaign, and carted off a gold-plated candlestick for Girolamo's mother, and this wonderful whiskey flask. In fact . . . but there was hardly time for a story.

"I don't expect to be gone for more than a year." Achille seldom drank spirits and he looked dubiously at the flask before putting it into his pocket.

"Wars end when somebody wins, and this one could be long. Do your duty, but save your heroics for a day when Italy really needs you."

"I will, Papa. Look, I'll go and tell the others that I'm leaving. And then come back to see you when I've packed."

"No," Leonida decreed as he swept him into his arms for a hug. "We've said good-bye, and your unit is leaving. Soldiers get used to quick farewells."

"Good-bye, Father."

Leonida released his son silently, no longer trusting his voice. Achille waved and walked out the door.

"You are the one I love the best," the old man whispered. There were tears streaming down his face as he stood in the sudden emptiness of his study repeating, "My son, my dearest son, my little boy!"

*   *   *

In his own quarters, Achille found Girolamo cramming extra socks into his leather suitcase. The Castello was silent.

His head was whirling from all the farewells. Giorgina had pecked him coldly on the cheek while Bruno had shaken his hand absently, talking about the exchange rates for Libyan currency. Terenzio had broken down and sobbed.

And Father is terribly upset, Achille thought. Will I see him again? What will it be like for me when he dies? How will I manage without him?

This is a real going away, he realized as he stepped into a neatly pressed pair of khaki field trousers and then put on his light-tan uniform shirt and field jacket. There were two round first-lieutenant's pips on each shoulder. Leaving for the Military Academy had been just a rehearsal. Packing one's bags to fight a war on another continent was the real thing.

"You need to change your socks twice a day when you're in the field."

"I'll remember, Girolamo," Achille promised, strapping his pistol around his waist and putting on his garrison cap.

"Wash your feet whenever you get the chance, and watch out for blisters," Girolamo insisted. "That's more important than all the grand strategy your father's been pouring into you. And keep your head down, boy. This war isn't worth getting killed in."

Achille felt the old man's frail shoulders shaking as they hugged at the door.

Outside, it was cloudy and cold. There was a wind coming down off the Apennines and it brought him the scent of the fields, his father's land, the smells of mulching hay and cow manure and drying grapes. He inhaled deeply, trying to fix it all in his memory.

Corporal Franco Grassi was checking the tires as Achille tossed his bag into the back seat. "Ready to go, sir?"

"I have one last errand, Franco." With his father's bottle of cognac under his arm, Achille Leone walked through the formal gardens at the front of the Castello, circling the servants' quarter in the north wing. He could smell the fresh cement from the cottage's new bathroom. Rosi would have her own tub and indoor toilet to remember him by, and he wondered if the flow of running water could keep love alive.

There was no light in the cottage. He knocked at the door, expecting to be greeted by a sleepy Sandro in his underwear.

Inside, there was the whisper of bare feet on a flagstone floor, and the scratch of a sulfur match against sandpaper. The wooden door creaked on rusty hinges, and Achille came face-to-face with Rosaria Lombardi. She was holding a candle in one hand, and for a moment all he could see was the brightness of her eyes.

"Rosi?" He squinted to see her clearly in the shadows. "We've got our orders and we're going overseas at last. I wanted to say good-bye to you and Sandro."

"So soon?" She seemed distraught. "Sandro is at a meeting in Cederna. They're planning a protest against your war."

"It's not exactly my war," he said ruefully. "But I've got to leave right now. We sail from Naples tomorrow."

"Oh, Achille, I . . . I'm going to worry about you so much."

"I'm going to be fine." He realized that Rosi was dressed for bed, wearing only a shawl over her thin cotton nightgown. "Listen, this is Sandro's favorite cognac. The two of us used to steal it from my father when we were little. Would you give it to him, and tell him good-bye for me?"

"Come inside," she begged him, backing into the cottage and putting the candle and the cognac on the table. "Someone might see me talking to a soldier in my nightdress and get the wrong idea."

"Look, there's a wrong idea I wanted to tell you about," he confessed. Rosaria was standing between him and the lamp, and he could see the outline of her body through the frail texture of her nightdress. The silhouette of her breasts and thighs thrilled him and for an instant he was tempted to take her into his arms and perhaps even kiss her. It would be reasonable, he assured himself. I am marching off to war, and I would be forgiven. If I am going to be a soldier, I should learn to take love where I find it.

"What . . . what wrong idea?"

"My sister is worried about you and my father. She has this ridiculous idea that he is becoming too fond of you."

"What does that mean?" she asked in alarm. "I'm just his secretary. You arranged it."

"Rosi, look, my sister is on the warpath, but no matter what happens, I want you to be there when my father needs you. Don't let Giorgina scare you away."

"I'll take care of him for you." She spoke in a choked voice and then abruptly turned her back on him. Was she crying? Hell, she was just a little girl when father took us all off to the embassy in London, and she cried then. And she wept again when I left for the Military Academy two years ago. If I'm going to be a soldier, he thought, I will spend my life going away.

I could take her in my arms and give her a hug, he told himself, but his body began to tremble as he stepped forward and he recoiled from the temptation. If I touch her, he thought it will never stop with hugging.

"I'll see you when I get back then," he heard himself saying stiffly, wanting to ask her to wait for him, but not finding the words. "It won't be too long. A year at the most. Perhaps . . . perhaps nothing will have changed while I am gone, and perhaps you'll be glad to see me again. Do you think . . . you might be glad?"

"A year!" Sobbing brokenly, she thrust herself into his arms. "Achille, I know that I have no right to say this, but I love you so much. I've always loved you!"

Achille felt his body burning. For a healthy young man, lust was a simple everyday sensation, but the sensation within him now was intense, almost a physical pain that demanded relief at any cost. He wrapped his arms around her, kissing her hair and wondering if she could feel his hardness.

"Rosi, I—"

"No, don't say anything you don't mean. Don't tell me a lie to make me feel better. If you're going to go away tonight, then tell me the truth about us."

"I've thought so much about us . . . ," He began to blurt out the truth, feeling her breasts pressing against his uniform jacket. "I've tried to imagine what we could mean to one another someday . . . and how it could be organized."

"Someday? What do you mean?"

"A relationship . . . I mean that we could be friends," he stammered. This is not going well, he agonized. She must think I am demented.

"Friends? Just friends?" Rosi seemed thunderstruck, and he felt her body pull away from his. "What kind of friends?"

Suddenly, he tugged her back to him and kissed her so hard on the mouth that he could taste blood. She did not resist, but let her arms hang limply at her sides, as if overcome.

"The kind of friends who kiss each other like that!" he panted when they finally broke away. "Rosi, there would be endless difficulties if we tried to have a formal marriage, and I haven't wanted, I mean, a vulgar seduction would dishonor you, at least now, at your age, but someday . . ."

"You don't have to marry me!" She kissed him furiously, her hands running over his face. "Just say that you love me!"

"I love you. I do love you. Ti amo," he swore. "And what I wanted to say tonight is that if you can wait until I come home, then we will explore . . . I will have no other women, and when I return . . . I don't know what will happen, but we will find some way to be together if you wait for me. Don't marry anyone else!"

He released her, realizing that he had been stammering like an idiot, that he had never before felt that kind of passion. His body was tormenting him with a violent yearning, but he retreated, knowing that another touch would lead irrevocably to sex. And I cannot do that to Sandro, he told himself. If Rosi and I are to have a relationship, then we must first talk to Sandro. We owe him that.

"Where are you going?" He backed toward the door. In the candlelight he could see that her nightdress had fallen off one smooth white shoulder in the confusion of their embrace, and she seemed somehow more desirable than ever.

"I've got to go." He felt a strange jubilation within him. Now I know for sure that she loves me, he told himself. I am certain that she will wait. She will not marry Emilio or Tommaso or the mayor's wretched son. When I come home she will be here, with indoor plumbing and electric lights. We will send her to school, and get a small apartment somewhere in Rome.

"Please don't go!" She followed him to the door, holding out her hands in supplication, but Achille knew he had to leave now, before anything dishonorable occurred. If I love her, I must not shame her, he ordered himself, or leave her pregnant. He waved good-bye one last time and stepped out into the darkness. This is the most difficult thing I will ever do, he thought, feeling the ache within his loins, but my honor demands that I go . . .

He is really going to leave, Rosaria realized as Achille crossed the threshold. He came and said he loved me, and now he is going to march off and kill Arabs.

This is crazy, she thought, darting into the darkness after him and catching him by his coattails. "Don't go!" she pleaded, pulling him back into the cottage.

"Oh, Rosi," he murmured as she leaped again into his arms.

"Come into my room, and hold me for a few minutes."

He drew back. "It would lead to something we would both regret."

"I'll never regret anything we did together." She felt a wild, unfamiliar passion. I must seal this business, her brain thundered insanely. I need to bind him to me. Words are too light for all the time he must be away.

"But Rosi . . ."

"Don't be honorable," she pleaded. "Just come into the bedroom."

She tugged on his sleeve, and he followed her toward the room, but she sensed his hesitation. In desperation, she reached down and seized the hem of her nightdress. With a quick, impulsive gesture, she pulled it over her head and threw it behind her on the bed.

She had never before been undressed in front of a man, but she felt strangely natural. Naked, we are no longer peasant and lord, she thought, attacking the buttons on his jacket with trembling fingers. We are just skin touching other skin.

She clung to him, and the feel of his hardness filled her with triumph. He wants me, she realized. He wants me the way a man wants a woman.

Pulling him toward her, she tumbled backward onto the bed, and Achille's resistance melted as he knelt over her, tearing off his jacket. He loves me, she rejoiced. The man I have always loved loves me in return, and now I am going to be his secret wife. It doesn't matter what the world thinks or knows. I will be his forever!

"Rosi, I'll always love you."

"Then come into me." She was astonished at her own boldness. "Don't worry if I cry out. It's the first time."

"The future . . ."

"Don't think about the future," she commanded him. "Make love to me."

She felt his hands on her hips, arranging her on the bed. She moved her legs apart, amazed that a lifetime of modesty should have fallen away so suddenly. Now everything changes, she told herself. Now my life begins.

Achille was kissing her breasts when she heard Sandro's rough voice. Her brother was outside the cottage, and he was not alone. There were two sets of footsteps converging at the cottage door.

"Who the hell are you?"

"I'm Corporal Franco Grassi," said a man with a Neapolitan accent. "I'm looking for Tenente Leone. If I don't get him to Camp Bracciano by midnight, they'll court-martial us."

Rosaria half-surrendered to panic. Sandro has been guarding my chastity for so long, she thought. He will feel so betrayed.

"Sandro will kill us," Achille whispered. There was a sudden coldness on Rosaria's bare skin as he staggered to his feet, working frantically to refasten his buttons. She closed her eyes and lay still, covering her nipples with her hands and crying under her breath.

"Maybe he's on his way here to say good-bye," Sandro told Corporal Grassi helpfully, and Rosaria tensed as the hinges on the front door squeaked. "Come in and wait for him if you like."

"I'll go out the window," Achille hissed. "We can't . . ."

"I know," she sobbed, her emotions clanging back and forth. On one hand, she felt the intense joy of knowing how strongly she was loved. But then there was a sense of intense physical loss, an emptiness inside her, a rage that the war should steal Achille from her in what ought to have been the best moment of her life. "Come back to me," she vowed. "I'll take you on any terms."

"I'll come back. And you can name your own terms," he promised. He bent one last time to kiss her parted lips and run his hand lightly over her breast. Then there was a cool breeze as he opened her bedroom window and threw his leg over the sill.

"I love you," she said one last time, hoping he might still be there, but there was no reply. In the front room, Sandro was talking to the soldier from Naples, explaining that the war in Libya was a blatant exercise in capitalist imperialism.

Rosaria turned on her side and pulled a blanket over her nakedness, pretending to be asleep.

Book
Two

1912 — 1913

1.

. . . .

"It's New Year's Eve, Comandante!" Guido Rosselli sang out.

Achille Leone looked around warily as he crawled from his tent. The sun was two fingers above the horizon, burning in a stark blue sky with an intensity they never saw in Italy. The air was still cool, and he buttoned the collar of his gray-green field jacket. Blinking his eyes in the harsh desert light, he climbed to his feet and searched the horizon for danger.

The encampment was calm. In the week since their arrival, the men had been digging defensive trenchworks, and they were already hard at work with their shovels, filling burlap bags with sand to serve as barriers against hostile fire. Achille's troopers were equipped with army-standard 6.5-millimeter semi-automatic rifles and six-shot Mannlicher magazines. Under the supervision of Sergeant Major Papafava, a fire team was preparing one of their six Breda light machine guns to cover the open field between them and an oasis-town called Sidi Osman. The company mechanic was working on their trouble-prone Fiat cargo truck, cleaning sand from the carburetor.

"I'd forgotten. We seem so far from the holiday season here." In Cederna, he knew, there would be music tonight. At the Castello, Terenzio would play the Blütner all day. Out in the fields, someone would be squeezing an accordion, and everyone would be singing.

Giorgina would be screaming at the kitchen staff as they prepared for her traditional New Year's dinner. The servants would politely serve all the stuffed shirts from Cederna, and then Rosaria and Girolamo and Valeria and Sandro and the others would stage their own festa in the kitchen. After offering insincere toasts to Mayor Mosconi and Don Maurizio, Leonida would infuriate Giorgina by slipping off to drink with the servants.

And with his beautiful secretary, Rosaria Lombardi, Achille thought. Who almost became my mistress that night we went crazy in her bedroom.

I wonder if Rosi is getting my letters? When will hers start arriving?

"Coffee's waiting." Plummeting back to reality, he followed Guido into the company's command shed where the faithful Franco Grassi was standing by with a pot of espresso. Official army-issue coffee was undrinkable, but the resourceful Grassi had located a source of real coffee for the five officers assigned to B Company of the Lupi di Lazio Infantry Battalion. Lieutenant

Leone had no illusions about the legality of Grassi's ever-expanding supply system, but he sipped the rich black brew gratefully and decided to ask no questions.

"Comandante, you're going to ruin your eyesight if you sit in your tent every evening trying to decipher those Arab squiggles," Guido Rosselli said. "We need to get out and have some fun."

"What did you have in mind?" Although he had mastered Latin, English, and French as a schoolboy, Achille was finding Arabic difficult.

"In Benghazi, there is an officers' brothel of some magnificence," Guido proposed. "Why don't we celebrate New Year's by inspecting the facilities?"

"A brothel? Oh, I don't know . . ." As a student at the University of Rome, Achille had enjoyed several discreet love affairs, but the notion of going to a brothel made him uncomfortable.

"Are you religious?" Guido persisted. "Thinking about the Blessed Virgin?"

"No, it's not that." He was thinking about his promise of fidelity to Rosaria, but this was not something he intended to share with the cynical Guido. "How about you?"

"Me? My family has been frantically religious ever since my great-grandfather decided that Catholicism was a safer superstition than Judaism." Guido laughed. "But the nuns never managed to beat much religion into me, so I am Hebrew by ancestry, Catholic by education, and a libertine by inclination. Now tonight, we could leave Lieutenant Siciliano in charge, and take the truck into Benghazi."

"You go if you want. It's too early for both of us to be away at the same time," Achille said, scanning his company area. Circling the wooden command post, there were several dozen small canvas tents where the officers and men slept, and one larger canopy that served as a day room and mess tent. The land around them was uneven, torn by erosion and scarred by a dry, meandering riverbed, or wadi. There were a few sand dunes in the distance, but the terrain was mostly sun-baked mud, littered with large rocks and boulders, providing good cover for an enemy who could come very close before he was spotted.

"Nothing is ever going to happen here, Comandante," Guido complained. "The damn war is at a standstill."

Poor Guido, Achille chuckled. He will never forgive the citizens of Benghazi for surrendering before he could get there and shoot some of them.

In fact, the wiry Venetian was turning out to be a magnificent deputy company commander—loyal, hard-working, intelligent, and full of animal enthusiasm—but Guido was convinced that they would never win any medals for heroism until they went looking for the enemy out in the desert.

And he was right about the war standing still. What the Italians called Libya had turned out to be two rather separate provinces of the aging Ottoman Empire. In the west, near Tunisia, there was a large city called Tripoli, where the Americans had once fought the Barbary pirates. In the east, around the port of Benghazi, was a province known as Cyrenaica, the homeland of the Senusi, a fanatic Muslim sect of bedouin Arabs.

There had been a brief, furious firefight in mid-October, when the first wave of Italian troops had come ashore, but now Libya's Arab irregulars had disappeared into the desert, while the Turkish Army had retreated toward Egypt.

Arriving in mid-December as part of the Seventh Infantry Regiment, Major Tobino's Lupi di Lazio Infantry Battalion had been sent to form part of the perimeter around Benghazi. Lieutenant Leone's B Company had drawn Sidi Osman, due east from Benghazi along a main road that led from the coast toward an enemy-held town called Benina.

"I'm not worried about the bedouin, but there are Turkish regulars out there somewhere, and if they should ever hit us in force, we'll be in trouble," Achille explained his anxiety. "You know our beloved Major Tobino gets drunk every night, and the headquarters in Benghazi is too far away to send help. I've got a hundred and eighty enlisted men, green, half-trained recruits who want to go home to their mothers. I have three second lieutenants who want to go home to their wives. Sergeant Major Papafava is the only combat veteran among us, and my second-in-command is a sex-crazed Jewish Catholic who thinks war is going to be amusing."

"Achille, there's nothing out there," Guido told him dryly. "The duty officer ran patrols through the night, and the only exciting thing they found was the skeleton of a camel. No bedouin and no Turkish regulars. And a dispatch came this morning from the intelligence people in Benghazi saying that enemy activity was unlikely for forty-eight hours."

"My father once told me to plan assiduously for anything Army Intelligence regarded as unlikely," Achille muttered. "Let's take a walk into Sidi Osman. I want to take another look around."

Guido groaned. Both men strapped Beretta automatic pistols to their Sam Browne belts and put on their flat-topped field caps. They were wearing the standard Italian Army field uniform of shiny black calf-length boots and a *giubba,* or field jacket, over tan linen shirts.

"When are we going to see all that wonderful farmland the government promised?" Achille wondered aloud as they passed their sentry and crossed the open field toward Sidi Osman. Prime Minister Giolitti had been talking about capturing enough arable real estate to give farms to the tens of thousands of Italian immigrants who would someday flock to Libya.

As far as they could see, North Africa did not even have enough farmland to keep the Arab population adequately fed. The village of Sidi Osman was surrounded by cultivated fields, and in the distance a half-starved cow was turning an ancient wooden contraption designed to lift water from a well to the surface of the prairie. Date palms and olive trees dotted the horizon, and all around them stalks of barley struggled for survival.

"Assalam Aleikum!" Nearing the mud wall that surrounded Sidi Osman, they encountered an elderly Arab on a camel. Achille greeted him with the Arabic phrase for "Peace be with you."

The old man was wearing the standard dirty white thobe, a garment that began on top as a man's shirt and continued down to his ankles like a dress. On his head, he wore a white cotton scarf with blue stripes. The camel spat halfheartedly in their direction, but the rider passed without response.

"Unfriendly sods," said Guido. The Libyans showed no gratitude for Italy's generosity in rescuing them from the Ottoman Empire, a fact Lieutenant Rosselli resented almost as much as their unwillingness to come and fight with him.

Just inside the town wall they heard a high-pitched, undulating voice, the muezzin of Sidi Osman's mosque calling the faithful to prayer. Achille assumed that only old men and young boys would be answering the call, since women seldom attended services and there did not seem to be any young males around. Had Sidi Osman's men all joined the guerrilla forces in the desert?

"What's he saying?"

"Allah Akbar means 'God is great,' but I can't get the rest of it," Achille confessed. "Keep your eyes open."

Thus far, there had been no violence against B Company, and Sidi Osman seemed to contain more misery than menace. It was a town of perhaps fifty small houses. On the periphery, the poorer inhabitants lived in wretched mud-brick dwellings with no roofs at all. As the two Italian officers made their way toward the piazza in the center of Sidi Osman, the standard of habitation improved: the houses were larger and the mud-brick walls were splashed with a coating of whitewash and covered by roofs of corrugated iron.

There were flies everywhere. The main avenue into town was empty except for one little girl of four or five wearing a filthy cotton smock, who was squatting in a corner, urinating. They saw that she was blind, her eyes covered with a white film.

In the town center, there were several veiled women drawing water from a well.

"I bet they're all young and beautiful," Guido guessed optimistically, but each woman was covered from head to toe with a solemn black chadour. On the far side of the square, there was an old oak tree with great soaring branches and a small, one-room mosque. On the roof of the mosque was a platform where the muezzin climbed five times every twenty-four hours to issue the *adzan,* the Islamic summons to prayer.

"My father always told me to notice what wasn't there," Achille said. "What aren't we seeing?"

"Children." Guido's reply was prompt and accurate. "When we were here the other day, this place was crawling with kids, and today there was only that blind girl. And look, Comandante! Don't Arabs take their sandals off when they enter a mosque?"

"Oh Cristo!" Achille quickly glanced away because the women were watching them, their brown eyes flashing beneath their veils. But he had seen enough. In front of the mosque, there were dozens and dozens of the crude leather sandals. The door of the mosque was closed. From inside they could hear the murmur of deep voices. Many voices.

Sidi Osman's men had come home.

"Did you catch them yourself? Tell me quickly."

Corporal Grassi was puzzled at the strident tone in Lieutenant Leone's voice. In the past, his Comandante had always been delighted with the Neapolitan cuisine his aide-de-camp managed to produce here in the North African desert.

"I wanted to make *spezzato di lepre*." Grassi was resentful. These two splendid hares weighed at least two kilos apiece, and he had gone to a lot of trouble to get them for dinner.

"You traded for them?"

"Just two tins of bully beef."

"Rabbit stew is wonderful." Achille controlled his impatience while Guido swept the horizon with his field glasses. Inside the B Company encampment, Achille's three rifle platoon leaders, all second lieutenants, frantically organized their defensive positions and issued ammunition, field rations, and water. "Ti prego, Franco, I need to know exactly where you got these animals."

"From the other cook." Grassi pointed east. "I met him about a mile that way. We were both gathering parsley."

"What other cook? There are no other Italian units in this area."

"He didn't speak Italian, signore." Franco frowned, recalling his own perplexity at discovering that there were cooks who did not speak Italian. "He wore a brown uniform with a funny-looking hat."

"A fez!" Arab men wore head scarves, and Italian soldiers wore field caps. Turks wore a conical affair called a fez, and the existence of a parsley-gathering cook in a fez meant there was an Ottoman Empire unit bivouacked not far from his eastern perimeter.

It was insane. Out there was a Turkish commander preparing to attack the Italian invaders. In the meantime, their cooks were amicably exchanging rabbits for tins of dried beef.

"I still can't believe it." Guido returned to the table, where Achille was pondering a Royal Army ordnance chart of the area. "Sidi Osman is just a pimple on Benghazi's ass. Why would the Turks come through here?"

"Look!" Achille turned the map upside down, remembering what his father had said about seeing the terrain as the enemy commander would see it. With his finger, he traced the wadi, the dry riverbed running past his position and winding off toward Benghazi. "There's a village called Benina about twenty kilometers to the east of us. There must be a Turkish unit there. Now if that commanding officer wants to attack Benghazi, what route will he take? What would you do?''

"You're right." Guido's finger slashed across the map. "If he can get by us, this is his most direct route."

"It's a good plan. That force of Senusi irregulars in Sidi Osman must have been ordered to distract us with an attack from the north while the Turks try to overrun us from the south. And tonight . . .''

"Tonight is New Year's Eve, Comandante. They will expect us to be having a celebration."

"It's going to happen tonight. Are you frightened?"

"I'm not sure. Should I be?"

"It would show a modicum of good sense, Guido. Let's get ready."

At dusk, a cannon fired twice.

Thanks to his training at the Military Academy, Lieutenant Leone recognized the faint, distant *pufft!* of a Krupp two-wheeled field cannon, but it was difficult to believe that three pounds of high explosives were now flying in their direction. Except for Sergeant Major Papafava, a veteran of Italy's 1896 Ethiopian campaign, none of them had ever been shot at before.

There was a moment of silence as the projectile reached its apogee and they tried to persuade themselves that the danger had gone elsewhere. Then there was a high-pitched whine as gravity took hold and the Turkish shell fell toward them.

"It's going to miss," Giuseppe Papafava informed them. Achille nodded, resolving that he would not duck until his sergeant major ducked.

The impact was fifty meters south of their position, but the blast was terrible, throwing hot sand and pebbles over them. A few men cried out with fear, but most of Achille's troopers hunkered down defiantly in their trenches, shouting horrible curses at an enemy they could not see.

"Another incoming, sir." This time, even the grizzled Papafava ducked and Guido Rosselli dived into the trench beside them, landing on top of a terrified Franco Grassi. The shell screamed across the evening sky to fall harmlessly into the barley field between them and Sidi Osman. A shower of topsoil sprayed into their area and Achille looked around apprehensively, but one by one, his platoon leaders signaled that their men were unhurt.

They braced for a third round, but silence settled over the desert.

"One too short and one too long. And then nothing?" Guido looked perplexed. Both officers glanced questioningly at Sergeant Major Papafava.

"That Turkish gunner's done his bracketing," the veteran noncom grunted.

"You're right. He's zeroed us in," Achille agreed. "He now knows what calibration on his sights will put the next shell into our position. And he's holding his fire."

"Until his infantry is ready to attack?" Lieutenant Rosselli asked. "Look, shouldn't we try to hit that Ottoman commander before he hits us? Achille, give me a platoon and I'll bring you his balls on a platter.''

"Guido, there could be a thousand Turkish soldiers out there." Achille was trying to project a calmness and confidence he did not feel. I hope I know what I'm doing, he thought. If I get this wrong, most of us are going to be dead before morning. "No, we're going to have a party with singing and feasting.''

"I suppose this means I can't go to the brothel?'' Guido climbed out of the trench.

"Admit it,'' Achille challenged him. "You're loving every minute of this.'' They spoke in whispers, as if in church. The desert's stillness had become oppressive.

With a grin, Guido dashed through the fast-fading light to put in motion the defensive arrangements Achille had devised. Two of their three rifle platoons quickly jumped down into trenches facing Sidi Osman, while the third moved east to cover the desert approach to their encampment. A moment later, the company cook lit a huge fire in front of the dining tent and a half dozen voices began a ragged chorus of an old army drinking song. After checking his eastern perimeter to calm a nervous Lieutenant Siciliano, Achille strolled west to where Guido was waiting with the other two platoons. The enlisted men were poised over their rifles, straining their eyes in the dark.

Behind them in the mess tent, the company cook was now banging pots and pans together, creating as much cheerful racket as possible. Corporal Franco Grassi was bellowing a Neapolitan drinking song involving a boy and a girl and repetitive violations of the Sixth Commandment. Achille waited, staring in the direction of Sidi Osman and listening to Grassi's obscene ditty. Absurdly, he wondered what Rosaria was doing at this precise moment.

"Machine guns are ready.'' Guido moved near him in the trench, holding a Very pistol. "Spot anything?''

"There!'' Achille suddenly caught sight of a shadowy movement two hundred meters in the direction of Sidi Osman. "How many do you see?''

"Cristo! There must be a hundred of them.'' Guido spoke in a whisper. The barley field was now filled with Senusi warriors, wearing thobes and head scarves and carrying rifles, moving silently toward the Italian position. They were counting on the dark and the fecklessness of their enemy, since there was no cover, and the grain was not high enough to offer much concealment.

"Cannon fodder.'' Achille wonder if his father had ever suffered a moment's hesitation before giving the order to open fire. "I suppose we had better start killing them.''

The flare was beautiful. From the Very pistol in Guido's hand, it soared a hundred meters into the sky, turning the darkness of a barley field into a festival of phosphorous light. Franco and the others stopped singing.

Achille shaded his eyes, watching the Senusi. In this situation, professional soldiers would know that their only hope for survival lay in pressing the attack, taking heavy casualties until they could storm into the Italian perimeter. But the Arabs froze, uncertain and perplexed. Then they turned and bolted, foolishly hoping to outrun the bullets and regain the safety of Sidi Osman.

"Open fire!" On Achille's command, the Breda machine guns burst into action, firing four hundred rounds a minute, and the six savage automatics tore into the crowd of confused Arabs, knocking them down in droves. The Italian riflemen concentrated on the edges of the mob, picking off those who tried to flee laterally into the desert and the few who stood and fought.

Only a few hostile bullets flew into the Italian trenches. A few steps to Achille's right, a man screamed "Porco Dio!"—dying with the ultimate blasphemy "God is a pig!" on his lips. I'll have to write to his mother, Achille thought, watching as a squad leader checked the man and then shook his head.

Achille turned away from the dead trooper, knowing he would have to defer his grief. Right now, there were decisions to be made despite the noise and confusion. Acrid smoke and the smell of cordite filled the air, making it difficult to breathe.

"We've got them." Guido was on his feet, straining his eyes to see into the battlefield, ignoring the bullets flying around him.

"Cease fire!" Achille shouted, but it took a full minute to get the shooting stopped. Quickly, he drove his two platoons across the encampment at a dead run, leaving one solitary rifle squad to preside over the blood-soaked barley field.

It was the first half of his first battle and he allowed himself a moment's pride as he watched his troopers shift into their new positions, facing the desert to the south. I command a hundred and eighty men, he reflected, and not one of them ran away when the bullets began flying. Only one of them is dead.

Attentively, Achille watched his riflemen reload their weapons. On his right and left flanks, machine-gun crews were orienting the Bredas, pointing them at white aiming stakes planted that afternoon a few meters east of their position. In the dark, the gunners would fire at their aiming stakes and hope they were hitting something.

There was a murmur of conversation up and down the line, as friends reestablished contact. The men touched each other and hugged with the innocent intimacy of survivors.

"Quiet!" Achille hissed, and the command rippled down the line. Then they heard voices coming from the east, the rumble and crunch of hundreds of boots moving across the desert floor.

There was a sliver of a moon, and they could barely see the Turks as they approached, stopping two hundred meters from the Italian position, cautious and puzzled at the silence.

Achille cupped his hands and screamed, "Allah Akbar!"

"Allah Akbar!" Guido and Sergeant Papafava joined in and quickly the entire Italian force took up the chorus, shouting the Arabic words they had heard the muezzin sing out five times a day from the minaret of the mosque in Sidi Osman.

"Allah Akbar!" came the answering cry from the desert as the Turks agreed that God was indeed great. They surged innocently forward, assuming that the Italian position was taken and the Senusi were praising Allah.

"When the doing of nothing is what the moment requires," Leonida had once counseled him, "then do nothing."

Achille recited his father's advice beneath his breath. For a few hundred seconds, he did the obligatory nothing, watching as the front ranks of the Turkish infantry blundered guilelessly up to the Italian position. At their head was a Turkish colonel shouting exuberantly in Arabic, and Achille watched him until he was only a stone's throw away.

"The poor bastards." He picked up a Sipe hand grenade.

"That's the enemy, Comandante," Guido reminded him.

"They're poor bastards anyway," he said. "We're all poor bastards. Open fire!"

A Blériot biplane rumbled across the sky on a reconnaissance run, soaring a thousand meters over their heads. Seeing that the fighting along the Benina Road had come to an end, the pilot dipped his wings in a graceful salute and swung back toward Benghazi.

"This is going to look very good in the newspapers," announced the commander of the Seventh Infantry Regiment, putting his hand on Achille's shoulder as they gazed out toward the oasis of Sidi Osman. Colonel Frederico Adamo had a magnificent white mustache and he twisted the ends into fine little points as he spoke. "If we hadn't stopped them here, Leone, we'd be fighting them in Benghazi right now. I'm not sure your father could have done it any better, and Rome is going to be very happy with the Seventh Infantry Regiment."

"Grazie, signore." Achille's eyes were fastened on the distant figure of Giuseppe Papafava, who was moving among the bodies in the barley field. From time to time, he heard a pistol shot as the Sergeant Major dispatched an Arab who was badly wounded but still alive. Following their sergeant was a squad with shovels, digging quick and shallow graves.

"How many Arabs did we get?" Colonel Adamo seemed to think uniquely of how it was all going to look in the newspapers. Battalion Commander Tobino had arrived at dawn, long after the shooting was over, and had spent the morning explaining how his tactical brilliance had turned the tide.

"Perhaps fifty, sir. I'll have an exact count shortly," Achille promised, irritated by the presence of all these high-ranking intruders in his company area. He tried to snap out of it, ordering himself to be cheerful, but he knew he was depressed. Do I want to do this the rest of my life? he wondered. I could be home with Rosi.

"And how many Ottoman troops did you get?"

"Signor Colonnello, we killed or captured about half a battalion. Most of the others retreated." Achille repressed a shudder, recalling the worst moment in the battle. Heroically, an Ottoman lieutenant had led a handful of troops through the confusion of the battlefield into the forward Italian trench, abruptly transforming a relatively sanitary firefight into savage hand-to-hand combat. Battling suicidally, the lieutenant had bayoneted an Italian trooper to death, and then surged murderously toward Achille himself. Caught off-guard, Achille had been trying frantically to get his automatic out of his holster when Guido Rosselli had appeared with his Beretta and fired a round into the Turk's skull. The lieutenant's head had disintegrated.

"You must have taken out a couple of companies. Your own casualties?"

Achille cleared his throat to disguise the emotion he felt. "I have two men killed, and thirteen wounded. I was hoping to get the Bronze Medal for Valor presented to the families of the two deceased men."

"Certainly, certainly, medals for everyone." Adamo waved his hand dismissively as he moved to his waiting staff car. "And a promotion for you. You can sew on your captain's pips today."

"Ah . . . thank you, sir!" For a moment, Achille was too stunned to react. A battlefield promotion! The after-action gloom lifted slightly as he realized that he was going to be a captain at twenty-five. Plenty of officers finished thirty-year careers as captains.

It did occur to him that he had not quite won the Battle of Sidi Osman single-handedly. "Ah, Signor Colonnello, I also want to commend my executive officer, Sottotenente Rosselli. We planned the battle together and he saved my life during the fighting."

"Oh, your Hebrew officer?" The colonel shrugged with a certain genteel distaste. Italy prided itself on being free from anti-Semiticism, but there were few Jewish officers in the army, and the general staff preferred it that way. "Fine, put him in for a medal as well."

"Perhaps promotion to full lieutenant?"

"I can't promote everyone, Leone."

"Ah, well, I would find it difficult to accept a promotion for myself unless . . ." Achille began diplomatically, but Adamo laughed, aware that he was being gently bullied by Leonida Leone's son.

"Bene, send me the paperwork on Rosselli, and I'll sign it," he growled. Achille saluted politely and the staff car pulled away.

*   *   *

His body aching with fatigue and a dozen bruises, Achille wandered out into the desert, looking for Guido. I've just won my first battle, he told himself firmly, searching for the exhilaration that ought to have been there. This was what being a soldier was all about, what his father had done all his life, and his father before him.

About three hundred meters east of the encampment, there was a single pistol shot. Achille tensed and drew his service automatic before following the sound down into the dry riverbed that ran west from the desert toward Benghazi.

"Guido!" The Venetian lieutenant was standing over the body of a Turk. Achille saw that the dead soldier was only a boy, no more than seventeen, with massive, terrible wounds in his loins and abdomen.

"He was dying," Guido said brokenly, and Achille saw tears on his friend's face. "He must have been lying here all night with his stomach torn open. I didn't know what else to do, so I aimed at his heart to put him out of his agony. He opened his eyes and looked at me just as I pulled the trigger."

Instinctively Achille put his arms out, and the two young men embraced. Then they pulled apart, both embarrassed at the spectacle of two commissioned officers hugging in a wadi with a dead Turkish adolescent at their feet. Together, they walked away quickly until they reached the shade of a date palm.

"Here, have some of this." Achille reached into the pocket of his *giubba* and produced his leather-covered whiskey flask. "Let's celebrate! They're promoting both of us."

"We'll be generals before we're forty." Guido took a long, grateful drink before returning the flask. "Where did you get this?"

"My father stole it from the Archbishop of Palermo." Achille still did not much like the taste of whiskey, but he took a gulp and felt the liquor revive him. "It's rather a long story."

"The battle was exhilarating while it was happening, but now I feel a little . . . cast down," Guido admitted as they walked slowly back to the company encampment. "Do you think we were meant to be soldiers? Maybe I should have been a businessman like my father, and sometimes I think you would be happier as a schoolteacher."

"In my family, we have been soldiers for five hundred years." Achille shrugged. "I suppose we would all have been happier as schoolteachers."

2.

· ·

"That's not a proper gallows," Lieutenant Rosselli said indignantly. "They're going to hoist them up there and let them strangle. Shooting a man in battle is one thing, but can we really hang them just for carrying weapons?"

Captain Achille Leone shook his head grimly, knowing that his father would never have stood for this barbarism. But did they have any legal right to intervene?

There had been another massive Arab offensive in the first week of March 1912, and the Italian Army was desperate to deter the Arab population from supporting the Ottoman Army. Consequently, three months after B Company had shot most of the men in Sidi Osman during that now-famous New Year's Eve battle, a carabiniere military police detachment had trooped into the little oasis and arrested seventeen of the town's male survivors. The charge was illegal possession of firearms, a capital offense under Italy's emergency martial law code. The carabinieri were now preparing to execute the guilty men with a rope thrown over the lowest branch of Sidi Osman's only oak tree.

The town seethed with misery and all around them was the shrill sound of keening, the high-pitched undulating cries of wives about to become widows. At the foot of the tree, a carabiniere lieutenant was fashioning a crude noose from one end of the rope. Nearby, there was an enclosure made of wattle that had previously been used for camels. Guarded by a squad of carabinieri, it now held the men caught with rifles. They gazed impassively at Achille as he looked at them.

It will take them all afternoon to execute seventeen men, he calculated, one at a time.

"Look, that one's just a kid," Guido observed. "He doesn't belong in there."

Achille saw that the Arab boy was barely into his teens. He had a bruise on his forehead; like the others, his arms were tied tightly behind his back. The child's thobe was torn at the knee and dirty, but his pale face was composed as he stood among the condemned men.

"Tenente, one of your prisoners is just a child."

The police lieutenant looked up coldly, not bothering to salute. The carabinieri provided Italy with both military and civilian police forces, and they had a reputation for ruthless obedience. Send the carabinieri a notarized written order to decapitate the contents of a convent, thought Achille, and you get a bunch of headless nuns and no questions.

"My orders are to execute any male found with a weapon. That kid's old enough to pull a trigger. Now get out of my way!"

Behind him, Achille heard angry muttering as several of his Lupi di Lazio troopers wandered over to the hanging tree, their rifles slung casually over their shoulders.

"Giuseppe, bring that child here," Achille ordered his sergeant major, pointing to the young man in the torn garment.

"Capitano, these are my prisoners!" snapped the lieutenant. His men looked up quickly but made no move to intervene as Sergeant Papafava marched the Arab boy out of the enclosure, holding him by the scruff of the neck. The child stumbled as he was pushed in front of Achille, but he caught his balance and looked up defiantly.

"Assalam Aleikum." Achille decided to test his Arabic. "Peace be with you, boy. What is your name?"

"I am Mustafa al-Sharif." The young man's voice crackled with puberty.

"And how old are you, Mustafa?"

"I am twelve, sir."

"And you live here?"

"I live in Benghazi, sir. I am visiting my cousin who lives here in Sidi Osman."

"And what were you doing with that rifle?"

"Defending my country, sir." Guileless but precise, Mustafa raised and lowered his shoulders to suggest that the answer was obvious.

Achille turned to the carabiniere lieutenant with a smile. "Just a misunderstanding, I'm afraid. He's a ten-year-old who was out hunting rabbits. We'll send him home to his mother."

"Not your decision, Captain." Defiantly, the carabiniere lieutenant motioned to his own second-in-command. "Corporal, put that prisoner back with the others."

Behind him, Achille heard a faint popping sound of a holster flap being unsnapped. With the barrel of his Beretta automatic, Guido scratched himself carefully under one ear while several of B Company's infantrymen unslung their rifles, pointing them casually in the direction of the execution squad.

"Go home, Mustafa, and don't play with rifles in the future," said Captain Leone, using his bayonet to cut the rope holding the boy's wrists together. Mustafa bowed respectfully and then sprinted out of the square as fast as his legs could take him.

Then Captain Leone turned and walked away while his men watched his flanks. The carabiniere lieutenant shrugged and got down to hanging the sixteen other prisoners.

• • •

Achille did not see Mustafa al-Sharif again until the end of April, when the Lupi di Lazio were pulled off picket duty at Sidi Osman and sent back into Benghazi for rest and reassignment.

On his first free day, Achille walked into the marketplace, what the Arabs called a souk, looking for a present for Rosaria.

The Benghazi souk was a tangled maze of tiny streets and winding avenues, where women in veils hawked goats and sheep and vegetables, and men in soiled thobes urged him eloquently in fragments of Italian to come in and buy. After the sober monochrome of the desert, the market was a riot of color, and Achille was dazed by its intensity, the noise and clatter of the merchants, and the smells of incense and spices.

There was a whole quartermastery of military gear on sale: helmets, boots, and bayonets, the flotsam and jetsam of a European army. Even pasta was available, long yellow strands of homemade tagliatelle wrapped in palm leaves and tied with bits of string. Despite the *Koran*'s stern prohibition against alcohol, there were *fiaschi* of good Italian wine.

Since Benghazi was now a garrison town, there were also women on offer, lurking in darkened corners of the souk and flashing quick invitations at him. Venturing into one tent to inspect some linen, Achille was confronted by a dark-skinned waif, not more than fourteen, who casually lifted her dress to display her belly and loins and then reached between her legs to spread the lips of her vagina.

Achille shook his head and turned away to encounter another girl, her shoulders bare and her body concealed behind the flaps of a tent. Her brown, oval face was marked with smallpox scars, and she put her middle finger between her lips and moved it rapidly in and out of her mouth, giving him a blank, dead stare.

Not even Guido would take a chance on you, he decided with a combination of desire and disgust.

He walked away quickly, concentrating instead on his memory of Rosaria's clean, splendid body and that fragment of unfinished time they had spent together in her bedroom. In her letters, all neatly typed on the new Olivetti, she was restrained, saying simply how much she missed him.

It will be wonderful when I am home, he fantasized. We will go somewhere safe from interruption and finish what we had begun, and then sit up in bed and talk and plan. Now, if I send her an expensive, romantic present, tongues will wag, so I'll buy gifts for everyone as camouflage. She will understand.

That means a souvenir for my wretched sister. Eastern fashions are all the rage right now; perhaps Giorgina would like a white linen dress. Father would appreciate an elegantly hand-printed Koran, while my musical little brother shall have one of these Arab mandolins to strum. A jeweled dagger for Girolamo, and Sandro gets a book on famous Arab revolutionaries. For Rosi, something feminine and delicate, a silver necklace, perhaps, or even a ring . . .

He was studying a tray of handmade filigree jewelry when someone touched his arm.

"Signor Capitano." Achille turned quickly, his hand moving to his pistol. It took him a moment to recognize Mustafa al-Sharif because the young man was now expensively dressed and followed by two servants carrying packages. It occurred to Achille that he must have rescued a number of the Libyan aristocracy.

"Oh, hello there. No rifle today?"

"Please come with me." Smiling with a natural sense of command, Mustafa shook hands with his Italian benefactor, and then led him through the tangle of stalls and booths to the far edge of the bazaar. Crossing a wide boulevard, they entered an upper-class neighborhood and—after a few minutes' walk—halted in front of an elaborately decorated iron gate.

An ancient manservant appeared, bowing respectfully to the young Arab, but Mustafa sent him quickly into the elegant two-story building with a message. For a few moments, Achille admired the spacious courtyard with carefully trimmed grass and a marble fountain. Then he followed Mustafa up the stairs into the villa itself.

At the door, Achille removed his boots as Arab custom demanded, although he felt foolish in his brown wool army socks. He wondered if etiquette required him to leave his side arm behind. Then he recalled Mustafa's fondness for guns and decided against it. He followed the boy into a large foyer, simply decorated with an Afghan carpet and cushions along the wall. Waiting for them there was a woman whose entire face and body were covered by a black chador.

"I don't know Italian." The veiled woman spoke near-perfect English with an upper-class British accent. "Do you by any chance speak English? Or perhaps French?"

"My English is better," Achille replied in the language he had learned from Helen Higgens. "Although I was taught by my Irish nanny, so my accent isn't as aristocratic as yours."

"I can hear Dublin in your voice, and it's lovely. I wanted to thank you so much for saving my son. I know you risked your life."

"There was no risk, and I was happy to be of service."

Achille bowed and they all sat on cushions on the floor. The woman clapped her hands briskly, and a servant entered with a samovar and served them mint-flavored green tea in tiny cups.

"Mustafa must thank both Allah and you for his deliverance." The woman's voice was appealingly deep and throaty, but the all-encompassing black veil gave no hint of her appearance.

"How is it that you speak such excellent English?" Achille asked.

"We are an Arab family, of course, but my late husband was an official in the Ottoman diplomatic service. He served for three years at the Turkish Embassy in London, where I had the opportunity to learn the language. May we know your name? I am called Anfi al-Sharif."

"I am Captain Achille Leone."

"Leone? Is that a common name in Italy? There was a famous Leonida Leone who was the Italian Ambassador in London when we were there. He fought in your country's war of independence and his name is in all the history books."

"Leone is a common name, but the famous one is indeed my father." Achille was gratified that an Arab woman had heard of his family. Leonida Leone was well-known to Italians, but few foreigners would know that much about Italy's past. "Do you like history?"

"Yes. Are you surprised?" she asked with a silvery, exciting laugh. "My father and husband were both educated men and we have a wonderful library here. Mustafa tells me that you are learning our language, and all the great works of Arabic literature are at your disposal. Shall I show you?"

"I need a better Italian-Arabic dictionary," Achille said as he followed Mustafa's mother down a passageway into a large vaulted room with thousands of books, mostly in Turkish and Arabic but many in English or French.

"You Italians seem determined to be our guests." Anfi al-Sharif's voice went a little cold. "I suppose we shall all need Arabic-Italian dictionaries."

"I should tell you that my father was very angry at the government's decision to send the Royal Army here. I myself had hoped your people would see that we were rescuing Libya from Ottoman domination."

"For several thousand years now, we have been rescued by one imperial army after another, and our liberators never seem to leave until someone else comes to rescue us," she told him dryly. "After five hundred years of Ottoman rule, it was time for our Turkish brothers to go home, but we had hoped for independence. Instead, we have another set of colonial masters. It is very disappointing."

"I understand your feelings," Achille said. "But the French have conquered Tunisia and Algeria and they will have Morocco before long. The British rule Egypt and the Sudan. Some colonial power would inevitably have taken this territory, and you are better off with Italy, because we intend to bring you modern science and medicine and farming technology and European culture."

"We shall perhaps be grateful for the science and medicine." There was now a distinct edge to Anfi's voice. "But we already have a culture based on Islam, and our literature and . . . ah, well, our culture demands courtesy to guests and I am on the verge of being rude. Captain Leone, you seem to have inherited great kindness from your illustrious father. If you are really interested in doing something for my people, then you need to know more about us. This library is available when you are ready to learn."

"Thank you. I want to learn to speak and read the Arabic language," he told her sincerely. "I have made a very slow beginning."

"Our language was formed by the Koran." She ran her fingers lightly over a row of leather-bound volumes until she found a pocket-sized Arabic text. "Let me give you this copy. Infidels are not supposed to touch our holy book, but we will make an exception. You need not believe in it, but it will teach you to love our language."

"That is very gracious of you." Achille accepted the Koran, impressed by the force of Anfi's personality. Arab women were reputed to be uneducated and submissive, but this one spoke with a certain blunt brilliance. He pocketed the Koran and followed Anfi toward the door, wishing he could see her face. *She must be older than I,* he estimated, *but she has the voice of a beautiful woman.*

"What you have done for Mustafa has made you very special to us, although our countries are now at war." She extended a hand from beneath the chador. Her skin was honey-brown, and on her middle finger she wore a simple golden ring. "You must come to us should you ever need sanctuary."

He was puzzled by her comment. "I would love to look again at your library, although I hope that I shall never be forced to ask for your protection."

"Your army conquers today." Anfi al-Sharif squeezed his hand with surprising force. "But Allah may require that you have some sorrow on another day. And there are various kinds of sanctuary. Good-bye, Captain Leone."

3.

....

Outside, it was windy and overcast, but they were all sitting cheerfully in the Castello's salotto where Girolamo had built a roaring fire to keep them warm. Leonida had poured out a late-afternoon brandy for everyone. Terenzio was at the family Blütner, playing all the latest songs from Paris.

Rosaria was wearing a new white linen dress that had cost a month's salary. Around her neck was a gold filigree necklace that would have cost her a year's earnings had it not been a present, arriving in a discreet package from Libya. She felt beautiful. She wished Achille were there to see how she looked.

Approaching from behind, a maid whispered discreetly in her ear. Sandro was at the kitchen door and wanted a word with her.

Her first reaction was irritation at being disturbed. She had already done a full day's work. Then she felt guilty. I'm turning into a cheap imitation of Giorgina, she rebuked herself, and went to the kitchen.

"Did you ask him?" Sandro demanded.

"I . . . I haven't had a chance," she quavered, worried that he would notice the necklace and demand to know who was presenting her with expensive jewelry.

Suddenly she was struck by the increasing social distance between them. She stood just inside the Castello door, wearing a linen dress. Her brother was standing on the back step with a cloth cap in his hands. There was dirt beneath his fingernails and his trousers were covered with mud.

"Look, sorellina, we absolutely need to know today."

"It's only the first of May."

"Look at the sky! We could get a spring rain at any time," Sandro exploded. "Once that field turns to mud, I won't be able to do anything with it."

"Leonida finished another chapter of his memoirs today, and now he's relaxing with Terenzio," she excused herself lamely. "I didn't want to interrupt his concentration, and we normally deal with farm business on Fridays when Bruno comes up."

"Oh, do we?" Abruptly, Sandro was angry. "Listen, this job of yours can only be justified if you use your position to the advantage of your compagni. If you become a handmaiden to the nobility, people will see you as a class traitor."

"All right, as soon as I can get him alone." She turned away with a shake of her head, knowing this would all become much worse when Achille came home to claim her as his special compagna. Would Sandro ever accept it? He was still talking about marrying her off to his friend Emilio Lodi. He would always demand solidarity with the working class. Even in bed.

As she returned to the salotto, Leonida looked up and smiled at her before continuing his argument with Terenzio. "Play something authentic," he teased his younger son. "How about some Verdi? That's real music."

"Papa, this is real music. Now listen carefully!" The normally frivolous Terenzio was totally serious about playing the piano. "These are three short pieces called *Gymnopédies*. Do you remember? We met the composer in Paris three years ago and he gave me the sheet music."

"That funny little piano-playing man? We bought him dinner?"

"We bought him lunch," Terenzio remembered. "Listen."

He began to play again, with softness and deliberation. Rosaria settled herself by Leonida's side, trying to absorb the performance. Accustomed to nothing more complicated than bouncy peasant songs, she found this music strange and sophisticated, whimsical and yet filled with a cool, controlled sadness.

She tried to get her courage up, telling herself that today was a good day to ask for a favor. Achille had just won another battle and Terenzio had finally passed Latin.

He won't be angry, she reassured herself. Giorgina and Bruno get furious whenever I interfere with the estate, but I've been His Excellency's secretary for a year now, and we are friends, despite everything. He knows all the famous people in Italy and the King writes him letters and the Prime Minister calls him on the telephone.

But when he is depressed or worried about Achille, I am the one he wants to see. Me!

Terenzio's music ended with incredible softness, and the pianist rested his fingers on the keyboard, waiting for comments.

"It's very gentle," Rosaria offered hesitantly.

"Of course, but it lacks, ah . . . *testicularità*," Leonida searched for a word. "Now listen, if you want delicacy, listen to this. "Teri, play 'Caro Nome' for Rosaria."

"Dear Name" turned out to be light and exquisite, at least the way Terenzio performed it. Rosaria closed her eyes and saw a very young girl with long blond hair pirouetting through a garden of immaculate white flowers.

"It's from *Rigoletto,* one of Verdi's most savage operas," Leonida explained in an undertone, conducting with his right hand as he leaned toward her. "But in the middle of all the anger and hatred, there is this gentle moment when a pure young girl named Gilda sings of her love for a man whom she believes to be an impoverished student. He is really the villainous Duke of Mantua in disguise, but when he tells her that his name is Gualtier Maldé, she falls in love with him and his silly name."

"When people fall in love," she said, thinking of Achille, "names don't make any difference."

"Names always make a difference." Leonida disagreed. "When you fall in love, fanciulla, make sure you know your man's real name. It isn't always what's written on his birth certificate. Maybe that's what Verdi is trying to tell us. You've never seen *Rigoletto?*"

"I've never been to an opera." For an moment, she was almost angry at him. Do you think peasants sit around in your fields, she wanted to ask, playing our grand pianos and listening to *musica lirica?*

Leonida seemed uncomfortable, as if overcome by memories. "Then we must take you to see something by Giuseppe Verdi," he promised. "My father knew Verdi well, and I met him in 1861 when we were both elected deputies to the first Italian parliament after unification. Neither one of us was cut out for that kind of politics, and we lost contact when I went back to the army and he returned to writing music, but after my wife died, I used to go to hear his *Requiem* whenever I got the chance, because it . . . well, it meant a great deal to me."

"Do you miss her, Signor Conte?" Rosaria leaned forward impulsively and touched his hand.

"I . . . well, I miss . . . yes, of course." He was now horribly embarrassed.

"I'm sorry. It was a stupid question."

Rising abruptly from the sofa, he smiled and touched her cheek with the back of his hand. "You need never regret anything you say to me as long as it is honest, fanciulla. Remember, we have a date to go listen to some Verdi. And now, this old man needs a pre-dinner nap."

Oh, Sandro's field, she suddenly remembered, and she caught Leonida at the top of the stairs.

"Signor Conte, I wanted to ask you something. You know that empty field out by the chestnut grove? Last night, the workers had a meeting and decided to ask you whether they could plow it up. Sandro would be in charge, and they would work . . . I mean, we would work during our time off, in the evenings and on Sundays."

Leonida looked puzzled. "There's about three hectares out there, but I haven't actually looked at the field for years. I don't remember it as being very good land, which is why we never used it. What would your friends do with it?"

"Plant wheat," she explained, following him into the study. "Then, if we could use the *mola* to grind the wheat into flour, we could do our own baking. Right now, we have to buy bread from Mayor Mosconi's store in Cederna, and he keeps raising his prices."

"Let's go have a look at it," he said, taking a hacking jacket from behind the door. "I don't mind irritating Mosconi, but I'm not sure you can grow much of anything in that field. You need something to put over your shoulders."

"I'll run home for a coat."

"Oh, there should be something here for you." Leonida ducked into a closet and reappeared with a long, heavy black cape of virgin wool, which he draped over her. With a shock, Rosaria realized that the elegant garment must have once belonged to Contessa Maria Pia.

"Oh, it's lovely."

"Keep it. No one else wears it."

Stunned, she followed him down the front stairs, hoping she would not be seen by Giorgina while wearing her late mother's cloak.

Outside, they trudged toward the *castagneto*, the chestnut grove, where young men from Cederna sometimes took their girlfriends for romance among the bushes. The sky was darkening and there was a cold mist over the fields, and Rosaria guessed that no one would be there in this weather making love. This was the same *castagneto* where she had gone as a child with Sandro and Achille and Terenzio and Tommaso Savarino to play red Indians among the trees, hiding in the tall grass and building campfires to roast chestnuts.

They left the shelter of the grove and walked out onto the deserted field, feeling an icy wind off the Tyrrhenian Sea. Not far off in another field, Sandro and a group of men were leading a pair of oxen back and forth.

"Sandro!" she shouted, and watched nervously as her brother approached with his assistant, Emilio Lodi.

"Signor Conte?" Despite their shared advocacy of revolutionary socialism, both Sandro and Emilio took their caps off when they reported to Leonida. Emilio Lodi was a skinny, bearded twenty-year-old man from Cederna who had once been arrested for thievery. He would have been sent to the penitentiary had Leonida not intervened with an offer of honest employment.

"This is the field you want for wheat?" Count Leone inquired. "Can you get a plow through that clay?"

"I'll take the responsibility for the whole operation," Sandro said stoutly. "All we want is a little land to grow some *grano duro* for ourselves, especially if our salaries are going to be cut."

"Who said anything about cutting salaries?"

"Signor Benelli said it would be necessary if grain prices fall again this year," Emilio burst in.

"That's ridiculous." Leonida was angry, but he controlled his temper quickly. "The price of wheat is not going down, and it would hardly be your fault if it did. Listen, you can have the land for your own wheat if you want to do the extra work. I'll contribute the seed, and my son-in-law can go to hell. Good luck."

"Were we wrong to ask to use that land?" Rosaria and Leonida were halfway back to the Castello before she broke the silence.

"No, I'm sorry I didn't think of it myself. I need to spend more time worrying about the men and women who work for me. Why didn't you tell me Bruno was threatening to lower wages?"

"We thought you knew."

"I didn't know, and now that I do, it's not going to happen. You need to tell me these things, fanciulla, now that you are my secretary. You can always trust me."

"From now on I will always trust you." She shivered. The afternoon was getting colder.

"Hai freddo, tu? Are you cold?" he asked, seeing her shoulders quiver. Only after a moment did it strike her that he had—for the first time—addressed her with the intimate pronoun "tu," which was used only among friends.

"Sì, e tu?" she answered. It felt natural. She wondered when Achille would tell his father about their relationship. Or did Leonida already know?

"Yes, let's go back. I know a shortcut." He turned to the right and they climbed over a hedgerow into a field of last year's corn stubble.

"Can you jump the stream?" Leonida asked courteously as they reached a narrow brook that ran down to the Tiber.

"I can if you can." Rosaria had been casually leaping this stream since infancy, but on this occasion she accepted the Count's hand as she gathered her skirts and skipped across.

"That's my personal little test," he sighed after he had bounded strenuously to the opposite bank. "I'll know I'm getting old when I can't jump this damn stream anymore."

"I don't think of you as old."

"I'm glad, because I could never get used to the idea." He took her arm again as they walked up onto the lawn. The wind was swirling around them now, and she pulled her cape more tightly around her.

"Do you think of me as young?" she asked impulsively.

"Yes, fanciulla. Very beautiful and very clever, but also very young."

"Is that why you call me 'fanciulla'?"

"I don't know." He looked at her in puzzlement. "It's just my word for you."

"Sandro calls me 'sorellina.' After Signorina Higgens taught Achille English, he started calling me 'Rosi,' as if I were British. And now you call me 'fanciulla.' It would be wonderful when people became friends if they invented secret names for one another, like you calling me 'fanciulla,' and I would call you . . . ."

"Yes, what would you call me?" he asked eagerly as they passed beneath the balustrade that united the north and south wings of the Castello Leone. Rosaria had never before come in the front door; like the other servants, she had always used the kitchen entrance.

"I don't know. Did you ever have a secret name?"

"Yes." His voice was abruptly tinged with emotion. "When we landed at Marsala in 1860, the Bourbons were shelling us and I had a moment of fear. Garibaldi saw me hanging back and he called me 'topo.' I was so angry at being called 'mouse' that I rushed to the beach and fought like a madman all day. Later, when we took Palermo, Garibaldi made me a captain, but he said that he knew there was a mouse inside of me, and whenever we were alone he always called me 'topo.' I didn't mind because I loved him.''

"Did your wife call you 'topo'?'' She regretted the question the moment the words had left her mouth. It's none of my business, she reprimanded herself.

"I never told my wife my secret name,'' he confessed as they stood in the formal gardens at the western entrance. "I should have, but somehow—well, it's late. You'll be wanting to get home.''

"Letting us use that land was very kind of you.'' Impetuously, she stood on her tip-toes and kissed his cheek. With a chuckle, the Count swept her into his arms for a mammoth hug, and for a moment they stood together with her head on his shoulder.

"Ask me for anything you want, fanciulla,'' he said.

"Thank you, topo.''

The moment was chaste and sincere, but as Leonida released her, Rosaria looked over his shoulder and saw Giorgina's furious face watching them from the window.

"We played Ghibellines off against Guelphs,'' Leonida Leone explained cheerfully as he turned onto the path toward the chestnut grove. "My family got this land five hundred years ago from a misguided Pope who had persuaded himself that we would transfer our loyalty from the Holy Roman Emperor to the Vatican.''

"Did it work?'' Sandro's mastery of Renaissance history was frail, but His Excellency seemed to be in a good mood. Was this a good day to ask for time to attend that Socialist Party training conference for new district leaders? After Amadeo Bordiga's visit to Cederna, Sandro had quickly organized a formal section of the PSI, even renting a ramshackle old two-story building in the Piazza Bixio as a headquarters.

Leonida chuckled. "No, because we were never loyal to anything except the idea of a united Italy. My ancestors hated German emperors and Roman pontiffs with equal fervor. We managed to hang on to everything from the hills over there to the Tiber.''

"Generations of my people have worked this land,'' Sandro reflected wistfully as the two men followed the path through the chestnut trees and came to what people in Cederna were beginning to call "the peasants' field,'' the tract Count Leone had allowed his employees to harvest for their own benefit. It was not the best soil, but Sandro's people were working it hard and the wheat shoots were already a few centimeters high.

"In an ideal world the land would belong to the people who till it,'' Leonida agreed. "But the real world is a rough place. If this land had been handed over to the peasants a hundred generations ago, it would have been long since ruined or lost.''

"Perhaps, but this is the twentieth century," Sandro objected. "Don't you think that we workers need to have some control over our own lives?"

"Yes, and that's what I wanted to talk to you about. The misunderstanding with Bruno over pay has made me feel the need for a general manager. Maybe it should be you. Naturally, there would be generous financial terms."

For a moment, Sandro was tempted. I'm twenty-five, he reasoned. I would be made for life. I could have a proper house and a wife. "This is like that scene in the New Testament when Lucifer tempts Jesus."

Leonida snorted. "You sanctimonious socialists! What is so diabolical about me offering you a decent job?"

"I've just been elected chairman of the PSI in Cederna, and we're organizing a labor union. How could I make a career in a capitalist corporation and also lead the workers?"

"You might be forced someday to call a strike against yourself." Leonida nodded. "Damn! I really do need a general manager, and I hate the idea of bringing in an outsider."

There was only one solution. Farming fundamentally bored Leonida, and his management style tended toward good-natured anarchy. Valeria oversaw the house and kitchen garden while Giorgina administered Valeria and tried to supervise everyone else. A forceful middle-aged man named Mercuzio Mercatelli performed many of the actual functions of a general manager, but poor Mercuzio had always been handicapped by illiteracy. Sandro was in charge of livestock while Bruno Benelli did the accounts, purchased seed and fertilizer, marketed what the estate produced, and complained about wage levels. As things stood, the only person who ever pulled together all the loose strings was Rosaria.

"Why not let my sister coordinate things?" he suggested lightly. "She's popular with the people who work in the fields, and you see her every day."

Count Leone frowned. "I realize she's smarter than the two of us put together, but I could hardly name a nineteen-year-old girl as general manager."

"Of course not, but she could be your administrative assistant, a kind of go-between. She wouldn't need a title, so long as people understood that she spoke in your name."

"So you wouldn't mind calling a strike against your little sister?" Leonida teased.

"I don't know anything about Ghibellines or Guelphs, Signor Conte," said Sandro as the two men turned away from the peasants' field and headed back toward the Castello, "but I can call a strike against anyone."

"Eccellenza, I've just seen your daughter, and . . ." Girolamo began hesitantly.

Leonida prepared himself for the worst. Ever since he had raised salaries across the board and allowed the work force to plow up that abandoned field for their own use, Giorgina had been sharply antagonistic. When he had announced that Rosaria Lombardi would be taking on some extra responsibilities in the running of the agricultural estate, intrafamilial warfare had broken out.

"Is the sun shining in my daughter's beautiful eyes?"

"Storm clouds have been gathering, M'lord."

"Old friend, we will require a preemptive cognac. A glass for each of us, if you please." Capping his fountain pen, Leonida gazed with affection as the crusty old soldier poured out two snifters of Vecchia Romana. He is only a few months older than I am, he remembered, and yet his body is twisted with arthritis. We have been together for fifty years. Time has been kind to me and cruel to him.

"You daughter wants you to see Don Maurizio Padana. He's outside and would like to speak with you before dinner."

"The priest was invited to dinner?" Leonida took a deep breath in an unsuccessful attempt to control his temper. "Girolamo, my daughter has taken to treating me like a senile old man whose wishes can be ignored whenever they conflict with her own. After that last horrific dinner, did I not give specific instructions that the vulture was not to be invited again?"

"You did, sir."

"I will murder him after the pasta course. Perhaps ecclesiastical bloodstains on the table linen will remind Giorgina to obey my orders."

"Very good, sir," said Girolamo. "Shall I load a pistol or will you be using table cutlery?"

Leonida laughed, pulling himself to his feet and straightening his collar. "Giro, you are the only man who always tells me the truth even when I'm having a tantrum. Tell me, am I getting to be an old fart?"

"Do you still have fantasies of women, Eccellenza?"

"I do, Girolamo, sometimes." A vision of Rosaria's lithe body skipped through his mind.

"Then you are still a middle-aged fart," Girolamo advised. "Don Maurizio is waiting. Shall I send him away?"

"Oh, show him in, Giro." A cloud of depression sank over him. The priests always start coming around when you hit seventy. But what did you expect from old age? I am rich and famous and . . . pointless.

Stoutly he tried to snap out of the blackness. You are the father of two fine sons, although Terenzio still needs to find himself. And unless he gets himself killed, Achille will be a great man, much greater than I was. He is smarter than I am, and more sensible. Or is he too sensible? He seems to lack madness. He never gets drunk, and one cannot imagine him making a fool of himself over a woman. Unlike his esteemed father.

"Leonida?" came Don Maurizio's stentorian voice. "Are you worried about your son?" The priest waddled into the study. Leonida studied him with distaste, noting that Cederna's curate had grown fat, but otherwise seemed as vigorous as ever in his sixtieth year. His black soutane stretched tightly over a bulging stomach, but the old clergyman moved with a certain grim energy.

"Of course. I would hate to see him perish in this foolish war."

"It is hardly foolish," countered the priest. "When the conquest is complete, the Church will send missionaries and convert the pagan Muhammadans."

"Islam is an ancient monotheism," Leonida reminded the cleric. He sat down and pointedly refrained from inviting Don Maurizio to do the same. "You can hardly call it paganism."

"Muhammadanism is a vile superstition."

"Priest, all religions are vile superstitions. Including yours. What do you want?"

The pastor walked boldly up to Leonida's oak desk. "Your family has come to me with their concern over your relationship with this young subversive woman," he said. "You have never accepted the authority of the Church, but I am apparently the only man in Cederna who is not afraid of you."

"What are you suggesting? I have no cause to reproach myself as far as Rosaria is concerned." Leonida was stunned that Giorgina should have raised this issue with an outsider. "She is merely my secretary, an arrangement suggested by my son."

"You have given her authority over your son-in-law, who feels humiliated. The situation has caused a scandal in Cederna, where the innocent townspeople believe that you have fallen in love with her. Have you, Leonida? It is one of the trials of our human condition that sexual desire should still be a bother to us even in our declining years, but God expects us to conquer our lusts."

Lust? Is that what this comes down to? Leonida rose abruptly and walked to the window. Old Leonida wanting a girl he cannot have? Ah, once there was a time when the lord of a manor could exercise the droit du seigneur over a pretty peasant wench, but this is the twentieth century.

And worse than destroying Rosaria's virtue would be taking her to bed and discovering that the destruction of virtue was now beyond your power. Be an old man, Leonida. It's time.

"Signor Conte?"

"If there is a God," said Leonida, looking down at the lights from the little cottage where Rosaria and her brother lived, "we should thank him for the gift of lust. It is the only reliable emotion we have."

"What?"

"Desidero ergo sum. As long as I still hate priests and lust after young girls, I know I'm still alive. Now get out!"

4.

....

"Grassi was always an idiot. Imagine, wandering off in enemy territory to hunt for herbs. If he comes back, he shall be court-martialed." Major Tobino stood before a map of Cyrenaica and examined the topography of Libya's eastern province. Wiping the perspiration from his forehead with the sleeve of his *giubba,* he marked the battalion's position with a lead pencil.

"We'll find him, sir." Achille Leone gazed at his commanding officer's chart for a moment, frowning as he studied the contour lines. Then he moved toward the door of Tobino's little wood hut.

"Leone, I don't want you sending out another patrol," Tobino shouted, feeling the need to exert his authority over his famous subordinate. "You can't risk lives to save your silly aide-de-camp."

"Sì, signore," Captain Leone assented, although he fully intended to disobey orders, locate his insouciant Neapolitan aide, and try to explain the difference between a war and a shopping expedition. "Ah, by the way, should we be making preparations to evacuate this encampment?"

"Are you telling me my business, Leone?"

"Signor Maggiore, I'm just asking you what you intend to do." Achille kept his voice level, but Tobino's behavior was beginning to worry him. First of all, the major had moved the entire Lupi di Lazio Infantry Battalion into the least defensible position in North Africa. Then he had apparently decided to settle down for the duration while Senusi troops gathered in the wilderness around them. Tobino's headquarters company had built him this fine little wooden hut, and he seemed indisposed to leave it.

"We will depart when we have accomplished our mission."

"Sì, signore." Achille saluted and left. It was too hot to argue, at least until after they had located Franco. August in North Africa was turning out to be warmer than anticipated, and nobody was functioning very well.

Pulling down the brim of his field cap to shield his eyes from the mid-afternoon sun, he walked back toward the B Company command post, which had been assigned the western perimeter of the battalion encampment.

Everything was going wrong. They had been ordered to conduct a reconnaissance patrol, but Tobino had nervously decided to bring the whole battalion, twenty-four officers, one thousand enlisted men, a battery of field cannon, and nine Fiat transport trucks. They were now deep in the desert with only enough ammunition, rations, and water for another week. The wilderness was populated by hostile bedouin tribes. Men were dropping from heat exhaustion. And Major Tobino seemed to be going crazy.

On his way back to the B Company sector, Achille saw that their precious trucks were being used at the moment as a source of shade. The big Fiat *autocarri* had proved hopeless in the desert. Their crude carburetors were constantly fouled by particles of desert dust, and their small, rubber-rimmed front wheels kept getting stuck in the sand, while the big back tires whirled uselessly. Most of the time the battalion ended up pushing nine heavy trucks across North Africa while the Senusi hunkered down behind rocks and took potshots at them. B Company was still intact, but the other three companies had already lost a total of nine men to sniper fire.

As a good engineer, Achille had been noting the design modifications that needed to be made on the Fiats before they could be deployed again in the desert, but the more immediate problem was getting back to headquarters in one piece. By his calculations, they were now one hundred kilometers southeast of Benghazi and eighty kilometers inland from the Gulf of Sidra, camped uncomfortably on the edge of a vast plateau that stretched off toward Egypt. They had left behind them the low, rolling sand dunes of the desert, and climbed into hilly, uneven terrain. The surface of the land here was baked mud, crisscrossed with deep ravines and wadis. There were mountains in the distance, but no water anywhere.

He stumbled into the torpid heat of the B Company command tent. "Any sign of Grassi?" he asked his second-in-command. Even the normally ebullient Guido looked shattered by the temperature.

"No news, Comandante."

"Guido, listen, poor Franco isn't the only bad geographer in the battalion," Achille blurted out. "Tobino is lost. I finally got a look at those charts of his, and he has us fifty kilometers closer to the coast than we actually are. And he doesn't seem to be making any plans to move out of here. Even if he knew how to find his way back, we can't push those Fiats all the way to Benghazi. We don't have enough water."

"Merda! Suppose the Senusi hit us in force while we're straggling back across the desert?"

"Suppose they hit us right here? If it were up to me, I would order a forced night march due west and try to make it to the Bay of Sidra. It looks like soft sand all the way, so we'd need to abandon the trucks and the field cannon, but at least we'd be in open country where we could use our firepower."

"The trucks? Cristo! They'd murder us if we came back without their trucks. Tobino would never agree. It would be the end of his career."

"I know." Achille Leone took a supply of ammunition, some dried beef, a pile of Guido's figs, and an extra canteen of water. "When the time comes, Tobino is going to try to walk back to Benghazi the way he thinks he came, taking all the trucks with him. I'm just telling you that we aren't going to make it, whether the Senusi attack or not.''

"What do we do? What would your father do?''

"A mutiny, maybe,'' Achille wiped the perspiration from his eyes, remembering what Leonida had said about disobeying stupid orders. "Father was always good at mutinies. Look, I'm going to take a patrol out for one last look for Franco.''

"When will you be back?''

"By sundown.'' Achille moved toward the entrance to the tent.

"Here, take a Sipe grenade, Comandante.'' Guido handed him a *bomba a mano*. "You might meet someone you don't like.''

Five hours later, Achille began to feel his legs going rubbery. The patrol had been a waste of energy. Franco could hardly have wandered this far, and the men could not be asked to search any farther.

"The sun's going down, sir,'' said Giuseppe Papafava. "I wonder if Grassi is back there right now roasting somebody's camel for dinner.''

"Give the men a break and we'll start back.''

Papafava nodded his agreement. "It's time for my daily duty,'' he said, picking up a folding field shovel. "These days, shitting on Cyrenaica is the only thing that gives me any pleasure.''

Capitano Leone watched as the veteran sergeant major set out four perimeter guards, one for each of the cardinal points of the compass. Several members of the patrol were going lame, and Papafava checked their ankles for signs of swelling. When he was satisfied with the condition of his men, the sergeant wandered off toward a nearby wadi for some privacy. Nearing exhaustion, Achille hunkered down in the shade of a large rock. We have done all that is humanly possible, he told himself. I have no right to risk my men on a night patrol. Unless we locate him on the way back, it is over for Franco Grassi.

Achille closed his eyes for a few moments, imagining himself home in Cederna. He would have a long talk with his father, he thought, and go for a ramble in the countryside with Sandro to argue about politics, and visit Rosaria, although not, perhaps, in that order. Sweet little Rosi, I wonder if she . . .

"Sir?''

Achille opened his eyes, and saw that Giuseppe Papafava's features were strangely taut. "What is it?''

"It's Franco. Not something you'll want the men to see,'' Papafava murmured quietly. Achille rose stiffly to his feet, shading his eyes against the late-afternoon sun. The noncommissioned officer led his commander through a maze of boulders down to the dry bed of the wadi.

The remains of Corporal Franco Grassi lay behind some rocks, and Achille suppressed a choking sensation as he surveyed the body. After nine months in Cyrenaica, the sight of a corpse, Italian or Arab, had become familiar, but he had not been a soldier long enough to adjust quickly to the death of a friend. Poor Franco had been robbed of his boots and his belt. His knees were drawn up against his chest and his hands had been tied behind his back. One sleeve of his field jacket had been cut off and used as a gag. There was blood coming from his groin and his face had that special paleness of men who have bled to death.

Achille knelt beside him, using his bayonet to remove the gag.

"What's this?" There was something pink and fleshy in Franco's mouth.

"That's his *cazzo*." Sergeant Papafava put a steadying hand on Achille's shoulder as he used the succinct old Roman word for "penis." "It's an ancient Arab custom."

Achille took a deep breath, sucking the air into his lungs in an effort to relieve the fainting sensation he felt sweeping over him. Papafava had brought him out alone to avoid any chance that he would pass out in front of the men.

"I'll bury him, Giuseppe." He wondered if his voice would reveal the savage emotions he was feeling. "Leave me your shovel. Give the men another few minutes' rest and start back. I'll catch up with you."

"Shouldn't we stay together?"

"We haven't seen an Arab all day." Achille shook his head as Giuseppe Papafava moved away. "And some of our boys can barely walk. We'll have trouble getting back by sundown as it is."

Thinking that digging a grave was the loneliest job in the world, he went to work with the shovel. The ground was soft, and within fifteen minutes he had created a shallow trench, large enough to encompass Grassi's tortured body. He wondered how they would ever make anything of a world in which such things could happen as he lowered the corpse into the grave.

Then he stood wondering if he ought to offer a prayer of some kind. As far as religion was concerned, Leonida's legacy had been firmly negative, and at the moment Achille could think of no prayers to recite. The only prayer book available was the Koran that Mustafa's mother had given him, and a prayer in Arabic seemed inappropriate for a Neapolitan who had just been tortured to death by Arabs.

Instead he found instead a phrase from a half-remembered English poem Helen Higgens had taught him. "The grave's a fine and private place. But none, I think, do there embrace." Or cook. Or laugh. Or find real coffee in the desert. No one will disturb you here, my friend. This place is not very fine, but it is exceedingly private.

"Atque in perpetuum, frater, ave atque vale," he quoted a verse by Catullus he had learned at the lyceum. "Forever, my brother, hail and farewell."

Then he heard voices coming from the south. Dropping the shovel, he scrambled up the side of the dry riverbed, hoping that Papafava and the patrol were still somewhere in sight. But the old sergeant had made the assumption that Leonida Leone's son must know what he was doing. The patrol was gone.

When the Arabs came into view, he saw that there were about twenty of them, carrying rifles and sauntering along the edge of the wadi. They were moving due north, and if they continued their present line of march, they would have to descend into the dry riverbed and walk right past him. There was no concealment anywhere.

For a moment, his mind reeled out of control as he saw himself captured, his hands roughly tied behind his back as the guerrillas laughed at his terror, their callous faces grinning as they ripped open his trousers, sliced off his penis, and stuffed it . . .

Achille was sweating so profusely that the automatic pistol was slippery in his hands. Gravel crunched as the first of the Arabs jumped down into the wadi, calling happily to his companions, not more than twenty meters away from where Achille was hiding.

One pistol against twenty. He calculated the odds as he listened to them coming closer. There are eight rounds in the magazine and one in the chamber, which makes nine. But I can only fire eight times because I am going to need the ninth.

For myself.

The Arabs were only a few meters away. He knew that if they spotted him, there was only one course of action. You can die quickly with a bullet in your brain, or slowly with your *cazzo* in your mouth. Take a few of them with you and then, quickly, before your hand betrays you with its trembling, put the barrel squarely against your temple and pull the trigger.

It will be quick. There will be no pain. Or very little and soon over. You must die like a Leone.

"Rosi," he prayed as the Arabs came closer, "Rosi, I'm going to die now. Why didn't I give you a baby before I left home? Because now I'm going to perish and leave nothing behind me. Oh, Rosi!"

He shot the first Arab very carefully through the heart as the guerrilla stumbled over a rock and lurched into his presence. It was the first time he had ever actually killed anyone. The shell tore into the bedouin, twisting his body and ripping open his chest.

That's one, he counted, struggling to stay calm. Got to keep a tally.

He shot two more men quickly before the rest of the squad dived for cover. There would be no time to reload, and three rounds were gone. He had to keep count and save the ninth round for himself.

The Arabs shouted in panic and Achille shifted his position among the rocks to make himself harder to find. They were calling instructions to one another and he listened to the harsh metallic clicks of rifle bolts being jammed home. They'll all charge at once, he thought, and they're sure to catch me with a ricochet. Oh, Christ, here they come. I've got to do it!

Suddenly he remembered the Sipe grenade attached to his web belt. Desperately he tossed it into the midst of the Arabs as they stormed his position.

The violence of the concussion knocked him down, filling the air with fire and noise. Instinctively, Achille staggered to his feet, fired wildly into the smoke, and then dashed up the side of the wadi. He tensed the muscles in his back, waiting for a bullet to come crashing into his flesh as he raced away. He hoped that if the bullet came it would kill him cleanly. There were shots behind him as the surviving Arabs screamed and cursed, but no bullet found him. There was too much sweat on his face to see clearly now, and too much pain in his head to think, but he ran as he had never run before, galloping away from the setting sun as the darkness gathered over the desert.

There was shooting all around them. Once in a while, someone would send up a flare in a desperate effort to see what was going on, but most of the time the darkness was absolute, and so was the confusion.

A Company was getting the worst of it, and Guido could hear screaming in the north as a wave of Senusi poured over the battalion perimeter, killing the men in the forward trenches with long knives. With fixed bayonets, the officers and noncoms were trying to push the Arabs back. Some of the young enlisted men fought well, but there were others who cowered in their trenches or fired wildly into the sky, or ran away.

On the Italian side, nobody seemed to be in charge. Only the Senusi knew what they were doing.

"Where the hell is Captain Leone?" Lieutenant Rosselli demanded. At the moment, nothing was happening in their sector of the battalion encampment, except for fire from a confused Italian infantryman in D Company who kept shooting in their direction. Early in the attack a runner from Major Tobino had brought orders that they were to maintain their position. Since then there had been no further word from battalion headquarters.

"I told you, I don't know where he is," Giuseppe Papafava repeated stolidly as he crouched in the forward trench next to Lieutenant Rosselli.

"Christ, what are we going to do?" Guido shouted. As he spoke, he heard the hard edge of hysteria in his voice, and realized that he was seriously rattled for the first time in his military career. "Tobino is stupid, and Achille is gone!"

"And you're in charge of this company." The sergeant major put an arm around Rosselli's shoulders and gave him a firm shake. "The captain made you his second-in-command because he knew you were the best there is, and I agree with him. Now calm down and take charge."

"All right." Guido took a deep breath, sucking the hot desert air into his lungs. Blood and glory is what you wanted, he reminded himself. It starts now. Let us pray for a minimum of blood and a maximum of glory. "I'm going to locate Tobino and find out why no one is giving us any orders."

"Keep your head down, Tenente." Guido Rosselli bent over double as he dashed across the encampment. The battalion's artillery section was now firing blindly into the wilderness, and the flash of the field cannon provided sporadic illumination. The battalion's four companies were all deployed around the periphery, leaving the center of the encampment almost empty, except for the trucks and a few corpses. Tripping over shell casings and ammunition boxes, Guido made his way to Major Tobino's hut.

Inside, he found the commanding officer of the Lupi di Lazio Infantry Battalion. Despite the carnage around him, Major Tobino was sitting alone at his desk, drawing arrows on a map by the light of a glass hurricane lantern.

"The record will reflect that this was not my fault," he announced. His voice was high and reedy. "Reports have been made on those who betrayed my trust."

"Signor Maggiore," Guido interrupted, wondering why Tobino was not out directing the defense of his battalion. "We need to stabilize our flank. My sector is calm. I could led a platoon over to help A Company."

"Where's Leone?"

"He did not return from patrol."

"He has disobeyed orders."

"Achille felt we needed to evacuate this position and move west."

"The Royal Italian Army does not retreat. Any man who moves from his position will be executed."

"Major, armies retreat all the time," Guido shouted. "The Senusi are chewing up A Company, and you have to do something. We could lose the whole battalion unless we push them back, and then get the hell out of here under cover of darkness."

"My officers have been given their orders," announced Tobino, placidly returning to his map. "They will fight to the death."

"Shall I take my men into A Company area, and try to—"

"You are relieved of command, Rosselli," Tobino suddenly screamed. "Leone has always undercut my authority, and you, Rosselli, are a coward. A coward from a race of cowards!"

He's gone mad, Guido realized, stepping behind the major and drawing his side arm. He's going to get us all killed.

He shot Tobino carefully in the back of the head. The major never saw it coming and his body slumped to the floor of the command hut. On his way to the door, Guido smashed the hurricane lantern with his automatic.

"A little something from my race of cowards, Major," he said, watching as the kerosene poured out and fire swept across the table, igniting the map and the dry wood. Guido jumped free of the command hut, and the building burst into flames.

"Pig!"

Achille woke up fast, his pistol already in his hand. He fired once before his eyes were properly open, and missed, but the Arab who had called him a pig dropped his rifle in surprise. He was a big bearded Senusi wearing a blue-gray burnoose, and he was still looking perplexed when Achille fired a second time, catching him in the forehead and knocking him over backward.

Assuming that there were other Arabs who would come running when they heard the shots, Achille leaped to his feet, whirling and crouching in panic. But he was alone, standing in some tall coarse grass, and the Arab scout was dead. It was very early morning. In the east, off toward Egypt, the sun peered over the horizon, and there were no enemy troops to be seen.

"Merda!" he groaned, dropping to his knees for any concealment the grass might offer. "Is this never going to end?"

There was a pain in his side. His head ached massively and the muscles in his legs were stiff and strained. After the gunfight in the wadi, he had run for hours and hours, with the Senusi patrol firing wildly whenever they caught sight of him in the shadows. The Arabs had tracked him implacably, kilometer after kilometer across the plateau, and whenever he stopped to rest he would hear them muttering in the dark as they searched for their revenge. It had been after two in the morning before he had felt safe enough to curl up in this grass and surrender to exhaustion.

Father had been right about the Arabs. They were neither fools nor cowards, and Italy's whole military strategy had been based upon the assumption that the Libyans were simpleminded and craven. At this rate, the war would last forever.

Field glasses in hand, Achille got cautiously to his feet and scanned the horizon, thinking about his beloved Lupi di Lazio. During his wild flight east across the plateau the previous night, there had been flashes in the sky from flares and cannon shells, indicating that the battalion was defending itself against a major attack. Where were they now? If Tobino had somehow managed to rally his remaining sanity and win a battle, they would by this hour have packed up their wounded and retreated toward Benghazi. If the Senusi assault had been successful, the Italians would be dispersed or dead. Either way, there was no point in trying to return to where the encampment had been, even if he could find it.

He reviewed his situation, finding that he had one Beretta automatic pistol and three clips of ammunition, one full water bottle, a compass, a bayonet, a pair of binoculars, a copy of the Koran, and a map of Cyrenaica. His lunch of figs and dried beef had been lost during the wild chase across the desert.

Furthermore, thanks to his father's foresight, he had four hundred British pounds in his wallet, handy in the event that there was a really good restaurant out here somewhere.

Finding a source of water seemed to be the first priority, since his canteen would not last long once the sun reached its zenith. Spreading out his map, Achille saw that Benghazi was simply too far to walk without water. Nor could he hope to make it west to the Gulf of Sidra. To the east, on the other hand, there were several small oases, although this would take him toward the Egyptian border. As he measured the distance, trying to decide if he could possibly walk five hundred kilometers to Egypt, a small brown lizard ran across the map, paused to look at him quizzically, and then darted away.

"Be careful, little friend," he chuckled. "I haven't had breakfast yet."

Unless you're going to start eating lizards, there isn't going to be any breakfast. And getting served in the nearest oasis will depend upon not looking quite so much like an enemy, he decided, realizing that he needed a disguise.

It was a grotesque chore. Removing the dead Arab's sandals was not difficult, but stripping off the man's heavy cotton thobe nearly made him vomit. Leaving the corpse clad only in a dirty pair of drawers, Achille then slipped out of his own uniform and put on the dead man's garments, his flesh crawling. The sandals fit perfectly. Arranging the head scarf was complicated, but the thobe covered his pistol and binoculars. From a distance, he could pass as a local.

"I've got to find water," he told himself, shading his eyes as he scanned the hill country to the east. The sun was barely above the horizon but it was already hot. He looked at the Arab, and saw that the brown lizard was sitting on the dead man's forehead, tasting his blood.

Achille nodded to the lizard, and started walking east. Egypt was a long way away.

"Our major died heroically." Lieutenant Guido Rosselli squirmed uncomfortably in his bed at the Second Division Field Hospital. The shrapnel wound in his left shoulder was not serious, but it itched furiously beneath the bandages. The sheets were rough against his flesh, and it felt strange to be lying down while talking to a senior officer.

"And you say he ordered you to abandon the trucks?" Colonel Frederico Adamo was the commander of the Seventh Infantry Regiment, of which the Lupi di Lazio Battalion was a subordinate element. Adamo had never liked Luciano Tobino, and the colonel found it difficult to believe that the major had got himself killed quite so heroically.

"That's right." Guido decided that his story improved with the telling. "When the Senusi penetrated our northern perimeter, Major Tobino ordered me to push them back with B Company. He was giving me my instructions when an enemy bullet came through the wall and killed him. I tried to rescue his body, but there was a fire and, well, we were in the middle of a battle."

"So you led a successful counterattack against the Arabs and then marched the whole battalion out to the coast, leaving the trucks behind?"

"Poor Luciano's last orders were to abandon the vehicles," Rosselli reported solemnly. The General Staff was furious at the loss of the precious Fiats, and Guido decided that the posthumously audacious Tobino could take the blame.

"I'm not quite sure I believe all this, Rosselli." There was a long tense silence while Colonel Adamo finished scribbling his notes. Guido Rosselli knew that it they ever found out what actually happened, they would put him in front of a firing squad. But there had been no choice. Achille might have managed something less emphatic than shooting the major's head off, but Tobino would have gotten them all killed.

"I assure you, Signor Colonnello . . ."

"Your loyalty to Tobino's memory is admirable, but the real hero of this dreadful affair is you," the colonel said. "With your own company commander missing and your battalion commander dead, you took charge of the entire unit, including several officers senior to you who clearly did not know what to do. And you rescued nine hundred and fifty Italians from an impossible situation. I'm going back to Rome for a few days, and I'll see about getting you a medal."

"I don't want a medal. I want a search party and permission to look for Achille."

"Out of the question, Tenente." Colonel Adamo walked to the door. "It's a tragedy, but Leone is dead, and you know it as well as I do. You're dehydrated and weak. Report to me when you can walk, and we'll see about putting you back to work."

The colonel disappeared and Guido Rosselli tried to relax, watching the ceiling fan rearrange the hot air in his room and occasionally disturb the flies buzzing around his bandage.

"What did he say, sir?" Giuseppe Papafava asked softly as he entered.

"He said a rescue mission was out of the question."

"I'm sure the colonel knows best, sir." The sergeant major nodded. "I got the four camels you ordered. Do you know how to ride a camel, Tenente?"

"We didn't have a lot of them in Venice." Guido winced as he swung his legs off the hospital bed. "You realize they'll court-martial us for this?"

"I've been court-martialed before. Can you stand up?"

"Let's go," said Guido Rosselli, deciding to ignore the pain in his shoulder. His vision blurred for a moment as he got to his feet, but he put his hand on Papafava's shoulder and the sensation passed. "If he's alive, we're going to find him."

"It's not for me to say, Tenente, but that was good work out there the night that Tobino died," the sergeant major muttered as they made their way out of the hospital. "Getting most of the battalion out of the desert was not something many other officers could have done."

"If Achille had been there, we wouldn't have lost as many men as we did."

"Captain Leone wasn't there, and you did damned well."

"It wasn't good enough, Giuseppe." Guido shook his head. "He's the other half of me, and I've got to find him!"

5.

· ·

"Watch Mercuzio," Girolamo instructed. "These are things you need to understand."

"I'm watching," Rosaria promised dutifully. The men trudged in with baskets of black olives and spilled them gently onto a canvas tarpaulin stretched across the flagstone floor. Most of the olives had matured from green to black, and the master oil maker—the hawk-faced Mercuzio Mercatelli—was using a stick to segregate those not yet ripe, or already sour.

As Emilio Lodi left for a second load with an empty wicker basket on his shoulder, he winked flirtatiously at her. She glared back at him coldly. You silly little man, she wanted to tell him. You just want to tumble me into a haystack. Down in Africa, there is a great man who loves me.

It was October, and getting cold. More olives were coming now, and Rosaria shivered in the coolness of the shed, wrinkling her nose at the twin smells of rancid olive oil and ox manure. This was the oldest structure on the Leone estate, a vast, gloomy stone building with tiny windows and centuries of dark green moss on the roof. Even as a child, she had always avoided the place, although the boys used to enjoy exploring an ancient tunnel that ran from the cellar of the shed to the basement of the Castello.

"A harvest is so complicated," she complained to Girolamo. Leonida's autobiography was almost done now, and the master of Cederna had begun to assign her more and more responsibility for the day-to-day management of his agricultural estate. Bruno Benelli still did the accounts while Sandro continued to oversee the livestock and Mercuzio worried about olive oil and wine production, but everything else seemed to have become her job.

"This part is simple," Girolamo assured her. "Every second year, God tells those trees to make olives, and they obey. We squeeze out the oil and sell it."

"Why doesn't God tell the trees to give us olives every year?"

"God is a stingy old bastard." Girolamo clarified his theological position. "Now watch."

"Siamo pronti." Mercuzio Mercatelli raised his staff to announce that the pressing could now begin. At his signal, the men moved forward to pile the olives onto the *frantoio,* a huge circular stone with a vertical iron shaft in the center. Using long poles, they spread the olives out evenly, and then touched the flanks of the patient ox harnessed to the grinding stone. As the ox walked around the *frantoio*, he pulled a great granite cylindrical roller over the olives, crushing them into a pulpy mass of broken pits and marrow. After a few circuits, the ox was halted and the men shoveled the residue back into wicker baskets.

Mercatelli watched intently as his assistants spilled the crushed olives onto the bed of the oaken olive press. When the olive pulp was arranged upon the *torchio* to his satisfaction, he ordered his team to begin winding the capstan down, bringing the two hardwood surfaces of the press together.

"Rosaria, watch," he muttered after the third turn of the capstan. The green virgin olive oil, so thick it was barely liquid, came down in a narrow, steady stream through a filter into an earthenware jug beneath the *torchio*. Rosaria dipped her baby finger into the oil and tasted its rich, warm flavor. "What do you think?" Mercatelli asked.

"It tastes good."

"How it feels is important too." Taking her hand, he showed her how to rub the oil gently into her palm to sense its texture and viscosity. When the container beneath the press was full, it was capped and taken down the tunnel to be stored in the vaults of the Castello, along with Leonida's most prized vintages. The door to the tunnel would then be locked until the oil was sold, since *olio vergine d'oliva* was the farm's single most profitable crop. It took twenty years before a tree generated its first usable olives, and the Leone estate had more mature olive trees—some hundreds of years old—than any other farm in the Cederna region.

"Now we'll do the second pressing." Mercuzio signaled to his men, who began turning the capstan again, with a fresh jug beneath the press. "It can be made to look the same, but the feel is different. The Mayor's family has been sending their first pressing to Milan for big profits. The stuff Signor Mosconi retails in town as virgin olive oil is really their second pressing, with chemicals in it. The Signora Giorgina would do the same someday if you let her."

"How could I stop Giorgina from doing anything she wanted to do?"

"The day is coming when you will run this estate." Mercuzio spoke as if stating the obvious.

"I'm not ever going to run this estate," she snapped back. "And I'm certainly not running it now. I'm only nineteen years old."

"It has to be you," Mercuzio insisted. "Achille has got a long military career ahead of him, and Leonida is getting old. Bruno is wicked and Giorgina is crazy and Terenzio likes to play the piano. Your brother wants to overthrow the government, and the rest of us are illiterate. Who the hell else is there? We depend upon this land for our daily bread."

The men brought in more olives, but Mercuzio's words had upset her and she found it difficult to concentrate. Emilio Lodi winked at her again and

Rosaria told Girolamo to make him stop. Then the great gray ox, still yoked to the *frantoio,* halted and deposited an enormous quantity of pungent manure at her feet, filling the air with a frightful odor. Feeling short of breath, she stumbled out of the olive shed into the late-afternoon air.

It was crisp but still sunny. She had started toward the kitchen to fetch a cup of coffee when Valeria suddenly appeared at the door, looking distraught and waving a tea towel to attract her attention.

"Come quickly!" The cook's face was white and Rosaria raced into the kitchen.

"What's wrong?"

"I don't know. A colonel named Frederico Adamo just went up to the study and a moment later Leonida came to the top of the stairs, shouting for you."

Rosaria bolted up the staircase and into the study, where she found Leonida talking to a short, stout officer with a pointed mustache.

"It may be time to begin facing reality," Colonel Adamo was saying. Leonida's face was stark-white as he stood erect behind his desk. Neither man looked at her.

"You're telling me he became lost while searching for his aide-de-camp?" Leonida Leone seemed unable to accept that a son of his could simply get lost. "Cyrenaica is a big place. He could be anywhere."

"Achille's lost." Rosaria chewed on the words, feeling desperate. He never got lost when he and Sandro and Tommaso went camping in the hills. Would they send a colonel all the way to Cederna just to tell us he was lost?

"When there isn't a body, death can sometimes be difficult for families to accept," Adamo said. "But shortly after Captain Leone disappeared, a large force of Senusi attacked his battalion and forced it to retreat."

"Then he was taken prisoner."

"These guerrillas do not take prisoners, Signor Conte."

"Has no one gone to look for him?"

"The area is now completely controlled by enemy forces, and we have been unable to conduct a formal inspection. However, your son's second-in-command has mounted his own private search. It was done in defiance of my orders, and I'm afraid we may never see Lieutenant Rosselli again either."

"Perhaps he is hiding somewhere in the desert?" Leonida seemed convinced that he could save Achille's life by winning the argument with Colonel Adamo. Yes, yes, Rosaria agreed desperately. He's hiding in the desert, and he will come home to us with a grin and a sack of souvenirs, and a wonderful story about how it all happened.

Adamo was losing patience. "Captain Leone had only a day's supply of water when he was last seen, and the temperature in the desert in August was routinely reaching fifty degrees Celsius. After nearly ten weeks, I fear we must abandon any hope."

"Dead? You are telling me that he is dead?" The Count's voice had gone cold. Concerned, Adamo rose from his chair and approached the desk. Rosaria put her back against a shelf of books, feeling the room starting to spin.

"I am sorry, sir. I regret to say that there are some forms to fill out, and—"

"Go away," Leonida gasped. "Just go away!"

Rosaria's mind moved slowly. This is how Sandro kills pigs, she found herself thinking. He hits them on the head with a sledgehammer, and they feel nothing when he cuts their throats. I've been hit. My throat is ready for the cutting. If he's really dead, then there is nothing more, no, nothing more . . . Her legs went weak and she sat down on her bottom. As Colonel Adamo walked past her stiffly, he stopped and bowed.

"My condolences, signora. Your brother was a fine man and officer."

It was difficult to think, but she finally understood that he had mistaken her for Giorgina. "No, he was my compagno," she replied indistinctly. "I loved him."

"Ah, yes, of course." The confused colonel bowed his way backward out of the office, and closed the door.

The tears started to come. Rosaria rolled over on her side and covered her face with her hands, ignoring the rest of the world. I'll never see Achille again, she realized. I'll never hold him in my arms again, or have his baby.

"God, I . . . I can't breathe!" gasped Leonida.

Rosaria looked up. It was difficult to focus her eyes, but through her tears she saw the old man collapse across his desk, face down among his scattered papers, trying to suck air into his lungs. His face was ashen gray.

Her first coherent thought was selfish. I can't lose both of them, she told herself, and she got to her hands and knees. Where is Girolamo? Valeria must have guessed what was happening. Why doesn't she send help? Why have they left us alone?

"Signor Conte?" Getting to her feet with difficulty, she staggered to Leonida's side. "Signor Conte?"

At first the old nobleman seemed almost unconscious, but she pulled one of his arms around her neck and lifted him off the desk. He was heavy, and when she got him standing up, he leaned against her, his weight nearly forcing her to her knees.

"Fanciulla . . ." he moaned, still gasping for oxygen. His eyes were tightly closed and there were tears flowing down his cheeks. For a moment she feared that he would lie down and die because the sadness would be too great for him to go on living. I should die too, she sobbed. There is no point now in carrying on.

"Let me take you to your bedroom," she panted. He mumbled and gestured toward a door at the far end of the study. Since the death of Contessa Maria Pia, the master of Cederna no longer ventured into the master bedroom, preferring to sleep in a tiny room off his study. It had once been his wife's sewing room.

With one foot, she kicked upon the door, helping him into a little chamber with a tiny window that looked out to the east over the Castello's formal gardens. Next to the narrow bed, there was a little desk with a diary and some letters and a fountain pen. Opposite, there was an old-fashioned lacquered *armadio* with dozens of tiny drawers.

"I'll lie down." As he collapsed onto the bed, his breathing seemed marginally better. She sat next to him and loosened his collar, watching color come back into his complexion. To make him comfortable, she took off his shoes and covered him with a brown cotton army blanket.

Then her own grief returned in full force, and she put her face in her hands and began to wail, softly but persistently. In one part of her brain, she could hear herself braying like a sick donkey, making an obscene, ludicrous noise, but there was no way she could stop herself. Nor was there any reason to try. It seemed easier to let her body take command.

"Oh, fanciulla, I should . . . I should have had more sons." In a strange, harsh voice, Leonida suddenly began talking furiously. "They are so easy to lose. You spend twenty-five years raising a lad, and then he wanders off in the desert one day . . . God, they might have savaged him. My Achille might have been tortured to death. Oh, Christ, the horror of it. My boy! They sent that awful man to tell me that my precious boy is dead."

"Oh, topo, I loved him so much," she confessed.

"I know," Leonida groaned. "Even when you were children, I wondered if the two of you might not fall in love . . . you and I, we loved him the most."

"Topo . . ." Rosaria felt the last strength go out of her arms, and she collapsed onto the mattress beside him, now absolutely howling. Instinctively, the count turned on his side and took her in both arms as if they were lovers. She put her head on his chest, and the two of them cried and cried and cried.

"Your hair is a mess."

Two days after Colonel Adamo's visit, Leonida sat up in bed and looked accusingly at Rosaria Lombardi, who had been serving him the minestrone and red wine prescribed by Dr. Beniolo. I hate Beniolo, he snarled mentally. I hate minestrone.

Blankly the girl put her hand to her auburn hair. It was dirty and disordered, and she stared at him with irritation. "I'm sorry, but what . . . what difference does it make?"

"We can't help Achille if we fall apart like this. You need to look pretty for when he comes back."

"Don't torture me," Rosaria begged. "He's not coming back. You know that."

"If my son were dead, I would feel his absence within me. This may seem like metaphysical nonsense to you, but I sense that he is alive somewhere."

Leonida spoke with great intensity. "You have to believe me. You loved him."

"But what—"

"Go brush your hair. Find Girolamo, and tell him to get me packed for a long trip. Then tell my family I want to see all of them in my study. Now!"

"Oh, topo . . ." she pleaded with him sadly. "Don't be crazy."

"I'm not crazy." He took her hand and squeezed it. "I'm an old man in a hurry, and if you don't trust in me, then nobody will. Now do as you're told."

She doesn't believe me, he guessed. She will do as she is told because she is my fanciulla, but she thinks I am mad. Maybe so, but I am not ready to let Achille go.

He swung his feet to the floor and got a good English tweed suit out of the *armadio*. He dressed quickly and went out into his study, where letters and telegrams of condolence were piled high on his desk. With an impatient sweep of his arm he brushed them all into a wastepaper basket, and made a long telephone call to the War Ministry of the Ottoman Empire in Constantinople, speaking in French. Then, switching to English, he had a chat with a friend at the British Embassy in Bern, Switzerland. He had just finished a conversation with a staffer in the military intelligence branch of the Italian Army General Staff in Rome when Rosaria led his stunned family into the study.

"Father, you're up?" Giorgina began protesting immediately, while Bruno Benelli looked appropriately concerned about this display of manic behavior from the grieving father of the family. "Didn't Dr. Beniolo say that a week of bed rest would be—"

"Be quiet!" Leonida ordered briskly, turning to his ancient majordomo. "Giro, get everyone a chair, and sit down yourself."

Girolamo had taken Achille's death particularly hard, but he obeyed with the patience of an old soldier. "We're ready, m'lord," he said with an air of hopelessness.

Looking sad and bewildered, Terenzio wandered in and sat down next to Rosaria. With innocent affection, the young man took her hand and held it.

"Signor Conte, I . . ." Bruno Benelli began officiously, but Leonida rapped his knuckles against the desk for silence.

"I am not satisfied that Achille is dead," he explained quickly. "I propose therefore to go to Constantinople and investigate the possibility that he may be a prisoner of war. I shall require cooperation from all of you. Girolamo, have you packed me something warm? You sometimes get a cold snap at this time of the year in Constantinople, and it will be wintery in Bern."

"Everything is ready, sir. Your pistol is in the pocket of your great-coat."

"I won't need a pistol."

"You may wish to shoot someone, m'lord. You often do."

"Bern?" Bruno demanded. "Why go to Switzerland?"

"The British Embassy there is going to issue me with one of their passports," Leonida explained. "Italians will be unwelcome in the Ottoman Empire for some time, so I shall pose as a British subject and slip into Constantinople on the Orient Express."

"Father, what can you possibly hope to accomplish?" Giorgina wailed. "If Achille is gone, we must try to carry on as best we can."

"You'll be in danger!" Rosaria blurted out. "Let Girolamo go with you. Don't go alone!"

Leonida ignored his daughter, but turned to Rosaria with a smile. "Girolamo doesn't speak English. Constantinople is still enemy territory, and if someone heard the two of us muttering in Italian, we could be executed as spies."

"I speak English," Bruno Benelli announced quietly, approaching Leonida's desk. "I won a prize for it at school. I'll go with you."

"Bruno, don't be ridiculous," his wife burst out contemptuously. "We have a child. Who will run the estate while Father's away?"

"I can run the estate," Rosaria volunteered quickly. "Signor Conte, go to Constantinople and find Achille. We'll take care of things here."

"You aren't going to run anything!" Giorgina screamed. Suddenly everyone was bellowing. Rosaria lost control and began sobbing. Girolamo demanded to be allowed to go to Constantinople in place of Bruno, while Giorgina screamed that her husband was an accountant and not an international spy. Bruno Benelli took offense, and—for the first time in their marriage—shouted back at Giorgina. The room dissolved into bedlam.

In the middle of the chaos, Leonida deliberately drew the pistol from the pocket of his overcoat and fired a single shot directly into the ceiling. Plaster dust floated down around him as the master of Cederna stood with a smoking pistol in his hand, but the room went utterly silent.

"My train leaves in three hours," he continued as if nothing had happened. "Giorgina, while Bruno and I are away, take that fat priest of yours to the Vatican and put him to work. The Pope has contacts all over the eastern Mediterranean, and perhaps the papal diplomatic corps can make itself useful for the first time in history. Bruno, get packed. Girolamo, find Bruno a gun, and then bring the car around front. Rosaria, you are in charge of the estate until I return. Anyone who fails to obey you is fired."

He put the pistol back into his pocket and walked to the door, looking at them with a strange, cold expression. "If you'll excuse me, I have a son to find."

"Wait," said Terenzio. "Wait! I'm going with you."

"No, look, boy, Bruno and I . . . ." Leonida began the obvious explanation, but then he caught a glint of hardness in the young man's eyes. Terenzio had stopped crying, and he was no longer clinging to Rosaria's hand.

"I'm Achille's brother, and if we're going to find him, then I deserve the chance to help," he said. "If we don't find him, then you need to teach me everything you taught him, and we can start on the train."

"No, look, son, it's dangerous, and you could be useful here helping Rosaria."

"I'm a Leone, Papa," said Terenzio. "I'm coming with you."

There was a long pause. Leonida looked at Girolamo, silently asking for advice. The old man nodded succinctly.

"Find him a gun, Giro," Leonida said. "Come on, we have a train to catch."

6.

. . . .

It's been a month. No, perhaps two. Wait, no, after I shot the Arab scout, there was a long time when I walked toward the east, getting lost and drinking a few sips of water every day from my canteen, until it was all gone. That was a week, at least, and then I found the little well. Was there one well or two? I don't remember. It wasn't much of a well.

Time was blurring. He had walked for many days, sometimes finding places in the desert where he could sponge out a few drops of moistness. Then, for a long time, there had been no water at all, and he had grown a little weaker every day.

At some unremembered moment in the past, he had stumbled upon this cave in an outcropping of shale. Inside was refuge from the killing heat of the sun, and insects to eat, although he had never been fast enough to catch a lizard. Each morning, there was a little condensation on the rocks for him to lick. There had been periods of unconsciousness . . .

He got to his hands and knees and crawled through soft sand to the cave's entrance. There were different Arabic words for different sorts of sand. This kind would be called *sogog,* the soft, restless, fine sand that penetrated your eyes and ears and mouth and anus, and itched and tortured. Outside, it was late afternoon, still hot even in . . . what month would it be? October? Or November?

I am Captain Achille Leone of the Royal Italian Army, he recited, trying to get his brain functioning. It is 1912 and I am eating bugs in a cave in North Africa, a thousand kilometers from nowhere and a lot farther from home.

Blinking his eyes, he looked out at the desolation around him, thinking that God must hate North Africa to have cursed it like this. No wonder those angry prophets in the Old Testament always came out of the desert.

His body trembled as he pulled himself to his feet, and his hands were quivering uncontrollably as he read his compass. I must get going, he told himself as he stumbled away from the setting sun. I get weaker every day. I will die if I stay here. I will die if I don't find water.

At first, he had conscientiously consulted the map provided to all company commanders by the Istituto Geografico Militare, but it seemed wrong as often as it was right, and he was now in a perfectly featureless sector of the desert. As far as he could see, there was flat, dried mud, broken only by a few dunes moving in from the south and occasional rocks, sandblasted to smoothness.

There was a wind blowing sand, and he fastened his kaffiyeh scarf around his face as he walked, covering his mouth but leaving his eyes exposed. It was hard to see, partly because of the gathering night, and partly because of the sand, but also—it seemed to Achille—because his vision was not as good as it used to be. His eyes hurt all the time now, and he fantasized about plunging himself into clear, cool water and washing away all this sand, bathing his eyes until they were clean again.

It made him recall how he and Sandro used to swim in the Tiber, splashing in that spot where the river loops around Cederna and turns south toward Rome. In those days, Rosaria had been a persistent little sister, sometimes tagging along when she was not wanted, and once the two boys, buck–naked and soaking wet, had climbed out of the Tiber to find little Rosaria inspecting them with a clinical gaze. She could only have been four or five at the time because her mother was still alive.

I wonder if she still remembers. Achille smiled at the reminiscence, and found that his lips hurt. I've got to keep walking, he told himself, but the wind was slinging the sand around fiercely now, and it was impossible to see. If I want to hold Rosi in my arms again . . .

"Bur-r-ro!" someone shouted as he staggered through the sandstorm. Confused, Achille stopped, and tried to wipe the sand out of his eyes. Who was speaking? *Burro* was the Italian word for "butter." Why would someone shout "butter" at him in the middle of the Sahara Desert?

"Bur-r-ro!" Dead in front of him, there were thirty or forty camels in a circle, hunkering down beneath the wind. A group of men and women were standing among them, looking in his direction. They seemed hostile, and it suddenly struck him that "Bur-r-ro" was the imperative mood of an Arabic verb that meant "Go away!"

These are not soldiers, he reassured himself; they have women among them. He remembered the wad of British pounds in his pocket, and lurched forward. I must convince them that I represent an economic opportunity and not a threat. They would kill an Italian, so I will tell them I am an Englishman. No one dares kill an Englishman. My name is Charles Lion, and I have been living in Tripoli, where I have been buying products for export to England, barley for our infidel beer, and esparto, that Spanish grass that we English use in the manufacture of paper. I was on a purchasing trip to the Fezzan Oasis when my caravan was attacked by Italian soldiers. My guides were dispersed, and I have been wandering ever since. My father is a wealthy London banker, who will pay handsomely for my rescue.

As he approached, the Arabs all began shouting at him, and one of the tethered camels became alarmed, struggling up on its skinny, preposterous front legs.

"Sadiq," Achille tried to say, "I am a friend." He managed to force air through his throat, but no sound came because he had been too long without water and his vocal cords would not function.

"Kill him!" one of the cameleers shouted. Four males confronted him, an old man with a stick, and three younger bedouin with guns. One of the rifles was a flintlock with an impossibly long barrel; Achille saw he was about to be murdered with a weapon that was obsolete before his father was born.

Realizing he could never get to his side arm in time, he turned, vaguely imagining that it might still be possible to flee. The world was getting dark, and he thought it might be possible to hide in the darkness.

Then he stopped, because the darkness had somehow become absolute, and he wondered how the sun could have gone down so fast. Have I blundered into a cave? Where am I? Behind him, the Arabs were talking in their ancient language, but he could understand nothing of what they were saying. The gift of tongues had deserted him.

Other gifts will leave me soon, he thought and he realized that the darkness was within him, that he was blind.

My body is shutting down, he realized as the floor of the desert came up and hit him. "Good-bye," he said, addressing no one in particular as he lay face-down in the sand. You're all alone when you die. Momma? Momma! I can't feel . . .

7.

Without warning, Leonida and Bruno and Terenzio came back on the first Friday in February of 1913. Valeria brought the news out to the cottage, knocking at the door just as Rosaria was saying good-bye to Sandro and Emilio Lodi, who were leaving for a weekend Socialist Party meeting in Rome.

"Valeria? Come in . . ." Rosaria found herself trembling.

"No, it's late and everyone is tired," said the cook. She stood in the darkness outside the door, making her sad, flat announcement before turning away. "They didn't find him, that's all."

The door closed. There was a long silence. Sandro poured himself a glass of peasants' wine and gulped it while he stared through the window into the gathering darkness, doing his own private grieving.

For her, there was no renewed plunge into sadness. She had never believed that Leonida would find his missing son. Achille had disappeared in August, and six long months had passed. It was time to stop trusting in miracles and let go. For his own peace of mind, Leonida needed to go looking, but she was glad that he was home safely. Now it could be over . . . although, of course, it would never really be over.

"Are we still going to Rome?" asked Emilio.

"I suppose so." Sandro's voice was flat, but Rosaria knew he was hurting inside. These days, young Emilio was his constant companion, but Lodi was a disciple, and Achille had been a friend. "We'll be back Monday and His Excellency won't be needing us until then. Get your bag and meet me in front of the mansion."

"I'd better go and see Leonida." Rosaria pushed back from the table as Emilio darted off.

"He's probably exhausted. I'd let him rest," Sandro suggested. "Look, I've got to go to this Rome meeting because the leaders of all the regional party sections will be there, and Cederna needs to be represented. But if you're feeling bad, I could leave Emilio behind to keep you company."

"No, I'll be all right." The weekend would be sad enough without fending off Emilio's adolescent ardor. "You go and plan your revolution."

"It's strange." Sandro unfolded his tall body and rubbed his eyes. "Achille's death really does make it easier for me to think concretely about the revolution. When he was alive, I was always horrified at the notion of violence between us. And, in a sad way, his death will make things easier for you.''

"What are you saying?'' Rosaria felt the fury building within her and she wished he would go away.

"Sorellina, there are still some things that are hard for me to say, particularly where Achille is concerned.'' He turned at the door, and put his arms around her. "I'll always wonder whether Achille would have ended up by supporting our movement against his own class, or whether he would have become an absentee landlord who exploited us. And you'll always wonder if . . .''

"I don't want to talk about this.'' She pulled away, looking at him sharply. She had always resisted the temptation to tell Sandro that she and Achille were in love. And now that Achille was dead, the secret was too private to share with a socialist big brother. Sandro would see their fragile little conspiracy as sexual capitalism, or demand to know whether she had lost her all-important virginity.

"I'm just saying that you loved him. And I think, in a way, that he loved you too.''

"Did he ever tell you that?''

"No, of course not.'' Sandro frowned, as if she were missing the point. "When Leonida was younger, there were always rumors about actresses and rich ladies from England. It bothered Achille to see his mother suffering, and he decided not to exploit women. This he told me explicitly. But he had the Leone blood in him, and the two of you were so fond of one another that I always worried about something happening to compromise your honor and make it impossible to find you a reasonable husband from your own class.''

"Achille would always have been honorable,'' she began hotly, but he cut her off.

"Maybe so, but as long as Achille was alive, it was hard for you to settle on another man, a normal man, somebody nice like Emilio. But now you need to think about your future. At your age, most girls are married. You don't even have a fiancé.''

Too furious to respond, she raced into her bedroom and threw herself sobbing on the bed. There was a moment's silence, and then the outer door closed quietly as Sandro went off to his meeting.

He wants me to marry his deputy revolutionary and breed good little socialists. How could I think about another man after being loved by a Leone?

Damn you, Achille, she swore. You could have stayed home and had me. Instead you wanted to have your great Libyan adventure. Well, you had your war. And it had you.

Rosaria cried for a while, but the room was cold and she needed the warmth of her bed. From her window, she could see the bay window of the Count's study, but there was no light, no flicker of a fire, suggesting that Leonida had gone straight to bed, probably knocking himself out with brandy.

She longed to talk to him, but he would have sent for her had he wanted company. Perhaps in the morning . . . Quickly she undressed and washed, and slipped into a flannel nightgown. She was about to crawl beneath the covers when her gaze fell upon the bottle of Vecchia Romagna, the expensive cognac Achille had left with her the night of his departure. Romantically, she had been saving it for his return.

It promised oblivion. She twisted off the corktop and filled a tumbler to the brim. She drained the glass, and then poured herself another. It made the room seem warmer, and she snuggled under the wool covers, feeling sleepy.

She dozed for a while, since the day had been long and exhausting. At some point in the night, she awoke, or half-awoke, in the midst of a dream about Achille. Her body was curled up with her arms thrust between her thighs, a strange warmth in her stomach. She tried to sink back into the fantasy, caressing her breasts with her fingertips and assuring herself that she was not responsible for what fatigue and cognac could do to a woman's body.

Suddenly a light from the Castello refracted off the dust on her bedroom window and she sat up in bed, confused and a little ashamed. The air in her room seemed stale, and she went to the door of the empty cottage and stepped outside. It was cold, and she stood shivering on the step, hearing nothing but the howl of a sheep dog somewhere in the distance. The Castello Leone was dark except for Leonida's study, where someone had lit the 40-watt electric bulb over her Olivetti.

Then Leonida appeared, framed by the window, staring blindly into the darkness. She wondered if he could see her white nightdress in the shadows beneath him, and tried without success to read the expression on his face across the hundred meters that separated them.

Is this the alcohol? She sensed that she was about to commit an irrevocable act with unknowable consequences. Am I drunk? A little, perhaps. Afterward, I will say that I was very drunk.

Over her nightgown she threw the cloak that had once belonged to Leonida's contessa. Then she scampered barefoot through the garden and into the kitchen. The house was silent, and she skipped quickly up the main staircase to the study. The door was ajar.

"Leonida," she whispered when she saw him still standing at the window, wearing an old pair of tan slacks. His white shirt was left open at the throat, and his sleeves were rolled up to his elbow.

"Fanciulla? Is that you?" He turned, and she saw that he had grown a beard during his trip. It was short and white and made him look like an Egyptian pharaoh. For a moment she feared that he might be displeased by her intrusion, but he crossed the room with that boyish, springy stride, kissing her deliberately on first one cheek and then the other. His beard tickled.

"Do I disturb you?" she asked.

"No, I couldn't sleep and I'm glad to see you." He seemed calm and self-possessed as he took her arm and walked her to the couch before the fire. "Well, you've heard, I suppose, that there was no news about Achille."

"Yes. I was so worried. You were gone so long."

"I know, but we covered a lot of ground. After a lot of quiet negotiating with the Turks, I realized they honestly had no idea what happened to Achille. So we deposited some reward money in a Constantinople bank and took a steamer to Cairo, where we alerted the Egyptian authorities to the situation. Then I went to Benghazi to light a fire under the Second Division Command there."

"Did you see Guido Rosselli?"

"I found that brave, noble young man in a military prison facing a court-martial," Leonida snapped bitterly. "Rosselli had gone absent without leave to mount an unauthorized search for Achille. Guido covered all the desert near where Achille disappeared and found nothing. I got the charges against him dropped, but . . . well, so much time has passed. There wasn't much else to do."

"Oh, topo, you did your best."

"I suppose I was merely making it clear to myself and everyone else that I had done the maximum to find him. You know, I miss him. All fathers love their sons, but they don't always like them, and I really liked Achille. And now that he is gone, I have no one except . . ."

"You have me." She finished his sentence for him. "The night he left, Achille asked me to take care of you, and I'll do it as long as you want me to."

"I'm glad . . . I have you," Leonida stammered. Rosaria had never before seen him at a loss for words. "During our voyage, Terenzio and I actually managed to have a few real conversations, but I missed seeing you every day."

"I missed you too." She reached up and touched his whiskers. "But I hate your beard. It makes you look old."

"I am old," he laughed. "But I'll have Girolamo shave me tomorrow."

"I could shave you. I always do Sandro before he goes off to give a speech."

He looked at her strangely, as if noticing for the first time that she was wearing his late wife's cloak over a nightdress.

"My shaving things are in here." He led her to the little sewing room where she had taken him the day Achille's disappearance had been announced. Nothing had changed. The bed was not made. On a low dresser with a mirror, she saw his toiletries: a blue porcelain bowl and an Oriental pitcher of water, a straight razor with an ivory handle and a Sheffield blade, a camel's-hair brush, and a pot of soap for lather.

"I'll sit here," he offered, moving a chair before the mirror. Rosaria took a deep breath, wondering if her hands would be steady enough for the task. Then she created a supply of lather and went to work, shaving him systematically with clean, deft strokes.

"The harvest was the best ever." She tried to make conversation. "Remember the land you let us use for wheat? We got a good crop out of it."

He nodded absently, sitting with his eyes closed. When Rosaria had removed the last traces of white beard, she washed away the leftover soap and then brushed his hair back from his forehead. Clean-shaven, he looked much younger.

"Rosaria, you have your own life to lead." He spoke suddenly. "When I was traveling I came to realize that where you were concerned, my liking had trespassed into loving. My poor son loved you, and all the things he found about you to love I have also discovered, but for me it is not right . . ."

"It's all right," she said quickly, trying to stop him.

"No, I've been trying to analyze—"

"Be quiet," she said. "Don't analyze." Surrendering to the impulse that had been with her all along, Rosaria leaned forward, putting her hands on his shoulders, and kissed him fully on the lips.

Leonida Leone opened his eyes and looked at her questioningly. For a frightful instant, she feared that he might reprimand her or send her away. Instead, he favored her with a crooked, perplexed smile, and pulled her onto his lap. She nestled her head against his shoulder, feeling safe. Not particularly happy, but safe.

"Thank you, fanciulla." There was a certain calm finality in his voice. She wondered if he was thanking her for the shave or the kiss.

"There will be trouble if anyone finds me here."

"It's the middle of the night. There will be no trouble."

"No trouble?" Her body trembled as she tried to dismiss the sure and simple knowledge that there would be an infinity of trouble. She could feel him growing hard against her thigh, and a voice in her head ordered her to flee before her life was utterly changed.

"Are you afraid, fanciulla?" His voice seemed to be coming to her from a great height.

"I'm cold."

"Then come under the covers."

They moved to the bed and Leonida pushed the cloak off of her shoulders. She let him kiss her slowly on the lips and then lower her head gently to the pillow.

She took a deep breath as his hand searched for her breasts beneath the nightdress, knowing that she was about to be ruined. After tonight, she would not be a virgin, and no other man would have her. I shall not have to marry Emilio or the Mayor's crazy son, she told herself. I will be disgraced, and whether or not Sandro has his revolution, I will be free.

Leonida seemed confident now, and very strong, and she found she could imagine him thus on a battlefield, giving orders and leading the charge. When he pulled back the covers, she snuggled into the bed and closed her eyes, letting him touch her where he wanted. There was a moment's confusion of arms and legs as he kicked off his trousers, and then they found each other again beneath the woolen blankets and linen sheets. Wordlessly, Leonida pulled her into his arms and kissed her and she felt again the hardness of his penis against her belly.

Although he was gentle, it was painful at first, but she forced herself to relax and accept this strange fierce presence within her body. After a while, the sensation became merely uncomfortable, and later, vaguely pleasant. Growing bolder, she ran her hands over Leonida's hard body, feeling the bristle of iron-gray hair on his chest, and the firm, straining muscles on his back.

There was a special tingle of excitement at the very end as things seemed to become very urgent and he rose up over her like a stallion.

"Fanciulla," he groaned and she felt the sudden moistness within her.

"Oh, topo! Topo!" she cried, curling up against his body with her head on his chest.

Leonida watched the girl fall asleep. She must have been exhausted because she dropped off almost immediately, lying on her back, the sheet gathered about her waist and her arms raised over her head, as if in surrender. The old general sat on the edge of the narrow bed, looking down at her vulnerable breasts, wondering if he would ever sleep again.

With a rush of tenderness he brushed a strand of hair out of Rosaria's eyes. With a murmur, she turned on her side and presented him with her bare back. There was a candle on the bedside table, and in the flickering light he saw that the sheet beneath them was moist with blood.

A virgin! It had not occurred to him to ask, and Leonida was uncertain whether to be surprised or not. Of course her brother had always watched her like a hawk, but he had always imagined that Achille would have . . .

For a moment, the discovery made him ashamed. Your poor dead son was a more honorable man than you, he thought. You have taken something that did not belong to you.

Or do I have the right to be selfish? When I first learned that Achille was dead, I believed that I would crawl into this very bed and die. Willingly. Now everything has changed. I will mourn my son forever, and I am still seventy-three, but I no longer have the slightest interest in dying. There is more pie on the table, and I have just taken another slice. I feel young and strong. I could conquer Sicily again.

"I wanted you from the first moment I saw you," he said softly to the sleeping woman. She stirred and turned back to him as he stretched out beside her, pulling the blanket over both their bodies. He put his arms around her. "And I'm keeping you. Forever."

8.

....

"O Lion, I challenge you!" cried Ali Mohammed el-Sayeed, a big, energetic man with a missing front tooth. He pointed to a steep hill a kilometer to the east. "To that dead tree on the *jebel* and back."

"Our guest is still too weak," his father objected. Still agile despite uncounted years of trekking across the desert, Ahmad el-Sayeed jumped to his feet and shook his head. "Do you remember how we had to tie him to the camel? How the women had to feed him by hand?"

"But your kindness has made me stronger, Ahmad." The man they were calling "Lion" spoke up, having decided to race and to lose gracefully. The defeat would have to be managed with finesse, since they had assigned him the strongest camel. It might be hard to convince the recalcitrant Souffa to lose for the sake of politeness.

I wonder if my strength is really back, Achille Leone wondered as he rose from his place by the fire.

Six months ago, when they had found him in the desert, Achille Leone had been nearly dead from exposure and dehydration. Ahmad's senior wife had nursed him back to consciousness, feeding him tiny cups of milk still warm from the nipples of a nanny goat. Since the bedouin needed to keep moving toward the next source of water, Ahmad's sons had lashed him to Souffa's back as soon as he had regained consciousness. As he slowly recovered, the tribe had marched all the way to their home base in Murzuk, a Libyan oasis in the still-unconquered Fezzan District.

Bouncing in agony on the camel's back through those early, awful days, he had suffered from constant hallucinations and nausea, but the tribe's rough kindness had restored him to health by the time they had reached the central Sahara. Now they were heading northeast again, making painfully slow progress toward the Mediterranean. Months and months had passed since his last contact with the Lupi di Lazio Battalion.

"Souffa, bella mia," he muttered as he approached his kneeling camel. "Behave yourself for once, and let me mount without a battle."

Achille had always regarded camels as badly designed horses, but he had quickly discovered that the irascible, half-wild bedouin *jimel* was a different animal altogether. A big, powerful mare, Souffa routinely disputed Achille's

96 · · ·

status as passenger, biting and kicking and never passing up an opportunity to spit in his face.

On the other hand, Souffa's stamina amazed him. Ahmad el-Sayeed managed to locate water for his bedouin family about once a week. They were frequently forced to dig into a damp patch in the sand to find a *bir*, or underground stream, affording the camels no more than a few mouthfuls of brackish water. Sometimes they would locate a proper *ain*, or open pond, usually surrounded by an oasis, and then the camels would drink voraciously, swallowing gallons and gallons of water. During the long days of slogging through the desert, the humans drank sparingly from huge watertight sheepskin sacks called *girbas*, but Souffa and her mates got only a few handfuls of dried dates every morning and no liquid at all. No wonder they were perpetually irritable.

Achille approached Souffa from the rear and before she had a chance to bolt, he sprang onto the *mahklufa*, a wood-frame saddle that fit around the camel's soft single hump. He braced himself. Instantly, Souffa rose on her slender front legs, throwing Achille backward. Giving him little time to recover, she then reared up on her powerful hind legs, lifting him more than three meters off the ground. With one hand on the saddle and the other holding the single-stranded rope rein, Achille brought his mount under control. Souffa snorted, turning her head belligerently to see if there was anything within biting range.

A second later, the young Ali Mohammed el-Sayeed sprang expertly into his saddle, striking his animal savagely across the flank. Like most horsemen, Achille prided himself on seldom using a riding crop, but the bedouin had taught him that camels responded only to pain. He administered a sharp tap to Souffa's bottom, and the animal bounded aggressively away from the encampment.

This long, strange interlude is coming to an end, Achille thought as Souffa settled into a steady pounding gallop, threatening to disarticulate his backbone with every step. It must be February or March; and it has taken three months to come from Fezzan to Egyptian territory.

If Ahmad was right, they should reach the Mediterranean Sea and the Egyptian coastal town of Sidi Barrani tomorrow. Then, if he could find a ship back to Benghazi, real life would begin again.

Dio, I've been out of touch for over half a year, he thought. Father must be frantic. Did they give my company to someone else? Or were my men all killed when the Senusi attacked? And poor Rosi could be . . .

Unfortunately, there had never been a safe opportunity to let anyone know he was still alive. Occasionally, they had passed villages in the Sahara, but he could not have sent a letter to Italy without exposing himself. Nor had there been any way of getting to Egypt any faster. A bedouin caravan moved about five kilometers an hour, and a long day's riding would put at most fifty kilometers behind them. When the ground was rough, they would cover a great deal less, and there had been hundreds and hundreds of kilometers to travel.

"O Lion!" Reaching the dead tree five meters ahead of his rival, Ali Mohammed interrupted Achille's meditation with a taunting call. Not wanting to lose disgracefully, Achille slashed at Souffa's thighs and began to close the gap. From high on the *jebel,* he thought for a moment that he saw the Mediterranean to the north, but he had learned that distance vision is unreliable in the desert, and he concentrated on guiding Souffa back down the uneven surface of the hillside.

As they pounded down the homestretch, he could see that the whole family was watching the race with passionate interest. Even the African girls were cheering. Since he was a male and a foreigner, he had been segregated from all the women, African or Arab, ever since his return to manly good health, but he had observed that there were five young black females traveling in Ahmad's caravan. He had made delicate inquiries and was troubled by what he had learned.

The kindly Ahmad el-Sayeed was basically a general-purpose merchant. His clan maintained a permanent home in Murzuk, now fifteen hundred kilometers behind them, but once a year they made this epic odyssey to the coast with a consignment of camels and dates, as well as a supply of ostrich feathers and ivory from tropical Africa. After he sold his wares in the Sidi Barrani market, Ahmad would purchase sugar, sandalwood, tea, and colored silks for resale back in Murzuk.

But Ahmad's most lucrative commodities were slaves. The girls, were Sudanese, thirteen or fourteen years of age, sold by their parents and brought to Murzuk by slave traders from the hook of Africa. Ahmad had explained nonchalantly that a wealthy city dweller would often purchase a Nubian girl as a sexual toy for his sons, since Arab men were not expected to be celibate before marriage. Once the girl had lost the sensual luster of youth, she became a domestic servant.

This traffic in human beings presented Achille with a powerful conflict of emotions. The slave trade was one of the things the Italian Army had come to Libya to stop. And yet this particular Italian officer owned his life to a kind, fatherly slave trader.

They were close enough to the camp now to hear shouts of encouragement. The two riders were now almost neck and neck, and Achille shifted his weight to one side of the *mahklufa,* subtly hindering Souffa. Encouraged, Ali Mohammed lashed his camel into greater effort and began to pull slightly ahead.

With Ahmad's son leading by half a camel's length, the two riders rumbled into the camp. The bedouin went wild with joy, since their guest had displayed his return to full strength while the clan's future leader had demonstrated that he was even stronger than this powerful Englishman.

"It is time for prayer," Ahmad decreed as the two riders dismounted to receive his blessing. Like all Muslims, the el-Sayeed family worshiped before going to bed at night, and then again at sunrise, at noon, in the late afternoon, and now, just as the sun was setting. Since water was always too scarce to perform five ritual ablutions every day, the men cleansed their hands with sand, and then fell into place behind Ahmad, who was facing east.

"In the name of Allah, the Merciful and Compassionate, praise be to Allah, Lord of the Universe, Ruler on the Day of Judgment. We worship you and ask your assistance to guide us along the Straight Path, the road taken by those you have favored." The old man recited the first words of the Holy Koran while his family performed the ceremonial *rakas*—bowing, then kneeling to place their foreheads against the desert floor.

"Bismil laahir rahmaa nir raheem," Achille murmured the sonorous Arabic phrases, having grown comfortable with the ritual after many months in the Sahara. Leonida regarded religion as an irritating superstition, and at home in Italy Achille had never been able to pray. Here in the harshness and finality of the desert, however, he found it almost possible, although he was still never sure that anyone was listening.

After their prayers, Ahmad's family began to prepare a festive evening meal, marking both the end of their journey and the departure of "Charles Lion," their honored British guest.

For a few minutes Achille watched the scene, trying to memorize every detail so that he could recount it all to Rosi. Two of Ahmad's grandsons nursed a fire of twigs and camel dung, while the older men cut a billy goat's throat, hanging it up by its hind legs on a tripod of crossed tent poles to allow its blood to drain out into the sand. With the animal's body still twitching, Ahmad sawed through its abdominal wall and removed the liver, which he washed carefully in a bucket of water, and then sliced into fine segments. As the guest of honor, Achille was offered the first piece of this Arab delicacy, and he took it willingly, since the race had made him hungry. The liver was delicious, although he realized with less enthusiasm that his status as guest of honor would later qualify him for one of the goat's testicles.

While the food was being cooked, Achille wandered away from the encampment with his map and compass, wanting to make one last set of observations before the sun disappeared.

"O Lion, is that not the devil's mechanism?"

Startled, he turned to find that Ahmad had unexpectedly followed him away from the encampment. This was no time to get careless. Were they to suspect that he was an Italian and a spy, the bedouin would cut his throat as casually as they had butchered the billy goat.

"No, it is a machine for seeing directions," he replied with an easy grin. "Let me show you. For example, I can tell you precisely in what direction you must face in order to pray toward Mecca."

Ahmad smiled benignly as Achille unfolded his map. Remembering that the family had faced in the direction of a cliff on the side of the *jebel,* he took a quick compass reading and then plotted that azimuth on his chart, running the line over Egypt and across the Red Sea into the Arabian Peninsula. To his amazement, he saw that the line neatly bisected the holy city of Mecca.

"How did you know where Mecca is?" he asked.

"My father told me," the old bedouin explained. "But this would be a good machine to use during sandstorms when we cannot see."

"Then you must have it." Achille folded the compass into Ahmad's hand, and the old man looked at it with pleasure. "I can get another when I return to . . . uh, England."

"It will give me great sadness when you go home, O Lion," the old man told him sincerely. "At first, we believed you to be an Italian infidel and we would have left you to die in the desert had we not found your holy Koran and learned you were a Muslim, although not of our race. And now you have become like one of my sons."

"I will be sad to leave you as well, Ahmad." For the first time, Achille realized that Anfi's little Koran had saved his life.

"Do you have a woman in England?" Ahmad took Achille's arm as the two of them strolled toward the encampment.

"There is a woman whom I love, yes, but there is also a difficulty." Achille suddenly found himself impelled to confide in his substitute father. "She is not of my class, and there would be difficulties about a marriage."

"Then have her as a concubine." Ahmad found it difficult to understand the problem. "Make an arrangement with her father."

"Her father is long dead, but she has a brother who is my friend."

"Of course, the brother's honor must also be satisfied." Ahmad squeezed Achille's hand, leading him back toward the fire. "You must have been lonely without a woman. I have been a poor host."

Achille was trying to work out the significance of this remark when he sat down to a massive bedouin feast. The Arab approach to eating, it seemed to him, had been borrowed from the camel. While caravanning through the desert, Ahmad's family rose at dawn, prayed, and then consumed a hurried breakfast of black coffee, dried figs, and unleavened bread. At lunchtime they ate nothing beyond another handful of figs, but after dark they routinely consumed enough food to stagger an elephant.

As soon as Ahmad and Achille had taken their places, the younger men hunkered down on their haunches around a huge oval platter holding a mountain of rice and the roasted goat. As the senior member of the family, Ahmad tore off great hunks of tender meat with his right hand and tossed them first at Achille, then Ali Mohammed, and then his other sons and grandsons, urging them all to eat as much as they wished. The women had withdrawn into one of the tents. The serving was done by the youngest boys, who delivered boiled sweet potatoes followed by a granular pasty substance called couscous and then freshly baked bread. To drink there was only water, warm and tasting of the sheepskin bags in which it was carried, and Achille privately wished he could wash down this extravaganza with a bottle of Cederna's vino bianco.

At the end of the meal, after he and Ahmad had ceremonially eaten the goat's chewy testicles, the company devoured a kind of pancake made with honey, followed by green mint tea. From an old canvas sack, Ahmad produced an large, irregular lump of sugar. With a small iron hammer, he expertly knocked a chunk into each cup, producing a potent solution that was about half liquid glucose and half tea.

The women were allowed to eat the leftovers, and they were clearing away the platter as Achille staggered off toward the tent allocated to him. As the family's guest of honor, he was not obliged to share his quarters with anyone, although the other unmarried men and boys all slept in a great untidy heap in another tent. It was growing cool, and he pulled the rough wool blanket over him, trying to get comfortable on the sand.

"O Lion," came an unexpected whisper. Achille sat up in some alarm, but it was only Ali Mohammed. "This girl's name is Meeya. My father worried you might be cold tonight."

Standing shyly behind him was one of the Sudanese girls. She seemed very young, perhaps twelve or thirteen, but her breasts had already begun to sprout, and Achille felt a sudden fire in his loins.

Then the officer and gentleman in him took control. This is a child and a slave, he told himself fiercely. It would be the worst crime of his life.

"My thanks to your father." He took Ali Mohammed's rough hand and squeezed it. "But tell him that today's race has tired me and I wish to sleep."

"If you wish it thus, Lion." Ali Mohammed himself had never found camel racing quite that exhausting, but he withdrew good-naturedly. The Nubian girl would fetch a higher price in Sidi Barrani if she could be advertised as a virgin.

Achille lay back on his bed of sand. The night wind was whipping up, pattering fragments of sand against the sides of his tent.

Oh, Rosi, Rosi, he repeated as the darkness gathered over the desert. We need to make some decisions, don't we? I want you.

I want you.

I want you.

In the morning, they trekked across a plateau so stony and featureless that Achille wondered if Ahmad had finally lost his way. By noon, Souffa went sore-footed and started to limp, but the land was already tilting toward the Egyptian coastal plain, and they began their descent through fields where goats were grazing on new spring grass.

It was mid-afternoon before they saw the minaret of Sidi Barrani thrusting into a peaceful blue sky, and, behind the mosque, a cluster of houses with whitewashed walls, and then the sparkle of low, rolling waves, white-crested in the distance.

The sea! For a moment Achille wondered if this was not another cruel mirage, but a kilometer later the bay itself came into view, dirty brown harbor water melting into the deep cobalt blue of the Mediterranean. As they rode closer, he could see little fishing vessels tied to a jetty and, on the far side of a massive stone sea wall, an oceangoing craft of some size.

"Whoa, Souffa," he commanded, sweeping the landscape with his field glasses. At first he could scarcely believe his eyes, but he refocused and the mirage refused to disappear. Riding serenely at anchor was a *cacciatorpediniere,* a torpedo boat, flying a flag with three vertical stripes of green, white, and red.

La bandiera italiana! His eyes abruptly moistened, although this sudden rush of emotion made him feel foolish. Achille had always imagined himself to be a thoroughly modern man, a technician in a technocratic century, too sophisticated for maudlin nationalism. And yet there were tears on his cheek at the sight of an Italian flag.

We are all tribalists at heart, he reflected, nudging Souffa and following Ahmad's clan down toward the city walls. And the sailors on that torpedo boat are members of my tribe. Bella Italia! I want to go home.

The caravan made camp in an empty field on the outskirts of Sidi Barrani. Since the bedouin had a well-earned reputation for carrying off women and property, they were not very welcome within the city walls. With an affectionate farewell gesture, Achille attempted to pat Souffa's nose, but the beast tried to bite him good-bye, and they parted enemies. Saying farewell to the el-Sayeed tribe meant kissing all the men in the family, and Ahmad's sons lined up for the honor. Warmly Achille performed the ritual with each of them, the handshake, the hug, and then dozens of great smacking kisses on both cheeks, followed by pledges to see one another again, promises that were as fervent as they were impossible to keep.

Walking a little way away from the others, he sought out the patriarch of the el-Sayeed family. "I will always be a man with two fathers," he told him. "Thank you for everything."

"Listen, my English son, do you have enough money for your voyage to England?" the old bedouin fretted.

"I have enough money." Achille produced the wad of British pounds sterling his father had given him, and counting out five five-pound notes. "About the girls you have brought for sale," he inquired. "Will this cover your expenses if I take them with me?"

"Ah, then you are no longer quite so tired," Ahmad teased him, making the automatic assumption that Achille wanted the girls for the usual carnal purposes. Achille decided against a lecture on the iniquities of slavery as he observed the speed with which his money disappeared into the small leather pouch Ahmad carried around his neck.

Then the old man kissed him on the nose in the ancient bedouin fashion, asked that his best wishes be conveyed to the King of England and sent him on his way with five veiled African slaves.

At the harbor, no one paid much attention to them until he approached the

Italian torpedo boat, where they were intercepted by a nervous sailor with a rifle.

"Buon giorno," Achille said cordially to the stunned seaman. It felt strange to be speaking Italian again. "Pardon my attire, but I am Captain Achille Leone of the Royal Italian Army. May I know your name?"

"Seaman Rodolfo Lazzari, sir." The guard came to attention and saluted. "Are you the Capitano Leone we're supposed to be looking for?"

"I suppose I might be." Achille wondered if there might be a bottle of reasonably cold white wine aboard. He led the five young Sudanese girls up the gangplank. "And these ladies are my guests. Could we find a cabin for them as well?"

"I'm not sure we can transport civilian passengers," objected Lazzari. "Our orders were to collect you and your property."

"Well, that's all right then," Achille laughed. "I've just purchased them, so they qualify as my property."

"I wish I were an officer," said Seaman Lazzari soulfully. "Welcome aboard, sir."

"We can leave within the hour." The commanding officer of the *cacciator-pediniere* stood in the wheel house, inspecting his charts as Achille Leone drank his first glass of wine in over six months. "Will I be court-martialed for running slaves or decorated for finding you?"

"Maybe neither," Achille said. "The girls aren't slaves anymore, since I've purchased their freedom, and you didn't find me until I walked up your gangplank."

"Well, we were there so you could find us," the naval officer countered. "The generals had written you off as dead until your father turned up and got everybody looking for you again. Then this demented Lieutenant Rosselli insisted you might have come this way along that string of oases, so we got orders to check every port city from Tobruk to Alexandria."

"You've been more than kind," Achille said. Guido must have made an magnificent nuisance of himself, he thought warmly. And Father went the distance to find me. "Before we leave, is there time for me to send a couple of letters from Sidi Barrani? If we're a week's sailing from Benghazi, a letter might get to Italy through international post faster than Italian military mail."

"Sure! Sounds like there's an anxious *fidanzata* waiting at home." Reading Achille's mind with some accuracy, the naval man located a pen with a steel nib, a bottle of black ink, and some Marina Militare stationery.

Settling himself at a table in the corner of the cabin, Achille dashed off a quick note to his father in which he explained briefly what had happened, sent his love, and promised a longer letter as soon as he arrived in Benghazi.

With a second piece of foolscap, be began a letter to Rosi, explaining that after six months as the guest of a Libyan family, he could no longer regard the Arab people as enemies and would prefer not to meet them again in battle.

Of course, I am still a loyal officer on active duty [he explained]. But I shall be requesting a transfer back to Rome, and when my legal obligation to the army expires next year, I want to return to the university to study more engineering and physics. Africa interests me greatly, and there is much that a competent European engineer could do here to help these people . . .

"She'll be glad to hear you're all right," the naval officer said. "When you've finished your letters, Lazzari can take them to the post office, and we can get under way."

Achille nodded silently and quickly scribbled a second paragraph.

Rosi, in all the nights I slept alone on hard sand, your face was never absent from my dreams. I love you. I don't underestimate the social difficulties we're going to face, and there will be antagonism from your community as well as from mine, but what I have endured has sharpened my thinking. I want to live with you and I don't want to keep it a secret. I want to finish what we began the night this terrible war took me away from you. I want to show you Africa. I love you. I have always loved you.

He folded the paper and addressed the envelope to Signorina Rosaria Lombardi, Castello Leone, Commune di Cederna, Provincia di Roma, Regno d'Italia.

Rosi, I'm coming home, he thought as Lazzari collected his letters. Wait for me, girl. I'm coming home!

9.

. . . .

"Pink gin, Loretta, and quickly!" Signora Giorgina Leone Benellis swept into the Castello Leone. The morning in Cederna had been simply exhausting. "Bring the mail into the salotto."

It was the fourteenth day of April in 1913, and Giorgina had spent four hours at the Cederna Municipal Hall with the Don Maurizio Padana, Pastor of Santa Teresa's Church, Enrico Mosconi, Mayor of Cederna, and Junio Mosconi, the Mayor's son and Giorgina's personal adviser on social, economic, and political issues.

With the help of these distinguished community leaders, Leonida's daughter completed her planning for the erection of a cenotaph honoring Captain Achille Leone (1887–1912), who had perished in what was presumed to be a heroic fashion during the liberation of Libya. The monument would be designed by an expensive Milanese architect and constructed with the finest Carrara marble.

To provide a site on the Piazza Bixio, Mayor Mosconi would now persuade the municipal council to order the demolition of Sandro Lombardi's Casa del Popolo. This "House of the People" was a run-down meeting hall occupied jointly by the Farmworkers' Labor Union and the Cederna Chapter of the PSI.

In Giorgina's considered opinion, a ramshackle Marxist hut would scarcely be missed, but they had been obliged to listen to a tiresome appeal presented by Tommaso Savarino, a Cederna lawyer who represented thieves, drunkards, and socialists. It had been nearly lunchtime before Savarino had finished his long-winded appeal and the committee had voted unanimously to reject it.

"Your letters, signora." Loretta fearfully presented a stack of envelopes on a tray, along with a large pink gin, the first of several Giorgina intended to consume before her afternoon nap.

"Can't you read?" Giorgina demanded irritably, discovering that the mail had not been sorted, a task normally performed by the wretched Rosaria Lombardi. Among the letters addressed to Giorgina and Bruno Benelli there was one meant for Leonida, postmarked Sidi Barrani, wherever that was, and another one . . .

"No, madam," Loretta confessed in terror, but Giorgina was already on her feet, moving toward the staircase. In the stack, there was a second letter, also dispatched from the Egyptian post office in Sidi Barrani, and it was addressed to Signorina Rosaria Lombardi. The handwriting looked familiar, but in her haste Giorgina was unable to identify it.

Who would send letters to both Count Leonida Leone and his secretary? Nobody writes to peasants. She frowned on her way up the stairs. Is it time to begin another anti-Lombardi campaign?

Giorgina halted before the door to Leonida's study, considering her options. She had tried once before to send Rosaria back to the kitchen garden, even enlisting Don Maurizio's assistance, but her noble father had staged such an elaborate tantrum after the priest's appearance that she had been forced to back down.

To make matters worse, while Terenzio, Bruno, and the old man were off on that fool's errand, chasing around the Mediterranean looking for Achille, Rosaria had brought in a record harvest, neatly cementing her position. The profits from the agricultural estate had been unprecedented, even after Red Rosaria had talked silly old Leonida into paying supplemental bonuses to the work force.

Our little contadina is beautiful and thoroughly competent, Giorgina admitted to herself. But she wants to get her hands on my family's fortune, and this shall not happen.

I will be friendly, Giorgina decided as she entered the library. I will give Father his letter first, and then pretend to discover Rosaria's.

Leonida's office was empty, and the grandfather clock near the door suggested that the Count might be enjoying an extra-long afternoon nap. The door to the little sewing room where he slept was closed, but not locked, and Giorgina entered softly.

She stopped breathing the moment she saw them, Leonida and Rosaria, curled up together in the narrow bed like spoons. They were both asleep, a sheet drawn up over their waists. Giorgina's father was lying on his side, breathing sonorously. There was perspiration glistening in the iron-gray hair on his chest, but his face looked serene. Rosaria lay facing away from him with her head resting on his bicep, her auburn hair sprayed against the whiteness of the pillow, her nipples dark and delicate in the afternoon light from the window.

Stunned, Giorgina let the letters slip from her hand and fall to the Persian rug.

You stupid old man! The rage built within her as she backed out of the sewing room and stumbled downstairs to the salotto. It would have been cheaper to go to an ordinary whore, Father. You could have paid once for your pleasure, and been done with it. You will be paying this particular *puttana* for the rest of your life.

"Signora?" Down in the salotto, Loretta became petrified when she saw Giorgina's rage. Somehow this would turn out to be her fault. "I'm sorry about the letters, signora."

"Damn!" Giorgina seized the pink gin with a vague intention of drinking it, but fury overcame her and she smashed the glass violently against the wall. It shattered, covering the carpet with ice crystals and tonic and gin and the Angostura bitters they imported especially from Trinidad to put the pinkness in Giorgina's gin.

Loretta backed away. In rages like this, Giorgina had been known to strike her servants and then fire them. "Signora, please . . ."

"You stupid mule, get me another drink!" Giorgina screamed, whirling on the maid. "Fetch my husband! Clean up this mess!"

"Yes, signora." Loretta fled and Giorgina inserted a Turkish cigarette into her silver cigarette holder. Her hands shook when she tried to make the lighter work. "I'm going to finish you," she hissed in the emptiness of the salotto. "Finish you, finish you, finish you, forever and forever and forever . . ."

An instant later, Rosaria awoke. She was not sure why, because she always felt safe in Leonida's little room, and slept soundly there. But somewhere in the distance there had been a shout and a crash—the sound of breaking glass followed by a shouted curse.

Leonida snored softly and turned on his side, and she looked down at him with the usual medley of emotions. I know this . . . this friendliness we have between us is not right, she told herself as she began to assemble her clothing. But it's all that keeps me from going mad.

In the two months since their first lovemaking, a comfortable connubial rhythm had developed between them. Lord and secretary worked together in the morning, writing, typing, filing, making decisions and phone calls. A few days a week, instead of going downstairs for *pranzo* with his family, Leonida would casually suggest that she bring up something simple from the kitchen for them. Sitting side by side on the davenport, they would dine on soft rolls and provolone cheese and chilled white Cederna wine.

Afterward, Leonida would mention that it was time for his nap. For a man who had spent a lifetime taking what he wanted, Count Leone was strangely gallant when it came to afternoon naps, always leaving it up to her to suggest that she would lie down with him if he so desired.

Leonida always made love to her very gently, sometimes stopping to ask if he was hurting her. She accepted his caresses calmly, although sometimes, when they had finished, her body still tingled with tension, a sense of incompleteness that she found difficult to understand.

I do love him, she decided, although not the way I loved his son. We are both still grieving, he is not my substitute for Achille, and I do not think that I am a replacement for anyone. He is . . .

"Oh, Christ!" Suddenly she saw the two letters on the rug, and gasped aloud with the realization that there had been a foreign presence in their little nest. Leonida's eyes opened. "These were on the floor." She handed him the letters. "Someone saw us together."

"It must have been Girolamo," he assured her, peering at the first envelope and then putting on his reading glasses. "No one else would have entered without knocking. Ah, I suppose it was inevitable. I've never been able to keep anything from Giro. He will be furious at me for your sake, but our secret is safe with him. These letters must be important . . ."

"He will be so angry." Rosaria put on her shoes, knowing that the old majordomo's rage would be directed primarily at her, since chastity was a woman's responsibility.

Girolamo would keep his silence, for everyone's sake, but the knowledge that someone had seen them wrapped in one another's arms made her feel tawdry. In a way, she had begun to enjoy the conspiracy of being Leonida's clandestine mistress. He sent her secret notes and seldom returned from Rome without a present, a gold ring or scent from Paris. She thrilled at sharing the interior life of a great man, leaning on his shoulder while he wrote letters to Prime Minister Giolitti or made rude jokes about the King after a ceremonial dinner at the royal palace.

But now it all seemed crude. She and Leonida understood what had happened to them and why, but to the outside world, it would appear depressingly conventional, the rich old nobleman and his pretty peasant plaything. If my secret were known in the town, she realized as she laced up her shoes, they would say I was a whore, a *puttana* . . .

"Achille is alive."

Achille is dead, she contradicted him mentally. What are you talking about? That's why we're here, in bed with each other, because Achille is not alive.

"Topo?" she turned to reason with him. Then she looked at the letter he was holding and recognized that meticulous rectangular handwriting she had once copied with the Olivetti. "How could he be alive?"

"He was rescued by some bedouin who took him to Egypt." Leonida seemed unable to believe his eyes. Unconscious of his nakedness, he paced the tiny sewing room. "He's on his way by ship back to Benghazi, and will write us all the details later."

Rosaria's mind was whirling. Her first reaction was joy, an exuberant lightness that seemed to take possession of her body. Then she felt angry at Achille for plunging them all into protracted grief while he caravanned across the desert with the bedouin, having wonderful adventures.

"Fanciulla, he's written to you as well." Leonida passed her the second letter, and she tore it open, her hands trembling. She was so excited that it was difficult to comprehend the words, and she had to scan the two short paragraphs twice to comprehend their meaning. "He wants to leave the army and go back to the University of Rome," she reported in amazement. "And he says . . . oh God!"

"What else does he say?" Leonida demanded. "The university, yes, that would be fine. He's got the best brain the family ever produced, and there is no law that he has to be a soldier. Does he mention ... does he say how he feels about ...''

Without asking permission, Leonida took the letter from her hands. Rosaria surrendered it, suddenly feeling faint. "He says here that he loves you, fanciulla. He wants to live with you. Openly."

"Yes, I knew that he loved me. I ... I don't know what to do." Her mind flooded with machinations and plots. I will say nothing. I will confess everything, and throw myself on his mercy. I will keep both men, father and son, and be a proper whore. I have bungled everything, and I will end up losing them both. "Oh, topo, what will we say to him?"

There was a long silence. Suddenly embarrassed by his nudity, Leonida put on his heavy cotton dressing gown and Rosaria mentally said good-bye to his muscular body, thinking that she would not be seeing it again. You are only an old man with your clothes on, she decided, and you age a decade with every layer. Undressed, you are still a young man.

"We are all going to be very happy." Leonida's face was pale. There was a slight quiver in his voice, as if words were not coming easily. "My love for you would not have been expressed in a physical way had we not been quite certain that Achille was dead. So we need not feel guilty. For me, at least, it was lovely, and I will never regret the moments of tenderness that we shared. But we must never, never tell Achille."

"How can I deceive him?"

"Cristo! Just don't tell him, girl. He doesn't want to know!"

"How can I base our life together on deceit?"

"Fanciulla, trust me. Every love affair that lasts is based on mutual deceit. Don't you tell him, and I won't ever tell him, and he'll be a happy man."

"Topo, I don't know ...'' She was laughing and crying at the same time. "He's coming home. He talks about an apartment in Rome. I feel so happy. But I feel sad for you."

"You needn't." He swept her into his arms and kissed her firmly on the forehead. "There! That's the only place I shall kiss you from now on," he chuckled. "My son will have to kiss you in all the other places."

For a moment they stood silently together, and she tried to draw strength from him. You're magnificent, she thought. I have been loved by the two greatest men in Italy. And I don't regret ...

Then there was a nasal tenor voice from the study, calling insistently. "Signor Conte! Signor Conte!"

"My wretched son-in-law." Leonida commanded silence with a warning finger to his lips. "Stay here and I'll get rid of him."

As the door closed behind him, Rosaria put her ear to the door, beginning to worry when she heard Giorgina's shrill voice. Bruno and his wife were both trying to talk at once. Rosaria wondered if Leonida would lose patience and shoot another hole in the ceiling.

"Will you listen to me?" the Count cried. "I have just learned that Achille is alive. He was rescued by bedouin, and we will have him home here in Cederna before very long."

There was a buzz of animated conversation as Leonida explained the circumstances of Achille's return to the living. Retreating from the door, Rosaria combed her hair, wondering how the Leone family had managed to produce Giorgina. Contessa Maria Pia had been a mild, quiet, undemanding woman. Leonida was open and generous, and neither of his sons was capable of being vindictive or mean. Yet somehow, in the midst of all the nobility, there was this dreadnought of a woman who cared for nothing but the enforcement of her will.

"Father, this is wonderful about Achille, but we are concerned about another issue." Giorgina recovered from the news of her brother's survival with remarkable speed and returned to the attack, her voice harsh and confident. "We have decided that the time has come for you to concentrate on your memoirs and enjoy your retirement. You need to hand executive authority over to Bruno. Immediately."

Instantly worried, Rosaria pressed her ear against the walnut-paneled door.

"Bruno already handles our family investments, and he does it very capably." Leonida's voice was tight with controlled anger. "I feel good, especially with this happy news about Achille, and I enjoy running my farm."

"But you're not running this farm, are you? Every substantive decision for the past six months has been made by Rosaria Lombardi," Giorgina argued, "I never understood why, until I brought those letters into your study just now. I saw—"

"You saw nothing!" Leonida shouted back at her, but Rosaria felt the blood rush to her head, and she sat down heavily on the bed, understanding that she had been delivered into the hands of her worst enemy.

"I saw everything. Wait until Achille hears."

"You will say nothing!" Leonida thundered. "You saw nothing and you will say nothing, girl! That is my order! I forbid you to communicate with Achille on this matter."

She's going to tell him! Rosaria collapsed on the bed in despair. God, she will tell him everything . . .

10.

· ·

Mustafa's mother inspected the Sudanese girls one by one, looking for signs of disease, and found that they were all healthy.

"Someday they will understand what has happened to them." She turned to Achille. "And they will be grateful to you."

"They should thank you," Achille commented as sipped his mint tea. "It is very good of you to take them in. Of course, I'll provide money for their schooling."

Meeya and her friends still looked frightened, but they knew so little Arabic that it was impossible to explain that they had been legally emancipated, and would henceforth be under the kindly protection of the al-Sharif family. Time and gentleness would make them understand.

"There are no schools for girls in Cyrenaica," Anfi explained. "But if they can learn the domestic arts, then we can find them good husbands because they are all pretty."

Her inspection concluded, Anfi signaled one of her maids to escort the five Sudanese girls from the room. "Give them baths, and change their clothing," she ordered before turning to her guest.

"I admire you greatly for what you have done." Mustafa's mother spoke in the same throaty voice he remembered so vividly from their first meeting. She was still dressed in a frustrating black chadour that concealed her features and enveloped her body. Achille wondered why his brain insisted that Anfi al-Sharif was a beautiful woman. She could be as homely as a cow shed. But she sounded beautiful.

"The abolition of slavery is high on my lists of things Italy needs to accomplish here," he assured her. "It's a question of social engineering."

"Is that what you think you are doing?" There was a harshness in her voice. "Social engineering with long-range artillery, and airplanes and bombs? My dear Captain, allow me to observe that you were never cut out to be a soldier."

"I have had the same realization," he confessed. "After knowing you and your family, and then spending nearly half a year with my bedouin friends, it would be difficult for me to go back into combat against your people. I have been contemplating leaving the army and studying physics as a post-graduate at the University of Rome. Perhaps I could come back here someday and design irrigation systems and wells for your people."

"We need fresh water more than colonialism. And your spoken Arabic is now very fluent. Perhaps you will become a Muslim."

"That seems unlikely, although the Koran literally saved my life. The el-Sayeed family were about to abandon me to certain death when they saw I was carrying your little Koran."

"I'm glad something saved you," Anfi told him sincerely. "Mustafa was horrified when we heard you were missing, and he will be delighted to know that you survived your ordeal."

"And you?" He regretted his imprudence as soon as the words escaped his lips.

"I am glad as well," she said dryly, taking his hand in both of hers. He noticed that she still wore her wedding band. "Good-bye, Captain Leone."

"The mail room will be closed tomorrow for Easter. But the courier boat just arrived from Rome, so I brought these right over." The duty corporal from Colonel Adamo's office had found the two officers on their balcony, just finishing dinner. He deposited one pile of correspondence at Lieutenant Rosselli's end of the table, and another, smaller stack, in front of the celebrated Captain Achille Leone.

"This one's from my sister Cristina, but the rest are from girls of poor moral character," Guido said as he sifted through his stack of letters. "Bless their impure little hearts. Anything back yet from His Excellency?"

"No, Father's letter must have missed this boat." Achille was disappointed. There would not be another mail boat until well after Easter, which meant an agonizing two-week wait for Rosi's reply. Paradoxically, an envelope from Bruno Benelli had slipped through, although he assumed that it would contain nothing more exciting than his brother-in-law's customary statement of family finances. There was a communication from the army payroll office about back salary during his absence, some forms needing to be signed, and a postcard from a cousin who was visiting Paris.

"Ah, Cristina has graduated from nursing school." With fraternal pride, Guido displayed the photograph of a slender blond young woman wearing a white dress. Timidly, she was peering through spectacles at the camera. "Someday, our Crissi would make a splendid contessa for you. Or will you be forced to marry a woman from the nobility?"

"There will certainly be that kind of pressure." Achille knew that Giorgina maintained an updated list of eligible girls from aristocratic families. "But if I ever do marry, it will be for love."

"I myself am going to marry for lust." Guido went to the sideboard and returned with whiskey and ice crystals. "Listen, how about a drink? It's not every day we get to celebrate your return from the dead with five slave girls."

"Whiskey goes right to my head," Achille laughed. "You have one and tell me what it was like in jail."

"The stockade?" Guido Rosselli chuckled at the recollection as he sipped his whiskey. "Ah, a scene of classic drama! After weeks of chasing around Cyrenaica looking for you, Giuseppe Papafava and I ride up to headquarters on our camels, and the guards nearly shoot us because we're still dressed as Arabs. Adamo is too furious to look at any of the intelligence we've collected, and the carabinieri arrest us for desertion. Desertion! Poor Papafava and I languish in jail until a sovereign blast comes from your exceedingly noble father, who explained to the commanding general that going absent without leave to search for your best friend is not the worst crime in the world. Thanks to His Excellency's intervention, we were promptly released with an apology."

"What a life!" Achille laughed. "So much has happened to us in eighteen months. Do you remember our first battle, when we beat everybody in sight at Sidi Osman?"

"And we've been winning battles ever since." The mercurial Guido was suddenly serious. "Achille, you and I are arguably the two best desert fighters in the Italian Army, and they want to make you the commanding officer of the Lupi di Lazio and me your second-in-command. Stay here in Libya and you'll be a major in another year and I'll make captain. How can you leave now?"

"I . . . I just feel that this chapter in my life is over," Achille said awkwardly. "I've got an idea for a hydraulic pump that could make desert wells ten times more efficient, and—"

"But your career!" Guido was crestfallen. "Achille, you're the golden boy of the Second Division. One good war can make you a general."

I want to go home to Rosi, he said to himself, but this was not yet something he felt able to share with Guido. "Perhaps they will give command of the battalion to you."

"They won't give it to a 'Hebrew officer,' and even if they did, I wouldn't want it alone," Guido said passionately. "We're a good team, but separately we make mistakes. If we'd gone together to look for Franco Grassi, I'd never have let you be cornered by that Arab patrol. And if you'd been at headquarters with me when the Senusi attacked, things could have . . . gone more smoothly."

"It wasn't your fault Tobino was killed, and getting the battalion out of there was sheer brilliance. How could I have improved on that?"

"I lost fifty men." Guido took a quick drink of his whiskey, as if to drown an unhappy memory.

"Tobino would have lost the whole battalion." Achille realized that there was something about the night of Tobino's death that Guido had never shared with him. He had rejected any praise for saving nine hundred and fifty Italian lives and created a minor sensation at division headquarters by refusing the Bronze Medal for Military Valor.

We've all got our secrets, he mused. Someday he'll tell me his, and I'll tell him about Rosi. Or should I tell him now?

"Did you ever lose your heart to a contadina?" Rising from his place at the table, Achille put his elbows on the balustrade of the balcony and gazed out over the harbor, thinking that he would miss Libya when he went home. Guido had found them a wonderful apartment, a kilometer from that old Moorish castle the army had comandeered as a headquarters, and only a few steps from the officers' brothel where Guido sometimes sought relaxation. It was cool and pleasant, like a September in Cederna, and there was a soft, cordial breeze off the Bay of Sidra mingling the smells of salt water and tar from the fishing boats and nets drying on the beach.

"About seventeen times! In bed, the daughters of the proletariat cannot be matched. Once, there was this girl on my father's estate outside of Venice who—"

"No, I meant were you in love?" Achille explained. "For example, could you marry a girl from the working classes?"

"Ah, that would be carrying democracy too far, amico mio. You remember when that colonel at the academy married his maid? It took the army about twenty minutes to retire him without a pension."

"I remember, and it seemed unjust," Achille argued, but Guido laughed away his objections.

"Achille, if you will stroll with me down to the brothel, I will find you a half dozen peasant girls with whom you may temporarily fall in love. Perhaps if we can get your sexual life sorted out, you might condescend to hang around and help me win this war."

Achille chuckled and shook his head. The junior officers' brothel boasted a meticulously inspected selection of very acceptable girls from three continents. Senior officers, of course, had their own separate facility, a luxurious apartment stocked with a bevy of authentic beauties for the exclusive enjoyment of full colonels and generals. There was also a *casa di tolleranza* for enlisted men, free and functioning around the clock, although Giuseppe Papafava complained that it featured only a cluster of weather-beaten hags. Some of the farm boys preferred uncomplicated relationships with ewes and nanny goats, but everybody had something.

Everybody but me, Achille reflected, getting pen and paper from his desk as he prepared to write Easter greetings to his friends and relatives. And perhaps another note to Rosi, explaining and amplifying what he had said in that first quick note?

"Then I will leave you to appreciate the serene joys of chastity," Guido chuckled. "But someday, Comandante, we have to think seriously about losing your virginity."

"Listen, I'm not . . ." he began hotly, but Guido only laughed and went off to change for the brothel.

Thinking it unimportant, Achille left the envelope from Bruno Benelli until the last. The writing was so bureaucratic that he was halfway to the bottom of the page before he realized that this was not an accountant's report.

> It is with profound regret [Bruno had written after a long preamble], that I convey to you further evidence of your father's declining mental condition. I have long been concerned about his business judgment, because he has taken to granting absurd and unnecessary salary increases to our work force. Recently, however, Giorgina had occasion to enter your father's room, and found him in bed with Rosaria Lombardi in a situation of mutual undress that left no question as to the debased character of their relationship. I need hardly tell you of the terrible scandal that could erupt should anyone outside our family learn of the disgraceful affair.

"O Cristo!" Stunned, Achille sat back in his chair, his body suddenly trembling. He discovered that he needed more oxygen than he seemed able to suck into his lungs, even by panting heavily, and for a moment the world spun around him. Knocking over a glass of mineral water in his dizziness, he managed to find the wine. Gulping directly from the bottle, he steadied himself with a long drink.

In a storm of furiously confused emotions, he quickly unscrewed his bottle of ink and moistened the nip of his pen.

> Signorina Lombardi [he scrawled on a sheet of regimental stationery]. Please forgive the impetuous tone of my previous letter, written in a moment of loneliness after a protracted sojourn in the wilderness. I would not wish to intrude upon your relationship with my father. In any case, I have been offered the command of the Lupi di Lazio Infantry Battalion, and propose to accept. I shall, therefore, remain here in Libya for two more years, perhaps much longer.

There were ink blotches on the paper, but he did not bother to rewrite it. He sealed the envelope and slumped back in his chair, covering his face with his hands.

"What's wrong, Comandante? Your father hasn't died?"

"No, no," he stammered as Guido returned to the balcony. "Father seems to be enjoying extraordinarily good health." Except for Sandro, this is the best friend I have ever had, Achille thought. But I will never be able to explain to him what I am feeling in this moment. Oh my God, it hurts. Christ, I never knew that anything could hurt like this!

"Well, I'm glad. Listen, are you all right? I think you need a whiskey."

Achille nodded, immobilized by the savagery of his feelings and unable to trust his voice. Guido quickly dumped ice into a beaker and added an enormous quantity of Scotch.

"Thanks," Achille muttered. He drank it in one gulp, coughed, and then banged the empty glass roughly on the table. Guido promptly refilled it.

"Do you want to talk?" his friend asked gently.

Achille shook his head and rose awkwardly, putting a hand on Guido's shoulder for support. "Are we going to that whorehouse?"

"Yes, well, if you've decided." Guido looked at him suspiciously, but did not press the matter. Achille was unsteady on his feet, but he managed to follow his friend down the street to the "convent," as they blasphemously called the officers' brothel. The liquor had numbed his nerves a little, blunting the intensity of the shock, but the question still burned in his brain: how could they have done it?

There were ways of rationalizing the matter. They had thought him dead and hence no longer a factor in anyone's emotions. Furthermore, he never confessed to his father that he wanted a role in Rosi's life. Yes, naturally, this line of reasoning made sense, but still it hurt, and he found himself hating the two of them. What did the old fool think he was doing? And why had Rosaria let him?

"Andiamo," urged Guido, and Achille reluctantly stumbled into the *casa di tolleranza*. He found himself in a large, dimly lit chamber with an absurd baroque crystal chandelier dangling from a high ceiling. Running around all four walls there was a balcony which led to a series of little rooms, each with a number on the door. In one corner of the lower floor, the Italian Army had established its presence by erecting a bar with the usual espresso machine flanked by bottles of liqueurs.

What am I doing here? he asked himself as he followed Guido to the bar. The prostitutes on duty were sitting on numbered chairs along the wall. Most of them were scantily dressed in short skirts or panties, their breasts exposed. Some looked demure, like schoolgirls waiting to be asked to dance. Others were brazen, sprawling with their legs apart in the best traditions of Italian whoredom, grinning lewdly at potential customers. A few looked shell-shocked, still trying to work out what detour on the highway of life had landed them in a brothel in Benghazi.

"I'll have another whiskey," Achille decided. "How about you?"

"Don't put too much *benzina* in your tank, Comandante," Guido advised. "Listen, how about those two over there? Take your pick." In one corner, there was a shy-looking pair of Arab girls who might have been sisters.

"Oh, look, you go and enjoy yourself." Achille suddenly wanted to to be alone. "I'll wait for you here at the bar."

"Come on, Achille, it's my treat." Guido stepped over to the cashier's booth and produced nine lire. The cashier patiently made out two receipts.

Achille ordered another whiskey, wondering why anyone would want a receipt from a brothel. Then Guido turned up with two keys and two Arab girls in tow. Before he could object, he found himself climbing the staircase with the girl from chair 17 holding his hand.

She seemed about fifteen and no more than an inch or two over five feet in height. Her hair was black and not very clean, tumbling over her shoulders in disorderly strands. She was moderately pretty, with dark brown eyes, and as she took the key from his hand and opened the door to room 17, she favored him with a quick, apprehensive smile.

This is too squalid, Achille thought as he surveyed the wretched little cubicle. There was a mattress on the floor. In one corner was a bucket of water and a portable porcelain bidet. Once the door was closed, girl 17 removed her only garment, a long shapeless sack of yellow Indian muslin, and stretched herself out quickly on a stained army-issue sheet, opening her legs. Something about the gesture reminded him of the way Rosaria had stripped herself the night of his departure from Italy.

I should have taken her then. He replayed the scene in his mind. Told my driver to wait and carried her out into the woods. I should have made her pregnant.

The Arab girl's body was not unattractive, and he gazed at her small breasts and dark protuberant nipples, her slender waist and comely thighs. Her pubic hair had been plucked, making her sex seem fragile and unnaturally exposed. He sat on the edge of the mattress and tried to work up some enthusiasm by running his hand lightly over her loins.

"What is your name?"

"Fatima." She seemed surprised, perhaps because so few of her clients spoke her language, or perhaps because no one had ever bothered to ask her name before. Half the women in Libya were named Fatima, and Achille was unable to think of another polite question. It seemed inappropriate to ask how she felt about having her frail body plundered a dozen times a day by the officers of the army that had invaded her country.

Fearful that this client was going to take all night, Fatima curled her body around his, putting her head on his thigh and trying to run her hands down the front of his trousers. His penis stiffened, but he shook his head, knowing that the whole experiment was doomed to failure. Gently, he moved her hand away from his groin, but not before she had felt his hardness.

"Why?" She was frightened that he would make some complaint against her.

"You can rest for a few minutes." He got a five-lire note out of his *giubba* and laid it on her belly. She looked at his face with renewed apprehension, wondering what kind of special service he was going to demand for this generosity. Then he left.

For a long time he stamped furiously through the darkened city with no destination in mind. There were adobe buildings on either side of the street, and sometimes music was coming from behind the high walls of the houses he was passing, but he kept his head down and stalked along one dusty street after another.

Bruno is an idiot, he told himself, becoming angrier by the minute. They want to have Father declared incompetent to get their hands on the estate, and I will never consent. The old man's mind has never been clearer. He knew nothing about the relationship between Rosaria and me. He assumed that I was dead and consoled himself by taking one more helping of love before it was too late.

Damn them, he cursed, damn her and damn him. A man that old and a girl that young. What on earth was she thinking of? What the hell is poor Sandro going to do? Challenge his employer to a duel? This puts the rest of us in an impossible situation. God damn it!

"God damn them!" he suddenly burst out, shouting aloud in the emptiness of a side street. "God damn them!"

The outburst passed and he felt exhausted. I've got to go home and drink myself unconscious, he decided. Where the hell am I? Earlier, he remembered passing the souk on the right, and then crossing the southern boulevard . . .

With a shock, he realized that he was a few steps from Mustafa's house. Is this, he wondered, an accident? Anfi once said that I was special to them, that if I were ever troubled, they would give me . . . sanctuary. Perhaps I could pretend to want to borrow a book from their library. Or I could ask how Meeya and her friends are getting on.

No, it's late, he reprimanded himself, and there is liquor on my breath. He half abandoned the idea, but headed down an alley running along the side of the al-Sharif residence.

He stumbled along, his head down, memories of Cederna burning in his brain. As he passed the rear of Mustafa's home, there came a whisper from somewhere above him, a hiss vibrating through the still air.

"Achille?"

He looked up in alarm, his hand traveling quickly to his pistol as his eyes made out the faint outline of a woman's face in the shadows above him.

"It's Anfi," came the softly accented English words. "I heard someone shouting in the street."

Since he had never seen her unveiled, he found it hard to connect her familiar voice with this stranger's face. She was younger than he had expected, somewhere in her middle thirties, a classical Arab beauty with a high forehead, a slender, aquiline nose, and a dark, piercing glance. There were lines beginning to form around the corners of her eyes, as if the death of her husband had taken its toll. She wore her hair long, and there was a severe intelligence in her gaze.

"Hello." His pulse quickening, he tried to think of a plausible reason for being in her alley at this hour. "It was me, I'm afraid. I'm a little drunk, and very angry."

"I knew that troubles would someday bring you here," she said deliberately. "I'll unlock the door. Make no noise."

Shivering with a strange excitement, he waited in the shadows until a door opened a few feet away. Once inside, he followed her along a corridor and into her bedroom. By the light of a candle on the windowsill, he saw she was wearing nightclothes, a simple shift that made her body seem very small.

"I learned something today which made me unhappy," he tried to explain. "So I went for a walk and quite by chance found myself . . ."

"It was a woman who made you unhappy?" She stepped closer to him and instinctively he put his arms around her slender waist.

"Yes."

"Pretend I am that woman," said Anfi al-Sharif and she opened her lips for his kiss.

Book Three

1914-1915

1.

· ·

"Do you suppose he hates me?"

The question popped out of nowhere, right in the middle of a business discussion. They had been walking across the high ground north of the Castello, looking at beef cattle. Ten more men would be needed for the harvest, and a mechanic should be summoned to repair the threshing machine. The vineyard looked good, but there were weeds that required hoeing, and the drying racks for the grapes had to be cleaned before the *vendemmia*.

It was only the last Sunday in June, but the spring growth had been good, and the *gran duro* was flourishing. Last year, 1913, had been a great year. But 1914 was going to break records. Still, Rosaria was finding it difficult to concentrate.

"No. I think he's unhappy and confused," Leonida replied. "Like the rest of us, I suppose."

"When he writes to you, does he ever mention me?" Over the past year, she had started a dozen letters to Achille, but her efforts had always seemed so flat and banal that she ended by throwing them into the fire. Everything sounded like an excuse, and all excuses were silly.

What was there to say? I was lonely. We had every reason to think you were dead. It was the nearest I could ever come to holding you in my arms again.

Leonida shrugged, reaching down to pluck a stalk of young wheat, already knee-high. "Not very much. After the Giorgina incident, I wrote to express my regret, and said that I was considering asking my daughter and her husband to leave the Castello. In his reply, he evaded the central issue but begged me not to break up our family. He now writes regularly, but his letters lack their customary warmth and he has never mentioned you or the . . . the episode. I'm sorry."

"Is he ever coming home?" She wondered what it would be like when Achille did return. What Leonida delicately called the "Giorgina incident" had detonated explosions in all their lives. Leonida no longer spoke to his daughter and took his meals in the study while Bruno and Giorgina haunted the ground floor of the Castello. Rosaria still occasionally joined Leonida for his afternoon nap, but they now merely hugged and went to sleep.

"Eventually, I suppose . . ." Leonida's voice trailed off, and she realized that she was upsetting him. "Well, have we made all our decisions? Shall we go back?"

"I suppose so."

The dream is over, she told herself soberly as they trudged back toward the Castello. And now it had become just a job, and a damned hard one at that. Although he had left Bruno in charge of the family's investments, Leonida no longer wanted his son-in-law involved in the farm. Hence the task of administering the Leone agricultural estate on a day-to-day basis had fallen exclusively to her.

Sandro might have helped, at least with the practical side of things, but her brother now spent most of his time on Socialist party activities. Loyally, Rosaria covered for him when he neglected his farm duties, but her irritation was growing.

"I have had one bit of news from an old army friend," Leonida told her slowly as they approached the Castello front gate. "There is apparently gossip in Benghazi about Achille being fond of a wealthy, well-educated Arab widow. This may be part of his reluctance to leave Libya."

"Oh." It really is over. She forced herself to accept it, a wave of stark unhappiness sweeping over her. Briefly she tormented herself with a vision of Achille naked in the arms of a dark-skinned Arab woman. He's a young man. It was inevitable that he would find someone else to love.

But it should have been me, she said to herself as the tears streamed down her cheeks. Blindly she stumbled into the Castello, turning away to keep Leonida from seeing her face.

That evening a dispatch rider arrived from the War Ministry, roaring up on an old Ducati motorcycle. Leonida tensed, remembering that awful day when Colonel Adamo had bumbled in to tell him of Achille's disappearance. Since then messengers tended to make them all nervous; he watched Rosaria and Girolamo exchange a worried glance as the young officer laid a letter on Leonida's desk.

It must be important to send an officer out on a Sunday evening, Leonida conjectured. When the young lieutenant had departed, he tore open the double-embossed envelope from the War Ministry.

"Dio mio!" he exclaimed. "Francis Ferdinand was murdered this morning by a Serbian terrorist."

Girolamo exhaled with relief. "A dead Austrian? For a moment, I was afraid it was something important."

"He was a good Austrian. And heir to the Austrian throne."

"Is the Minister of War worried?" Rosaria wondered.

"It could be serious. Between the Austrian Empire and Serbia, there is a province called Bosnia-Herzegovina, and . . . oh, Girolamo, find us a map, will you?"

"I know where it is," she snapped. Leonida reminded himself not to take his secretary for granted. When I hired her three years ago, she was barely literate, he remembered. Since then, she's consumed half the books in this library, and every day she reads the *Messaggero* from Rome and the *Corriere* from Milan.

"Then you see the problem. The Austrians will be understandably furious over this, and the Serbians . . . well, Serbians are lovely people, but they are born crazy and never get any saner when they get older. If Serbia is defiant, the Russians will support them because Russians are also crazy. The Germans will automatically back the Austrian Empire. Anyway, the War Ministry wants my views on the likelihood of British involvement, should there be a war."

"Why would the British become involved?" Rosaria frowned. "A quarrel over Bosnia has nothing to do with them."

"Not directly, but Britain has been getting nervous about Germany's growing sea power, and the French want to get Alsace-Lorraine back."

"How does this affect Achille?" Rosaria demanded.

Leonida's mind had already explored the consequences. "Achille's original three-year term of service with the Royal Army expired this May. But he's become involved in digging wells and building hospitals for the Libyans and he has signed on for another tour. So if there's a war, he will still be in uniform."

"Why would Italy be involved?" Rosaria's face grew pale.

"Whenever Europe gives a fancy ball, poor little Italia puts on her tight-fitting shoes," said Leonida bleakly. "And tries to dance."

It was a beautiful day. Rome could sometimes be brutally hot at the end of July, but today there was a steady breeze off the Tyrrhenian Sea. Even the paving stones felt cool underfoot as the crowd moved steadily up the broad avenue. There were five hundred of them. Sandro was proud to be leading fifteen men from Cederna and marching at the head of the procession.

"No war," they all chanted. "No war! No war!"

There were vendors on the sidewalks selling strawberry ices. Emilio Lodi and the other men from Cederna wanted to stop for a cone, since demonstrating was thirsty work, but Sandro decreed that it was un-revolutionary to lick ice-cream cones while marching on the Ministry of War.

Turning the last corner before the Ministero di Guerra, the demonstrators ran into a six-man squad of carabinieri. The police were led by an officer wearing a huge black cape and holding a bronze trumpet, sitting astride a stately white horse. To Sandro, he looked like an equestrian statue of himself.

The crowd shuffled to a halt, and a socialist professor from the University of Rome stepped forward. "We come in peace!" he shouted. "We wish to deliver a petition to the Minister of War. There must be no war over one dead Austrian."

There was a sudden silence. "You are in violation of the criminal code," the carabiniere officer replied. "Disperse immediately!"

The professor walked toward the police line, explaining that this was a nonviolent demonstration to express opposition to the futile war about to erupt on Italy's northern border. Furious at the death of their crown prince, the Austrians were convinced that the Serbians were trying to take over Bosnia-Herzegovina. Determined to humiliate them, the Austrian government had just delivered a long series of impossible demands, amounting to the surrender of Serbian national sovereignty. Serbia had rejected the ultimatum, and mobilized her army. Not only was the Italian government doing nothing to defuse the rush toward war, but some cabinet ministers were already debating the merits of Italian participation.

At a nod from the officer, two burly policemen leaped forward and seized the professor, roughly bending his arms behind his back and snapping manacles on his wrists. Stunned, the socialist crowd watched in disbelief as a policeman raised a truncheon and clubbed the handcuffed man to his knees.

"You bastards!" No one knew what to do. A young man standing between Sandro and Emilio suddenly began to curse and shake his fist. Dressed as a farm laborer, he had long black, disorderly hair tied in back with a string.

"Hey, steady," Sandro admonished him, but the lad surged past him, carrying a sign with the word PEACE painted on it in big irregular letters.

"Bastardi!" he shouted again, and rushed at the officer on the horse, brandishing his sign.

Drawing his side arm, the carabiniere officer casually shot the farm boy in the forehead.

The lad's body seemed to come unstrung, like a marionette with cut strings, and he collapsed on the cobblestones, his arms and legs flapping in the agony of death.

"You can't . . . you didn't need to shoot." Stammering in rage and dismay, Sandro rushed to where the boy had collapsed. There was blood pouring from his forehead, and Sandro felt the sticky warmth staining his shirt.

Behind him, there was a tumult. Knowing what was likely to happen next, a few older men turned and ran. Stunned, most of the peasants stood their ground, those behind asking those in front what had happened and if the boy was really dead. The men from Cederna looked belligerent, and some of them began shouting abuse at the police.

The officer on his horse put his pistol away and blew his trumpet. "Disperse!" he shouted. He had the deepest, loudest voice Sandro had ever heard. Gently, Sandro laid the dead farm boy back down on the pavement, watching as Emilio Lodi dropped to his hands and knees. With a short, stout-bladed knife, Emilio quickly dug up a paving stone and tossed it furiously in the direction of the police. Emilio was a bad shot, and the stone rolled harmlessly into the gutter.

"Watch out!" Sandro hurried back to his group of Cedernesi as the six unmounted policemen dropped to their knees, raised their carbines, and fired a single volley into the crowd.

Sandro felt a bullet whistle by, centimeters from his head. There were screams as two men dropped, badly wounded, and another grabbed his shoulder and began to shriek with pain.

"Disperse!" the mounted officer cried again. Emilio Lodi and the other unwounded men from the crowd were pulling more paving stones up off the street, and Sandro stood up in their midst.

"Together, lads, now!" Sandro commanded. It's a beautiful day, he thought. Perfect for a revolution. "Now!" And they all threw their stones at the police.

Inside, a baby was wailing.

"No, carissimo, no," a woman's tired voice crooned. "Don't cry."

"Benita, it's me," Rosaria called out. There was no door to knock on, only a soiled blanket nailed to the front of the shack. The structure was wattle, twigs and clay, originally built for pigs or goats, but great hunks of mud had fallen off and the frame was now leaning dangerously to one side.

"Oh Rosaria, come in." There was a shuffling from within and a haggard woman pushed aside the blanket. Rosaria was stunned at the sight of Benita's gray skin and skeletal figure. We used to be close friends, she remembered. She's my age and once she was pretty. Now she looks like a grandmother.

"I brought you some food." Rosaria put her sack on the floor. My life has become so comfortable, she reflected with a surge of guilt. I have come so far from this kind of wretchedness.

The floor of the hut was mud, dusty dry now in the summer's heat but destined to become a puddle once the winter rains began. There were holes in the ceiling. In one corner, some flagstones had been arranged to make a crude fireplace. In the center of the room, Benita had created a crib out of a wooden fruit box; a naked baby boy was lying inside, fussing.

"Oh, Rosaria, thank you." There was no furniture beyond a rough-hewn plank serving as a table, and Benita collapsed on a piece of burlap, as if her legs had failed her. "Sandro always made sure we had something to eat."

"He wrote that I should come and see you. You knew he was in prison?"

Benita nodded. "I knew because there were four men from the Mosconi farm with him the day of the demonstration. First they got beat up by the police, and then the Mayor fired them when they came limping home. How is poor Sandro? You know, someday Cederna will be famous because Sandro Lombardi was born here. He is going to be a great man."

"He'll have to get out of prison first," Rosaria said. Thinking of Sandro behind bars always made her depressed. "Leonida engaged Tommaso Savarino to represent Sandro, but they won't let anyone see him yet."

Benita sighed. "Poor Sandro! He was always so kind to me, the only one who never . . . took advantage."

Embarrassed, Rosaria looked away, knowing that others had taken advantage. As a young girl, Benita had been raped, or at least roughly seduced, by a foreman on the Mosconi farm. Her reputation soiled, she had drifted from man to man until she became the common-law wife of a kindly older peasant named Sergio, who had managed to get her pregnant just before getting himself crushed under the wheels of Mayor Mosconi's tractor. When Benita charged that the accident was the fault of the Mosconi family, Junio had fired her.

"What's the baby's name?" Rosaria touched the infant gingerly under the chin.

Benita seemed surprised at the question. She concentrated for a moment and then shrugged. "I just call him 'baby.' If he lives, I'll think of a name." Lifting the infant tenderly from its crib, she pushed her dirty cotton shift down off one shoulder to expose a flat, sagging breast and bruised nipple, which "baby" seized voraciously.

"When the winter comes, you won't be able to stay here," Rosaria said.

"He'll be dead before winter unless I can make more milk. He sucks, but there isn't anything there. Could you ask Signor Junio to give me my job back?"

Rosaria shuddered at the idea. "I'm so afraid of him. And he doesn't care what happens to anybody."

"But Junio used to like me. Once, before I went to live with Sergio, Junio took me into the bushes and I figured, well, if it means a guaranteed job, I'd better let him do what he wants. But he couldn't, so he hit me."

Rosaria shook her head, puzzled at the inconsistencies in Junio's sexuality. Once, when they were children, the Mayor's son had caught her alone in the woods, down by the Tiber. She had been twelve at the time, on the brink of puberty, and he had put his hand up under her jersey to feel her tiny breasts. She had wriggled free, but Junio had been after her ever since, always hovering in the background with some mocking, suggestive comment. What did he want? Was he impotent? Could he be searching for the one woman who could make it happen for him?

"He's crazy. You know that."

"I know, Rosaria, but he's powerful. Please, you have to see him for me."

She nodded and kissed Benita good-bye, leaving her with a one-lire note. The shack was on the outskirts of a poor section of East Cederna, where Rosaria had once played as a child. A lot of poor people lived here. The lucky ones worked for one of the half dozen big agricultural estates in the township. The girls became domestic servants or shop assistants until someone married them, or else went to Rome and never came back, because they were ashamed at having become prostitutes. Some of the boys joined the army or went to sea or worked as waiters in the city, leaving behind the old and sick and ugly and unlucky, hundreds and hundreds of people who would never find jobs.

Are these still my people? She left the slum with a shudder and began the long walk uphill toward downtown Cederna. What do they think of me? They must know that Leonida pays me more a month than they make in a year. Do they think of me as a moderately expensive administrator?

Or a moderately cheap whore?

Around the fountain in the Piazza Bixio, there was a crowd of women. Rosaria's heart sank as they waved to her. What would they think when they saw her entering the Mosconi mansion? Cederna lived on gossip.

"Ciao, Rosaria," someone called. She waved back timidly.

There were three imposing buildings at this end of the Piazza Bixio and Sandro called them collectively the Kingdom of the Wicked. First was Santa Teresa's Church, where they had gone to Mass as children, but never went anymore because Don Maurizio had excommunicated all the Socialists. Next to that was the Mosconi mansion, where the Mayor and his son Junio lived, and then the Carabinieri Station with bars on the windows.

Resisting the temptation to go around back to the servants' entrance, Rosaria knocked at Mayor Mosconi's front door. With a sneer, a serving girl led her to the second floor, where the Mayor's son had his office.

She climbed the stairs, telling herself that she had no reason to be afraid of Junio Mosconi. I am secretary to Count Leonida Leone. I am here on a legitimate mission. And Junio is a failure. No woman of his own class wants him, and he isn't even a proper attorney because he failed his exam. And Benito says that day in the bushes he couldn't even . . .

"Rosirosalina, I am so honored." Rising behind his desk, Junio seemed the same as ever, a short, pudgy man with a bulbous nose and an acne-scarred face, who strutted as if he sensed within himself something infinitely attractive to women. Hesitantly she entered his office, putting her back against the wall.

"Signor Junio, I've come about Benita. When Sergio was killed, she was left without any means of support. She and the baby could starve."

"It's not my fault Sergio got himself squashed," Junio began defensively. "We have witnesses to testify that Sergio had been drinking before the accident. And he never legally married Benita, so she has no rights."

"We're just asking you to let her come back to work." Rosaria edged away as Junio moved toward her.

"What can poor Benita do? She never was very bright, y'know, and she's losing her looks. The girl I want working under me is you, Rosirosalina, right under me." He leered with amusement at his own ridiculous double entendre. "We can't expect our poor Count Leone to keep it up forever, and I need a good secretary."

He knows, she realized with a feeling of desperation. Giorgina must have told him about finding Leonida and me together. Oh God, who else knows?

"Signor Junio, I want to talk about Benita."

Junio trapped her with one hand against the wall on either side of her head. "All things are possible for those who fulfill conditions."

She held very still. "What?"

"You must close your eyes and let me give you one kiss. On the lips. And tomorrow Benita goes back to work in the laundry."

Bribery and ransom, concessions and betrayals, ideas began to ricochet through her mind. Then her body rebelled at the notion of being kissed by him. No, I won't be a *puttana!*

"Get away from me!" she hissed, but he lurched forward and tried to kiss her, his hands reaching for the collar of her blouse. She broke away, but Junio was still holding her blouse, and she could feel the buttons pop as she pushed past him to the door.

"I don't think our brave Achille likes you anymore, and Sandro will be an old man before they let him out of jail," he shouted as Rosaria stumbled down the stairs, holding her torn blouse together, red-faced and panting with rage. "When Leonida kicks the bucket, girl, you will need a protector, and it is going to be me."

She made no reply. At the front door, Rosaria collided with Mayor Mosconi, who was coming in with Father Maurizio and Dr. Beniolo and several members of the Cederna Municipal Council. There was a round of rough male laughter at her ruffled appearance, and even the priest smiled. At the fountain, all the women stopped talking and turned to stare.

"Have a good time, dearie?" asked the Mayor, and he patted her bottom as she swept past him into the Piazza Bixio.

"My name is Tommaso Savarino," said the lawyer. He was a short, stocky man in his mid-twenties and he gazed at the prison official through thick spectacles. "I am here to see two men from Cederna."

"Their names, if you please, Avvocato?"

"A tall man named Sandro Lombardi, and a youth called Lodi."

Tommaso drew himself to his full height and tried to look the part of an important provincial *avvocato,* knowing that the holes in the elbows of his distinguished dark suit were almost invisibly patched. His cheap patent-leather shoes were shined. And his watch fob extended majestically across his waistcoat even though the timepiece itself no longer ticked, and he did not make enough money getting socialists out of jail to buy a new one.

"Ah, the two gentlemen from Cederna." With a wave, the guard led the lawyer through a door and down a steep flight of stairs. "Mind your feet, Avvocato. It's wet down here."

They passed a checkpoint. The guards were sullen, diffident men with short wooden clubs who presided over a huge rectangular gallery filled with rows of steel cages. There were five hundred prisoners in this one room, packed ten or fifteen to a cell. The smell from their bodies was atrocious. The floor was covered with a lethargic brown river, two or three centimeters deep, carrying feces and fragments of food from the cells to the sewer. Visitors crossed over a haphazard bridge of stout planks, and Tommaso followed his escort from board to board, remembering how Dante had shadowed Virgil into the Inferno.

"Your customers, Avvocato." When they halted before a cage, Tommaso peered into the dim light. The walls were moldering cement covered with centuries of mildew. On the other side of the bars, a gaunt, filthy Sandro Lombardi pulled himself painfully into a sitting position.

"Tommaso?" His voice was raw. "We weren't sure you'd come."

"Who is it? Is it Tommaso?" Thinner than ever, Emilio Lodi splashed through the puddle to join Sandro at the bars. "Avvocato, have you come to take us home?"

"No. They've decided to put you on trial and I'm representing you. You've been charged with insurrection, homicide, and assault with a deadly weapon."

"We were merely a group of working men defending ourselves against an assault by the police," Sandro immediately insisted.

"Well, you managed to kill one of them, an officer. You even wounded his horse." Tommaso resolved not to rekindle their ancient debate. Sandro believed in revolution, talking like an Old Testament prophet about war and struggle and blood on the streets. As a lawyer, Tommaso advocated a peaceful redistribution of economic resources by a wise and moderate socialist government. Achille, the eternal technocrat, had always preached that modern science would bring the good life even to the impoverished. The three of them had disputed the issue since they were teenaged boys, and nobody had ever convinced anybody else.

"They opened fire and killed at least three of us," Sandro retorted. "But neither Emilio nor I threw the stone that hit that officer. Somebody else got him first."

"I think I hit the horse," said Emilio helpfully.

"No, you didn't. Listen, we need some kind of defense." Tommaso got out his fountain pen and a block of writing paper. "If you could say in court that you were not throwing stones, then we could make the case that you were mistaken for someone else."

"With my height, it will be hard to convince a judge that they got the wrong man. And Emilio was right next to me."

"Then we could say that you heartily regret the entire incident, and promise in the future to refrain from participation in political activities. At least we ought to be able to get you a shorter jail sentence."

"I can't stay in jail," young Emilio gasped. "It would kill my mother."

"Look, there is a way we could avoid a murder trial," Tommaso explained patiently. "The police actually know who threw the fatal stone, and I've had a word with a colleague in the Prosecuting Attorney's Office. They are prepared to waive custodial sentences for the two of you if you go before a magistrate, express regret for what happened, and volunteer to enlist in the armed forces.''

"Sandro, that's okay, isn't it?'' Emilio was pathetically happy. "In the army we'd have a salary and food, and we'd be home in a year.''

"You want to be a soldier?'' Sandro laughed and, with sudden gentleness, he turned and put his hand on Emilio's shoulder. "Okay, but steal a couple of rifles for the revolution. The next time the police use their guns on us we can return the favor.''

Tommaso was reluctant to push the enlistment solution under false pretenses. "Look, the army option is a good deal, but since you were arrested, this Francis Ferdinand crisis has gotten a lot worse,'' he explained. "The Austrians have issued an ultimatum that the Serbians can't accept, and the German government keeps threatening war. If fighting should break out, you'd be in uniform.''

"Anything is better than this,'' stammered Emilio Lodi. "Sandro, why don't we go together?''

"No. If our avvocato wants to represent me, he'll have to say that people have the right to defend themselves against the hired thugs of a murderous regime. Policemen who shoot down innocent demonstrators must expect a few paving stones bounced off their heads.''

"Sandro, I can make a famous speech,'' Tommaso snapped. "The morning papers will print my picture, and the Partito Socialista Italiano will pass a resolution praising you at their next annual conference. And the judge will send you to prison for a century and a half!''

"Don't you believe in democracy?'' Sandro asked him softly. "We were expressing our right to free speech in a peaceful demonstration when the police opened fire. Don't we have the right to defend ourselves?''

"Yes, of course.''

"Then put me on the stand, because that's what I want to say.''

"Sandro, they're offering you a good deal.''

"I don't want a good deal.'' Sandro turned away. "I want a good revolution.''

2.

· ·

The earth turned on its side, a wall of yellow stretching from endlessness to infinity. Achille's stomach lurched, but he swallowed and took the Blériot farther into the roll. For an inverted instant, nausea threatened to overcome him as the floor of the desert appeared over his head and he looked down into the stark blueness of an Arab sky.

He swung out of the roll and the airplane stabilized for a moment before running head-on into an invisible pillar of hot, rapidly rising air. The updraft battered the fragile airframe, but the sensation was irresistible. Turning into a tight curve, Achille rode the column skyward, soaring two thousand meters in less than a minute, until he spun off into calmer air.

He had never flown this high before, and the view was staggering. Adjusting his goggles, Achille took hold of the Blériot's upper wing and stood in the cockpit for a better view. On the left, he could see the Mediterranean and the coastal road to Tripoli. On the right, the minarets of Benghazi rose majestically into the sky.

This is so beautiful, he reflected. Has anyone ever flown this high over Africa before? If I could take Rosi flying with me, would she be fearful? No, nothing ever frightened Rosi . . . damn! He cursed himself. Why was it impossible to enjoy life without thinking about a woman he was determined to forget? He had not seen her for two years and she had never bothered to write a letter explaining what had happened. It was time to start forgetting.

Deliberately losing altitude, he cruised out toward the coast until he spotted the reservoir his engineers were digging. Consulting his compass, he turned southwest and plotted the trajectory of a certain shallow wadi that wound its way several kilometers through a field of sand until it floundered in a flat basin of dried mud.

He marked the wadi's location on his map, convinced that these mudflats could be transformed into prime agricultural terrain. If the General Staff would invest the money and man-hours, an irrigation canal could be constructed to bring thousands of potentially fertile acres under cultivation.

A glance at his fuel gauge told him that it was time to land, and he turned regretfully back toward the Benghazi military aerodrome. At two hundred feet, making about seventy knots, he lowered his flaps and eased the plane down onto the smooth mud surface of the runway. The aircraft shuddered as rubber wheels touched dry earth.

"Good landing, Comandante!" Achille heard Guido's gleeful shout the moment he cut the Blériot's engine and he sprang down eagerly from the cockpit.

"So how was the Promised Land?" Achille asked lightly as they strolled together across the hard-packed mud toward the aerodrome headquarters. The Lupi di Lazio had been on leave since early July. Achille had employed his free time with flying and engineering while Guido Rosselli had trekked off to visit Jerusalem.

"My ancestors have moaned for thousands of years about God giving us Palestine. So I go there and find mostly desert. Jerusalem is okay if you like lots of Arabs, which I don't, but the rest of Palestine is about as bleak as Libya. If our ancient Semitic deity was feeling generous, why couldn't he have given us Paris, or Manhattan, or even Venice? Why Palestine?"

"Does anyone there speak Italian? How did you communicate?"

"No, but there's a colony of insane Zionists there, and I've been learning a little Hebrew." Guido had always seemed troubled by the ambiguity of his Jewishness.

August in North Africa was hot, and the two officers were both perspiring freely as they stepped into the comparative comfort of the aerodrome engineering office. In the workshop, they found a crowd of engineers clustered around a wireless. There was a crackling noise coming from a loudspeaker, and one of the engineers waved at them in excitement.

"We're picking up a signal from Tripoli. Something's happening!"

"What is it?" Achille was unconcerned. Normally, it took two weeks for news to come from Europe, and this gave them a feeling of detachment about events there. The newspapers had been talking about some nonsense in the Balkans, dead archdukes and diplomatic crises, but there had always been trouble in the Balkans. Whatever it was, it had nothing to do with them.

"Attention, all units," came an indistinct voice speaking Italian. "We have just received reports that the Imperial German Army has crossed the border into Belgium. The British Empire and the Republic of France have declared war. The Russian Army is advancing along a broad front toward Germany, and Serbian units are defending against a large-scale Austrian attack. No immediate action is expected here in Libya, but the General Staff has ordered a pre-mobilization exercise for all Italian military units . . ." The voice fluttered and died as the atmospherics changed.

There was a moment of stunned silence in the engineering shed. Guido spoke first.

"We simply must help France." There was a murmur of agreement from the other officers. Most of the enlisted men shook their heads and turned away. Achille wondered how his father would feel. As a major, he was the senior officer present, and he realized that the others waited for his opinion.

"I don't know . . . On one hand, democracy is worth fighting for, and we could never let England and France be overwhelmed by a militarist dictatorship like Germany. On the other hand, are we ready to fight a major European war? We haven't even managed to conquer the Senusi yet."

"Listen, a big war is precisely what Italy needs right now." Guido argued persuasively. "If we could collect our energies and focus ourselves on some great goal, like beating the hell out of the Austrians, we could become one of the pivotal nations of Europe, instead of a backwater. And it would be the great adventure of our lives."

The engineers went back to work on their radio, searching for another signal. The two infantry officers walked to the door, where a staff car was waiting to take them back to Benghazi.

"An adventure?" Achille Leone shook his head. "Do you really enjoy fighting?"

"There are two times when I feel really alive. When I am ejaculating into a woman's body and when I am fighting. Sometimes, it feels almost the same. You know, when we lift our shelling and go at the bastards with bayonets? That's the moment I love. My whole body seems to come at once."

"It's not the same for me," said Achille. "How can you compare fighting to making love? For me, a woman's body is pleasure and peace."

"Then for your sake, I hope that this European thing is over by Christmas, and that Italy assumes its usual meek neutrality." Guido backed away from the argument as they settled themselves in the back seat. "Speaking of women, when am I going to meet your little brown-skinned friend?"

"Sometime soon." He spoke insincerely. Guido frankly disliked Arabs, and Anfi had once expressed polite contempt for Jews.

"This relationship has been going on for a long time now," Guido said as the driver took them down the dusty road to Benghazi. "Are you in love with her?"

Achille shook his head, wanting the conversation to be over so he could think about the war in Europe. "No, I will never possess the woman I love," he said succinctly. "So it is a question of finding a woman I like. And I like this one."

3.

....

"Why are you so worried, Eccellenza?" asked the Deputy Foreign Minister. "What is today? The sixth of August? I predict to you that the fighting will have stopped by this date in September."

"No, the forces set in motion are already too great." Leonida frowned, glancing around the salotto. "In a month's time, tens of thousands of men will have died and the momentum will be irreversible."

Twenty men had come to Cederna for this meeting, and most of them nodded in agreement. A dozen senators and deputies, three cabinet ministers, five generals and an inspector general of police had turned up at Leonida's invitation. They were all nervous. Since the beginning of the century, politics in Italy had been dominated by a cool, competent professional named Giovanni Giolitti, but in the spring of 1914, Giolitti had yielded the Prime Minister's office to a volatile right-winger named Antonio Salandra.

"Even assuming the war does continue," persisted the Deputy Foreign Minister, "I assure you that there is no risk of Italy becoming involved."

"The risk is very real," Leonida retorted. "The most serious fighting is close to our own northern border. The Russians have a huge army, and the Germans will hardly stop until it is destroyed. With the British and French supporting Serbia, the Ottoman Empire will almost certainly rally to the Central Powers, and this brings the conflict right into the Mediterranean. Can't you see the danger?"

"But the Prime Minister has already proclaimed Italian neutrality."

"Our new Prime Minister comes from Sicily," Leonida snapped back. "Sicilians are not natively very good at neutrality, and there will be unbearable pressure on him from abroad to join the madness."

"If we fight Austria, we could conquer the Province of Trentino and move our northern border to the watershed of the Alps, where it belongs." The observation came from a bright young brigadier general named Armando Díaz. "And we could also seize Trieste."

"Trentino and Trieste ought to be Italian, I agree, and with some quiet diplomacy we can have them both for the asking. The Austrians will cheerfully pay that price to keep us out of the war."

"I am surprised at you, Leonida." The speaker was Gaetamo Salvemini, a young professor from the University of Messina whose books on history Count Leone had always admired. "During the Franco-Prussian War you dashed off to defend *la belle France* against the brutal Germans. Forty-four years later, France is still a democracy, and the Germans are still Prussian militarists. What's changed?"

"My dear Salvemini," Leonida retorted, "our potential enemies now all have modern weapons and large, well-trained armies. My heart is firmly with France and England, you know that, but Italy is armed with nineteenth-century gunnery. Our best units are pinned down in North Africa."

"His Excellency is right." Police Inspector General Paolino Taddei spoke up from the rear of the room. "I am speaking confidentially, signori, but Italian involvement in a European war might provoke a Marxist insurrection. We have about thirty thousand policemen for the whole country, and the socialists could put a million rioters on the street."

"Well, Signor Conte, what's the answer?" one of the senators demanded.

If only Rosaria were here, Leonida thought as he formulated his response. Twenty of the cleverest men in Italy have come to Cederna to hear my advice. Thanks to you, fanciulla, I'm not a pointless old man anymore. God, is it possible that I have thrust myself back into international politics to impress a twenty-one-year-old girl?

"We must recognize that war in the rest of Europe will be a harsh fact of life for many years," he launched into his concluding remarks. "Since neutrality will grow more difficult as time passes, we need to watch the Prime Minister carefully, because the British will try to inveigle us into an alliance. We need to use our collective influence to persuade our government to wind down this Libyan nonsense and get our best combat units back on this side of the Mediterranean. When we have secured our borders defensively, we open negotiations with the Austrians over the question of Trentino and Trieste."

There was general agreement as the meeting broke up. Several prominent men stepped forward to shake his hand and offer congratulations, and Leonida decided that his initiative had been at least a preliminary success. A set of important issues had been clarified. General Díaz and Professor Salvemini were still cautiously favorable to Italian intervention in the war, but a number of key personalities had swung around to Leonida's point of view. An informal but powerful network of alliances had been established.

It was now time for coffee and liquors, and Leonida rang a small silver bell. The door opened so quickly that he wondered whether Rosaria had been there all along with her ear pressed to the door.

He noticed that she had a new outfit. In place of the usual black skirt and white blouse, Rosaria wore a smartly cut pink cotton dress. Hugging her hips, the garment buttoned down the side and left her ankles daringly exposed. The collar was high, and there was a ruffle of lace over her bosom. Normally, Rosaria wore her auburn hair in a tight bun, peasant-fashion, but tonight she had combed it out over her shoulders, as if she wished to proclaim that she was no longer one of the kitchen staff.

Heads turned as this unexpected beauty supervised the serving of coffees and cognacs. Leonida felt a sudden rush of male pride, almost wishing that he could announce to the men in the room that this splendid creature had been his mistress. Once, she had shuddered in his arms and said that she loved him . . .

"Coffee, Eccellenza?" Rosaria appeared at his elbow with a discreet smile before moving away to serve his other guests. Once, he thought, once she was mine . . . will I ever stop wanting her?

"Count Leone, I spoke to your son a few months ago in Libya." Leonida turned to encounter Armando Díaz, the general who had politely disagreed with him. "Achille is doing marvelously. Imagine, already a major at twenty-seven! When's he due home?"

"Ah, well, he seems to be having too much fun in Libya to bother coming back to boring old Italy." Leonida tried to cover his wince with a smile, but the subject was uncomfortable and he turned away.

As the room emptied, Police Inspector General Paolino Taddei raised one eyebrow to indicate that he wanted a private word. The two men strolled to the far end of the salotto and stood looking out into the garden.

"At your request, I looked into the matter of your two employees. Emilio Lodi was released this morning after he appeared before a municipal judge with a petition to be allowed to enlist in the Royal Army."

"Good. And the Lombardi case?" Leonida recognized that his emotions about Sandro were mixed because Sandro seemed intent upon becoming a serious revolutionary. But a Marxist revolution in Italy was neither possible nor a particularly good idea. How far was it reasonable to protect him?

"The paperwork on Lombardi has been, uh, misfiled, and the arresting officer has been awarded a long holiday in Sardinia. Therefore, when the defendant appears in court, the prosecution will drop charges."

"Thank you." Leonida exhaled slowly.

"Government documents are hard to lose twice, so keep him out of trouble." Paolino Taddei smiled as the two men walked to the door.

"I'll talk some sense into him." Leonida privately wondered if anyone could influence the headstrong Lombardi.

When the last guest had departed, he climbed the stairs to his study, expecting to be alone. To his surprise Rosaria was standing before the bay window, looking out into the darkness to the east. She is the most beautiful woman I have ever known, he decided. I hate myself for this, but I never loved my wife the way I love her. I never desired my wife the way I desire her.

"Topo? How did it go? What do you think?"

"Politically it went very well." Leonida took her hand. She looked up at him and smiled, resting her head against his shoulder. "There will be other meetings like this, of course, but this was an excellent start."

"If only Sandro . . ."

"Stop worrying. When Sandro comes to trial in September, the government will drop charges."

"Tommaso Savarino said he would spend years in prison," she exclaimed, hugging him in astonishment. "How did you do it?"

"Oh, a word to a friend. At any rate, your brother will be home in a month."

"Oh, amore mio!" Tears came to her eyes as she kissed his cheek. "How can I thank you?"

"Stay here with me tonight." He spoke without thinking. "Under the circumstances, there is no reason why . . . oh, fanciulla, I still want you."

She sighed, nodding slowly. Leonida Leone took her hand and led her into the sewing room.

4.

....

I am pregnant.

She lay on her narrow bed in the cottage looking at the cracks in the ceiling, trying to deal with sudden certainty.

The suspicion had been there for days, lingering in the back of her mind like a nightmare that refuses to disappear at dawn, but it was the end of September and the truth could no longer be shut out.

I'm pregnant!

I was always careless about what my body was doing, she rebuked herself furiously. I grew up on a farm. I should have known better. I always thought in terms of moments and never about cycles or periods.

It didn't seem right to refuse Leonida when he wanted me. There are things that prostitutes do to keep from getting pregnant, but I don't know what they are. You can only defy biology so long. I should have bled the third week in August and I didn't. I should be bleeding now, and I'm not. I feel nauseous and dizzy in the morning. I used to love coffee, and now it makes me gag.

I'm going to have a baby.

For a moment, she felt overwhelmed by the prospect. Her hands and feet went ice-cold, and she found it difficult to breathe.

There was no one in the cottage. From the angle of the sun, she calculated that it was already mid-morning and that she had overslept for the first time in her life. Today is the day that Sandro comes home from jail. And he will find me pregnant.

I need to get rid of it. I've got to! Otherwise, Sandro will throw me out. Leonida will think I have done it to blackmail him. Achille will be insane with anger. The women in the village will call me a whore.

In East Cederna, there was an old midwife named Medina. She was not a proper nurse and had no training, but for a certain sum of money, Medina would help girls in difficult situations. This treatment was not always successful because once a woman had died, and Sergeant Cirillo of the Royal Carabinieri had taken Medina away to prison.

After some months Medina had been released and resumed her practice. There had been no dead girls for some years now, but the women who went to Medina with their problem knew what the risks were.

Just as she thought she had made the decision, she felt her body crying out in horror. She rolled on her side, cradling her stomach. It could be a very beautiful person. There are such powerful lines running to it. It could be someone brave like Sandro. Or artistic like Terenzio. Or noble like Leonida. Or brilliant like Achille. Or even good with an Olivetti like me.

I want it. The decision created itself in her mind with the same abrupt vigor as the child in her womb. It will be a catastrophe, but I don't care. My head doesn't want it. But my body does.

She got to her feet. The room spun briefly, but she dominated it with an exercise of her will, and the dizziness diminished. Breakfast was unthinkable, but she took a long drink of water from the jug by her bed and put on her clothes.

We women will always be slaves, she told herself on the way to the door. Because we obey our bodies and not our brains.

He will take one look at me, and know that something is wrong.

It was ten-thirty, and in the distance she could see dust in the air as the morning coach from Rome rounded the last turn and rumbled into Piazza Bixio, coming to a halt in front of the municipal building. Sandro was the last man off the bus, ducking his head as he emerged, blinking, into the bright September sun.

He's so thin, she realized as she rushed to embrace him. He must have suffered terribly. I have never suffered. Not really. Not until now.

"I suppose I am the first revolutionary in history to have been rescued from prison by his little sister," Sandro said, hugging her so fiercely that her feet left the ground. "How did you arrange it?"

"Leonida talked to someone from the Interior Ministry." She took her brother's arm as they trudged up the dirt road toward the cottage. "Is that the way you wanted the experience to end? Tommaso said you wanted to have your day in court."

"It was a compromise," he admitted. "I didn't intend to beg forgiveness for what happened, but it seemed self-indulgent to sit in prison when there was so much to be done here in Cederna. Listen, were you able to do anything for Benita?"

Rosaria nodded. At least there would be this bit of good news. "Junio made problems about taking her back, so I talked Leonida into giving her a job in the laundry. We found an old woman to rent her a room and watch her baby while Benita works."

"How about the others who were arrested with me?"

"Not good," she admitted as they skirted the Leone mansion and strolled toward their cottage. "Emilio's in a punishment battalion near Milan and he's terribly unhappy. All the others lost their jobs."

Sandro's face darkened. "The landowners will either rehire those workers or face a strike during the harvest. I'll go right after lunch and talk to them."

They pushed open the cottage door, and Sandro smiled fondly at his books, his pen and ink, his desk and his fireplace. "Ah, I've missed this place. I'm going to have a glass of wine."

Rosaria stood with her back against the wall, fighting back the tears. Her brother was pouring out two beakers of Cederna vino bianco, but wine was the last thing she needed. It was warm, and the smell made her nauseous. Choking back the bile in her throat, she accepted the glass for the sake of politeness, and then felt her knees give way.

"Rosaria, what's wrong? Rosaria?"

Flat on her back on the flagstone floor, she heard his voice calling to her, and realized that she had fainted.

"I'm okay," she gasped as he helped her into a chair.

"Have you been eating properly? Here, drink this wine."

Meekly she sipped the wine, deciding that she needed whatever courage it contained. Slowly her head cleared.

"I'm pregnant." She was not sure whether she wanted to be defiant or apologetic.

"You? Who is the . . ." he stammered.

"Leonida." She hated herself for bringing this sorrow to him.

"Puttana!" He snarled the ultimate insult at her, his face a mask of fury as he lurched into the table and upset the wine. For the first time in her life she felt afraid of him, knowing he was going to hit her.

Then she rebelled. Why should I always be frightened of men? I don't want to be beaten like one of his horses. I belong to myself!

Sandro's arm swung wildly, catching her with a stinging, open-handed blow on the side of the face, but instead of cringing in the corner, she stood her ground and kicked back with all her strength, hitting him squarely in the testicles.

"Ahhhhh!" He doubled over with the unexpected pain.

For an instant she rejoiced, as if a special corner had been turned in her life. No one will ever beat me again, she decided.

Then the pure sensuality of having fought and won collapsed around her and she threw herself on her brother's shoulders, crying and kissing his hair. The battle was over. Sandro crouched on the cold flagstone floor, breathing heavily, and she knew that he would not speak now until he had reestablished his iron self-control.

"Oh, Sandro, I'm sorry."

"Sì, sì, sì," he muttered, pulling himself into a sitting position, and putting his arms around his legs. He did not look at her. "All right, why did you do it?"

"How can I explain?" Was there any way of making him understand? Had Marx ever written anything about young girls who went to bed with older men?

"Cristo! We'll never make a decent marriage for you. I couldn't even ask Emilio to take you under these circumstances."

She started to giggle. If nothing else, being an unwed mother would free her from the danger of ever having to marry Emilio Lodi. "I's sorry for Emilio. Anyway, you always said we were going to have a revolution."

"We could have ten revolutions and nobody would marry you."

"I don't want to get married," she exclaimed. "You've always said socialism was going to make us free. Why shouldn't I be free too? Is socialism just for men?"

"Sorellina, this is peasant country. It could be centuries before people change how they think about marriage and virginity," he said sadly. "Count Leone isn't going to marry you. Do you love him?"

"I feel happy when I'm with him. He's gentle." There was nothing more that she could say about her friendship with the master of Cederna, not even to Sandro. Sometimes Leonida seemed so young, and when he embraced her she felt a wonderful calmness. It was not something she could explain and she had no intention of trying.

"Is that love?"

"I don't know. What's it supposed to feel like?"

"I don't know either." Sandro got to his feet and splashed water in his face. "I've avoided getting involved with a decent girl because love would be a distraction from my main purpose in life. I had hoped that we would work for the Party, and you would get married eventually to a socialist."

"I'm sorry I've disappointed you. I'm still a socialist."

"You won't do us much good now." He shrugged. "Well, I'd better go and see about those men who were fired."

Turning his face away, he moved toward the door, and she realized with a shock that he was still thinking about the PSI and his everlastingly downtrodden proletariat. Not about her.

"Wait. How do you feel about me?" She caught him at the door.

"I will always love you as my sister," he said formally. "But if you're going to breed bastards for the aristocracy, then I don't think I'm going to like you very much."

She nodded. He headed for the door, hesitated, and then looked back at her over his shoulder, a long, unhappy stare.

"We'll work something out," he said gruffly, and then he walked back down the dusty road toward Cederna.

On her way up the stairs, Rosaria sorted through the mail. There was a letter for Leonida from Achille and she kissed it where Achille's lips would have moistened the flap.

Punctually, the young Major Leone wrote once a month to his father. Every three months, there was a postcard for Sandro. Nothing ever came for her.

She climbed the staircase, wondering what Achille looked like after three years in the desert. Would his skin be dark like an African's? Was he in much danger? How would he feel about having an illegitimate brother or sister? Can he hate me any more than he already does?

"Buon giorno, caro." At his desk, Leonida Leone was already at work. She came to his side and kissed his forehead while he put his arms around her waist and hugged her. She worried that he would think that her pregnancy was purposeful. She had never asked him for anything for herself, but she had talked him into spending money on the workers. Giorgina would try to persuade him that the baby was a socialist plot.

"Topo, something has happened." She turned away to avoid his eyes as she let the secret tumble out.

"Your face is white, fanciulla." He put down his pen and looked at her soberly. "I knew one day this would happen."

"I didn't plan it." He's going to throw me out, she thought.

"Inevitable," he muttered. "A younger man would have to come along eventually."

"What younger man?" She was perplexed.

"You have fallen in love with someone else." There was a rasp of resentment in his deep voice.

How could such a wise old man be so dense? "I am going to have a baby."

"Is it my . . . I don't know how to ask this, but . . ." He was on his feet now, moving toward her, astonishment on his face. If he hits me, she decided, I'll break his jaw.

"There has never been anyone else but you. But it can be just my baby if you wish it so. I will ask nothing."

"Fanciulla!" His voice was halfway between a groan and a cry of ecstasy and he took her powerfully in his arms. "Do you . . . I mean, do you want it? I know it will be embarrassing for you, but a child from you would make me very happy."

"I want it, yes, very much." She put her head on his shoulder as relief flooded over her.

"Then we will have it. And I don't like the idea of him being illegitimate. I think we ought to be married."

Rosaria disengaged and walked to the window. It's not necessarily going to be a him, she reflected. Below, the boys were driving Leonida's cows to pasture after the morning milking. To the north, women in black dresses were weeding their way through a hectare of ripening corn.

If I marry him, I become a countess, she realized. And a laughingstock.

"People would scoff if we were wed," she told him gently. "There is such a difference in our ages."

Leonida shrugged. "Garibaldi married a younger woman when he was long in years."

"And everybody laughed at him. You told me that."

"Only because the girl turned out to be a *puttana*."

"If you marry me, everyone will say that I am a puttana," she giggled.

The world intruded an hour later. They were talking about the baby, sitting in the alcove next to the Olivetti and holding hands while they argued the merits of marriage. This is as happy as I am ever going to be, Rosaria thought.

Then the telephone rang. With a gesture of irritation, Leonida picked it up. He listened for a moment, his face growing pale. Rosaria wondered if Achille had been killed. This time it would be for real.

"No, Prime Minister, I'm well," she heard him say. "Yes, I agree that there is great danger. Of course we should seal our borders and remain rigidly neutral. There is no reason for us to become involved unless they actually attack us."

The father of my baby has conversations with the Prime Minister, she thought, turning to the window and wondering what it would be like when the child actually came. What would Giorgina say? What could Leonida tell Mr. Salandra then? Yes, Prime Minister, I have impregnated this peasant girl . . .

"I suppose I had better go at once, if Joseph Joffre wants me," Leonida said into the telephone. Her ears pricked up. "Although I cannot promise to give anyone the advice they want to hear. Good-bye, sir. Sì, Sì, bene. Arrivederla."

Leonida sat for a moment in his chair looking at the telephone receiver, as if he was having difficulty in metabolizing the news. Then he came to her side and took her hand.

"This seems to be a day for momentous events," he said. "That was Prime Minister Antonio Salandra, and he has asked me to get back into uniform for a short time. Apparently, the commander in chief of the French Army wants me to advise him. Our General Staff thinks that it would be useful for me to spend some time at the Western Front and report on the new weaponry being used."

"Topo, don't go. It sounds dangerous."

"I know the timing is awful." He took her in his arms and hugged her with a new gentleness. "But I do need to go. There are people in our army who think that Italy should become involved in this war. This will be my only chance to demonstrate from the technical military point of view that it would be suicidal."

"When do you have to go?"

"There's that evening train to Paris. And when I come home, we might plan a private ceremony here in the Castello . . ."

She realized that she had to rescue him from his own nobility. "Sandro has been saying that Italy might be dragged into this war and only you could prevent it. Now if you married a contadina like me, you would lose all your influence with Mr. Salandra and the King. And then you would be powerless when the country needed you. Let's wait until the issue of the war is settled."

Reluctantly, Leonida conceded the point, although she sensed that he would return to it again. He kissed her forehead and moved toward his room. "I'd better let Girolamo get me packed."

"Oh, Topo, I'm so frightened for you."

"If I am young enough to beget a child, then I should be spry enough to visit a battlefield." Leonida turned at the door to his bedroom. He seemed relaxed and sure of himself. "And this child of mine needs a father, not a grandfather."

"But you're seventy-four."

"I know. And I will be long dead when he is old enough to understand these things, but someday you must tell him all about me."

"I will tell him." Rosaria began to sob. "Everything."

"Tell him that his father was General Leonida Leone. Tell him that Italy still needed me when I was seventy-four."

5.

. . . .

With Leonida gone, she had difficulty sleeping, and an obscure noise awoke her one night late in the middle of November. It was raining. Sandro was in Rome at a meeting of the Central Committee of the Partito Socialista Italiano, and she hated staying alone in the cottage when he was gone overnight.

"Who's there?"

No one answered and she ordered herself back to sleep. There was no point in lying in the dark, listening for ghosts. Sandro would either come home wet or find another bed for the night.

Wide awake, she wandered into the living room, feeling depressed. The morning sickness had passed, but she was exhausted from the strain of worrying about Leonida. In obedience to the Prime Minister's orders, he had spent weeks on the Western Front, studying the conduct of the war. He wrote with cheerful regularity, but Rosaria was frantic with the knowledge that her old warrior was once again dodging bullets in a combat zone.

Meanwhile, she was managing the entire agricultural estate alone, week after week.

And it had been a difficult harvest. Achille's mechanical thresher had broken down, and the men had struggled to fix it while torrential rains flattened fields of wheat. Sandro spent nearly all his time these days on Socialist Party activities, and Mercuzio Mercatelli had been sick in bed. All by herself, she had dealt with the olive-oil production and the grape harvest and the *vendemmia* and everything else that needed to be done.

Suddenly, she heard footsteps trudging through the mud, and then Leonida's hoarse cry. "Fanciulla!"

Thank God, he's all right! She threw open the door and kissed him hungrily. He was still in full uniform, a short ceremonial sword hanging from his waist. His water-soaked field jacket was covered with decorations, all of them won decades before she was born. With his white hair wet and plastered down against his forehead, he looked tired and yet somehow very tough.

"Oh, Topo, I've been so worried," she whispered. "Sit down and let me give you some cognac."

"I'm fine." He glanced at the gentle swell of her stomach. "Are you . . .

are we all right? How is my little friend? Your last letter reached me Monday night, just as I was leaving Paris. You sounded mournful.''

''I was just tired. Your little friend and I are well, and we only wish you could stay home with us.''

''When the Prime Minister has digested my report, there should be no reason for me to go away again.'' Shivering with the cold, he drank the cognac quickly, and Rosaria refilled his beaker. ''Fanciulla, it was awful. In all my years of soldiering, I never saw anything like the Western Front. The Germans and French are using poison gas, and long-range artillery, and barbed wire, and they seem to have an unlimited supply of heavy machine guns. Both sets of generals have run out of ideas, and they are now simply throwing divisions at one another.''

''Then there is no chance that Italy will become involved?''

''To send lightly armed Italian infantrymen into that nightmare would be genocide. I think I can persuade the General Staff, and it will be up to the Cabinet to keep us out of the war. God, it's cold in here.''

''I'll start a fire.''

''No, listen, you can't stay here,'' Leonida decreed, and she knew that he was going to have his way. ''Let's get your things together and move you into the house.''

''There isn't much to pack.'' She led him into her tiny room and he sat on the bed and watched as she threw dresses and toiletries into a bag. She decided to leave something she treasured behind so that Sandro would know that she was coming back someday. Folding the lovely black wool cloak Leonida had once given her, she left it deliberately in her cedar chest.

''I never meant for you to be poor.'' Leonida led her toward the door. ''When we became close, I worried that it would cheapen our relationship if I gave you money, but I intend to acknowledge this child as my own, and there is no reason for him to be born in poverty.''

''Oh, Topo, I—'' She stopped in mid-sentence, as they heard running feet and a shout. A second later Sandro stumbled in, soaked after his kilometer dash from the coach stop in Cederna to the Castello Leone.

''Rosaria, I . . . Eccellenza?''

The two men glared at one another, and for a moment Rosaria feared a quarrel. Oh, Sandro, she wanted to say, don't be angry with him. Great men take what they need and there was a moment when he needed me. You will do the same when you become a great revolutionary.

''Have you heard about Mussolini?'' Sandro burst out, and she turned away angrily. It's always politics with him, she fumed.

''What about him?'' Leonida had a soft spot for most revolutionaries, but regarded Benito Mussolini as a great charlatan.

''We have just expelled him from the Socialist Party.'' Sandro seemed stunned and hurt, having been a devoted reader of Mussolini's newspaper,

Avanti. "He has joined the war-hawk movement, the interventionists. He wants Italy to go to war to support the French."

"The French are undoubtedly bribing him. Don't worry! One cheap ex-Marxist journalist is not going to hustle the Kingdom into war. Listen, come and see me tomorrow and we'll talk."

"Eccellenza, the Central Committee of my Party believes that the King wants war and I am worried that—" Sandro paused abruptly as he realized that Rosaria was leaving. "You're moving out? You're not going to live here anymore?"

"It's a question of her comfort." The Count was irritated.

"This is the ultimate in class exploitation," Sandro exploded. "When you steal our little sisters!"

Leonida Leone grew red in the face, and Rosaria quickly stepped between the two men. "This has nothing to do with Marx and no one is stealing me," she explained. "If it were not for the baby, I would never leave."

"You left a long time ago," Sandro said quietly, and he closed the door in her face.

All of which, in the morning, he regretted.

Dressing quickly, Sandro presented himself in the Leone study and found the general alone.

"Sit down, Lombardi," the old man commanded. Sandro obeyed, wondering if Leonida was going to talk about Rosaria. Instead he launched straight into politics. "You said last night that your Central Committee believed that the King secretly wanted war."

Sandro nodded. "And most of the General Staff have become interventionists. They want to support England and France."

"Whom do you know on the PSI Central Committee?"

"Everyone."

Leonida tossed a heavy envelope into Sandro's lap. "Then perhaps we can be useful to one another. This is a blind copy of my report on the military status of the Western Front. It goes later today to the Prime Minister and the General Staff. If they decide to suppress it, then you need to make arrangements for it to appear in the socialist press. This document should make it clear that Italian military participation in this abbattoir of a war would be unthinkable."

"In return, you would expect . . ."

"I would expect an open-ended collaboration. I can keep track of our bloodthirsty generals if your colleagues can report on ex-socialist war hawks like Mussolini. If your Central Committee agrees, I would like you to act as the intermediary between us, since, if I am seen entering your headquarters, I would lose my standing with the army and the court. Any questions?"

"No, sir!" Sandro sensed that he was being dismissed, and he walked to the door as Leonida settled himself behind his desk. "I'll take this to Rome on the noon coach."

Leonida stood and raised his hand. "Sandro, about your sister, I . . . I'm sorry about the embarrassment this will mean to you and to her. Having behaved dishonorably, I am now prepared to act as honorably as I can. I think Rosaria understands that."

"Yes, sir." Sandro left the study, his mind whirling.

He met Rosaria on the stairs. Impulsively he put his arms around her and kissed the top of her head. So I'll become the uncle of a bastard, he thought carelessly. Maybe he'll be a socialist bastard.

"I love you," he whispered. "Ti voglio bene."

She hugged him back, sniffling, and Sandro held her for a minute. Then he broke away and raced for the noon coach to Rome.

6.

. . . .

Laid out before the turn of the century by the late Countess Maria Pia Leone, the *giardino segreto* was a few dozen square feet of grass around a little pond with goldfish and a bronze ornamental fountain. Screening the garden from the house was a tall row of cypress trees, a moss-covered wall, and then a massive hedge.

It was Giorgina's favorite place for a quiet drink, and she rang a silver bell to signal her desire for another gin and tonic. Their daughter was chasing a puppy around in a circle, and Bruno Benelli was reading the morning *Messaggero* with his usual concentration. Since August of 1914, Bruno had become a compulsive newspaper reader.

"How is the war going?" Giorgina asked, glancing at her wristwatch. Her appointment with Rosaria Lombardi had been set for two, and she worried that the maid would not appear with the gin in time. It would be awkward having to offer Rosaria refreshment. What did peasants drink anyway?

"Still stalemated," Bruno Benelli responded slowly.

"And you still think Italy should become involved?" For once, Giorgina was prepared to consider her husband's opinions carefully. When the world had gone to war in the summer of 1914, most Italians had favored safe neutrality, but Bruno—who was not a stupid man—had immediately joined the Interventionist Movement. It was now April of 1915; the interventionists had become the strongest political force in the country, and Bruno had quietly become the manager of their finances.

"The sooner the better," exclaimed Bruno. Giorgina had never before seen her husband this passionate about anything. He wasn't this excited when our daughter was born, she mused. For that matter, he wasn't even very excited when she was conceived.

"Even if this means consorting with men like Mussolini?" The upper classes had been puzzled and suspicious when Italy's number-one Marxist agitator had abruptly become the nation's leading patriot. "He's scum."

"He's our scum now," Bruno assured her. "Mussolini is the only man who can convince the working class that a war would be in their interest."

"Would it be in their interest?"

"Of course not." Bruno shrugged. "A declaration of war would send food prices sky-high, improving the profit situation for landowners. The government could introduce emergency legislation prohibiting strikes, so we could lower workers' wages without fear of a walkout.''

"We already pay them too much." Giorgina became irritated whenever she contemplated the salaries the Leone family dispersed every week to their employees. "Especially since that wretched girl took over."

"Your father does not understand the economics of running a large agricultural estate." There was urgency in Bruno's voice as he leaned forward in his chair. "Consequently, he is allowing her to make one concession after another to the work force. Furthermore, the girl's pregnancy is affecting our social prestige. Ah, here she comes."

Giorgina looked up to see Rosaria Lombardi enter the *giardino segreto*, infuriatingly elegant in a white linen maternity dress. Oh, you really are a beauty, she assessed her objectively. Once you have your figure back, you could do well in one of those fashionable brothels in Rome. And you must be eight months pregnant, so we need to move quickly.

"Signora? Did you send for me?" Rosaria stood a few steps away, obviously embarrassed by her distended belly. Collecting little Teresa, Bruno Benelli excused himself and left.

"Girl, my father is apparently under the impression that he is responsible for this bastard you are about to produce." Giorgina gestured toward an uncomfortable wicker chair. I will play this carefully, Giorgina planned. Father has not spoken to me in two years, but he shares his every senile notion with her.

"The Count knows that he—" Rosaria began hotly, but Giorgina cut her off with a sneer.

"Spare me the protestations. My father expects his orders to be obeyed. If he told you to jump into his bed, then you were only doing what you were told, obedient little thing that you are. It was hardly your fault."

"Signora, I—"

Giorgina waved her hand languidly. "But now an accident has occurred. A scandal must be avoided and a baby needs to be provided for. Let me explain how these little embarrassments are handled in our social class. A suitable father is found to take responsibility for the child, and enough money is made available to keep everyone deliciously happy. Do you understand?''

"Yes, but—"

"And there is an eminently suitable father for your child, much better than you deserve. You have known Junio Mosconi all your life, since he has spent most of it sniffing after you. He is a moderately handsome young man who will inherit a large farm and several stores in Cederna, a huge estate in the Abruzzi Mountains, and a considerable personal fortune. And when old Enrico Mosconi dies, Junio will have my family's support to take his father's place as Mayor."

"I don't understand. I've never been friendly with Junio."

"But he is prepared to be massively friendly with you. Listen, girl, my father is not going to live much longer. Junio has offered to find you a comfortable place to live in the Abbruzi Mountains. Generous provisions will be made for your financial security. Papers will be drawn up in which Junio publicly acknowledges paternity of your child. He is a powerful man and no one will treat you with disrespect."

"And what does Junio want in return?"

"I really couldn't guess." Giorgina smiled to herself. "Perhaps he would expect you to be grateful in some fashion."

Rosaria grew so pale that for a moment Giorgina wondered if she was about to pass out. No, peasants don't faint, she reminded herself. Only a woman with a large private income can afford to swoon over a question of lost honor.

"If Junio Mosconi comes anywhere near me, my brother will deal with him." Rosaria stormed out of the *giardino segreto* so furiously that she nearly colliding with the maid who was bringing Giorgina's gin and tonic.

"In these matters there are hard options and soft options," Giorgina said to herself as she sipped her drink. "And hard options can be so . . . so very hard."

7.

. . . .

"We have precise information," said Sandro Lombardi as he stood nervously before Leonida's desk. "The Central Committee has instructed me."

"Sandro, stop making speeches and sit down," Leonida Leone ordered with gruff affection. "What do you have for me?"

Sandro sat down obediently, irritated that Leonida still had the power to intimidate him, despite his own growing importance in the Socialist Party. Peasanthood, he decided, is more psychological than economic. He glanced quickly at his sister, who smiled at him reassuringly but did not speak.

Sandro took a deep breath and said what the PSI Central Committee had told him to say. "We have obtained a copy of a secret treaty in which Britain guarantees that Italy gets Trentino and everything this side of the Brenner Pass as well as Trieste and most of Dalmatia. Our government has accepted fifty million pounds sterling and the promise of more Arab land in North Africa. In return, we march against the Central Powers."

"This is hard to believe." Leonida was shaken. "The King assured me that he had no intention of allowing our neutrality to be breached, and he specifically promised to inform me of any change in his thinking."

"Here is a copy of the treaty." Sandro placed a packet of papers on Leonida's desk. "The King has not yet signed it, but we think that he will."

There was a long silence while Leonida read the purloined document.

"If this document is authentic, I have been played for a fool. It would mean that the government recalled me—a well-known neutralist—back to active duty to send a deliberately false signal while they quietly negotiated with the British. Oh, the villains!"

"What should we do?" Sandro was frightened. The PSI leadership was uncertain, indecisive, and Mussolini's defection had left them paralyzed.

"I will go to see the King tomorrow and tell His Imperially Stupid Majesty that he is playing with forces beyond his control. He has got to fire this Prime Minister and appoint someone with enough brains to put Mussolini and the interventionists in jail."

"Eccellenza, suppose he refuses?" The question shot across the room like an arrow.

"Are you socialists still planning that monster rally tomorrow in Rome?

Tell your Central Committee that I am prepared to address their meeting after I have talked to the King. If the government intends to declare war, I join your party publicly, and call for a mobilization to close down the railroads and harbors and telegraph centers and major highways. We will shut Italy down and keep it shut until there is a new government."

"Hurrah!" He is more of a revolutionary than I will ever be, thought Sandro as he reached forward to shake Leonida's hand.

"Be careful, Topo," Rosaria cried, rushing up and putting one arm around each of them.

"I have been careful too long," roared Leonida Leone. "Let the King and his ministers be careful!"

"We need to talk." Bruno Benelli entered the room quietly and stood before Giorgina like a plaintiff facing a judge.

"Junio is coming, and I'd prefer to see him alone," she snapped.

"There are two things you need to understand before you talk to Junio." Bruno spoke mechanically, as if delivering an auditor's report. He was avoiding her eyes and she sensed that something was devastatingly wrong. "Your father intends to carry his opposition to the war all the way to the King, over whom he continues to exercise some influence. If he fails to sway His Majesty, he proposes to join forces with the Socialist Party and oppose the war with extra-legal measures."

Giorgina exploded. "He's gone mad!"

"This political crisis could have private consequences for you and me." Bruno consulted a slip of paper in his hand. "For many years, I have been diverting a portion of the profits from the autumn harvest, investing them in the Milan Stock Exchange, and putting the profits into the account that we control. These investments have been carefully chosen. You and I are now moderately affluent in our own right."

"What are you saying? Did you have Father's permission to gamble with his money?"

"No, it was entirely illegal, but in the past I have always been able to return the borrowed money and cover any trace of the operation. Last December, Junio and I received inside information that the King intended to negotiate a treaty with the British and declare war in early spring. I took all of our money and the entire 1914 profits from the farm and invested heavily in munitions stocks. If war is declared soon, we will become extraordinarily wealthy, and there will be no problem about replacing the money in your father's account. On the other hand—"

"What are you saying?"

"If Count Leone blocks this declaration of war, we will be bankrupt, and I will go to prison. I will perhaps share a cell with Junio Mosconi, who has borrowed funds from the Cederna Municipal Treasury and finds himself in the same disagreeable position."

There was silence. Giorgina lit another cigarette and paced through the salotto, dropping ashes on the Persian carpet. My obedient little adding machine has become an embezzler. She chuckled. I like him better already.

"What do we do?" she asked quietly.

"Junio is coming with a specific proposal to deal with all these areas of unpleasantness." Bruno moved toward the door, putting the slip of paper back into his pocket. "Consider very carefully what he has to say."

Junio was late, as usual. It was getting dark.

Where the hell was he? Strangely restless, Giorgina paced into the hallway, thinking that a drink might improve her mood and wondering what had happened to all the maids. Then the front door opened and Sandro Lombardi came in.

Neither of them spoke. Giorgina gazed at him with an expression of what she hoped was haughty contempt. Sandro glared back with proletarian animosity and then bounded up the stairs toward Leonida's study.

The reds were plotting something. She frowned, drifting back into the salotto. Girolamo had been servicing the Fiat, which meant that her father was going someplace. The phone had been ringing since dawn, and Sandro had been in and out of the study all day.

Bruno and Junio are my only allies and they are weak men, she thought, sinking into the softness of the couch and smoothing her silk dress down over her thighs. She inserted a yellow Turkish cigarette into an ivory holder and lit it with a sulphur match. The oriental tobacco made her head spin with pleasure as the heat from the fireplace radiated against her legs.

Sandro Lombardi is my enemy, she told herself, but he is also the strongest man in Cederna . . . suddenly she remembered herself as a silly teenaged girl, prancing around on her pony. Sandro had been alone in the field that day, digging fence-post holes. She had expected him to doff his hat and bow as she passed, but he had ignored her.

To get his attention, she had hit him with her riding crop. Sandro had caught her arm and pulled her down and she had scratched his face and got on top of him, her legs around his hips, struggling as he held her wrists.

I remember, she said to herself. I remember how I twisted and squirmed until I felt that electricity sear through me. I wept and then climbed back on my pony thinking that some more appropriate man would send me that electricity again.

But it had never, never happened again.

"Signora?" Loretta was calling her and Giorgina realized there were tears on her cheeks. Christ! The girl will tell the other servants she saw me having a fit. This must never happen again. I cannot afford the luxury of weakness.

"Signora?" The maid's eyes avoided Giorgina's. "Signor Mosconi is at the door. He says he has an appointment."

"Bring whiskey!" Giorgina heard the tremble in her voice as she checked her makeup in the mirror over the fireplace. She took a deep, unhappy breath, and then prepared a face of icy sovereignty with which to greet the Mayor's son.

"Giorgina, we've got to talk." The younger Mosconi barged into the salotto with his walking stick. You are a cheap little man, she sneered as he dropped uninvited into a chair. Your grandfather was a peasant who poached chickens from our land, and your father is a crooked, bribe-taking small-town politician. Once I could look down my nose at you, Junio, but now I need allies. You will have to do.

"How's your leg, Junio?" she said maliciously, Just before his scheduled induction into the Italian Army a few years back, Junio had injured his knee in a mysterious fall from a horse. Dr. Beniolo had duly certified that he was physically unfit for military service. The damaged knee had then healed rapidly, at least until August of 1914, when the mobilization of the German Army seemed to have made it worse again.

"The pain comes and goes," he answered impatiently. "Look, I'm just back from a meeting of our Interventionist Committee. Has Bruno explained the situation? We're getting very close to getting a declaration of war, and your father simply must not be allowed to interfere."

"How can you stop Leonida Leone from doing anything he chooses?"

"Tomorrow, when he leaves the royal palace, there will be a minor incident on the street, after which your father will be escorted to a hospital, where a psychiatrist will decide that he is no longer competent to administer his affairs."

There was a long pause. Then Giorgina seized Junio by the ears and pulled him roughly to his feet.

"Listen, you little shit," she said distinctly. "Do what needs to be done to get my father into that hospital, but if anything serious happens to him, we send you to the cemetery. Do you understand?"

"Of course, signora." Junio's face went suddenly pale.

"We need to think about the Lombardi family. Leave Sandro to me, but have his wretched sister killed."

"Kill Rosaria?" Junio backed away. "We hadn't planned on going that far. Did you talk to her about my offer? I've had papers drawn up to establish my paternity of her child . . ."

"She was furious."

"How did you put it to her?" Junio's face flushed as he digested the humiliation.

"Pimping has never been one of my strong points," Giorgina snapped at him. "When she realized that the offer involved going to bed with you, she nearly fainted."

"Who the hell does she think she is?" Junio's male vanity was aroused.

"She is smarter than you are, Junio, and tougher, and unless we get rid of her, she will someday have your balls for breakfast. Kill her, or the deal is off and you can rot in jail."

"All right!" Junio's face hardened. "An incident . . . will be arranged."

8.

....

"No Leone in history has ever been a policeman," grumbled Girolamo.

"It's just that the carabinieri have offered me a commission," Terenzio explained uneasily.

"Why not make a career with the piano?" Rosaria was appalled at the idea of the gentle Terenzio's joining the national police, but she understood his motives. For several centuries now, Leone men had been university-trained military officers. Terenzio hated school, and if the carabinieri would commission him without a university degree, he would achieve a shortcut to respectability on the family tree.

"Well, it's not very heroic, is it, being a musician?" Terenzio said wistfully. "Besides, after my training as a carabiniere officer, I could be assigned to Libya with Achille."

"Well, the carabinieri have nice uniforms." Rosaria turned in her seat to gaze across the courtyard at the Quirinale Palace, a massive, square two-story building where King Vittorio Emanuele III of Italy lived.

Terenzio had parked his father's luxurious Fiat Tipo 51 Zero beside Cleopatra's Needle, the tall granite Egyptian obelisk that towered outside the entrance to the palace. At the front, there were carabiniere police guards standing at parade rest, rifles at their sides. They wore ceremonial Napoleonic hats and long, romantic-looking black capes.

"Here comes Papa now," Terenzio remarked. "O Dio, he looks mad. It always makes me nervous when he shouts at the King."

Feeling the sudden tension, Rosaria watched the honor guard snap from parade rest to attention as Leonida's angry figure surged past them. An officer saluted, but Count Leone ignored him and headed toward the car, his face dark.

"Take this and put it under the seat." Girolamo handed Terenzio a snubnosed pistol.

The younger man stared at it in puzzlement. "Father said nothing about bringing guns. I don't think he was anticipating any trouble."

"Only your father could threaten a King with insurrection and not expect trouble," growled Girolamo. "Start the engine."

Terenzio pulled the starter lever and the Fiat's two-liter engine sprang into life. A moment later Leonida climbed into the back seat next to Rosaria.

"Father, are we going to have a war?" asked Terenzio.

"I don't know." Leonida was angry and perplexed. "The King denied that he was considering any specific arrangement with Great Britain, but admitted that the Prime Minister might have been negotiating behind his back. He made me a firm promise that I would be consulted before there was any drastic change in our foreign policy. I'm just not sure I can believe him."

"What do we do now?"

"I want to see Prime Minister Salandra. Terenzio, take us to Palazzo Chigi."

"Don't you need an appointment to see the Prime Minister?" Terenzio wondered.

"I don't need an appointment to see anyone."

That ended the conversation. As Terenzio pulled slowly from the courtyard of the royal palace, Rosaria gazed out the window, wondering if she would ever live in Rome. Perhaps later, after the baby has come, she reasoned, it will be awkward for me to stay at the Castello. It would avoid embarrassment when Achille returned. I could have one of those prams with a parasol and pneumatic wheels and take the baby for walks down these twisty little streets. They sell lovely dresses here for little girls. I won't mind if it's a little girl.

Who are you, little person? she wondered, putting her hand on her belly and feeling the baby kick. Will you become a revolutionary socialist like your Uncle Sandro? Or a famous soldier like your father? Or will you be a little girl, and a secretary like me? The baby kicked again, refusing to commit itself.

After another turn, the Quirinale Palace disappeared from view and the Tipo 51 Zero coasted down the hill away from the King's residence and into a maze of narrow streets. Suddenly, a horse and cart blocked the road ahead of them and Terenzio brought the car to a halt.

"Back up!" Girolamo growled, but there was a truck behind them, and Terenzio stalled the motor. Suddenly the arthritic old majordomo kicked open the Fiat's door and spilled out onto the street, a gun in his hand. Girolamo fired once and Rosaria saw the barrel in his revolver turn, aligning the next shell with the chamber while smoke poured from the muzzle.

"Giro!" Leonida cried out as men in rough clothing swarmed over them. Rosaria grabbed desperately for his hand, but he bounded out onto the cobblestones, battling heroically with their assailants. Then someone yanked open the car door on her side, seized her hair, and hauled her out onto the road.

She landed on her back, screaming and doubled up, with her hands across her stomach, thinking, my baby, my baby, they mustn't hurt my baby!

"It seems a shame," said one of the men standing over her. He held a butcher's knife in his hand. He was cross-eyed and a birthmark spread like a stain down his neck. From somewhere, she could hear Leonida's deep voice. She tried to wriggle away, but the man with the birthmark dropped to his knees and straddled her with his legs.

"Get it over with," snarled the other.

"Please, I'm going to have a baby," she pleaded. She watched the man's eyes as he selected a spot on her breast, looking for her heart. Then there was a gun shot and his arm dropped. The knife clattered onto the cobblestones, and she watched a bloodstain spread down the front of his shirt.

He opened his mouth and spit and sneezed, trying to clear the blood from his throat. Then he fell forward, covering her body as if he were going to make love to her, the blood seeping from the bullet hole in his chest.

"Stronzo!" She heard Terenzio cry the old Roman vulgarity, triumph and pain in his voice. There was the sound of a fist hitting someone in the face, and the noise of bones breaking, but Rosaria felt herself fading from the battle. She could feel the warmth of the dead man's body on her breast and the coldness of the cobblestones against her back, and then there was blackness all around her.

"Porco Dio!" Sandro blasphemed, striking his knee against a pile of firewood he had cut and left carelessly by the cottage door.

Where the hell is everyone?

Blundering into his cold, dark cottage, Sandro felt water dripping from his clothing onto the flagstone floor. Imagining how nice it would be to come home to a dry, warm house, he struck one damp sulfur match after another until he managed to ignite the kindling and dry pine on the hearth. As the flames threw heat into the empty room, he stripped off his wet clothing and climbed into fresh cotton underdrawers and trousers.

He was still shivering. Impatient, Sandro dug out a bottle of grappa he had been saving for an emergency and took a few thirsty gulps directly from the bottle. The alcohol made him cough, but it gave him the energy to pile more wood on the fire.

It was strangely quiet. He covered his bare shoulders with a blanket from the couch and listened to the patter of rain splashing against the slate roof and the hiss of droplets coming down the chimney to vaporize in the fire. He tried to relax, since there would be no news until the morning, when Leonida and Rosaria came back. In the meantime, there was nothing to do but find a book and read himself to sleep.

Of course, there were other ways of getting to sleep. If one of those bright-eyed Roman girls were here, he thought, I could sleep with a woman's body pressed against mine. That would be good. I am tired of sleeping alone.

But a woman in my bed would mean babies and family and an end to everything I ever meant to accomplish. In the final analysis, a book is better. You can always get rid of a book in the morning.

With a sigh, he thumbed through his tiny library. Leonida had once given him an expensive three-volume leather-bound set of Dante's *Divine Comedy,* and Sandro decided that *L'Inferno* best suited his present mood.

"In the middle of our life's journey"—he read the familiar opening lines sprawled on the rug before the fire, a cushion beneath his stomach and the comforting bottle of grappa by his side—"I found myself, having lost the path, in a dark forest . . ."

Suddenly his ears detected the whisper of footsteps moving lightly across the wet grass, and a second later a soft, tentative knock at his door.

"Rosaria?" he called hopefully as the door opened.

"It's Giorgina." There was an unexpected voice from the doorway. "Am I disturbing you, Horse?"

"What do you want?" She's still calling me "Horse," he thought. She always called me "Horse" when we were teenagers, and I had to call her "signorina . . ."

"I have some bad news." Signora Benelli moved into the illuminated half-circle around the fireplace. I'm not going to stand up and bow, Sandro decided, rolling into a sitting position and staring up at her. Her long brown hair was loose and hanging over her shoulders. She was clothed from head to toe in a thick black cloak that looked familiar, although Sandro could not place it.

"Bad news?"

"This afternoon in Rome, my father was attacked on the street by a gang of anarchists. I've just come from the hospital."

"Rosaria was with him. Is she hurt?"

"A few bruises on her bottom, I am told." Giorgina took another step forward and stood over him, enveloped in her majestic black cape. "Terenzio will bring her home tonight, but my father was badly beaten and will be in the hospital indefinitely."

"If I had only been there to protect him! Are you sure they were anarchists?"

Private tragedies have public consequences, he calculated. How badly was the old man hurt? They needed at least one senior military man to denounce this war as suicidal and Leonida Leone was the most famous general in Italy.

"The police said they were anarchists." Giorgina did not seem overly interested in the question. She pulled the cloak more tightly around her and glanced about the cottage. "You live here all alone, Horse? In your lonely little stable? With no nice mare to keep you warm?"

"What do you want?"

"Sandro, I believe that we should all get whatever we can out of life," Giorgina sank down to the rug and rested on her haunches. Sandro noticed that her feet were bare. "Don't you agree?"

"You're describing the ethic of capitalism. It has nothing to do with me."

"Look, I was born in that big house over there, and what I want out of life is every penny this estate can give me. You were born in a shack and you became a revolutionary to redistribute the wealth. I understand this completely. We should have realized long ago that you were too big a man to leave out in the cold."

"Get to the point."

"With my father in the hospital, you and I are the only two people who count. You control the workers and I control the land. So we make a deal. It's as simple as that."

"The workers should have power over their own lives," he retorted as Giorgina burst into laughter. "This estate should be run by a committee."

"Sandro, Sandro, you're so loyal to your lovely little proletarians." She chuckled. "Pay attention to what I am saying, dear. Nothing was ever run by a committee. Things happen when strong men make them happen, and you are the strongest man in Cederna."

"Wait a minute!" Sandro sat up, trying to fathom the situation.

"You want a share of the pie? Run this estate for me and take as much pie as you can eat. Think about it! No more cold cottages and lonely nights."

Closing his eyes, he gave the proposal a moment's worth of consideration, stunned by the force of the temptation. I am tired of talking to silly people who are too frightened to take what socialism has to offer. Suppose we never have a revolution? Will I go on for fifty more years breaking my bones every day in a field, smelling of horses, going to meetings at night to make futile little speeches?

"And there's a bonus, Horse." He heard a subtle, softening change in her voice. "A very special bonus for horses who don't try to throw their riders."

He opened his eyes. One bare arm emerged from beneath the cape, and she tossed a riding crop into the space between them.

"Do you remember when I hit you with this? I've kept it all these years. With this whip I thee wed, Horse. The bonus is me."

Her body quivered. She undid the bow that fastened the cloak at her neck and pushed it off her shoulders. It fell to the floor, and in the flickering light from the fire he saw that she was naked. Giorgina closed her eyes and sat utterly still.

Sandro felt a heat within him as he looked at her taut athletic body, the small breasts and sinuous thighs he had never expected to see, or be offered. You've always wanted her, he admitted. Since you were an adolescent she has been the fantasy dancing behind your eyes when you caressed yourself at night.

There was a tightness across his forehead as he got to his feet, suddenly short of breath, and he leaned against his bookshelf. Is this the moment when I sell out? Blindly, his hands ran over the cheap cardboard covers of the thirty-seven books he had accumulated, the collected works of Marx and Engels in Italian translations, the writings of Bakunin and Turati.

"Horse, this isn't going to happen again. I'm on my knees."

"Get out!" He closed his eyes and clung to the bookshelf for support. When the door closed, he turned and saw that she was gone.

So was the riding crop.

Sometime before dawn, there was a hubbub at the door.

"Go away, you bitch!" In the confusion of sleep, he assumed that Leonida's daughter had returned to haunt him. Then he heard the splintering of wood and understood that someone had just kicked in his door.

"Sandro Lombardi?" Sergeant Virgilio Cirillo of the Royal Carabinieri was standing at the foot of his couch, backed up by two enlisted men who were pointing carbines in his direction.

"Why are you arresting me?" Move slowly, he cautioned himself as he climbed deliberately into his trousers. People get shot resisting arrest. He put on a work shirt and a heavy woolen jacket before extending his hands for the handcuffs. Going to jail is something that happens to revolutionaries, he reflected. You need to get good at it.

"Draft evasion." Sergeant Cirillo snapped the handcuffs shut and the two privates relaxed immediately, digging in their pockets for Nazionale cigarettes. They offered Sandro one, but he shook his head.

"That's silly. Giorgina will have to do better than that," he laughed. "Look, when I was eighteen I was exempted from the draft because I was an orphan and responsible for my little sister. It was your office that did the paperwork, Cirillo. Look in your files!"

"Your sister now earns five times as much as you do," the sergeant sneered. "She is very well paid for whatever it is that she does and hardly needs your support. Nor does she live under your roof. And Signor Junio Mosconi has filed papers with the North Lazio District Court acknowledging paternity of her unborn child and accepting financial responsibility."

"What?" Sandro surged forward. The two privates dropped their cigarettes and picked up their rifles.

"When you ceased being your sister's source of financial support, you should have reported this fact to the district conscription office."

"I want my lawyer. Notify Tommaso Savarino."

"It won't do any good. We're going to take you to a military judge in Rome who will decide that you're the sort of fellow we want in the army. They send draft dodgers to a punishment battalion."

"You won't get away with this," Sandro muttered, but he realized that argument was pointless. The carabinieri were acting under orders from someone. And Leonida was lying in a Rome hospital, hurt, maybe dying.

"I won't get away with it?" Sergeant Cirillo seemed amused at the idea that there was anything a policeman couldn't get away with. "Come on, Lombardi."

With growing unease, Sandro trudged outside to where a truck was waiting. The upper rim of the sun was edging above the mountains to the east while rain clouds fled west across the Tyrrhenian Sea.

It's going to be a sunny day, he thought as he climbed into the back of the truck. When will I see this place again? Where is Rosaria?

"This is a frame-up, Cirillo!" he shouted.

"Life is pretty much of a frame-up, Lombardi," Sergeant Cirillo agreed, and they drove him away.

"Is she all right?"

"Peasant women are very tough." It was the cold, professional voice of Dr. Beniolo, the rich people's physician from Cederna. "She has a bruise on her scalp and some abrasions on her legs and buttocks, but nothing seems to be broken. The sedative should be wearing off soon."

Consciousness returned and Rosaria reassembled the recent past in her mind. Yes, she had awakened in a hospital, where they had given her a pill for the pain in her back. Then they had brought her to the Castello, where Valeria had put her to bed with a sleeping potion.

"She's my father's secretary." There was a new authority in Terenzio's voice.

"Ah, I remember, this is the wench that Junio . . . well, the last time I saw her she was dashing half-dressed out of the Mosconi place."

"I find that difficult to believe," Terenzio replied coldly as the two men walked to the door. "In my absence, she is to be shown every courtesy,"

Rosaria opened her eyes. She was lying in the little bedchamber adjoining Leonida's study. Her back ached.

"Are you awake?" Terenzio was businesslike as he sat next to her on the bed. One of his eyes had been thoroughly blackened. "Someone will come up with coffee."

"Teri, what happened to us?" Instinctively, she used his childhood nickname.

"I'm not sure. When those men attacked, I ran around the car and shot a man who was trying to stab you. Don't you remember? The gang ran away, and left father unconscious."

"Where is Leonida now?"

"The Ospedale Militare in Rome. He hasn't regained consciousness. He has a fractured skull, and they say several of his ribs are broken."

"Oh Christ!" The thought of that gallant old man lying unconscious in a hospital made her furious. "Teri, who did this to us?"

"That's what I'm going to find out," the young man replied. "I went to Carabiniere Headquarters to report the incident and the Commanding General invited me to take part in the investigation. They seem very keen to have me, and I go on active duty immediately."

Rosaria wondered why the Carabinieri would want an untrained schoolboy interfering in their inquiries, but she was too worried about Leonida to probe the matter. "I need to go and see Leonida."

Terenzio shook his head. "Girolamo will take you to see him in a few days, but now you need to rest and take care of that baby."

"Teri, I'm sorry if this child is an embarrassment to you."

Terenzio turned at the door, and looked back at her. "If father dies, this baby will be the last gift we'll ever have from him. So take care of yourself."

He smiled, a little sadly, and left.

She slept for a long time. About noon, she awoke to find that someone had left coffee and fresh clothing by the bed. The pain in her back had subsided, and her head felt clear. The baby was kicking, and it made her feel happy, despite everything.

She began to organize the counterattack, deciding to confer first with Sandro and then go to Rome and find Leonida. She dressed quickly, gulped the coffee, and walked into the library.

Girolamo was standing at the window staring intently at the road from Cederna. There were angry black bruises on his face, and one of his front teeth was missing.

"Look! It's the whole awful crew." He gestured toward the front gardens, where cars were being parked. Over his shoulder Rosaria could see Giorgina and Bruno Benelli and Junio Mosconi and the fat priest and Sergeant Cirillo and his two enlisted men. "This feels like the end."

"The end of what?"

The old majordomo shrugged. "I don't know. There are always cops and priests around when things come to an end."

Oh, don't let Leonida be dead, she tried to pray. Oh, God, please save my Topo.

"Where is Sandro?"

"Gone," Girolamo told her. "The entrance to the cottage has been smashed."

Then the door to the study opened and Father Maurizio entered alone. "I bring you good news," he said. "Count Leone has made his peace with God."

"What, did God apologize?" asked Girolamo.

"Oh no, I want to see him." Rosaria gave way to grief and began to cry. This is my fault, she told herself. He tried to be young for me.

"His Excellency stands on the brink of eternity." The clergyman took her arm with surprising gentleness. "He needs what time he has left for reflection, and I believe he wishes to pray."

"He's recovered consciousness? Listen, priest, did you actually see him?" Girolamo advanced on Don Maurizio with such fury that Rosaria feared that there would be violence.

"Did you talk to him?" Rosaria knew the old priest was lying. "Did he say he didn't want to see me?"

"Child . . ." For a long moment Don Maurizio hesitated, uncomfortable with his role. Then he turned and opened the door to admit Giorgina and Bruno Benelli, Junio Mosconi, Sergeant Cirillo, and two carabiniere patrolmen. Giorgina was clearly in charge.

"You have stolen from us." Leonida's daughter pointed an accusing finger at Rosaria. "After all our kindness, you looted my poor mother's possessions."

"What?" I've got to fight back, Rosaria told herself. This is serious, and I'm on my own. Where the hell is Sandro? O Dio, she's going to have me arrested!

"This garment was found in your cottage." Sergeant Cirillo held up the cloak Leonida had given her that day they walked in the fields, the black mantle that had once belonged to Contessa Maria Pia.

"It was a present."

"That's absurd. Gentlemen, I will leave this to you." Giorgina waved at Rosaria as if she were furniture to be removed. "For the sake of my family's reputation, I prefer to avoid placing criminal charges, but I shall sign the papers if . . ."

"Leave her alone!" Girolamo stormed up and stood between Rosaria and the carabiniere sergeant. "You bastard!"

"And get that old fool off my property." Giorgina turned at the door and pointed at Girolamo. There was triumph in her voice. "Gentlemen, will you excuse us? We have an estate to run."

Giorgina sailed through the door, waving her hand in dismissal as her husband stumbled along behind. Junio Mosconi was wearing a smart gray Borsolino, which he tipped with heavy irony as he left. "Listen carefully to what Don Maurizio has to say, Rosirosalina," he advised her. "And remember that I have come to rescue you from all of this. You will be grateful someday."

Feeling weak, Rosaria sank into a chair, picturing Leonida, inexplicably beaten half to death by terrorists, now dying alone in a hospital somewhere. Oh, Achille, she pleaded across the Mediterranean. Come home now. We need you now!

Fingering the heavy silver cross he wore on a chain around his neck, Don Maurizio sat by her side and leaned toward her. "You are with child," he said. "I understand there is some question about the father."

"The father is Leonida Leone," Rosaria was amazed that she could still find her voice.

"Girl, if you have been with many men, then only the Holy Ghost knows precisely who put this infant into your womb." The old priest's voice grew menacing. "And you must not go around saying that Count Leone was the father. It would be terrible to have your baby in prison."

"She hasn't committed any crime." Girolamo began shouting and shaking his fists. At a nod from Sergeant Cirillo, the two enlisted policemen frogmarched him from the room. Rosaria could hear Girolamo shouting curses and threats on the staircase. Poor Giro, she thought miserably. He was my last ally.

"Listen, little slut, let me explain something to you." Suddenly Sergeant

Cirillo was standing over her. "There is a crime called slander. It means saying something untrue about someone. Dr. Beniolo has signed a certificate attesting that the old man is no longer physically capable of begetting a child, so if you claim in public that he fathered your bastard, you will be slandering the Leone Family and I will arrest you."

"Where is Terenzio?" she demanded. "Terenzio knows the truth . . ."

"Terenzio has left for Milan," the priest intervened. "Tonight he will be commissioned as an officer in the Royal Carabinieri, and tomorrow his training begins. In Milan."

"Now? With his father in the hospital, dying? He had to report right now?"

"You don't ignore an order from the General Staff," Cirillo explained.

Orders from the General Staff? This is a massive conspiracy of some kind, Rosaria realized. Something bigger than me and my baby is at stake. And I have run right out of friends. "What do you want of me?" she asked in a very small voice.

Father Maurizio moved closer to her, as if this were a confessional. "Young Mosconi has told me how he seduced you and how you later quarreled. In fact, the day of the spat we saw you storming out of his house, don't you remember? It must have been just after the baby was conceived. He now wishes to accept his responsibility as a Christian by providing you with a residence in the Abruzzi Mountains, where you will be comfortable while you have your baby."

"No," she cried wildly. "I won't go."

From the other side, Sergeant Cirillo seized her arm roughly, his fingernails digging into her flesh. "For someone with a reputation for brains, it's taking you a long time to understand," he snarled. "Signora Giorgina Leone Benelli is downstairs waiting to sign a complaint against you for grand larceny. As a courtesy to Signor Mosconi, she will refrain from demanding your arrest, but only if you accept his hospitality."

"But I'm not guilty of anything." Nearly surrendering to panic, she tried to get to her feet, but the two men held her arms and forced her back into the chair.

Father Maurizio lost his patience. "You are guilty of a great many things," he snapped. "And you have just one simple decision to make. Either I take you to a lodge in the mountains as the guest of Junio Mosconi, or Sergeant Cirillo takes you to jail. Choose!"

There was a long moment. The two men perched on either side of her like vultures, holding her arms. The two enlisted policemen stood at the door watching. She could feel her heart beating wildly. Think of the baby, she told herself. Do what would be best for the baby.

"Choose!" hissed the priest.

Prison sounded like a hard place to get out of. "The mountains," she said finally, and they led her away.

9.

....

"We were barfing over the gunwales when the coast of Sicily appeared." Girolamo bent down to draw a line in the dust on the hearth. "Leonida was already an acting lieutenant because his father, that's Count Massimo Leone, served under Garibaldi during the defense of Rome in '48 and his father before him had fought against the Pope when Napoleon conquered Italy. That's Ludovico Leone, and he's another story. Now when we landed in Sicily, there were enemy troops here and here."

Girolamo redefined the line in the dust, adding the forces of the Kingdom of Two Sicilies. Pierluigi's eyes glazed over, and the old man realized that his grandnephew wanted to play outside in the sunshine.

If I only had the words to tell him how it felt, he yearned. What a giant Leonida was in those days when we fought the Bourbons at Calatafimi and he led the bayonet charge that changed history forever. History doesn't change anymore. Politicians just keep making more of it.

"Afterward, we danced with all the girls." Girolamo decided to skip the Battle of Calatafimi. "After combat, there are always women around, kid. They're attracted by the blood. Like sharks."

"Uncle!" There was a shrill voice from the kitchen.

"Sì, nipotina," he said apologetically. There was a dull pain in his back as he got to his feet. Since coming to live with relatives in this damp and drafty cottage on the eastern edge of Cederna, his rheumatism had worsened. When Giorgina threw me out, I should have had a pension and a place of my own, he told himself bitterly. For fifty years I was aide and servant to a great man. Now Leonida is dying or dead, and I draw lines in the dust by the fire.

"The boy's too young for that sort of talk." Pierluigi's mother scolded. "And there's a woman come to see you."

For a moment he felt his heart beat faster, thinking that Rosaria might somehow have escaped from wherever the priest had taken her. But it was only Valeria.

"Giro, we've got to talk," said the Leone family cook. The slender gray-haired woman surveyed the squalid room with a glance and then put her arms around him.

"Have you come to take me back to the Castello?" he demanded eagerly.

"No, I've been fired too," Valeria reported. "Giorgina has cops guarding the Castello with orders to arrest us both if we set foot on the property."

"What do they say about the old man?"

"Listen," Valeria whispered urgently, drawing Girolamo down by the fire where they could talk confidentially. "I went to Rome to see the Conte, and one of the nurses at the Ospedale Militare told me that he came in suffering from some bruises, a cracked rib, and maybe a concussion. Nothing more."

"That's not enough to slow Leonida down." Girolamo was overjoyed at the news.

"I know, but when he regained consciousness, Dr. Beniolo came in and put him back to sleep with laudanum. Giorgina had him moved to a private psychiatric clinic where no one is allowed to see him."

"A madhouse?"

"Yes, and His Excellency isn't mad."

"Leonida has been crazy since the Battle of Calatafimi," declared Girolamo. He got to his feet, noticing that his rheumatism no longer hurt. "But we need him, crazy or not. Let's get him out of there!"

"Who are you?"

The night nurse was a tall, fat woman in a crisp white uniform. She looked up irritably at the crooked little man who had appeared before her desk. It was two o'clock in the morning.

"I am looking for Count Leonida Leone," said the visitor. "Where is he, per favore?"

"He is sleeping in that room." She nodded to her left. "But he is not permitted to have visitors."

"Is that what you give him to make him sleep?" The caller pointed to a tall medicine bottle on the nurse's desk.

"None of your business!" The nurse reached for the bottle, but the little old man had grabbed it first. After a glance at the label he pulled the cork out with his teeth and sniffed it. "Put that down or I will call the guardia."

"I want you to drink it."

"It's laudanum," the nurse objected. She was less imperious now, because the little man had just produced a large Colt revolver. "It will put me to sleep."

"You need your rest." Girolamo handed her the bottle.

"I can't." The nurse looked around quickly for help, but there was no one else on the ward, and the day shift would not arrive for hours. The intruder smiled pleasantly and poked his pistol between her voluminous breasts.

"Drink!" He cocked the Colt. Hastily, the nurse put the bottle to her lips.

Smiling pleasantly and pointing the gun at her heart, Girolamo watched the nurse until she fell off her chair, fifteen minutes later. When he was convinced that she was authentically unconscious, he opened Leonida's door, finding the Count stretched out beneath a woolen blanket, snoring. There was a neat white bandage on his forehead.

"Eccellenza!" Girolamo shook him roughly. "Wake up. They've taken the girl away."

Leonida moaned in his sleep, but his eyes remained firmly shut. "A baby," he muttered.

"And you'll never see it unless you get on your feet." Girolamo began slapping Leonida's cheeks. "Wake up, you old fart!"

"Fanciulla?" Leonida opened his eyes, and sat up in puzzlement. "Where is Rosaria?"

"The priest took her away, m'lord."

"You called me an old fart."

"Eccellenza, this is an insane asylum, where you have been committed by your daughter."

"Where did they take Rosaria?" There was more authority in Leonida's voice now. He rose unsteadily and opened the door and looked out at the nurses' station.

"The priest knows. Perhaps if we hit him a little, he will tell us."

Leonida seemed invigorated by the notion of hitting Don Maurizio. "I can walk. Listen, what did you do to that nurse?"

"She has had a hard day, m'lord," said Girolamo, pushing Leonida toward the exit.

IO.

. . . .

"Introibo ad altare Dei," intoned Father Maurizio. "I go unto the altar of
God." He glanced over his shoulder at the waiting congregation. There were
mostly old women and children there, since the men in Cederna rarely came
to church.

"Ad Deum qui laetificat juventutem meam," In high, boyish voices, the
altar boys chorused the response. "To God, who brings joy to my youth."

The old priest bowed to the altar, trying to clear his mind for the confiteor.
I represent this congregation before Almighty God, he reminded himself, and
I acted in the best interests of my community. Father Maurizio knelt and
struck his breast ritually.

"I confess to Almighty God, to Blessed Mary Ever Virgin, to Blessed
Michael the Archangel, to Blessed John the Baptist, to the Holy Apostles
Peter and Paul, and to all the saints, and to you, Father, that I have sinned
exceedingly in thought, word and deed. Through my fault, through my fault,
through my most grievous fault."

Should I have acted differently? I could have refused. Giorgina has no
special rights before God. He remembered the stark misery on Rosaria's face
when they drove her up into the ruggedness of the Abruzzi Mountains to the
shepherd's lodge where Junio proposed to detain her.

"Mea culpa, mea culpa, mea maxima culpa." He paused on the steps of
the altar, still trying to accommodate his conscience. I lied, he reminded
himself. I did not see Leonida, and he has almost certainly not repented of
his sins. Men like Leonida never repent. The girl will be lonely and frightened
when the baby comes.

"May Almighty God be merciful to thee, and, forgiving thy sins, bring
thee to life everlasting."

Look, Lord, you invented the Sixth Commandment, not us, Don Maurizio
launched into a spontaneous silent prayer. Leonida took this young girl to
bed and planned to acknowledge her illegitimate child as his own, and this
would have created a scandal among the faithful. So I am heartily sorry for
what we did, but I did not see any other options.

"Kyrie eleison," he proclaimed. The Lord has risen.

"Kyrie eleison," said the altar boys.

"Kyrie eleison." He paused. Outside, there was the clattering footfall of horses galloping over the cobblestones in Piazza Bixio.

"Christe eleison." The voices of the altar boys were muffled by the sound of the church doors crashing open. Christ is risen, Don Maurizio told himself. And so has Leonida Leone. No one else would knock in the doors of my church.

"Christe eleison." Don Maurizio closed his eyes. The church floor was paved with flat slabs of marble, and he could hear iron horseshoes striking stone as Leonida's mount stalked up the center aisle.

"Christe eleison?" There was no response because the people in the pews were all screaming and the altar boys had rejected martyrdom and fled into the sacristy. The priest turned and opened his eyes.

Leonida's big white mare was approaching the altar. The old man's head was bandaged, but he looked strong enough to slaughter the entire College of Cardinals. There was a naked sword in his hand and a brace of pistols at his waist. Girolamo was at the door with a shotgun in his hands, covering his master's flanks.

"Leonida, the nineteenth century has been over for some considerable time." The priest tried to keep the quiver from his voice. "Remove yourself and your animal from the house of the Lord."

Wordlessly, Leonida leaned over in the saddle and caught the priest by the hair, putting his sword to his throat.

"Lord, make it quick," the priest prayed feverishly. "Into your hands, Domine, I commend my spirit."

"Where is the girl?"

"A village called Simbruino," Don Maurizio confessed promptly. "In the mountains near Subiaco. She has not been harmed."

Leonida released him and Don Maurizio felt his knees surrender. He sat down heavily, his vestments billowing around him.

It was quickly over. Leonida turned his horse and rode down the aisle and out into the Piazza Bixio. The congregation returned fearfully to their seats. Don Maurizio got back to his feet and looked at his flock, seeing that everyone understood precisely what had happened.

"Christe eleison," he said as the altar boys scampered back from the sacristy.

"Christe eleison," they agreed as the Mass resumed. "Christ has risen."

It was sunset. Night seemed to come on quickly in the mountains, and there were long shadows slashing over the pasture from the rooftop of the lodge.

The shepherds were moving up the side of the hill and Rosaria Lombardi was watching them when she felt a faint twinge in her abdomen. It was not very strong, and quickly over, but it frightened her.

"I've got to escape." Over the past two weeks she had fallen into the habit of talking to herself for lack of companionship. An silent old woman arrived every day to empty the slop bucket and leave her food. At night the shepherds returned, but they were afraid to speak to her, and Rosaria could barely comprehend their harsh mountain dialect.

Her confinement here was Junio's idea of punishment. At first they had taken her to a big comfortable house in the village of Simbruino, but she had scratched Junio's face and tried to climb out a window. Furious, he had ordered his men to move her into the shepherd's lodge with a warning that she would stay there until she countersigned a document identifying him as the father of her child.

I can survive this, she told herself. I am a tough peasant woman. I will run away and find Sandro and Leonida. Unless Leonida is dead.

The idea was unbearable. Quickly she gathered together some salami, sweet provolone cheese, and a loaf of the hard, unsalted bread the Romans called *panioto,* putting it all into a canvas bag along with a sharp kitchen knife.

There was little else to take. She had been sleeping in a windowless back room of the lodge. There was a table of roughly hewn timber in the front room, and blankets on the mud floor where the shepherds spent their nights. They were always gone in the morning, but they never went very far from the lodge, and someone was always watching.

Bravely she hoisted her bundle but the cramp came again, low in her belly, this time a lingering presence.

It was a labor pain and a wave of fear swept over her. She had lost track of the calendar and no longer knew what day of the week it was, or what date in the month. Here in the mountains, the days all resembled one another.

She had not expected to be this frightened. The act of bearing Leonida's child had once seemed romantic, the provocative act of a socialist woman defying bourgeois morality.

Now it seemed terrifying. Every year in Cederna, she knew, a woman would die in childbirth, her legs apart, her swollen belly covered with blood, and a baby inside who would not be born. Whenever it happened the word would spread and women would grow silent for a few weeks, and refuse their husbands. Virgins stayed virgin until the memory faded, and the men would talk about it in Tommaso's father's restaurant, shaking their heads and touching their genitals for luck.

She stepped outside. Her guards were all presently busy with their sheep, driving the flock slowly up the side of the hill toward their night pasture near the shack. Rosaria edged around to the side of the building, hoping that the hut would block their view as she moved toward the main road. It was her only chance.

"Aiiiiyah!" She heard the man's voice, shouting at her in his rough Abruzzese accent, and looked up to see one of the younger shepherds sprinting up the side of the hill. "Come back!" he bellowed, waving a stick.

I'm not going back, she vowed, quickly pulling the bread knife from her sack of provisions. She climbed over the stone wall that rimmed the pasture and walked defiantly toward the road. In the distance she heard what sounded like a motorcar and wondered if Junio was already on his way to thwart her bid for freedom. Could he have been warned so soon?

"You don't go! Signora!" panted the shepherd, but Rosaria kept on walking, holding her enormous stomach until the shepherd caught up with her.

"Leave me alone!" She slashed out with the knife, grazing his forearm.

"Strega!" the man yelped, swinging his stick wildly and clubbing her on one shoulder. "Witch!" She grunted with the sudden pain and nearly fell. They both recovered their balance at the same time and grappled as he tried to get an arm around her neck and she wiggled free. Then she lost patience and slashed his left arm for a second time, feeling the blade go deep into the biceps.

"I'll kill you!" Rosaria reeled blindly away. Maddened with pain, the shepherd swung his stick brutally. Trying to defend her stomach, she spun and took the blow on her shoulder, but it knocked her to her knees, and the knife tumbled from her hand.

She curled up in a ball as the shepherd hit her again, and she could hear the shouts from the other men as they rushed to recapture her. There was the sound of tires squealing over pebbles as a motorcar bounced down over the dirt road toward them.

Then a shotgun cursed through the early-evening air. Getting to her hands and knees, Rosaria saw Leonida's Fiat roaring toward her with the barrel of Girolamo's old Sicilian *lupara* extending from the window. The old major-domo had fired into the air, but the shepherds were prudently retreating behind the stone wall. One of them threw a stone, and it bounced off the roof of the Tipo 51 Zero with a metallic thud.

"Papa, don't kill anyone!" It was Terenzio, wearing the uniform of a carabiniere sub-lieutenant. His father ignored him, storming across the field and waving a pistol at the shepherds, who were now all throwing rocks.

Rosaria tried to get to her feet, but another contraction swept through her abdomen, and she doubled up with the pain. It passed, slowly, but she felt a wetness flowing out of her.

"My God, Rosaria!" Terenzio shouted, and a second later he and his father were at her side and lifting her up. There was another lupara blast as Girolamo fired at the shepherds. Leonida's face was gray with fatigue. For the first time Rosaria looked at him and saw an old man. He'll never make love to me again, she realized.

"My water has just broken." She felt surprisingly calm. Leonida supported her as they staggered toward the Fiat. "The baby is coming soon."

The back seat of the Fiat felt soft and spacious. She cradled her belly, wondering if the baby would be born in the car. Did any of these men understand what to do? Leonida seemed to know everything else, but she suspected he would be hopeless at delivering babies.

Desperate to keep the car from leaving, the shepherds charged a second later, delivering an absolute hail of stones in the fast-fading light. In the front seat Girolamo reloaded his shotgun while Terenzio climbed behind the wheel. Stones bounced off the roof, and the windscreen on the passenger side suddenly shattered. Then, as Leonida turned to fire a warning shot, a rock the side of a walnut sailed in from the pasture and struck him on the head.

Rosaria used the last of her strength to haul him onto the seat. "Go," she screamed at Terenzio, who accelerated up to the main road, the Fiat's engine roaring as rubber wheels spun over loose gravel.

"Topo," she cried, cradling his head on her lap. "Are you all right?"

"Sì, sì, sto bene." He tried to sit up so that he could give orders. "We're taking you back to the Castello. Everything is going to be all right. Not so fast, Terenzio."

"I don't want to see Giorgina." She shook her head firmly.

"My traitorous daughter is gone," he told her. "And I've dismissed her husband. It is something I should have done a long time ago."

"Then take me home," she said. The contractions were coming steadily now, and she concentrated on each one, trying not to cry out as the pain reached its crescendo. Leonida pulled her into his arms and she clung to him while Terenzio maneuvered the car down off Junio's mountain.

The clock tower of Saint Teresa's Church had just struck three. The Piazza Bixio was dark as Terenzio Leone killed the Fiat's engine and looked at Girolamo. This is a hell of a place for a piano player, he told himself.

"Is this right?"

"It feels right to me, boy," Girolamo muttered. The Fiat drifted to a halt in an alley a short distance from the Mosconi residence.

"I'm a policeman now. I should be serving him an arrest warrant."

Girolamo got angry. "Junio kidnapped a woman under your protection and his employees assaulted your father! You have to slap him down, or he's going to take over the town."

Nervously Terenzio watched the murderous old majordomo load shells into a double-barreled shotgun. Then he followed him down the darkened street, carrying his own shotgun and a jerrican of gasoline.

Silently they took up positions on either side of Mayor Mosconi's front door. Pulling his cap down over his forehead, Girolamo shouldered his weapon and casually fired a round through one of the front windows. The roar resounded through the sleeping town, and there were screams from inside Palazzo Mosconi as Terenzio nervously shot out the other window and then sprayed the front door while Girolamo took out all the glass on the second floor.

"Go!" the old veteran commanded and Terenzio rushed up with the *benzina*. The Mayor and his family all slept in the rear of the house; by now, the Mosconi tribe should be out the back door and running for their lives. Terenzio kicked in the front door and splashed the gasoline into the vestibule.

Girolamo produced a match, and the whole front of the edifice was in flames before they reached the safety of the Fiat.

The old trooper chuckled as Terenzio eased the car quietly into the main road. There was no one behind them. "How do you feel?" he asked.

After a moment's introspection, Terenzio told the truth. "I feel absolutely wonderful."

"Doesn't it feel good? Nothing like a little mayhem to get the blood moving."

"Suppose Junio realizes it was us?"

Girolamo shook his head in despair. "Teri, he's supposed to realize it was us."

"And if he counterattacks?"

"Then we kill him." Girolamo shrugged. "And that'll feel even better."

At dawn, after nine hours of labor, Rosaria felt the baby begin to move within her. Valeria and a midwife named Caterina had been sitting with her through the night.

Leonida had been exiled to the couch in the sewing room, since the women believed that childbirth was complicated enough without a wounded general lurching around giving orders. Dr. Marco Beniolo had spent the night in the Castello to look after Leonida. The physician believed that peasant women ought to be able to have babies without his professional help, but he had grudgingly inspected Rosaria several times during the course of the night, pronouncing himself satisfied with her progress.

"Spingi, spingi!" Caterina called. "Push harder, girl, you're almost there."

Nearing the end of her strength, Rosaria bore down, and felt the infant leave her body. Immediately she began to sob, partly from relief that the hurting was over, and partly from a sudden sense of separation. She had been two for so long, and now she was only one again.

"Oh, Rosaria, it's a little boy." Valeria wiped her face with a flannel and propped her up on the pillow. "Look, he's strong and healthy. Stop crying! The Conte will be so happy."

There was a thin wail from the child, and Rosaria got her eyes focused as Caterina held up the infant for her. He was covered with mucus. His eyes were closed, and a few centimeters of umbilical cord dangled from his tummy. Rosaria gazed at his minuscule fingers, his tiny penis, his little nose, still flat from the trauma of being born.

Until this moment, she felt she had never known what love was. "Oh, please, give him to me, please."

Methodically Caterina sponged the child clean before she presented him to his mother. The baby felt fragile, almost weightless as Rosaria opened her nightgown and arranged him across her breasts so that he would be able to feel her heart.

With rapt attention she watched as her son attempted to put his fist into his mouth, and missed. With a grunt he tried again, punching himself in the nose. "You're going to be a stubborn young man," she told him, pressing her lips on his wrinkled forehead. "You come from a long line of uncompromising people. If you think your father is hard-headed, wait until your Uncle Sandro comes home from the army."

For a while there was a flurry of activity around her. Beniolo treated her to another disdainful examination, gazed at the infant without interest, and informed them all that Leonida had finally dozed off and should on no account be awakened. Valeria helped Rosaria to the toilet and then combed her hair before going downstairs to make breakfast. Caterina tidied up the room and darted off to deliver another baby on the other side of Cederna.

Suddenly Rosaria was alone. For the birth they had moved her into the master bedchamber, a room big enough to be a barn. It was beautiful, with oil paintings of Leone ancestors on the walls and a balcony overlooking Cederna, but she felt uncomfortable in the bed where Leonida had once slept with Contessa Maria Pia.

On a table next to the bed, there were framed photographs of the Leone family, the cheerful Terenzio, the loathsome Giorgina, and the gallant Achille, dressed in the uniform of a lieutenant in the Royal Italian Army.

"Oh Achille, I'm sorry," she said to the picture. "If you hadn't stayed lost so long that we thought that you were dead, then I would have waited and this would have been your baby. I'm sorry if this little brother brings you unhappiness, but I will always love your father, even if it's not the way I could have loved you."

But you're not part of my life anymore, and I have this new little person to think about. So I'm going to try to let go of you now.

The baby murmured on her breast. She tried to coax him into taking her nipple, but he seemed more interested in having a snooze. It seemed like a good idea, so she put her head on the pillow and went to sleep also. For the first time in a long time, there were no dreams.

"Eccellenza!" The doctor shook his head as the patient sat up on the couch. "You need absolute quiet. You still have a concussion and a deep scalp wound, and your ribs need time to heal. Furthermore, your blood pressure is still alarmingly high. Surely a few days in a hospital . . ."

Leonida Leone shook his head impatiently and glared at Beniolo. Girolamo claimed that Cederna's physician had been part of Giorgina's conspiracy to keep him locked up in a mental hospital. If it turns out to be true, he decided, I will have you struck from the rolls.

"Is the girl all right?" Leonida asked levelly.

"She is fine, and so is the child." The physician made a gesture of impatience. "However, there is this question of the birth certificate, which I am obliged by law to complete."

"Lombardi. The mother's name is Rosaria Lombardi."

"I know, but I was concerned about the identity of the father. A fictitious name is normally used, but Junio Mosconi has offered—"

"I am the father." Leonida was puzzled. "Didn't anyone tell you?"

"Eccellenza, a birth certificate is a legal document." Terenzio was sitting at the foot of his father's bed and Beniolo turned toward him for support, but the young man shook his head angrily.

"What you suggest is dishonorable." There was ice in Leonida's voice. "You know my name. Do me the kindness to write it on this *certificato,* and I will sign it."

There was a long silence. "I have many conflicting obligations," Beniolo said vaguely as he walked to the door. "Perhaps you should consult another physician."

"Sign that certificate!" shouted Leonida, but Beniolo ignored him and stalked away.

"I'm not sure I understand it all," Terenzio explained. "But our dear Giorgina seems to have been very thorough. First she had Sandro drafted and arranged for me to be called to active duty so neither of us could interfere. Then she got Beniolo to certify that you were impotent so that they could arrest Rosaria for slander if she identified you as the father. Junio Mosconi has filed papers claiming paternity."

"Impotent!" Leonida shouted, deciding to destroy the physician's practice at the first opportunity. "Of course our Beniolo can hardly reverse himself now. Could Giorgina have known in advance that we were going to be assaulted that day in Rome? She seems to have miraculously prepared to exploit the situation."

"I don't know," said Terenzio bluntly. "But I'm going to start my career as a policeman by finding out. What are you going to do about that birth certificate?"

"Teri, go down to Cederna and fetch Tommaso Savarino for me." Leonida climbed into his trousers and pulled a shirt over his broad shoulders. "First, I need to alter my will to include Rosaria and the baby, and then Tommaso can make me out a formal declaration of paternity. We'll sue Junio for slander unless he retracts that ridiculous document of his."

"I'll get him, Papa." Terenzio headed for the door.

"Teri?" Suddenly Leonida felt awkward in the presence of his younger son. "Teri, these geriatric passions of mine must be embarrassing for you, but this new baby changes nothing between us, you know that, don't you? There is plenty of money for all of you, and more than enough love to go around."

"I know that, Papa." Terenzio paused at the door and smiled. "Go see the baby, and then rest until I get back with Tommaso, alright?"

"Yes, but listen to me. I haven't paid enough attention to you. When all this settles down, we need to talk. We can get you out of the carabinieri if you still want to think about the Academy of Santa Cecilia and a musical career.''

"I'd like that." Terenzio nodded thoughtfully. "Perhaps I could do composition and orchestration."

"Tonight we'll have dinner, just the two of us," Leonida promised enthusiastically as Terenzio sped down the stairs.

In his bare feet Count Leone walked down the corridor from his study to the master bedroom. He paused at the door, his mind suddenly flashing back to the day when Terenzio was born. I was downstairs drinking with friends, he remembered, while Maria Pia was in labor, here in this room. After Teri was delivered, I drove into Rome and celebrated in the arms of another woman. I have been a wicked man. Not always, but sometimes. Achille would never have done such a thing, nor Terenzio.

Inside the master bedroom, Rosaria was sleeping, exhausted, lying on her side, with the baby napping against her breast. My beloved, he thought, my fanciulla, my second chance. He touched her soft auburn hair but she did not awaken, not even when he picked up the sleeping boy.

"Hello, little man," he whispered as he carried his son over to the window for a better look. "For an uninvited guest, you will sit very high at the table. I will be your father for as long as I can stay, and then you will have two strong brothers to look after you. Come and meet the family."

The child stirred and gazed at him with one half-opened brown eye as Leonida walked the length of the bedchamber. At first he felt awkward about holding the baby, but the old familiarity quickly returned.

"Here is Count Massimo Leone, my father and your grandfather." Leonida halted in front of a huge formal oil portrait. "Pope Pius the Ninth once put him in jail for insurrection against the Papal States. He was a good soldier and he taught me about geography and history. Shall we name you after him? Massimo? I like it, but we must consult your mother."

The boy began to gurgle in his father's arms. The old man patted him lightly on the back and continued. "And this is your great-grandfather, Count Ludovico Leone, who commanded a squadron of cavalry the day Napoleon's forces took Rome. It was a famous battle . . .''

Rosaria awoke reluctantly, disoriented, feeling immediately that something was missing but not knowing what it was.

"Achille?" she said in confusion, sitting up in bed and seeing a tall figure at the far end of the room talking to a picture.

"What?" Leonida turned with a smile, not having quite heard, and walked back to the bed. "Ah, young man, your mother has returned to the world of the living. Fanciulla, he's absolutely beautiful!"

"Oh, Topo, I'm so glad you're all right." She reclaimed her baby and snuggled against Leonida's chest as he put his arms around both of them. "It was awful up there on that mountain thinking you were dead. Oh, I think he's hungry.''

While Leonida watched entranced, Rosaria opened her nightgown and maneuvered one brown turgid nipple toward the baby's lips. "That's the most beautiful sight in the world," he said as the child began to suck clumsily. "I love you so much. I don't know if I ever said it, just like that, in so many words, but I wish I could be a young man again for you.''

"Oh, carissimo! You're going to make me cry," she protested. "What do you wish to call him?"

"My father's name was Massimo. I wondered, unless you had another name, whether Massimo would do?"

"Massimo is lovely. Your father's name is . . . is more than I expected."

"I am becoming conscious of my own mortality," Leonida began slowly. "Tommaso is coming up now to help me rewrite my will, and I want our Massimo to bear my family name. He was born here in the same bed as his brothers, and if it takes a short, silly ceremony to make him a legal son and a real Leone, then I think we owe him that.''

He would be Massimo Leone, she considered. A nobleman. Should I deny my child his birthright?

She was about to say that she needed to think, that there was plenty of time, when the bell in the tower of Santa Teresa's Church began to peal. Normally the bell sounded the hour and stopped, but the ringing now was insistent, and passionate.

"What's that?" Leonida rose from the bed and walked to the balcony. Little Massimo had fallen asleep, and Rosaria buttoned her nightdress and followed with the infant in her arms. "Maybe the Pope has croaked."

"What day is today?" Rosaria asked. "It's not Sunday, is it?"

"It's Friday, the twenty-third of May." Leonida frowned as he strained his ears. "I hear shouting, like a chorus of people all chanting . . . chanting what?"

With her sharper hearing, Rosaria listened intently, more curious than afraid. "Italia! Italia!" the voices were chorusing. Someone was blowing a horn.

"What does this mean?"

"I don't know." Leonida put his arm around her shoulders. "It doesn't matter.''

"Here comes the car," Rosaria observed, watching the Fiat bouncing up the dirt road from Cederna with unusual speed. Something is wrong, she realized, seeing Terenzio and Tommaso Savarino tumble out at the front entrance to the Castello.

She had just slipped a dressing gown over her shoulders when Girolamo burst in. "I don't like the news, m'lord."

An instant later he was interrupted by Terenzio, who pushed past waving a copy of a newspaper. "They've declared war!" he panted. "The King announced a declaration of war against the Austrian Empire, and the army is moving north! Papa, it's happening!''

"No!" Leonida shouted, his face going quickly red. "I had the King's word, not a fortnight ago. The bastards, the bastards, we have to counterattack. Girolamo, get my uniform!''

"Eccellenza!" Tommaso Savarino stumbled in, out of breath from dashing up a flight of stairs. "We need to form a committee.''

"The idiots!" Leonida smashed a table with his fist and Rosaria retreated to the bed, hugging little Massimo against her breasts. I've never known him like this, she told herself. He's out of control.

"Topo, be calm," she pleaded.

"I've seen what those guns are doing on the Western Front. Those fools will kill a whole generation of young men and win nothing worth having. They cannot feed my sons into that meat grinder! No!''

Then he stopped talking, abruptly, as if some overpowering notion had just occurred to him. "Tell Massimo . . ." he said in a normal voice, turning toward Rosaria. He hesitated, looking puzzled, took a deep breath, and fell over backward like a dead tree.

"Topo!" Rosaria screamed. Leonida lay spread-eagled on the smooth varnished oak floor. His face was turning purple. He looked a thousand years old.

"Don't die, Topo! Don't die!" she sobbed.

Tommaso knelt by the old man's side, touching his neck and then holding his pocket watch beneath Leonida's nose to see if condensation formed on the burnished gold. "He's gone." The lawyer shook his head. "He's not breathing.''

"M'lord!" Girolamo threw himself on Leonida's chest.

"Papa, don't leave us," Terenzio groaned. "The world is going crazy, and we don't know what to do.''

"He's gone," repeated Tommaso, and the baby began to cry.

Book

Four

1915—1917

1.

. . . .

"Oh, sweet man," she cried out as the moment again took possession of her. "You sweet man!"

"Anfi!" He pinned her to the bed with his hands on her wrists, captured by that special wildness he had only ever shared with her. The moment passed between them and he groaned, collapsing with his head on her breasts.

The sheet was tangled and soaked with perspiration. After a time they drew apart, exhausted. Motionless and naked, Anfi gazed at the blades of the silent fan that swirled the air above them and then closed her eyes. Feeling his usual post-coital restlessness, Achille sat up and touched the beads of perspiration on her belly. After Anfi, he decided as he ran his hands over the rich brownness of her skin, every European woman will seem pale.

"I find such pleasure in you." This is more of a carnal friendship than a love affair, he told himself, but it is still wonderful. Will I ever find anyone I like as well? Rosi and I might have made love like this, but it isn't ever going to happen, and the time has come to stop thinking about it. My father knows what Rosi is like in bed, but I don't suppose he will ever favor me with a description.

"You make me so wild," she whispered. "I am always ashamed afterward."

"You are the only woman I have ever known to whom it could happen more than once."

"I am fortunate it can happen at all. In this country, little girls are usually . . . circumcized." In her lightly accented English, she stumbled over the unfamiliar word.

"Little girls are what?"

She guided his fingers to a soft place between her legs. "This is removed in order to make a woman less lascivious. But my father was stationed at the Foreign Ministry in Constantinople when I was little, so the operation was never performed."

"I'm glad." With a shudder, Achille added female circumcision to the list of barbarisms the Italian Government would abolish.

"I am glad too." She smiled at him, and blushed. "Now that you have become my friend."

There were footsteps in the corridor. It was the middle of the night, and Achille tensed; their relationship was highly irregular, illegal in Italian eyes and a capital crime under Koranic law. Anfi quickly covered her body with a robe while Achille retreated behind the door.

"A servant must have heard me cry out," Anfi whispered. "I shall say it was a peculiar dream."

It was Meeya, one of the Sudanese girls, and she passed Anfi an envelope with a murmured explanation.

Anfi shut the door and handed the message to Achille. "An Italian soldier brought this to the front gate."

"Please return immediately." Achille recognized Guido's scrawl.

"What does it mean?"

"I'm not sure. Perhaps Italy has declared war on Austria." He felt a coldness in his body, although war had been expected since the beginning of May. These days at the officers' mess they talked of little else.

"This does not please you?"

"My father has been concerned that changes in military technology will make the casualty rate very high," he conceded. "And I have been worried about tackling another war before we have finished our job here, but . . . well, it is just something we will have to do. And we will succeed, I'm sure of it."

"Your nation has gone mad." There was no anger in her voice, but Anfi spoke with great clarity. "It began when you invaded us, and now you want to fight half of Europe. You Italians make good wine and lovely operas. Why do you pretend to be Prussians?"

Achille shook his head, irritated that Anfi should reproduce all his father's arguments so glibly. "Look, there is a large territory called Trentino in northern Italy inhabited by Italian-speaking people but under Austrian control. It is part of our inheritance, and we mean to redeem it."

"Is it worth a war?"

"What's worth a war is the defense of democracy," he insisted, although he was only half-convinced. "If Britain and France are defeated, German militarism will spread from the Urals to the Atlantic, and poor little Italy could hardly hope to survive as a free country."

"Britain and France? So you will defend two colonialist powers in the name of democracy?"

"Oh, Anfi, the Germans are colonialists too." Achille tried to back away from the argument. "They just aren't very good at it."

"So you will go home to fight the Central Powers?" There was a catch in her throat, and she walked to the window and looked out into the garden. "You made love so fiercely tonight and pushed so hard inside of me. Did you want to make me pregnant and leave something of yourself behind?"

"You misread my body's message." Achille said what he had been thinking all evening. "I can't let you go, war or no war. I want you to come back with me. I want to marry you."

She looked at him hard for a moment. Then she sighed and reached up to caress his face with her fingers. "That's impossible."

"Nothing is impossible. We could be married privately here according to the rites of your people and then go to England for a European marriage."

"Achille, we are wonderful as lovers, but it would be a mistake to marry. I am a woman of color and older than you. I would be scorned in Italy."

"Anfi, I am the son of a wealthy and famous man. You would be my wife, and someday, my countess. No one would dare scorn you."

"How could I go to Italy and surround myself with the people who are raping my country? Oh, Achille, we speak English together and your lovely Irish accent helps me to forget who and what you are."

Achille felt ready to explode. It had never occurred to him that she might refuse.

"What Italy and Libya have done to one another is one thing. What you and I could mean to one another is something else. You were never meant to be my Butterfly. I am not your Lieutenant Pinkerton."

"Achille, I loved my husband very dearly. Not the way I love you, because there was not the same passion between us. But he gave me a beautiful son and I will always treasure his memory. You never asked how he died."

"It seemed indecorous to ask. You said he was old."

"He was not that old. When he heard the guns of your ships at the beginning of the invasion, he took his rifle and went with the other men to defend Benghazi. He was killed by cannon fire from your ships."

"I'm sorry." Instinctively, he released her and walked away.

"Go home, Achille," she whispered, and he realized that she was crying. "Go home to the woman you really love. Did you know that you sometimes say her name in your sleep?"

"Whose name?" He already knew the answer. Christ, I have been sleeping in her bed and dreaming of my father's mistress!

"Go marry your Rosy, whoever she is," Anfi told him. She turned from the window, and Achille could see there were tears on her cheeks. "You only love me when you're awake, and that's not enough."

"Anfi!"

"Please, you have exhausted me." She stumbled toward the bed. "I want to sleep."

At four in the morning, Achille Leone returned to the apartment he shared with Guido Rosselli.

Strangely agitated, the Venetian was pacing through the living room in an old dressing gown. Through the open door, Achille could see into his friends's bedchamber where a young Arab whore was sprawled on her stomach, her head beneath the pillow and the sheet tangled between her bare legs.

"Now that it's happened, I'm afraid." Achille spoke first.

"You? Afraid?"

"I'm afraid, yes. Naturally, I support the government's decision, but a war with Austria isn't going to be like chasing bedouin around the desert. This will be serious fighting, and . . . it's just, damn, we have this beautiful battalion, the best men in the army, and we're going to get a lot of them killed. I hate that.''

"Achille, listen . . .''

"Aren't you afraid? Don't you have any normal emotions?''

"Yes, I'm afraid. Of course I'm afraid.'' Guido seemed impatient.

"So when do we leave?''

"Nobody knows. Adamo says there are no units available to replace us yet, and if they pulled us off the perimeter now, the Senusi would storm Benghazi. He thinks we'll be here for the summer.''

"You got me back here in the middle of the night because we might leave in four months?''

"That's not why I sent for you.'' His face pale in the lamplight, Guido crossed the room and took Achille's arm. There were letters in his hand, and Achille saw that one of them bore the royal crest, meaning a communication from the royal household.

It hit him like a bullet in the chest. A letter from the King could only mean one thing.

"My father?''

"It was a stroke. He went instantly.''

"Oh, God! Papa!'' His head spinning, he stumbled forward and might have fallen had Guido not wrapped his arms around him. "Oh, Papa! And I wasn't there where I might have done some good.''

"This wasn't your fault,'' Guido assured him. "Come and sit on the balcony. I'll get you a drink.''

Feeling leaden, Achille allowed himself to be led to a chair near the balustrade. Guido put a glass before him. Papa's gone, he forced himself to realize. He was only seventy-four and he died with a coldness between us over Rosaria. I wasn't there when it happened, and I wasn't there for the funeral. I have lost him. I am alone now.

Damn Rosaria! If she hadn't convinced him he was nineteen again, the old man might have taken better care of himself.

"I'm sorry.'' Guido lit the hurricane lantern and set it on the table between them, together with Achille's flask. "He was the last of the giants.''

"Thank you. I . . . I . . .'' Achille's voice failed him.

"Don't try to talk. I remember how it was when my father died. And I didn't even like my father.''

In the bedroom, the Arab whore awoke and began to sob, her thin body racked by some private sadness. Ignoring her, Guido pushed the flask across the table. "Drink,'' he commanded. "Whiskey is made for moments like this.''

Achille nodded dumbly and drank from the flask his dead father had stolen a long time ago from the Archbishop of Palermo. The Arab girl cried for a while, and then went back to sleep. Without speaking, the two men sat together on the balcony and watched the sun come up over Africa.

2.

. . . .

"Beate sponde." Achille remembered an old poem by Giacomo Leopardi as the ancient troop transport lumbered into the harbor of Naples. "O happy shore, I've come again to see you."

There was a soft September breeze coming in off Vesuvius and a band on the quayside played the national anthem. The Royal Navy troopship *Principe Amadeo* scraped its rusty hull against the pier and all the soldiers crowded over to the gunwales, listening to the music. Most of them were crying.

"This is embarrassing," Guido grumbled. "You quoting poetry and the men all bawling. I can't imagine this happening with a battalion of Germans sailing into Bremerhaven."

"Oh, Guido, it's been almost four years." Achille watched sailors throwing hawsers onto the quay, thinking how much his life had changed. Terenzio was now the family's first policeman. Sandro Lombardi was at the front, fighting for a government he would prefer to overthrow. Rosaria had become the mother of his illegitimate half-brother. And Giorgina had been exiled from the Castello Leone.

And Leonida Leone was dead.

He knew that the full impact would not hit him until he was home. I'll go into his study, he thought, and he won't be there. Damn! When I left, he was in perfect health. Who is to blame for this? That mysterious mob of assassins? Or my witch of a sister? Or Rosaria? Or did the two women wear him down with their absurd quarrel?

There was a bump, and the old troopship came to rest. There were families along the shore, cheering and waving Italian flags. On the wharf, there was a photographer setting up his tripod.

The sailors lowered a causeway, but the exit was immediately blocked by a platoon of military police led by a hard-faced carabiniere captain.

"Signor Conte?" The captain saluted while his men prevented the Lupi di Lazio from disembarking.

"What can I do for you?" It was the first time anyone had addressed him as "Conte," the title he had inherited from Leonida.

"General Adamo is waiting to see you on shore, sir," announced the carabiniere captain. "We will take your battalion under guard to the trains, and you can join your men there for a departure in thirty minutes."

"Under guard?" Achille frowned. "These men are heroes, not convicts, and they want to see their relatives."

"There will be desertions if we let them mingle with the crowd," the captain insisted. "They know they're headed for the front, and this will be the last chance they have."

"My men do not desert," snapped Achille angrily. "Have you heard about the Lupi di Lazio Infantry Battalion?"

"Yes," the captain shot back. "Have you heard about the Austrian Army?"

Achille understood the situation. There had been awful rumors of mutinies, of officers being murdered in their sleep, even of authentic decimations where the Military Police had lined up entire companies that had faltered in battle and shot every tenth man.

Ignoring the carabinieri, Achille climbed up on a capstan and raised his hand for attention. "Boys, listen to me," he shouted. "You have fifteen minutes to see your people and then you need to board that train. Anyone who goes absent without leave will disgrace me and the battalion. Do I have your word of honor?"

"Allah Akbar!" Ever since that famous first battle at Sidi Osman, this had been their battle cry. Obstinately, the carabinieri tried to hold their ground, but the veterans of Cyrenaica dumped two of them into the harbor and pushed the others aside as they swarmed ashore. The Lupi di Lazio were home.

"My young friend, welcome back." Speaking in an undertone, General Frederico Adamo took Achille's arm and led him a few steps away from where the officers of the Lupi di Lazio were assembling while a photographer focused his camera. "There is so much to tell you."

"Could you start with my father's death?" Achille demanded quickly. As a brand-new brigadier general, Adamo had been transferred to the Army General Staff in Rome, where he was in a position to know all the gossip.

Adamo spoke as if reciting from a report. "Your father was concerned about the army's preparedness for this war. After an audience with His Majesty, during which he had received reassurances on this subject, he was attacked outside the palace by a crowd of anti-war extremists. We were all, naturally, horrified when he died some weeks later."

Achille nodded silently. This was the same story he had received from Bruno and Giorgina, although Terenzio had written a far more complicated and troubling version of events.

"What are our orders, sir?"

"First of all, we're raising the Lupi di Lazio Battalion to regimental status, but keeping the present cadre of officers and noncoms," Adamo told him.

"You and your deputy go to lieutenant colonel and major, respectively, and we'll need your recommendations about promotions for your junior officers."

"We're a regiment?" Achille was too stunned to take it all in. "I'm being promoted again?"

"You're the youngest lieutenant colonel in the army," Adamo told him. "And you command what is now the Seventy-seventh Infantry Regiment. We're giving you two thousand more men and a few days in Rome to get yourself organized. Then you'll move to Udine for assignment to the Comando Supremo."

Achille nodded with satisfaction. Udine was a small provincial town on the Austrian border; the Leone family had stopped there overnight once on their way to Vienna. Terenzio was assigned to the carabiniere station there, and just a few miles out of town was the punishment battalion where Sandro Lombardi was serving. Achille had already intervened once through the bureaucracy to get his boyhood friend released, but Sandro had promptly belted a sergeant and got himself sent back to the punishment battalion. He and Terenzio would have to work together on the project of saving Sandro from himself.

"I see the photographer's ready for us, sir." Achille looked to see the officers of the Lupi di Lazio posing before the camera. The rusty hull of the *Principe Amadeo* served as a backdrop.

"After you, Colonel Leone," said Adamo.

In his heart, Achille found that this promotion did not excite him much, although he knew Guido would be ecstatic about becoming a major. Had things gone differently, he would be now working at the University of Rome, designing hydraulic pumps for irrigation systems. And living with Rosaria Lombardi.

With a sigh he joined his officers for the photograph, remembering how the bedouin believed that a *macchina fotografica* had the power to steal a man's soul.

Will this war steal all our souls? He gazed at the young men he would soon lead into battle against the Austrian Army. Some of them looked jubilant, innocently happy to be back on Italian soil. Others were pretending to be bored, while a few of the younger lieutenants seemed frightened by what lay ahead of them.

It is not unreasonable to be scared, he admitted to himself as he took his place in their midst. Before this war is over, most of us are going to be dead, the jubilant, the bored, and the frightened alike.

"Could you all smile?" the photographer pleaded as he ducked beneath a black blanket to look at his subjects.

"Smile, lads," muttered Achille, and they all smiled obediently into the camera.

· · ·

"Where are we?" Guido Rosselli awoke from a nap, gazing through a dirty train window at the passing scenery.

"Near Rome, and it's awful." Achille studied the panorama of shacks and shanties as the train chugged into a station on the outskirts of the capital. "The poverty here is appalling. It never used to be this bad. The peasants must be fleeing the countryside and flooding into these slum-cities to look for work."

"This war is going to involve sacrifices from everybody." Impoverished peasants did not interest Guido much. With a yawn, he opened *Il Mattino*, the Naples daily paper, putting his boots on the seat opposite him in defiance of railway regulations. "Speaking of bothersome peasants, there is a rumor that your family estate is now controlled by a pretty proletarian who was one of your father's lady friends. None of my business, Comandante, but if you want help, ask for it."

"It's an awkward situation." Achille was not sure how to explain it all to Guido. "Before my father died, he created a workers' council of some kind to run his farming operations in tandem with a peasant woman named Rosaria Lombardi. He also seems to have given her a child. My sister and brother-in-law bitterly resent Rosaria, although Terenzio supports her fully. So this is not quite a fight among strangers, and I have exactly three days to sort it out."

The train stopped for a moment at some anonymous suburban station, jerked forward again, as if indecisive about the wisdom of continuing the voyage. A ragged man with wild eyes appeared outside their window, selling fava beans in a vinegar-and-oil sauce, and he broke into an awkward trot as the train picked up speed.

"Is Terenzio in love with her?" demanded Guido suspiciously. "Difficult to imagine a carabiniere in love, but I suppose it must happen."

"We have all been in love with her," muttered Achille. "That's the problem."

"Down with her panties and up with her knees," advised Guido as he turned the pages of his newspaper. "Teach her some respect for the gentry."

Achille glared at him. Sometimes Guido could be painfully insensitive. "It's something I should have done years ago. Now it would seem like incest." He opened a book in the hope that Guido would take the hint and drop the matter.

"Bah! I always screwed my father's mistresses. It brings a family together."

"Incest brings a family together?" This is my closest friend. Achille winced inwardly. But he is a fucker and I am a lover and there are things he will never understand.

"Madre di Dio!" Guido exclaimed suddenly, folding his paper over and showing Achille an advertisement. "Look at that. How do you suppose it works?"

"For a more beautiful bosom," proclaimed the title over two line sketches of the same woman. In the first frame, she looked flat-chested and sad. In the second, she was smiling after having been powerfully endowed by the artist. Reading the text, Achille discovered that persons having bosoms requiring embellishment were requested to send five lire to a post-office box in Palermo.

"I don't suppose it does work." He pictured Rosaria, remembering the time she had shown herself to him naked, and felt an uncomfortable warmth in his loins.

"My future is settled," Guido joked. "I will buy one, whatever it is, and start up my own business, going from town to town enlarging bosoms."

"You'd go broke in Italy," Achille counseled. "Perhaps you should emigrate to America."

"Ah, Comandante," Guido sighed, his eyes resting on the twin with the sumptuous bosom. "It has been such a long time since my last woman."

"About a week, by my count. Didn't you disappear somewhere on our last night in Benghazi?"

"Caro mio, Arab girls are not what I require. At last we are home in Italy, where we have the best musicians, the best painters, the best cooks!"

"The worst politicians?"

"Ah, but the best whores in all the world. And of all the whores in Italy, the most magnificent are to be found in a brothel directly opposite the Sistine Chapel, doubtless because of the sanctifying presence of the Holy Pontiff. Shall I give you the address?"

"No, if I have trouble finding it, I shall ask His Holiness."

"How would the Pope know?" Guido exclaimed. "With all those nuns, he would hardly need to cross the street, would he? It is Via Santa Agatha, number thirty-nine."

"Enough! Guido, I can organize my own fun."

"You are good at organizing battles, my friend," His mood sobering, Guido shook his head. "But when it comes to fun, you are a disaster."

The coal-powered troop train finally snorted into the Rome Stazione Termine and Achille Leone swung out from the carriage door, scanning the crowd for his relatives. There were thousands of people milling about on the platform, but in the melee he could identify no one from Cederna.

"There are my folks," shouted Guido Rosselli. "Come on, I want you to meet my sister Crissi. You're going to marry her."

"What?"

"Don't worry, I'll pay for the wedding. We can work out the details later." When the train slowed to a quick march, Guido jumped down and dragged Achille across the platform to meet a plump gray-haired woman who was frantically waving an Italian flag at them. Standing by her mother's side, Cristina Rosselli turned out to be an extraordinarily handsome girl of twenty.

Guido had been showing him photographs of Cristina for years, but Achille was unprepared for the pale, almost translucent quality of her skin and the classical perfection of her features. Her body was so slender it seemed almost fragile, and her light blond hair was cut boyishly short. She seemed terrified of him.

"Buon giorno, Signor Conte." Guido's mother embarrassed them all with an elaborate curtsy, but Achille salvaged the situation by kissing her hand with equal ceremony.

I've got to get used to being Count Leone, he told himself, turning to Cristina with a smile. "Hello, your brother says we're going to get married. Would this afternoon suit you?"

"I think you should know that I'm a Jewess." Cristina stared at him with gray-green eyes.

"You're not Jewish." Signora Rosselli recoiled from her daughter in horror and then turned entreatingly to Achille. "Our ancestors . . . she's just having a crisis."

The whole family is demented, Achille thought. It's not just Guido.

"Crissi, what's the matter?" Guido was concerned. "Achille knows all about us."

"She wants to join the Red Cross and serve at the front," Guido's mother exploded. "Can you imagine our Cristina, who faints at the sight of blood, nursing a bunch of peasants with their arms and legs blown off?"

"There's a hospital in Udine," Cristina told her brother. "They've offered me a post there, and I would be close to you."

"You're too delicate," said Signora Rosselli. "Your health! It's out of the question."

"You're coming with us," shouted Guido. "It's settled."

"Signora, it will be fine," Achille reassured the old woman. "Nursing is a wonderful contribution for Cristina to make. Guido and I will be stationed nearby, and we will look after her."

"Oh, it's an awful war." The Rosselli matriarch crumbled with grief as both her children put their arms around her. "They've been bombing Udine. You could all be killed."

Achille turned away, embarrassed, and found himself face-to-face with his sister and brother-in-law. Giorgina looked pale, and there were more lines in her face than he remembered. She wore a flowing lavender dress and an ornate feathered hat, but still gave the impression of being as friendly as a field howitzer. Bruno had put on weight, but there are men who are meant to be fat and Bruno was one of them.

"Ciao," he said simply, briefly hugging Giorgina and feeling her body pulling away from him. He shook hands with her husband. "How are you both? Sorry not to have been here to help with the arrangements for the funeral."

"It was a beautiful service," Giorgina assured him. "King Vittorio Emanuele and Queen Elena attended, and His Holiness sent an archbishop to deliver the elegy.''

Achille winced, knowing what his father would have said about a prelate in scarlet robes preaching a homily at his funeral. "Listen, we have some problems to sort out, and not very much time.''

"We ought to wait for Junio,'' Bruno Benelli advised him cheerfully. "He should be here any minute.''

"What's Junio got to do with anything?''

"He's our adviser,'' Giorgina announced. "And he's an important man now. You should see how elegant his new home is. Did you know the socialists torched the old Mosconi house?''

"The socialists?'' Achille shook his head impatiently. In fact, the mysterious burning of the Mosconi residence was an issue he intended to raise with Girolamo and Terenzio at the earliest opportunity. "Listen, I want to meet with the two of you for dinner tomorrow at the Castello. I have seventy-two hours to get this mess resolved.''

"Then get rid of Rosaria and that horrid child,'' Giorgina suggested.

Achille was about to reply when he was confronted with the truly unwelcome sight of Junio Mosconi making his way through the crowd and waving his cane to attract their attention. The Mayor's son wore a semi-military suit with black leather boots and a high-peaked aviator's cap.

"Welcome back.'' Junio extended his hand in greeting, but Achille ignored it.

"Mosconi, if half of what I hear about your behavior is true,'' he growled, "you are lucky not to have been arrested for kidnapping. Hauling that young woman off in the ninth month of her pregnancy is the most reprehensible—''

"Ah, Signor Conte.'' Junio tapped Achille lightly on the shoulder with his unshaken hand. "What can I say? A disagreement between lovers.''

"What lovers?''

"The beautiful Rosirosalina and I had . . . oh, sorry, Achille, but if you go off and leave ripe fruit dangling on the vine, you must not complain when someone else plucks it.''

"What is this man talking about?'' Achille shouted.

"Didn't you know?'' Bruno looked down at the platform's cement floor to avoid meeting Achille's eyes. "Junio has acknowledged his paternity in the case of the Lombardi girl.''

"His paternity!'' Achille felt the last vestiges of his self-control disappear. "Do you seriously believe that Father would share a woman with this creature? Or that Rosaria would allow herself—''

"We have medical documents, Achille, proof positive.'' Junio smirked. "I will bring the papers to the Castello.''

In a flash, Achille drew his service automatic and slapped the barrel against

Junio's forehead, seizing the younger Mosconi's jacket with his free hand. "If you ever set foot on my property, I will feed your body to the pigs," he thundered, and then pushed Junio over backward, sending him sprawling on the cement floor.

"Achille!" Giorgina screamed. Around them the crowd began to make room while the junior officers of the Lupi di Lazio moved up to support their commanding officer.

"There will be a conference tomorrow evening at the Castello," Achille roared at Giorgina and Bruno. "Be there!"

"Isn't it nice to be home?" Guido took the pistol out of his friend's hand and guided him away from the stunned Mosconi. "Crissi won't marry you this afternoon since you seem to be in a bad mood, but we have negotiated a compromise agreement involving lunch."

"Lunch, yes, let's have lunch." Achille felt a measure of sanity return slowly as he walked back to the Rosselli family. Signora Rosselli had dried her eyes and was smiling bravely. Cristina was shaking uncontrollably. He took her arm, but it only seemed to make matters worse, so he let her go, and Guido carried them all off to a restaurant.

3.

. . . .

"You can't hide here in the kitchen." Girolamo proclaimed the obvious. "Put on a pretty dress. Then go into the salotto and talk to him nicely."

Trying to still the tumult within her, Rosaria pushed her papers aside and laid her head on the kitchen table, dreams and memories cascading through her mind. "I will consider being minimally nice to Achille once he has signed an agreement with Tommaso," she announced.

"No, that's the wrong attitude. Go and talk to him," Girolamo insisted.

And what, she wondered, do we talk about? Almost four years have gone by. I was just a girl when he went away, foolish and infatuated with my handsome lieutenant. The last time we saw each other I took off my nightgown and threw myself naked into his arms. Then I went to bed with his father and we made Massimo. What am I supposed to say now? Awfully sorry, my dear, but you were supposed to be dead?

"I don't think I can face him."

"Rosaria, whatever has happened, the two of you are old friends. When you were children, we all used to worry . . ."

"Well, you can stop worrying." She was suddenly furious. "They've got Sandro in a punishment battalion at the front where he could be killed at any minute. Our workers haven't had a proper salary in months, and Giorgina wants to fire us all. None of our problems are going to be resolved by me falling into Achille's arms, assuming he wanted me, which he doesn't."

The unaccustomed harshness in her voice awakened Massimo, who had been sleeping in his cot by the corner of the wood stove. Repentant, she soothed the startled infant in her arms.

"I'm going to feed him."

"What shall I tell Achille?"

"Tell him we've got a lawyer. He needs to negotiate with Tommaso Savarino." She carried little Massimo out of the kitchen. There was a fig tree at the foot of the garden, and she sat down on the grass beneath it, unbuttoning her dress and giving Massimo her breast.

Thirstily the child began to suck as Rosaria tried to sort out the situation in her mind. Getting Leonida to create the Workers' Council had taken her several years of persuasion, but now that the former master of Castello Leone was in his grave, there was no way of compelling anyone to respect the council's authority.

With Terenzio serving in Udine and Achille still in Benghazi, Giorgina had claimed plausibly that she was legally entitled to manage the Leone Estate. Rosaria and the workers had refused to accept Giorgina's dictatorship and a stand-off had begun. The peasants controlled the land, but since they had no hard cash, they were reduced to eating vegetables out of the field and slaughtering animals to put food in their stomachs.

We can't survive much longer without real money, she realized, but I can't let Achille see how desperate we've become, or else . . .

"Rosi?"

Her blood ran cold for a moment because the voice from the kitchen door sounded so much like Leonida's. Then she looked up and saw Achille. He was tan and fit, but thinner than ever. She wondered if he got enough to eat in the army.

"Oh, oh, it's . . . it's you." Embarrassed, she covered her breast with Massimo's cotton blanket and put the infant over her shoulder to pat the wind out of him. "I'm glad you're home and not hurt."

"I wish it could be under happier circumstances." Achille seemed ill at ease. He wore a formal gray-green uniform with medals and pips, with a short ceremonial sword at his side. It all looked uncomfortable. "Ah, well, how is . . . everything? And this is our little man? How old is he and what are we to call him?"

"He is nearly four months, and your father named him Massimo," she said timidly, since this was dangerous terrain.

"He has Grandfather Massimo's nose, so I guess it's a good name for him. Can I hold him?"

He seemed friendly, so she surrendered her son and quickly did up the buttons on her dress. The baby seemed happy in Achille's arms, and she observed that he held the infant with a certain domesticity. If he liked babies, he would soon start wanting some of his own.

"I was worried that you might have believed what Giorgina and Junio have been saying," she told him quickly. "Whatever else has gone wrong between us, I wanted you to accept Massimo as your father's child."

"He is my father's child?" The question seemed sincere.

"Yes," she breathed.

"Then I believe you. Terenzio wrote that Papa regarded the baby as his, and the matter is settled as far as I am concerned."

"Thank you." For a long time, neither of them spoke. Achille sat down on a tree stump and held Massimo on his knees. The mutual embarrassment was heavy.

"I feel awkward," he admitted finally. "I always imagined that when we met again, there would be a million things to say. In fact, whenever I saw something interesting in Libya, I would rehearse in my mind how someday

I would describe it to you. And now . . . well, I'm told I have to negotiate with your lawyer."

"Oh, no, it doesn't have to be like that," she said quickly. She had resolved not to apologize for anything, but the words began to tumble out. "I'm sorry you were hurt by what happened. But a man came from the army and said you were dead. Then months and months went by and your father searched for you from one end of the Mediterranean to the other. When he came home, we comforted each other in the only way we could."

"I understand," he said, but she could tell from his voice that he didn't. "I just wish . . . you could have waited a little longer."

"If you could only have found some way of getting word to us that you were alive."

"Rosaria, I was rescued by a tribe of Arabs who detoured a thousand kilometers into the Sahara Desert before taking me to the coast. There weren't any telephones along the way, and if anyone had suspected I was an Italian, they would have cut my throat. There was no way I could have informed anyone. Don't you think I suffered with the knowledge that you and Father were grieving?"

"You didn't suffer very long, did you," she lashed back instinctively. "You could have taken leave to come home and talk, and we could have worked things out. Instead you cut me off as if I were your worst enemy and jumped into bed with a native woman."

"Leave her out of this!"

"Why?" she shouted at him. "Is there one set of rules for peasant girls and another set for officers in the Royal Army?"

"Calm down," he ordered, and she heard the tone of command in his voice. "It's just the shock of losing my father. I've been given a half dozen different accounts of what happened, and I don't know what to believe."

"I'm sorry." She put her face in her hands and turned away from him, not wanting him to see that her eyes were brimming with tears. "I just want you to know that I cannot bring myself to regret being loved by your father. He was a wonderful man and . . . what have they told you about the attack outside the royal palace?"

"Terenzio has some crazy idea about a plot, but the police say that the bunch of you were assaulted by a gang of left-wingers who may have mistaken Father for someone else."

"Terenzio is right. There was a conspiracy." The baby was fussing and she took him back, although Achille seemed momentarily reluctant to surrender his little half-brother. "Leonida was in touch with the Socialist Party about keeping Italy out of the war. He . . . he had even been talking about an insurrection. The men who attacked us that day were interventionists in league with—"

"My father would never have rebelled against the King." Achille shook his head vehemently and got to his feet in irritation. "For all his radical talk, he had been a lieutenant general in the Italian Army and an ambassador in the diplomatic service. He didn't always like the system, but he worked within it."

"Those men were war hawks working with Giorgina and Bruno and Junio Mosconi!" Rosaria hissed at him.

"Look, my sister is a hard, rapacious woman, and she was anxious to avoid a scandal over you. But she would never have conspired to injure our father."

Rosaria sat up on her haunches, determined to make him understand. "Giorgina paid those men to wound your father, and they had orders to murder me. With my baby still inside of me. Then she had Sandro arrested while Junio held me prisoner in the Abruzzi Mountains. She must have known in advance what was going to happen because she was ready to move the moment Leonida was incapacitated."

"No!"

"Yes! At the end, even your father began to suspect the truth," she insisted. "Why do you think he made her leave the Castello Leone? Because she tried to have me killed!"

"That's not true," Achille shouted at her. "You must never say such a thing to me again. Never! Do you hear? Never!"

"As you wish, Signor Conte!" She spat out the words one by one, as if they were curses.

"Well, what are we going to do about the farm? I've got to leave tomorrow."

"Talk to my lawyer," she shrieked at him and Achille strode away furiously, his ceremonial sword slapping against his thigh.

"If I may direct your attention to paragraph six?"

"Oh Tommaso, please!" Still exhausted from the bruising encounter with Rosaria, Achille poured himself another glass of Cederna 1901 bianco and offered the bottle to his table companions. Bored and getting drunk, Guido nodded, but the abstemious Bruno Benelli shook his head, and Giorgina refused even to acknowledge the gesture.

"What?" The lawyer raised one quizzical eyebrow as he looked up from the sheaf of papers before him. Tommaso was a boyhood friend and they had been classmates at the University of Rome, but today he represented eight hundred and eighty-seven employees of the Leone agricultural estate, and he was giving nothing away.

"Do you want a glass of wine?"

"When we have concluded our business."

"Fighting the Arabs was easier than negotiating with you." Achille tried to lighten the moment, but nobody laughed. "But I think we have a basic agreement, don't you?"

"We have nothing of the kind," Giorgina interrupted. "I want Rosaria off this property. Ever since you made her Father's secretary, she has poisoned our lives."

"The members of the Workers' Council will never again serve under Giorgina or Bruno," Tommaso repeated stolidly. "Any attempt to reimpose Benelli authority over this estate will be met with a strike."

"Fine, we'll fire them all!" Giorgina shouted.

"I could not be responsible for any acts of sabotage or violence committed by eight hundred angry peasants." Tommaso was clearly uncomfortable making threats, but there was no mistaking his meaning.

"Please listen. We have an agreement and it will work," Achille intervened quickly. He had to be tough with everyone, or Giorgina and Rosaria would feud forever while the land decayed and the peasants starved.

"I'm not sure . . ." The lawyer shuffled through his papers.

"It's simple. Bruno and Giorgina will make their residence in Rome, and Giorgina will remain off the property in accordance with my father's wishes."

"How can you do this to me?" Giorgina was livid. She leaped to her feet, sweeping her dishes to the floor. "Father was not in his right mind at the end. That witch had twisted his mind. And it wasn't those anarchists on the street who sent him to his grave, because his injuries were minor. He died of a stroke, brought on by the strain of trying to perform bedroom athletics for the benefit of an adolescent strumpet."

"What finally killed him was a rock bounced off his head by one of Junio's employees," Tommaso corrected her quietly.

"He should have stayed in the hospital and let Dr. Beniolo take care of him."

"Shut up, Giorgina!" Achille got unsteadily to his feet, feeling the combined effects of rage and alcohol. "Terenzio says that you would have been disinherited had Father lived another day. What killed him was the strain of that perpetual war between you and Rosaria."

"I hate you!"

"And I hate you," he bellowed back. "But you're going to obey me, like it or not. Here are my orders. Bruno continues to manage our family investment portfolio, and he can come out here a day or two a week to market our produce and represent the corporation in the acquisition of seed and supplies. He will keep the books and offer financial advice generally, in return for which he receives a percentage of the profits. Girolamo remains on full pay as my counselor. Valeria runs the Castello itself, and Rosaria Lombardi continues as general administratrix of farming operations, to be compensated on the basis of the formula we have negotiated. And you, sorella mia, stay the hell off my land."

"You bastard!" Giorgina began sobbing as she staggered away from the table. She was bent over double, as if kicked in the stomach. "You're signing away our birthright."

Indecisive, Bruno Benelli rose to follow his wife, but Achille seized his arm.

"Bruno, I have to go and fight in this lovely war your interventionist chums have organized. We have some complex finances, and I think I need you to handle them in my absence, but if you walk out that door, I'm going to find a way to get along without you forever. So make up your mind!"

"But Giorgina?"

"Look, I may never find out exactly what led to Father's death." Achille kept the pressure on. "But whatever it was, our workers are now so hostile to Giorgina that we will have endless strikes and sabotage unless Rosaria is left in charge. Be back here next week ready to go to work, and keep your wife in Rome until she has my permission to return."

Bruno Benelli nodded miserably and stumbled off to explain the hard economic facts to Giorgina. Achille spun around in his chair and addressed himself again to the attorney.

"I'm waiting for an answer. Do we have an agreement from your side?"

"There is still the question of Sandro Lombardi," Tommaso Savarino said levelly. "Rosaria asks that you use your influence to ensure that he is released from the army."

"That's impossible," intervened Guido Rosselli.

"Sandro's a separate issue." Achille rubbed his eyes, feeling utterly drained. "I concede that Giorgina did arrange for Sandro's sudden conscription, but he would have been drafted anyway once the change in his draft status came to the attention of the military authorities. I can't get him out of the army, and if he keeps hitting sergeants, he's going to stay in a punishment battalion until the Austrians shoot him. I will try to thwart his self-destructive yearnings, but the fate of a man trying to overthrow the government does not belong in an agreement affecting hundreds of employees who just want to earn a living."

"Achille, I see your reasoning, but this is a very major point for Rosaria."

"Tommaso, if I leave tomorrow without an iron-clad agreement, I will have the carabinieri clear the land and leave it fallow until I return. Rosaria's peasants will starve, but my father left me comfortably well off, and I do not need the irritation. Will you try to make your client understand that subtle point?"

"I need to consult," Tommaso Savarino announced coldly, leaving the dining room through the door to the kitchen, where Rosaria had established her command post.

"You're doing well, Comandante." Guido poured them both another glass of wine. "I've never seen you quite this savage. Are you drunk?"

"A little," Achille admitted. "Guido, I love the people who work on this estate and I want to take care of them. But we have to achieve some kind of stable working relationship."

They could hear whispering in the kitchen. I once held her in my arms and said that I loved her, he remembered. Now we are communicating through a lawyer. When Tommaso reappeared, his face was impassive. "Your proposal has been accepted."

"Good." Achille took a bottle of his father's favorite cognac from the sideboard and opened it. "Would Signorina Lombardi care to join us for a drink to celebrate?"

Tommaso shook his head and moved toward the door. "My client would not be receptive to your offer of a drink, although I suppose under the terms of paragraph four of the agreement you could put it into the form of an order. You do seem unusually imperial tonight."

"Oh, Tommaso, tell her to come in," Achille said recklessly. "I want her to meet Guido, and—"

"She's angry." Suddenly the attorney stepped aside from his role and gave vent to his feelings. "Since you've left, she's done nothing but serve your family faithfully, in return for which she's been kidnapped, brutalized, and insulted. So she doesn't want to drink cognac with you, and neither do I."

He's in love with her too, Achille realized as Tommaso strode toward the door. God damn! Isn't life complicated enough? Quickly he sprang to his feet and caught the furious lawyer on the front steps.

"Tommaso!"

"Leave me alone. Our business is finished."

"Not quite." Achille seized him by the arm and turned him around. "I need your confidential help on a couple of legal matters."

Tommaso shook his head angrily. "I represent Rosaria Lombardi. Get your own lawyer."

"Okay. Who represents little Massimo?"

"I don't know. I suppose I do," Tommaso conceded.

"Good." Achille took a bank draft from his pocket and handed it over. "Use this to establish a bank account for any expenses that little Massimo may encounter."

Tommaso's eyes widened as he studied the check. "This is very generous."

Achille then produced a sheet of legal paper from his notebook. "I've written up a codicil to my will, and I need to know if it can stand up to a legal challenge from Giorgina. If I should be killed in battle, then obviously Terenzio inherits everything. But if both of us die, then I want both my property and the title to go to Massimo."

Tommaso scanned the document, pausing to reread several passages carefully. "You should have been a lawyer," he admitted grudgingly. "Why won't you let me tell Rosaria? It would make all the difference in the world for her."

"Because I'm not doing it for her," Achille Leone said shortly as he turned away. "This is for my little brother."

"What do you think of the settlement?" The night was cold for September, and Achille was sprawled before the fire, working his way stolidly through the cognac and reluctant to go to bed. Guido was gone, having decided upon a late-night visit to the famous brothel on the Via Santa Agatha.

"Your father would have handled it more gently, Signor Conte." Girolamo seemed stiff and irritable.

"What is this 'Signor Conte' business?" Achille protested. "Say, do you remember when you boxed my ears for throwing stones at the cows?"

"They're your cows now. Shall I get you some stones?"

"What's wrong, old friend?"

"You implied that Rosaria hastened your father's death, and that's not right. I waited on Leonida for fifty years and I never saw him so happy."

"What the hell was she doing in bed with him?" Achille exploded, the old resentment surging quickly to the surface. "And speaking of irresponsibility, what were you doing, running around in the middle of the night, burning houses down?"

"Could we leave it for another day?" Girolamo snapped back. "I'm tired and you're drunk." The old man turned and hobbled toward his quarters. "I've put your bags in the master bedroom."

The bottle was nearly empty and Achille swigged the rest, knowing that he would hate himself in the morning. Something has gone wrong in my life, he told himself as he climbed unsteadily up the stairs. In battle, I have always faced my enemies cold sober, but these days I seem to need alcohol to deal with people I love. Why?

In the master bedroom he wandered through a web of memories, looking at the great oil portraits of his noble ancestors and wondering whether he wanted them all staring down at him while he tried to sleep. He halted at the side of the big four-poster and took off his *giubba* and boots. This is where I was conceived, he thought. This is where Mother died. Did Papa sleep here with Rosaria?

When he made love to her, did she ever cry out, the way Anfi did?

I'll get a book from the study and read myself to sleep, he decided. Still unsteady from the cognac, he pushed through a connecting door into the little room where his mother had once done her sewing and where Leonida had once taken his naps.

The room was smaller than he remembered it. Beneath the window, Rosaria Lombardi was sitting in the narrow bed, her knees drawn up beneath a blanket, studying the text of the contract they had just negotiated.

She looked up at him, serene and unsurprised. Beneath her loose-fitting white nightgown, he could see the gentle rise of her breasts. Vaguely he wondered if it was the same nightdress she had worn the night he left for Libya, the one she had stripped off to offer him her body.

"I've been reading the fine print." There was no emotion in her voice. "You've tricked me."

"What's wrong?" Oh, let it be over, he said to himself, taking a few uncertain steps and resting his hand on the burnished oaken bedpost. This is where they must have made love, he realized, here in this ridiculous little bed.

"For administering this farm, I receive a percentage of your family's gross income, not a salary." There was a resigned tone in her voice, as if she too were weary of litigation. "This means that if I side with the workers in a conflict, I lose my own means of support and deprive my child of his inheritance. And if I favor your family, I will betray my people. So you have me walking a tightrope. Congratulations, Signor Conte."

"No, look, it just seemed a reasonable arrangement." He sat down heavily on the end of the bed as Rosaria hastily moved her feet out of the way. In a part of his mind that was still sober, he knew he should leave, since he was drunk, and she was hardly dressed to receive visitors. But he was too dazzled by the warmth of her body to move. With her auburn hair flowing down over her bare shoulders, she seemed more desirable than ever.

"Well, what did you want?" she demanded. "Why did you come in here?"

"I didn't know you were here. Don't you sleep in the cottage?"

"Leonida moved me here years ago," she explained. "I imagined you had gone back to Rome with your friend."

"Really? Or were you expecting me to come in and make love to you?"

She shrugged. "You are a drunken soldier on his way from one war to another. I am the nearest available woman and my honor has been very thoroughly compromised. I suppose it was inevitable that you would come looking for me."

"Aren't you going to scream 'rape'? Or is that too old-fashioned for a socialist woman?"

Why am I talking like this? he asked himself. Why can't we just love each other?

"You haven't come to rape me." Motionless, she stared at him as he reached out to stroke her hair. "You think I'm a whore and you've come to buy me."

"Then what's your price, little whore?" I want you, he thought. He pushed the straps of her nightgown down off her shoulders to reveal the fullness of her breasts. I am not responsible for any of this because I am drunk, he told himself. Now she will send me away, and in the morning I will return with flowers to apologize.

For a long moment's silence, Rosaria simply looked at him questioningly. Avoiding her eyes, he touched one dark nipple, watching it stiffen as he caressed it.

"My price is Sandro." She turned her face away as Achille slipped his arm around her waist and tried to kiss her lips. "You must arrange his transfer into your regiment and keep him away from the fighting."

"I can't do it," he said thickly. "It would be against regulations, and dishonorable."

"Then find yourself a whore with more reasonable terms, Signor Conte." She pushed him away, slowly covering her breasts.

"This is monstrous!" he shouted hoarsely, staggering to his feet. "You don't want me in the slightest."

"I have wanted you all my life," she cried, but the moment had already fractured. Blindly Achille stumbled back the way he had come, blundering into the master bedroom. In a fury he slammed the door behind him and then kicked it for good measure. He then staggered into a bookshelf and knocked it over, sending a hundred volumes crashing to the floor.

"M'lord?" When Girolamo hobbled in a moment later, alarmed, Achille was pulling on his boots. "Where are you going?"

"To the Via Santa Agatha," Count Leone mumbled as he stumbled toward the door.

"Don't worry, dearie," said a cheerful voice.

"What?" Awakening slowly, Achille Leone sat up in bed, noting that the sheets were of red satin. Where the hell am I?

"It happens to all the boys once in a while." He could not at the moment remember having been introduced to the woman lying between his legs, with her head resting against his thigh. She was a pretty lady, and she winked at him before rolling over on her side, languidly presenting him with a naked back. "Maybe you've had a drop too much to drink?"

"Cristo!" His head was aching from the cognac as he sat up. It was Guido's favorite brothel and he had just disgraced himself with an expensive prostitute.

There was a knock, and the door opened. "We need to leave, Comandante," Major Rosselli informed him blithely. "Maybe you'd better get your trousers on."

"Leave?"

"For Udine, Achille. There's a war on, remember?"

4.

. . . .

What are we going to do?'' There was naked terror in Emilio Lodi's whisper.

Get killed, Sandro thought, but Lodi's morale was bad enough without spelling out the obvious. The army had a policy of sending socialists to punishment battalions with the blunt intention of getting them killed. The two of them would have been a great deal safer in jail.

"I'm going to have a look.'' It was hot, and Sandro grunted with the effort of getting to his hands and knees in the little cave they had carved out of the forward wall of the trench. It was a refuge against Austrian artillery shells and a place to sleep when it rained; there were tens of thousands of similar cubicles along the front line. Unfolding his long body, Sandro dropped to the floor of the trench, his boots splashing into the perpetual stream running along the bottom. The water was yellow with urine, and a dead rat floated by.

He got his balance and sloshed through the muck to the nearest observation point.

All along the trench, men were crouched in their compartments. Permission to consume evening rations had come at five in the afternoon, and now they were all eating chocolates and drinking the cheap raw cognac that the army issued in abundance just before an attack. His comrades in the *battaglione di disciplina* all saw him, but no one spoke. Sandro understood their silence; prior to an attack, the men retreated within themselves. A few prayed, but not many; others looked at photographs of mothers and girlfriends. Some wept silently. One man lay curled in a corner with his face to the wall, masturbating frantically.

The sides of the trench were supported by burlap bags filled with dirt and stacked on top of one another to keep the walls from collapsing. The trench was nearly three meters deep, but narrow enough for Sandro to touch both walls at the same time. Every few meters, crude staircases had been constructed out of rough-hewn timber and stones to permit access to the surface. Moving carefully, Sandro climbed to the top, crouched behind a row of sandbags, and crawled into a cement observation post. Inside, there was an empty grappa bottle, a neat pile of feces, and a helmet with a bullet hole in it.

"Lombardi, go back down instantly.'' Sandro looked up to see the lieutenant commanding their company admonishing him from the next observation post to the south. "We don't want them to see any activity from this side."

"Yes, sir." But Sandro lingered where he was, trying to get a look at the ground immediately in front of them. They had only recently been moved to this position, and a surprise attack had been ordered for sunset, less than an hour away.

But there had been sporadic firing all day and he knew they would not take the Austrians by surprise. No one had ever surprised an Austrian.

"Now!" hissed the lieutenant, but Sandro ignored him and moved the stone that normally blocked the observation post's spy hole. He waited a moment and then held the discarded helmet in front of the hole. A second later a bullet whizzed through the opening with Germanic precision, knocking the helmet out of his hand. They must have that sniper's rifle in some kind of vice, permanently aimed at this hole, he reasoned, knowing that he had only a few seconds before the Austrian sharpshooter could reload.

He looked across thirty meters of no-man's-land, wondering about the men on the other side. They must be farm boys, like us, and yet we spend all our time trying to kill each other for a few centimeters of mud. If we could only make a deal, rise up together and kill our officers . . .

Another bullet spun angrily in his direction, but Sandro had seen what he needed to see, and ducked away. The Austrians had erected three successive coils of concertina, thick spools of heavy barbed wire to protect a line of well-built fortifications. Facing them were at least two machine-gun installations. Artillery rounds had broken up the earth between the two front lines, which would make it awkward to run in the fading light. There was nothing out there that offered much in the way of cover or concealment, except for one shell crater about fifteen meters straight ahead of them.

This was going to be a diversionary attack, he understood. Nobody expected them to succeed. We're going to soak up enough bullets to give a unit in some other sector half a chance of making it into the Austrian trench, he thought. And they're over there waiting for us. Attacking at sundown isn't going to make a lot of difference.

"Get down! You goddamn subversive, get down!" The lieutenant had his side arm trained on Sandro's chest. He was within his legal rights to execute a man who disobeyed a direct order.

"I'm going." He backed down the ladder, calculating their chances of escape. The trench ran north and south into other infantry units and the military police had established checkpoints at both ends. Behind them to the west, there was a maze of trenches and tunnels leading to battalion headquarters, but any enlisted man caught out of his assigned area without a valid excuse was automatically deemed a deserter. An hour before an attack, there was no valid excuse for being anywhere but on the line. Summary execution was the penalty for attempted desertion, and it was carried out with inflexible regularity.

He faced reality: the carabinieri would have all the exits blocked by now. There was a numbness in his body as he crawled back up into the shelf he shared with Emilio Lodi.

"What are our chances?" the younger man asked anxiously.

Sandro decided to spare him the worst. "Look, there's a big shell crater about fifteen meters in front of us, and if we're quick we might take shelter there until they call off the attack."

"We'll never make it that far. Why don't we give ourselves up?"

It was an option Sandro had already considered and rejected. Surrendering to the Austrians in the hopes of finishing the war in a prison camp had been attempted often enough in the past, but to his knowledge no one had ever succeeded.

"If we tried it in the dark, we'd be shot by the Austrians before we got close enough to surrender, and if we went over the top now with a white flag, one of our own forward observers would nail us."

"We could refuse to attack. We could mutiny."

"They'd execute the lot of us." Sandro put his head in his hands, weary of Emilio's wailing. They should have gone for a revolution before the war. Now they had to attack, because certain death at the hands of their own officers was worse than probable death from enemy fire.

"Lombardi, you there!" Sandro looked up in alarm. The major in charge of their punishment battalion stood in the trench below, flanked by the same lieutenant whom Sandro had just irritated. "You're wanted. Get your things and come with me."

Sandro tensed. Was it possible that they would take the time, just before a major attack, to shoot him for such a minor act of insubordination? Not seeing any alternative, he gathered together his field pack: a knapsack, a shovel, a canteen, four ammunition pouches, a bayonet and a gas mask.

He thought about ending it all right there. He could shoot these idiotic officers and then kill himself.

"Give me your rifle." Before he could react, the lieutenant took the rifle out of his hand and pushed him forward. He could hear Emilio behind him in the cave weeping but too frightened to say anything.

"Why?"

"Get moving!" said the lieutenant. The battalion commander turned on his heel and walked down the tunnel that led to the unit headquarters. Sandro followed, puzzled as they marched through their immediate rear area and out into the open air, with a small hill between them and the battle area. They halted by a roadside where several staff cars were drawn up. There was a squad of carabinieri in a field nearby.

He wondered if they were going to shoot him there. To encourage the others.

Then he saw Achille Leone. On each sleeve the newest Count Leone wore the five-pointed gold stars of a lieutenant colonel. On his field cap there was an embroidered insignia with the crossed rifles of the infantry and a "77" to identify his regiment. Stunned, Sandro followed his major forward, and the two of them saluted.

"Good evening, sir," asked the battalion commander. "Is this the Private Sandro Lombardi you're looking for?"

"Yes, thank you, Major." The voice was cold, but Sandro detected a twinkle in Achille's eye. "Stand at ease, private! There is a position open in the Seventy-seventh Infantry Regiment as my aide-de-camp. Are you interested?"

"Sì, signore." Sandro took a deep breath as it came home to him that he was not going to be shot. "Ah, we have Private Emilio Lodi here as well, sir," he added promptly. "A valiant soldier from Cederna and a great admirer of the Seventy-seventh."

"Is he really?" Colonel Leone smiled, turning to address the major. "If you could spare Lodi as well, I would take him off your hands."

"You are welcome to him, Colonel." The major did not seem distressed at losing the valiant Lodi. "Now, if you'll excuse me, we have an attack scheduled in a few minutes. If you'd like to watch, Private Lombardi can take you to an observation point."

They were suddenly alone. Sandro suddenly remembered that moment in the *Inferno* where the poet Virgil offers to escort Dante through hell. "Io sarò tua guida," he quoted. "I will guide you from here, and show you an eternal place."

"Look you first to see if my strength is sufficient," Achille quickly countered with a verse from the Second Canto. "Sandro, are you all right? My regiment just got into Udine last night and it took me a while to find you."

"I will be all right if your strength is sufficient to get us out of here. Emilio and I were going to be dead in about five minutes." Uncertain how to treat someone who had been his childhood playmate but was now a senior officer, Sandro extended his hand, but Achille impulsively hugged him. Trudging by on their way to shoot deserters, the carabiniere squad gazed at them curiously.

"Is it that bad?"

"It really would take Dante to describe it adequately." Sandro led him up the side of the hill. "The Austrians shell this observation post from time to time, but once the attack begins they'll have better targets, so we should be safe."

They reached the top of the hill and looked out to the east. Below, they could see the Austrian front lines and then the Isonzo River, winding down from the Julian Alps to the Adriatic Sea. It had become an article of faith among Italians that their country ended at the watershed of the Alps, on the far side of the Isonzo.

"Keep down," warned Sandro. "The Austrians snipers can see us from here. Look, there's our major."

They both watched as the battalion commander and his staff moved into the forward trench. The major carried a megaphone; there was a trumpeter by his side, ready to broadcast the attack.

"What's wrong with those men?" As Achille pointed, squad after squad of troopers began shambling unsteadily to the foot of the ladders. They were all desperately draining their canteens.

"They're drunk. If the troops can't drink before an attack, they'll balk at the last minute."

Achille shook his head in irritation. "And what's that man doing?" With his field glasses, Colonel Leone gestured to the far right of the line, where a soldier had climbed alone to the surface. Unobserved by his comrades, he was standing on his head, supporting himself with his arms against the wall of the barricade, waving his legs in the air.

"He's trying to get shot in the legs. He'll pretend later that it happened during the attack so they'll send him home with a pair of crutches and a medal."

Far below them the trumpet sounded, and men began clambering up ladders. Many were so drunk they could scarcely crawl as they spread out behind the sandbag barricade at the top of the forward trench. Sandro watched as the battalion commander shouted instructions through his megaphone. The officers were all standing behind their men with pistols in hand; they seemed stiff, and Sandro knew that they had each donned a *corazza*, the uncomfortable bulletproof vest issued to officers.

"Savoia! Savoia!" came a hesitant shout as the battalion ritually chanted the family name of Italy's ruling house. As Italian troops climbed clumsily over the barricades into no-man's-land, the Austrian machine guns barked fire at them and a few men fell immediately.

"Look!" Sandro pointed off to the center of the forward line, at the company area where he and Emilio had been serving until a few minutes ago. It was too far away to distinguish his face, but one man was refusing to go over the top, and Sandro's former company commander was standing over him, shouting. They watched as the lieutenant drew his pistol and repeated the order. The soldier dropped his rifle and knelt in the mud, crouching and putting his face in his hands, paralyzed with terror. The officer shot him casually and then jumped over the barricade behind his troops. An instant later a bullet struck the lieutenant so violently that his body was flung back over the barricade and out of sight into the trench.

"That was my officer," commented Sandro laconically. "I'm glad he's dead."

"How can you say that?" Achille seemed stunned.

Sandro shouted over the roar of the machine guns. "Look what's happening. What difference does it make?"

The battle proceeded rapidly. The men of the punishment battalion were thieves, cowards, psychotics, and socialists, and they seemed confused and unwilling. Few fired their weapons, and others blundered forward with their arms at their sides. The officers shouted and ran ahead of their troops, trying to encourage them, but the Austrian machine guns sliced viciously into the battalion, knocking men down in droves.

Morbidly curious to see if anyone would make it to the shell crater he had chosen as his personal sanctuary, Sandro watched the attack falter about ten meters from the Italian trenches as men began flinging themselves to the ground. Some of them used their rifles to fire at the enemy, but most of them tried to find cover behind rocks and tree stumps. When the Austrian mortars began delivering shells into the no-man's-land, the officers led the few survivors back to the safety of the Italian trenches.

"They lost half the battalion." Sandro grunted. "Let's get out of here before their artillery finds us."

Dazed, Achille Leone swept the battlefield with his field glasses, unable to believe that a unit could lose so many men so quickly and so pointlessly.

Then, in the distance, Sandro heard a hollow, deep-throated explosion, a sound he knew all too well.

"It's a four-twenty," he shouted. Colonel Leone seemed puzzled. There was a whistling in the air, and then silence.

"What do you mean?" he asked but Sandro hurled himself across the observation post, tackling Achille. The two men tumbled out and down the side of the hill. Springing to his feet, he dragged the stunned officer into a reinforced concrete anti-artillery shelter, flinging him behind the sandbags at the entrance.

The 420-millimeter artillery shell landed an instant later, obliterating the observation post, and showering the area with mud and rock and pieces of shattered concrete and shell fragments. The concussion was awful.

"What the hell was that?" Achille sat up, rubbing his face. He had a cut over his left eyebrow.

"Sorry, but there wasn't time to explain. A four-twenty is the biggest artillery piece the Austrians have. It lifts off like a cosmic fart and then goes silent on you. By the time you hear it again, it's too late."

Achille was brushing the dirt off his uniform. "I've got a lot to learn about this kind of warfare," he said slowly. "But I will never send drunken men to certain death like that. That's not why I became an officer."

"You saved our lives. Emilio and I would have been in the middle of that carnage," said Sandro, getting to his feet. Now I have to be a good soldier, he admonished himself. I have to give up hitting sergeants, and help Achille win this war. We can't have a revolution until this is over, and anyway I couldn't rebel against Achille.

"And you saved mine," Achille interrupted his thinking as they limped down the side of the hill toward the vehicles. Sandro could see Emilio Lodi standing next to the colonel's staff car, smiling beatifically. It seemed insanely peaceful on this side of the hill. The sun had just set. There were some cows grazing in a field, and the farmer in Sandro wondered if the shelling affected their production of milk.

"Well, perhaps we could make it a tradition." Sandro managed a chuckle. "Uh, am I supposed to call you Signor Colonnello?"

"Only when there are other people around. Tell me, when you become the Military Commissar of the Proletarian Defense Forces, what will I be expected to call you?"

"You can call me 'friend.' "

"I can call you that now," said the colonel warmly, taking his arm as they walked toward the staff car. "My oldest and best friend."

"Listen, did you see Rosaria in Rome? How is the baby?"

"Ah, the day before yesterday we chatted briefly. The baby is remarkable, really, a very beautiful baby."

There was an awkwardness in Achille's voice that should have warned him, but Sandro blundered ahead impulsively. "Did Rosaria ask you to get me out of the punishment battalion?"

"This has nothing to do with Rosaria," Achille snapped irritably. Emilio Lodi took his place behind the wheel, and they started down the road to Udine. The two men were silent for several kilometers, and then began to talk of other things.

5.

. . . .

The officers all came to a position of attention as the Supreme Commander of Italian and Allied Forces on the Southern Front cleared his throat.

"On this day, the twenty-fourth of July 1916, I, Luigi Cadorna, confer the Gold Medal for Military Valor on Colonel Achille Leone of the Seventy-seventh Infantry Regiment. Congratulations, Colonel Leone."

With great solemnity he stepped forward and pinned the decoration on the left breast pocket of Achille's gray-green uniform jacket. Cadorna was a short man, and Achille leaned over slightly to make it easier.

"Thank you, sir," he said, thinking what a silly business it was. His Seventy-seventh Infantry Regiment had been assigned to a quiet part of the front, anchoring the line northeast of Udine, but after nine months of relatively easy duty, the Austrians had unexpectedly launched a clumsy daylight attack. Achille had lashed back with an improvised bayonet charge, catching his enemies in no-man's-land and chasing them a half-kilometer past their own front lines. When the fighting was over, the Seventy-seventh had captured three rows of Austrian trenches and a thousand men and officers.

"Whatever made you think of a bayonet charge?" inquired the general. "An unusual tactic."

"My father often reacted to a difficult situation with a bayonet charge," Achille responded honestly.

"He was always a man for unconventional solutions," General Cadorna observed. "Did you know that my father commanded your father's unit in September of 1870, when we conquered Rome? Ah, if we had Leonida Leone with us today!"

"Yes, sir." And if we had your father as our commander, we'd have won by now, he reacted with mental sarcasm. Unlike his talented ancestor, the younger Cadorna was a remorseless military bureaucrat who confronted tactical problems by throwing men at them.

"Listen, Leone, I want your Seventy-seventh involved in our next offensive." Cadorna dismissed his staff and led Achille to a huge tactical map of northeastern Italy. The front was eight hundred kilometers long, a huge S running south of Trentino, which was still mostly in Austrian hands, to the north past the Julian Alps before following the Isonzo River south again toward the uncaptured Trieste and the Adriatic Sea.

"Of course, Signor Generale," Achille answered politely, although his blood ran a little cold. In their first year of fighting, the Italians had pushed the Austrians back here and there, but they were still a long way from knocking them out of the war. The politicians were pressuring Cadorna to make some progress, and in some recent offensives the casualty rates had run over fifty percent for enlisted men, and even higher among the officers.

"It's still secret, but we're going to take Gorizia in early August." Confidently the Supreme Commander stabbed his finger at an Austrian-held town on the east bank of the Isonzo, southeast of Udine and north of Trieste. "We can move a reserve unit up to plug your place in the line. Could you be ready to leave tonight?"

Say no, he told himself, or your regiment will be slaughtered in another fatuous general offensive. Explain that you would prefer to stay where you are, or claim that there are technical difficulties.

"Of course, sir," he said, and took his leave.

There were things that needed to be arranged. He would have to write to Rosaria and Girolamo and Bruno Benelli, explaining that he was likely to be out of touch for a period, and authorizing them to make any necessary business decisions in the interim. A long letter needed to go out to Anfi al-Sharif, who wrote him every month with news about Benghazi.

And I'd better tell Terenzio and Cristina we're being transferred, he decided. Win or lose at Gorizia, there is no way of knowing when we'll be back in Udine. He paused at the portals of the headquarters compound and glanced cautiously at the sky, since the Austrians occasionally blasted Udine with their high-flying Albatross bombers. But the sky was clear except for a pair of Italian SPAD biplanes prowling defensively over the city, so Achille walked quickly through the piazza to the Ospedale Militare.

Through ignorance or malice, the Austrians even bombed the hospital from time to time, and there were sandbags piled around the entrance and chicken wire covered the windows. Despite the heat of the day it was cool inside, and as he searched the corridors for Cristina, Achille shivered, although not entirely from the change in temperature. After every battle, the medical officers performed a triage on the wounded, and men who were going to die anyway were kept at the front, along with troopers suffering from relatively minor wounds. Only seriously wounded men with a chance of life were sent to this hospital. Those who survived were usually given medical discharges and allowed to go home.

"Schlaf, schlaf," he heard Cristina's soft voice in a room to his left, and he pushed open the door. "Try to sleep."

In this ward the beds were empty except for one at the far end of the room.

Cristina was sitting by the patient's side, wiping his face with a sponge. She looked tiny in her white Red Cross uniform, a delicate gold chain around her neck bearing a tiny Star of David.

When this war is over, Achille thought suddenly, nobody will have a homeland anymore. We will all be Jews.

Suddenly the wounded soldier began to thrash from side to side on the narrow mattress, gasping for breath and clawing at the frail blond nurse. Concerned, Achille moved to her side but the patient abruptly relaxed.

"Sleep." Cristina lifted his hand and kissed it impulsively. "You'll feel better in the morning."

"Mutter?" the soldier murmured, calling for his mother. Achille sat down on the opposite side of the bed and saw that the man's chest was swathed in bandages. There were great livid bruises on his neck. His eyes were closed and he was crying. Cristina glanced up at Achille, putting her finger to her lips.

"Schlaf," she urged her patient. "I'll stay here with you."

"Mutter?" he asked again, and then a gurgle came from deep in his throat. A moment later his chest stopped rising and falling and there was a urine smell in the room as his bladder relaxed. Carefully Cristina dipped the sponge in a saucer of water and wiped some phlegm from the soldier's lips. Then she pulled the sheet over his face. When she rose, Achille saw that she was sobbing violently, making no sound but shaking wildly as the tears poured down her cheeks.

He took her in his arms, feeling her tiny body quaking. It has been a long time since I have held a woman, he realized. We don't need field brothels or regimental prostitutes like the French have. Just a woman we can hug from time to time.

They walked to the door as Cristina struggled to control her emotions. "It's not getting any better," she managed to say. "We still don't have enough of anything. There's hardly any gauze or catgut for surgery. We're doing operations with cognac and chloroform and sometimes our boys wake up screaming before the surgeon has finished."

"There aren't many nurses who would cry for an Austrian prisoner of war." Achille took out his hankerchief and dried her eyes.

"I cry for all of them." She tried for a smile and managed only a crooked grimace. "They're so far from home and it hurts so much when they die. Dr. Carducci sometimes assigns me to the prisoners because I studied languages at school and I can weep in German. I don't know too much medicine yet, but I'm the best crier in the hospital."

"Crissi, you're doing fine," he assured her. "We're all so proud of you."

"Sometimes I think I should go back to Venice and take care of mother. They've been bombing Venice, and she's sick and terrified."

"You're needed here." Achille took her hand as they walked together toward the hospital's front entrance. She has such a sweet vulnerability, he mused. I wish I could stay and talk to her. "There are so few nurses," he said. "That young man needed you. We all need you."

"Then I'll stay."

"Look, I've just received orders to take my regiment to a new position some distance from Udine." He spoke evasively because the attack on Gorizia was still secret. "It may be a while before Guido and I can get back, but if you need anything, contact Terenzio at Carabiniere Headquarters."

"I'll be here if you need me," she said simply. "But be careful. I don't want to have to cry for you."

She squeezed his hand good-bye and he kissed her on the forehead. It seemed the only appropriate place to kiss Crissi. Out in the street, air-raid sirens were sounding and there were Austrian bombers in the evening sky.

"The men call him Colonel Shit." The commanding officer of the shattered 102nd Infantry Regiment pointed across forty meters of shell-torn hillside. "Colonnello Merda! There he is!"

It was a surreal moment, one of those tacit, temporary, unreliable truces that occasionally happened at the front. The Austrians were working on their fortifications and needed a quiet evening in which to finish the double wall of sandbags they were erecting. For their part, the Italians were changing units on the line, with Achille's Seventy-seventh replacing the remnants of the 102nd, the regiment Colonel Shit had massacred earlier in the week. In the last hour before sunset neither side wanted a fight, and the Italians stood boldly on the parapet looking at the Austrian front.

"Why is he called Colonel Shit?" Guido Rosselli shielded his eyes as he studied the enemy position. The Austrian officer was a tall, youthful man with an elaborate brown handlebar moustache. Except for a flamboyant red aviator's silk scarf around his neck, he was wearing the standard pike-gray uniform of the Imperial Austrian Army. Standing carelessly on the Austrian parapet, he turned toward the Italian trench and greeted his next victims with an ironic salute.

"We've attacked him seven times in a month," confessed the commander of the 102nd. "Each time he's chewed us to pieces. We had to pull back after the last assault leaving a lot of wounded on the field. He sat up there shooting them one after another with a rifle."

"Why didn't you nail him?" Achille was furious. There was an unwritten agreement that the defeated side would not be prevented from removing its wounded from the field.

"We tried, but most of my men were dead." The commander of the 102nd Infantry Regiment was too choked up to talk. He had lost nearly two thousand men in a month, and his eyes were hollow with grief. Unless he accepted the common option of suicide, he would end the war in a desk job somewhere, trying to grapple with his guilt.

"Leone, everybody says you're the best we've got." The commander of the 102nd turned to leave. "But Colonel Shit is the best they've got. Remember that!"

Achille nodded, turning his attention to his theater of battle. Sitting on some high ground behind the Austrian lines was a small village named Podgora. Barely visible in the distance was the Isonzo River, and on the far shore was General Cadorna's objective, the city of Gorizia. It seemed a long way away.

Grimly he surveyed the sloppy, haphazard system of trenches he had inherited from the 102nd. This was clearly the worst three hundred meters on this front. There was a road running into enemy territory to his right, affording clear fields of fire for the Austrian machine gunners. On the left, his men would have to climb uphill through endless circles of concertina barbed wire to get to the enemy trenches. No wonder Colonel Shit was smiling.

"Comandante, this is not the best battlefield I have ever seen." Even the irrepressible Guido Rosselli was subdued. "What do we do?"

"They won't ask us to do anything too serious too soon," Achille predicted. "But today is already the fifth of August and we may only have a few weeks before Cadorna's offensive, so we'd better get busy. What do you think of digging a tunnel over there, near that road? It might take us a week or more, but we could run it a few meters toward their position."

"Let's look." The ephemeral truce ended with sunset, and the parapet was no longer safe. The two officers jumped down and walked south at the bottom of the forward trench.

It was filthy. There were huge rats scurrying everywhere, feeding on piles of garbage and even eating flesh from a scattering of corpses abandoned after the last assault. Achille's three battalion commanders had already set out sentries, and squads were cleaning up the area, but it would be a long time before the Seventy-seventh would feel at home here at the scene of another regiment's disaster.

"Look, there's the Isonzo," Guido whispered as they climbed into an observation tower on the southern end of their regimental territory. The evening was overcast and the sun was now below the horizon, but an artillery battery somewhere behind them was shelling a target near the water. The flash from each exploding shell sent a reflection rippling across the placid surface of the Isonzo, several kilometers to the east.

"What a silly little river! It's not very wide nor very deep, and we seem destined to fight over it century after century," Achille said. "Did I ever mention that one of my illustrious ancestors won a battle here in 1507? He was helping you Venetians conquer Gorizia from the Ottoman Empire."

"I know. And the following year the Austrians took it back again and ... listen, haven't we had this whole conversation before? This is the part where you tell me how your great-grandfather Ludovico Leone got drunk with Napoleon."

"God, it's time for the war to be over. I'm running out of ancestors."
Achille yawned, feeling the fatigue sweeping over him.

"You were on your feet all last night." Guido was serious. "Get some
sleep and I'll hold the forces of evil at bay until dawn."

Achille agreed, knowing he would need a clear head in the morning to put
this shambles into some kind of order. Dragging himself to the regimental
headquarters area a few dozen meters behind the forward trench, he found
that Sandro had already erected his field tent. Sandro was turning out to be
the best aide-de-camp in the army.

Achille inspected his portable little world, the familiar universe Sandro re-
created for him whenever they moved. There was the usual oil lamp burning
on his foot locker. Anfi's Koran was there as well, together with a bundle of
her letters. A bucket of clean water was waiting for his nightly wash and his
bed had been made up with fresh sheets.

There was even a letter resting on the pillow. He undressed slowly and sat
down on the bed to read the letter, a short, formal report from Rosaria on the
status of the farm. The autumn harvest promised to be generally satisfactory,
and the 1916 vino bianco was expected to be the best in years. An old out-
building had burned down and was being rebuilt. A fuller report would be
rendered in September.

Achille read the letter a second time, and then a third, looking between the
lines for some subtle hint to her feelings, but it was nothing but an efficient
administrator's dry report.

He threw the envelope aside and a photograph of Rosaria tumbled out.

In the picture it was late summer because the carnations were in bloom
behind her. Rosaria was sitting on a wicker chair in the secret garden, wearing
a high-collared blouse over a white skirt, the kind of outfit young ladies wore
at fancy colleges. On her head was a saucy wide-brimmed straw hat with a
ribbon, and she was laughing without restraint, her hands on her thighs as
she kicked out with her legs to reveal high-buttoned shoes.

Father must have been standing behind the photographer, making her giggle, Achille decided. And where was I? Off in Libya killing Arabs? And why
did she send me this? He turned the photograph over, but there was nothing
written on the reverse.

What is the message here? What is she trying to say? Does this mean that
she has forgiven me for what I said? Oh, Rosi, what are we doing with our
lives? He inspected the photograph minutely again, and then fell back on the
cot with tangled emotions raging in his tired brain, the photograph resting on
his chest. What is going to happen to us?

He fell asleep a few minutes later and plunged immediately into a dream
in which Cristina and Rosaria were both wearing military uniforms and he
was trying to force them over the top with a pistol. Weeping, Cristina refused
to go. He executed her with a bullet in the head, in accordance with General

Cadorna's directive, but instead of dying she evaporated into nothingness, as if she had never existed. Meanwhile, at the top of the parapet, Rosaria had undressed and walked naked toward the Austrian trenches. In the distance Colonel Shit was laughing as he raised his rifle . . .

At midnight the barrage grew to a crescendo as thousands of massed guns poured fire on the Austrian lines.

It has nothing to do with us, Sandro told himself, pulling his parka over his head to block out the sound and keeping his eyes firmly shut.

Then he heard Emilio Lodi's hoarse whisper. After their rescue from the punishment battalion, Lodi had been assigned to one of the companies in the first battalion as an ordinary rifleman. Since Sandro now spent most of his time with Achille at regimental headquarters, the two peasants from Cederna seldom saw one another.

"Sandro, there's going to be an attack," Emilio hissed. "We're going over the top in a few hours."

"We can't." Sandro began the complicated maneuver of extricating himself from his sleeping bag and crawled out on his hands and knees. "Nothing is ready."

"We're all going to be killed unless we organize a mutiny. We'll refuse to go. The revolution can start here."

Sandro pulled on his boots, anxious to calm Lodi down before he was overheard. "Listen, the revolution is going to have to wait," he whispered, putting a hand on Lodi's shoulder and squeezing as hard as he could. "The Party's orders are to win the war."

Unexpectedly, an angry Major Rosselli materialized out of the darkness and threw Emilio up against the wall of the trench. Sandro backed away, trying to sort out his loyalties. He and Guido had disliked each other from the beginning, although they maintained a facade of politeness for Achille's sake.

"Lombardi, what is this man saying?"

"Sir . . ." he began to explain, but Guido was too furious to listen.

"Mutiny?" the major snarled, slapping Lodi violently in the face and then pounding him with his closed fist. "You socialists are cowards and traitors, every goddamned one of you. If I hear one more word about revolution, I will put you up against a wall and shoot you. Now get back to your unit."

"Major, listen," Sandro began as Lodi darted away.

"Shut up," Guido ordered brutally. "We've got orders from brigade headquarters directing us to launch a massed frontal attack at six. Wake the Comandante and tell him his battalion commanders are on their way."

Sandro saluted and turned away. Guido had nerves of iron, and if he was rattled, they were in trouble, he realized as he crawled into Achille's tent.

In the dim light, Sandro saw his colonel sleeping fitfully, his face bathed in perspiration. He was about to wake him when he spotted the photograph of Rosaria propped up lovingly against the lantern. For a moment he studied it intently, wondering how much of this mess was his fault.

I was always afraid their friendship would degenerate into the ultimate in class degradation, he thought, imagining a bad plot from a Puccini opera. It would start with the young lord of the manor seducing the pretty peasant wench, and end with his pensioning her off in disgrace when she complicated his life by getting pregnant.

Or would it have been the great love of both their lives? Now she is sending him her picture. Could anything be salvaged from the wreckage?

"Achille, wake up!"

The colonel opened his eyes reluctantly as Sandro touched a match to the wick of the kerosene lantern, bathing the tent in soft light. "What's happening?"

Feeling awkward, Sandro glanced at his sister's photograph. "Speaking as her brother, I wanted to say that it would be all right for you and Rosaria to mean whatever you want to mean to one another."

Achille rubbed his eyes, looking at him in perplexity. "Thanks, but it may be too late. There has been so much bitterness. Sandro, what's happening? You didn't come in here in the middle of the night to give me permission to love Rosi."

"We attack at six."

"That's not good." Achille was putting his trousers on as Guido entered with the three battalion commanders, Marcello Campione, Alighero Filippini, and Pierluigi Palumbino, followed by Sergeant Major Papafava.

"Why have they done this to us?" Major Campione asked plaintively. "After that bayonet charge at Udine we should be the apples of Cadorna's eye."

"It's just a stupid accident," Guido argued. "We were sent here as an afterthought, and when a hole in his line developed, the division commander plugged us in and forgot about us. Every unit on the line got the same order, and nobody is thinking about our situation. Comandante, what would your father have done?"

Achille shook his head. "My father was a nineteenth-century warrior. The technology is all different and the rules have changed. He would have improvised."

"Achille?" Guido Rosselli spoke softly but insistently. "If we take this regiment over the top in broad daylight, Colonel Shit is going to chop us up. What are we going to do?"

Achille put his head in his hands for a moment and they all watched him concentrate. For months and months now they had trusted him to get them out of one tough corner after another, but they had never faced a suicidal situation like this before.

When he looked up, his voice was steady. "We'll need to start right now. Pierluigi, start with a steady grazing fire into the Austrian position, with enough intensity to keep their heads down. Marcello, pound their rear echelon with your mortars but make sure nothing falls into the no-man's-land. Alighero, get your men over on the right flank to make as much racket as possible. Use that megaphone, and shout orders at people. Corporal Lombardi, you—"

"I'm coming with you." Sandro looked at Guido as he spoke. "There are some socialists who are not traitors."

"I made somebody a kind of promise about you," Achille said softly. "I think you should stay here."

"I know what you're planning, and you'll need my help." Sandro glanced quickly at the photograph beneath the kerosene lantern. "She'd want me to protect you."

"What's the Cederna Mafia up to?" Guido was puzzled and irritated.

Sandro grinned. "We're going to kill Colonel Shit," he said.

"Here's the barbed wire," Achille Leone whispered, reaching into the breast pocket of his field jacket for the wire cutters. The world was still utterly black, but his team would cease to be invisible when the first rays of the morning sun broke across the battlefield. And dawn was an hour away and they needed to hurry.

Achille snipped the barbed wire and passed one strand to Sandro, who tied it to a stake he had driven into the ground. The opposite strand he passed to Giuseppe Papafava, who secured it in the same careful fashion.

"We're about ten meters away," Sandro grunted as the trio inched forward, machine-gun fire masking their hushed voices. "I can just see the parapet."

Achille paused to wipe dirt out of his eyes. The Austrian commander had left the northern sector of no-man's-land covered by only one machine gun, the weapon directly in front of them. If they could destroy it, there would be a safe corridor for Guido and his volunteers.

"I've got the second strand," Papafava hissed and the team inched forward, methodically breaching the barbed-wire net. A moment later Achille put his hand out and felt the rough burlap of the Austrian forward position. The Austrian gun crew had been firing sporadically into the darkness, shooting over the heads of Achille's team, and he could hear them chatting placidly in German only a few steps away.

This is the tricky part, he thought as Giuseppe Papafava brought the seven-man infiltration team up to the Austrian parapet. They were too close now to risk speaking. Sandro handed him the signal rope and Achille tugged and then felt a distinct tug back, meaning that Guido had received the signal.

Then Achille's men gently drew apart the severed coils of concertina as Guido's three hundred volunteers followed the signal rope through the darkness. Pierluigi Palumbino elevated his machine-gun fire slightly to avoid hitting any of the Italians.

Suddenly they heard excited chatter as one of the Austrians spotted movement in front of them. There was no time to lose. Achille fired a flare directly into the Austrian position, momentarily blinding the gunners.

"Let's go," he cried. With a roar, Papafava's seven men all threw their hand grenades into the machine-gun nest and then ducked down behind the parapet as shrapnel killed the gunners.

"Comandante, we're here!" An instant later, Guido arrived at the head of his column and flung himself over the parapet. Achille quickly set off another flare to illuminate the Austrian position while Guido raced down the line killing the sentries one by one. He's good at that sort of thing, Achille thought fleetingly. I would hate to have to do it.

A moment later the remainder of Guido's assault force stormed down the parapet, firing into the trench and shooting the Austrians in droves as surprised enemy soldiers crawled out of their sleeping bags.

Except for a handful of dying Austrians, the trench beneath him was quickly cleared. With Sandro close behind him, Achille jumped down into the darkness, firing another flare to locate the lateral trench that led to the Austrian rear area. Colonel Shit was not the sort of man to faint because he had lost a forward trench. Somewhere back there, he was organizing a counterstroke.

"There he is!" shouted Sandro.

Ten meters away and white-faced in the phosphorous light from the flare, the aristocratic Austrian was unmistakable. With his automatic, Achille aimed at the red scarf and pulled the trigger.

A second later, an incoming mortar round detonated on the trench wall above them, knocking them all down as it threw mud and shell fragments in their direction. Dazed and concussed, Achille got to his hands and knees, seeing that Shit was crawling toward them, with a rifle in one hand and a squad of soldiers behind him.

Colonel Shit had to be stopped. If he managed to block the trench, he would have them cornered.

"I've got him!" Sandro was on his feet, bleeding from a cut over his left eye as he fired. He missed, and his pistol jammed. Colonel Shit sat back on his haunches with a snarl, aiming his rifle at Sandro's big body. Oh, God, if I let him be killed, Rosi will never forgive me, Achille thought, and he got off one quick shot from his automatic. The gun leaped in his hand, and the trench went dark as the last flare faded.

"Sandro? Sandro?" he shouted in the darkness, and then he heard the whistle of another incoming mortar shell. That's one of ours, he realized, and the world went black.

He regained consciousness slowly, aware that a great deal of time had passed. He expected to find himself in a hospital somewhere, and was perplexed to find that he was still lying in a corner of the Austrian trench.

"Achille?" A worried Sandro was bending over him. "Thank God, you've been out for hours, and we've been worried. Don't move. They're sending a stretcher.''

"Where's Guido?"

"He should be in Podgora by now," Sandro explained. "Once we broke through, the division sent in another two regiments, and we took the village. The Austrian line's collapsed and we'll be in Gorizia before lunch.''

"Did I shoot Colonel Shit?" Achille sat up, feeling confused. His ears were ringing, but his arms and legs seemed to be working.

Sandro nodded as he draped a red scarf around Achille's neck. "The colonel liked real silk. So, as it happens, does Rosaria."

"Rosaria? Sandro, do you think she still loves me?"

"I think she has always loved you," Sandro said slowly. "Why do you ask? I mean, why now?"

"I want to see her." He got to his feet, his head spinning. "I need to write and tell her . . .''

He lost his balance, and Sandro caught him as he fell. "Tell her what?"

"That I want her," Achille muttered. "I want her!"

6.

. . . .

He was eloquent, you had to give him that. It was the same mad dream that Sandro had chased his whole life, but no one could preach it better than Amadeo Bordiga.

Rosaria watched as the Neapolitan orator extended his arms like a prophet, reaching out to embrace the entire room. On their rough benches in the Casa del Popolo, the men leaned forward eagerly. The women lingered in back, some of them with children on their laps. They were attracted to Bordiga's charisma, but frightened of his words.

"This has always been the finest of our rural sections," Bordiga told them warmly. "You have built this splendid Casa del Popolo, headquarters and home for so many unions and proletarian organizations. When Comrade Lombardi returns from the war, the Central Committee expects to see even greater things from Cederna."

This was irritating. Rosaria glanced across the crowded meeting room at Tommaso Savarino, who was chairing the meeting. In Sandro's absence, Tommaso had taken over as leader of the Cederna PSI. Their eyes met, and she knew that he shared her annoyance because the two of them had not done badly since Sandro had been forced into the army. Every farm employee in the district was now represented by a union, and they were growing enough wheat out on the peasants' field to feed half the town. And the Socialist Party of Cederna did it all without a centesimo from the Central Committee.

"But Comrade Sandro cannot return until this war is over. And how long will that be?" Bordiga asked. "It is now 1917, and we have been fighting for exactly two years. On the home front our people are starving while our brothers in uniform are dying by the hundreds of thousands. We need to end this war. If it takes a revolution, then let us begin immediately, so that the troops will have the courage to rise up and kill their officers!"

Involuntarily Rosaria shook her head as Bordiga neatly summarized her private nightmare, the specter of Sandro turning his gun against Achille.

"Ah, Compagna Rosaria disagrees?" Bordiga had observed the pain in her face and gently challenged her to make her case. I can't debate with him, she worried. He's so smart and articulate, even though he's only a few years older than I am. But Benita poked her in the ribs and she rose hesitantly.

"Comrade Amadeo, we want revolution from the bottom, and you want it from the top," she told him. It was the first time she had ever spoken in public, but she drew courage as the women turned and smiled at her encouragingly. "There is a huge, complicated economic structure that puts food on our tables. It's not a good structure and it just barely works, but if there were a revolution tomorrow, it would collapse and people in Cederna would stop eating. We've been trying instead to build a counterstructure that we can control, peasant cooperatives and people's markets, so we can feed your revolution when it happens."

Bordiga sighed. "Oh, Rosaria, this is the same tedious reformism the politicians have been pushing on us for half a century. The war has provided us with a golden opportunity to wreck the system while it is desperately weak."

"Comrade Amadeo," Tommaso intervened. "The Central Committee has always said that we should neither support the war nor sabotage it. Even Comrade Sandro believes that a successful insurrection will have to wait for an Allied victory over the Central Powers. Even your ex-socialist friend Mussolini has joined the army and is doing his part. As far as the PSI is concerned, reform is all we can hope for at the moment because a revolution in the middle of the war is impossible."

"And yet the Russians have done precisely that."

"We don't really know yet what the Russians have done," Tommaso Savarino echoed the confusion they all felt about the events of March 1917. The news from Russia was slow and incomplete, and beyond the fact that Czar Nicholas and his royal family had been arrested, there was little hard information available.

Bordiga lowered his voice as if sharing a secret. "Comrade Lenin is on his way back to Petrograd. He intends to throw out the Provisional Government and lead the Soviets toward a real Marxist revolution. Then he will distribute land to the peasants and pull Russia out of the war."

Tommaso shook his head violently. "Removing Russia from the war will free the German Army for an attack on Italy. Comrade Bordiga, I think we should bring your motion to a vote, and I urge my friends here to vote against it."

Nodding, Amadeo Bordiga produced a slip of paper containing the text of his resolution and unfolded a pair of wire-rimmed glasses. Rosaria and Tommaso knew that Bordiga commanded only a minority of the votes on the PSI Central Committee, but he had visited all the provincial party sections to rally support for an immediate insurrection against the government.

"Be it resolved," Bordiga read to them slowly, "that the Cederna Chapter of the Italian Socialist Party calls for active sabotage of the imperialist war, for soldiers currently serving to desert with their weapons in hand, and for young men to refuse induction into the armed forces. We call for the disarming of the police and the army, and the transfer of political power to proletarian councils . . ."

It was more of a speech than a resolution. When he finished, Tommaso asked for any final debate before a vote. Rosaria rose again.

"We are grateful to Comrade Bordiga for coming to address us today," she said levelly. "He has our respect and our love, but I urge members of this chapter to defeat his motion, as the Central Committee of the Party itself has rejected it."

But the vote was stunningly narrow. Mercuzio Mercatelli and a group of young men at the front of the room raised their hands in support of the revolution; Bordiga's proposal was only defeated by the older men and almost all of the women.

When the meeting was over, Rosaria walked with Amadeo to the door of the Cederna Casa del Popolo. Before the war, the Neapolitan revolutionist had come frequently to Cederna; Sandro had once hidden him in the cottage for a week when he was wanted by the police.

"If there is no other way, I don't oppose a revolution," she told him seriously. "You know that, Amadeo. But we don't have any food stored, or any money, or even any guns. If Comrade Lenin isn't any better prepared than we are, a lot of Russians are going to starve."

"Vladimir and his colleagues are ruthless, violent men who don't care how many die." Bordiga shrugged. "They will have their revolution even if they destroy socialism in the process. We Italians are such nice socialists and we would make such a lovely revolution. I wonder if we will ever get the chance. Good-bye, Rosaria."

Bordiga kissed her hand. It made her shiver. Then he walked across Piazza Bixio toward the coach station. Rosaria waved, but he did not look back.

"You were very good."

It was the first time he had ever touched her. Rosaria was standing at the door of the Casa del Popolo, feeling a little dreamy as Tommaso put his hands on her shoulders and kissed her on the cheek. She liked it, but it did not make her shiver.

It's true, she thought. Revolution is sexier than reform.

She tried to relax, leaning back against Tommaso's chest for a moment as she sorted out her emotions. It had been difficult speaking out against an old friend like Bordiga, who was only saying what Sandro had preached for years.

"Amadeo pricked my conscience a little," she admitted. "Should we be more aggressive? For example, we have at least a hundred families living in shacks in Cederna while there are houses standing empty because no one can afford the rent. Perhaps a municipal public housing program would be—"

"Vetoed instantly by Mayor Mosconi," Tommaso cut her off. "What we need is a Mayor who cares about the people. Its a pity women aren't eligible for public office. You'd be perfect."

"I'm not going to be Mayor of anything until women get votes in this country." Some male socialists were wild-eyed revolutionaries like Amadeo and Sandro while others were cautious reformists like Tommaso, but to Rosaria's perpetual fury, they all saw women's suffrage as a political liability.

"Rosaria, if we got a bill through Parliament enfranchising women, we would hand the conservatives five million votes." Tommaso followed her up the stairs to the office they shared on the second floor of the Casa del Popolo. "Upper-class women would vote with their husbands, and working-class women usually obey their priests."

It was an old argument and Rosaria let it drop as she sat behind her desk and began to sort the morning mail. "The next Mayor of Cederna has to be you," she said. "There will be municipal elections as soon as the war is over, and if we started a campaign now, we could probably find the votes to elect you."

"Wouldn't Sandro be a more plausible candidate?"

"Can you see Sandro running a municipal housing program? He wants to overthrow the government and lynch the royal family."

"I would run if I had your support." Abruptly ill at ease, Tommaso stammered as he removed his spectacles and polished them on his tie. He sat on the corner of her desk, looking uncomfortable. "And there are other things we need to talk about as well. There's Massimo, for example. One wonders whether he needs a father, although no one could ever replace Leonida. What I mean is—perhaps, if we are going to continue working together . . ."

What is he saying? Rosaria had seen Tommaso skillfully arguing cases in court, deftly blending quotes from Machiavelli with high-sounding Latin phrases, but for the moment he seemed incapable of uttering a complete sentence.

Marriage, she realized suddenly. He's asking me to marry him.

"Oh!" She turned and touched his face, tenderly. I would be a lawyer's wife, she reasoned, and perhaps a Mayor's wife. I do like him so much. The Leone family could get someone else to run their estate and I could be a proper socialist without these endlessly divided loyalties. And Massimo seems to love Tommaso. On the other hand . . .

"Tommaso, we need to talk . . ." Mechanically she continued to open their mail. Then she stopped, realizing that the next envelope on the stack was not routine Socialist Party business but a letter from Achille Leone. She tried to project an air of insouciance as she tore it open, wondering if Tommaso saw her hands shaking.

Dear Rosi [it said], Just a note to tell you that we are all well here, despite everything. Sandro sends his love. I am so proud of him, because he is a magnificent soldier despite his political beliefs, and we just made him a sergeant. We have never been closer. Please kiss little Massimo for me. Why don't you come visit Sandro and me in Udine? There are some frescoes here by Giambattista Tiepolo that might interest you, and there are so many things we need to talk about. Oh, Rosi, we parted on such bad terms! Can you ever forgive me? I think about you all the time. The past is immutable, but the future is ours to choose. Yours, Achille.

I asked him to rescue Sandro from that punishment battalion, she remembered, feeling panicky. He has kept his part of the bargain. Does he want what I offered him in return?

What does he mean? How is the future ours to choose?

"Rosaria, about what I was saying?" Tommaso put his arm around her shoulders, but she broke away and walked to the door.

"Look, I've got to go on a trip," she said awkwardly. "I'll need to buy some clothing and pack and arrange things for Massimo and . . ."

"A trip? Where?"

"Udine," she murmured, her mind in a whirl. "It's just a question of . . ."

"Of what?" he demanded. "Of what is it just a question?"

"Of business." It sounded feeble, but this was nothing she wanted to explain to Tommaso. "When I get back, we'll talk about . . . what you want to talk about."

"Do you promise?"

"I promise we'll talk." She stumbled down the stairs. I need a new dress, she was thinking. Something with ribbons.

7.

. . . .

It was the twenty-third of October in the third year of what people had already begun to call the Great War. The sun had just set behind menacing clouds and a light rain was falling.

Rosaria Lombardi sat by the window gazing through the mist at the half-ruined castle that dominated the center of Udine. There is a precise purpose for this trip, she reminded herself as the train clattered to a halt. Before I can get on with the rest of my life, Achille and I need a stable relationship.

Our little sand castle has been knocked down by so many waves. Can we rebuild it again? Or should I go home and marry Tommaso?

"Udine." The conductor pulled the doors opened. "End of the line."

The platform was crowded with men wearing army gray-green, but Sandro stood a head taller than the others, resplendent in his sergeant's uniform. A grim Emilio Lodi stood by his side. She hardly recognized him without his scraggly beard.

"Rosaria!" Sandro caught her in his arms as she jumped down and he swung her around in delight. He had lost weight, but he still moved with the same vibrant energy.

"Sandro, it's been so long." She clung to him, beginning to cry. "My dearest brother! I've missed you so much."

"I've missed you too." Emotion in his voice, Sandro threw his free arm around Emilio's shoulders, including him in the hug. "Here, I brought along this humble private to carry your bags."

"Ciao, Emilio. God, the two of you look thin. Don't they feed you?"

"We're okay." Sandro led the way across the platform while Emilio struggled along behind with her suitcase. "Since our breakthrough at Podgora, we've become big heroes, and Achille got us moved into a reserve position near a town called Zaga. It's not far from here. We catch some artillery from time to time, but we'll live."

"We won't!" Suddenly Emilio lunged forward, seizing Rosaria's arm, desperation on his face. "Every two weeks they rotate us back on the line, and in the end we'll either get shot by the Austrians or executed by the carabinieri. Rosaria, you've got to talk to the colonel. Please!"

"Don't be a fool!" Angrily Sandro pulled Emilio out into the street as two military policemen gazed in their direction.

Suddenly Lodi put his back against the city wall and began screaming. "There's a revolution coming. We're going to throw down our rifles and go home. No one can take it anymore."

"Emilio," Rosaria cried.

Sandro pushed him roughly away and rescued Rosaria's bag. "Lodi, if you crack up now, you're going to fall apart when the revolution does come." His whisper was filled with authority. "And people who run around public places shouting about desertion end up in front of firing squads. Report back to the regiment and stay there."

"Rosaria, what should I do?" Lodi wailed.

"What Sandro tells you," she pleaded with him, and Emilio stumbled away, sobbing under his breath. Rosaria glanced quickly at her brother. That's the creature you wanted me to marry, she almost said, but she held her tongue.

"Damn! He was a good man once, and this war has driven him crazy."

"Is it that bad?" she asked gently.

"Morale is shot to hell," Sandro admitted. "We're in better shape than anybody else because every time we get into a real jam, Achille comes up with some fresh magic, but there are units here with very stupid officers and they have been taking a beating. And we've all been on the front too long. There's too much cheap alcohol, and not enough food."

"It's been awful at home as well," she confessed. "I feel guilty about being comfortable in the Castello when people in Cederna are getting so little to eat. Every night I lie in bed listening to people out in the forest chopping down Achille's trees for firewood. I'm supposed to be protecting his property, but there is absolutely no coal and the old people will die this winter without fuel."

"We'd better get to the hotel. The carabinieri would call this defeatist talk and arrest us as subversives," Sandro warned, leading Rosaria through the Aquileia Gate toward Udine's central square, the Piazza Vittorio Emanuele. They walked slowly down an arcade, and Rosaria gazed at colorful boutique windows, marveling at the prices of luxury goods. Udine had become the headquarters of the Supreme Allied Command for the Southern Front, and local merchants were making a killing.

They had just left the piazza when sirens began to howl and pedestrians scattered. Glancing at the sky, Sandro led her quickly down a side street toward the Hotel Italia, and together they hurried past the barricade of sand-bags around the entrance.

"What is it?"

"An air raid. The Austrians have been coming over every night recently, doing bombing and reconnaissance runs. Their long-range artillery can't hit us here in Udine, but up in Zaga the Seventy-seventh gets pounded every day. Sometimes it drives men mad."

"How can you stand it?"

"I'm preparing myself." Sandro dropped his voice to a confidential whisper as they entered the Hotel Italia. "This war is making revolution an inevitability, and the government has obliged us by radicalizing several million workers and peasants. I've been learning everything Achille has to teach me, and when the time comes, I will know how to command a proletarian fighting force."

"Don't be too brave in the meantime, big brother."

"I am seldom allowed to be brave. Somebody seems to have extracted a promise from Achille that her brother would be kept out of combat."

Rosaria smiled noncommittally as they crossed the lobby. She had never before stayed in a luxury hotel, and the opulence of the Italia was intimidating. There were deep carpets and lush curtains covering the windows. A row of porters stood along one wall, waiting to be of service while a concierge presided haughtily over the reception desk.

"Do we pay first or later?"

"Achille has arranged everything," said Sandro. To her enormous relief, he led her directly to the elevator. "I am under orders to keep you fed and entertained until he gets here tomorrow."

"And how has our Count Leone been?" she inquired coyly.

"He's amazing. It's hard to see someone you've grown up with as a hero, but Achille is simply the best regimental commander in the army. Whenever we meet an impassable obstacle, he and Guido devise some way to go over it or under it or around it. And he really cares about the men."

"No, I meant . . . is he personally happy? Does he like being a colonel?"

Sandro was unsurprised by the question. "I'm not sure. Being a soldier is something he and his family have always done, but he keeps talking about going back to Africa after the war and designing irrigation systems. He's good at orchestrating battles, but he doesn't actually like fighting very much. It even upsets him when we kill a lot of Austrians and sometimes he gets a little depressed, just like Leonida did. But now you're here, and that will change things."

"And why should I make a difference to the great Colonel Leone?"

"You'll make a difference," Sandro chuckled. "You always do."

8.

· ·

His fist raised to knock upon her door, Colonel Achille Leone detected the flutter of butterflies within his stomach. That's my going-into-battle feeling, he thought. Of all the women in the world, why should Rosaria Lombardi have the unique power to keep me permanently crazy?

I must . . . no, we must, together we must resolve this imbroglio. This time, I will declare my feelings.

He knocked and there was an immediate rustle from within. She has been waiting for me, he told himself with satisfaction. We will look back upon this as the first day of our real lives.

"Buon giorno, Achille." The door opened and he saw that she was wearing the secretarial outfit that had become almost a uniform for her, a dark blue wool skirt, tight around the hips but slightly flared at the ankles. Her long-sleeved cotton blouse was buttoned at the collar. Her only concession to fashion was a slender golden chain around her neck.

"Hello." Awkwardly they shook hands. Father must have given her the chain, he guessed. He left her with an education and a profession and a baby. Is there anything she needs from me?

"Am I dressed properly?" She seemed nervous. "I mean, is this appropriate for whatever we're going to do?"

"You are the most beautiful woman in Udine. You don't need to worry about being fashionable."

The compliment made her blush. "Leonida and Sandro once had an argument over how the upper classes managed to hang on to their power century after century," she told him. "Sandro claimed it was control over the means of production. Your father said it was a question of making everyone else feel badly dressed."

Achille winced at the unexpected reference to his father. "The Conte was good at aphorisms."

"I'm sorry." She caught his mood quickly. "Does it upset you when I mention Leonida?"

It was his turn to blush. "No, I loved you both, and when the two of you were led to believe I was dead, you turned to each other. It's taken me a while to accept that, but it's part of the past now."

Rosaria nodded. "I feel . . . well, a little nervous. It's been two years since I last saw you, and almost six years since we really talked, and back then I was just a frightened girl. I don't feel I know you very well."

"Well, let us take a stroll through Udine and renew our acquaintance." He spoke casually, but her remark stung. So you don't know me very well, he wanted to say. Who taught you to read? Who played Red Indians and cowboys with you in the chestnut grove? Who kissed you on the mouth for the very first time?

"In your letter, you said that there were some paintings by Giambattista Tiepolo in Udine." Rosaria extracted a small leather-bound volume from her handbag as they walked down the staircase to the lobby. "In the library I found this book about his life."

"Tiepolo's best work is supposed to be at the Archbishop's palace." Achille was happy to move to a neutral subject. "Let me check to see if I have any messages, and then we can pay a visit."

Leaving Rosaria by the lobby door, Achille turned to the reception desk, finding only a note from Guido confirming their arrangements for lunch. Glancing over his shoulder, he saw Rosaria in furious conversation with a Royal Army enlisted man. He was surprised, wondering whom she might know in Udine. It took him a minute to recognize the emaciated figure as Emilio Lodi, and he frowned, because there could be no legitimate reason for Lodi to be out of the regimental area.

"We need to talk," Lodi whispered urgently, unaware of his commanding officer's presence.

"Not here," Rosaria was telling him in a firm undertone as she pushed him toward the door. "Remember what we told you at the train station? You have to follow your orders."

What orders? Achille busied himself with the writing of an unnecessary note for Guido, giving Lodi time to get clear of the lobby before he turned around. Whose orders?

"Who was that?" he asked casually. "Were you talking to someone?"

"Oh, it was just a soldier from Cederna," she replied. "Shall we go? I think it's going to rain."

Outside, there were puddles among the cobblestones and the day was still overcast and cold. Rosaria was wearing a long black cloak that Achille recognized as having once belonged to his mother. They fell silent for a time as he led her toward the Piazza Vittorio Emanuele. In front of Cristina's Ospedale Militare, there was a row of parked ambulances. The drivers were mostly American volunteers, and they lounged on the ground in front of their vehicles smoking pungent Yankee cigarettes and passing a bottle of whiskey from one to another. In the center of the piazza they were passed by a column of sad-faced Austrian prisoners, shambling along in chains and guarded by a squad of carabinieri.

Farther on they encountered a group of Tommies in their baggy brown uniforms and flat tin helmets. Assigned to one of the British field artillery units on this section of the front, the *inglesi* were off-duty and already drunk as lords, although it was only noon. If the supply of alcohol were interrupted, Achille decided, the war would have to stop.

"I heard airplanes in the night." Rosaria was the first to break the silence as they strolled down the Via Lovaria toward the Archbishop's palace.

"There were some Austrian reconnaissance flights," Achille explained, turning to look at her. To his eyes, she was more beautiful than ever.

"Was there danger?"

"Here in Udine, the bombing is more of a nuisance than anything else." He was torn between the desire to be honest and reassuring at the same time. "Frankly, the tactical situation puzzles me. If I were the enemy commander, I would be attacking right now, and when their 308s opened up last night, I feared it was the start of a general offensive. But they only shelled for a few hours, and the front was quiet when I left early this morning. I guess we can get you back to Massimo in one piece. How is my fratellino?"

"He's beautiful and terrifyingly smart." Rosaria glowed with maternal pride. "Girolamo has become his great friend. The two of them go for wonderful rambles in the countryside and Masi comes home covered with mud and scratches, bubbling over with stories about Garibaldi."

"We used to hunt rabbits, Girolamo and I." Achille felt a hollowness in his chest as he remembered the Castello Leone, now his sovereign domain but so far from Udine and the Austrian Army.

They made their way to the Archbishop's palace. Achille identified himself to a footman, who led them through an elaborate throne room into the Tiepolo Gallery.

"According to this book, Tiepolo came here from Venice in the early 1700s to do these paintings," Rosaria whispered as they entered a long, narrow room. Arm in arm, they strolled across the brightly burnished marble floor while the attendant threw open the window shutters in order to shed light on the frescoes. As the chamber brightened, they saw that the ceiling and walls were covered with rich, brilliantly drawn scenes from the Old Testament.

"Our friend Tiepolo liked women," Achille observed, enjoying the dreamy, mystical quality of the work. It was difficult to imagine that artists' motives were altogether spiritual; most of the really interesting figures in his frescoes were lovely women, portrayed with a subtle, affectionate sense of humor. "Who do you suppose those two ladies are?"

Rosaria consulted her guidebook. "They were Leah and Rachel, and that's their husband Jacob over there."

"How did the story go? 'Leah was tender-eyed, but Rachel was beauteous and well-favored.' Didn't Jacob work seven years to earn Rachel and her father tricked him into marrying Leah instead?"

"How sad it must have been for Leah to get a husband under false pretenses." She glanced at him quickly and then looked away, shaking her head.

"I was thinking more about poor Jacob," Achille admitted. "Did he ever come to love his tender-eyed Leah? Or did he kiss her with his eyes closed, pretending she was the well-favored Rachel?''

There were times, he remembered, when I made love to my poor Anfi with Rosi's name screaming in my brain. Did Rosi ever lie in my father's arms imagining he were me? Or did she come to prefer the father to the son? Will we ever be able to talk about these things?

They climbed to the top of a monumental staircase to inspect a gigantic fresco of Saint Michael casting Lucifer down from the heavens. Tiepolo was teasing again because the Devil looked as if he were having more fun than the Archangel.

The celestial battle reminded Rosaria of the real war going on a few kilometers away. ''When do you think the fighting will be over?'' she asked suddenly. ''Cederna is suffering so badly. The young men are all gone, and so many have already been killed. Prices have risen sky-high and there doesn't seem to be any meat anywhere.''

''I don't think it could possibly end soon,'' he told her honestly. ''The Americans are arriving, but the Central Powers are still very strong, especially with the chaos in Russia. The men are utterly exhausted and their spirits are low. Frankly, all this anti-war propaganda being generated by the PSI is becoming a morale problem. When your friend Amadeo Bordiga suggests that the troops rise up and kill their officers, it does not help matters in the slightest.''

''The official Socialist Party has never advocated a military rebellion.'' She took offense immediately. ''But you have no idea what it is like for the poor. With inflation and unemployment—''

''People sacrificing their lives in the trenches have the right to expect a minimal amount of support from the home front,'' he interrupted hotly. ''I'm sorry about the inflation, but paying high prices for bread is not quite as catastrophic as being bombarded by Austrian artillery.''

They had reached the bottom of the staircase when Rosaria whirled on him.

''The people at home had no say whatsoever about this war, and they have a perfect right to complain. You, on the other hand, deliberately chose this profession.''

''You're wrong!'' Achille was stunned by her anger but he stood his ground as she blazed at him.

''I'm not! You could have been a farmer or an engineer, or a professor, or a playboy. You could have stayed home with your father. Or with me and I would have been your secretary or your serving girl or your mistress if Your Excellency had desired me in that capacity. It was your choice to go off and fight Arabs and Austrians, but there are three million men in your army who want to be home with the women who love them. You can hardly blame them if they fail to share your enthusiasm for patriotic bloodbaths!''

She was crying. Achille shook off his anger, realizing that they were getting close to absolute honesty.

''Rosi?''

"I hate this war," she sobbed. "Nothing will ever be the same again."

"We make our own destinies, war or no war." He followed her to the door of the Archbishop's palace, thrusting a half-lira coin into the outstretched hand of the puzzled footman. Outside, drizzle was falling from a gloomy sky. There was moisture on her face, but it was hard to distinguish tears from raindrops.

She looked down at the cobblestones, avoiding his eyes. "Achille, just before your letter came, Tommaso Savarino asked—"

"No, don't talk, please." It's time, he decided, to say what ought to have been said years ago. I will tell her that I love her and ask her to marry me when the war is over. I will adopt Massimo as my son and heir, and anyone who wishes to laugh at the arrangement is at liberty to do so.

"Comandante!" It was the worst possible moment for an interruption but Guido Rosselli had materialized at the end of the street, a dozen meters away. Beside him was Cristina, looking willowy in her Red Cross uniform.

"Ciao!" Achille called. A glance at his pocket watch reminded him that he had booked a table for one o'clock at the Ristorante alla Vite.

"Are we still meeting for lunch?" Guido asked. It was socially impossible to avoid introductions and polite conversation. Achille offered his arm to Rosaria and led her toward the street corner where the Rosselli siblings were waiting.

"I still love you," he whispered. "When the war is over, I think we should be married."

Rosaria looked thunderstruck for a moment, and shook her head. "Tommaso has asked me to marry him," she said faintly.

I wish he would go away. She glared at the waiter who insisted upon refilling her wineglass after every sip. To accompany their risotto and wild duck, Achille had ordered an exquisite Pinot Grigio, and the *camerieri* were pouring it out relentlessly.

Is this, she wondered, really the way the upper class relaxes? How can we talk freely with all these servile creatures bowing and scraping around us? Sandro should give them a speech on class consciousness and proletarian dignity.

Rosaria glanced at her brother to see if he shared her annoyance, but he was locked in a serious conversation with Major Guido Rosselli at the opposite end of the table. A strange relationship had developed between the two men. In politics, Guido was a reactionary conservative with an intense antagonism toward socialism, while Sandro still advocated a Marxist revolution as soon as the war was over. All they had in common was a fanatic loyalty to Achille, but it seemed to be enough.

Still upset, Rosaria stole a glance at Guido's stunning little sister, who was telling Achille and Terenzio about the supply problems the medical staff was experiencing at the Ospedale Militare. She makes me feel like someone's dowdy old aunt, Rosaria mused darkly, studying the Venetian woman's peerless features and slender frame. Even her nurse's uniform is tailor-made, and it fits better than anything I own.

Calm down, she told herself, taking a sip of the Pinot Grigio to dissolve the tension. It's been a difficult morning. Don't take it out on Cristina or the waiters.

"Do you like the wine?" Achille was playing the solicitous host and their eyes met briefly. Rosaria smiled before looking away in embarrassment. An hour ago, she recalled, he asked me to marry him. Did he mean it? Or did he just want to spend the afternoon in my bed?

"The wine? Oh, yes!" She found it difficult to make polite conversation. "But I prefer our Cederna bianco."

Grinning, Terenzio leaned across the table and took his brother's arm. "Achille, you know that tunnel that goes from the olive-oil shed to the wine cellar under the Castello? Do you recall the day we crept in and carried off a half dozen bottles of Father's best wine, and got stinking drunk in the forest by the Tiber? Remember? Tommaso passed out and Sandro threw up in the bushes and Rosaria jumped into the river with all her clothes on."

"Who could forget?" Achille said. "Sandro, we got into a fight over politics. You tried to hit me, and fell down. Remember?"

"With great clarity," said Sandro dryly. "Even thinking about it gives me a hangover."

"I didn't jump into the river." Rosaria smiled at the irresistible memory. "I was pushed in by a certain young nobleman, who then had to take off his trousers, jump in, and rescue me."

They all laughed. Rosaria wondered precisely what Achille was remembering about that picnic by the river. My breasts had just begun to grow, she reminisced. When my blouse got wet you could see my nipples and after you pulled me out of the water, I took off my skirt because it was soaking wet. It was innocent, or at least I thought it was until I saw your excitement, and you blushed and turned away. So right now, Terenzio is recalling the wine and the comradeship, and Sandro is thinking about wanting to hit his best friend.

But I am thinking about your body and you are thinking about mine. Oh, Achille, what are we going to do? Shall we become compagni at last?

"Having that wildness must have been lovely." Cristina frowned, suddenly isolated by their shared laughter. "I was always under such scrutiny as a child, and Mother was always terrified that her only daughter would disgrace the family. Guido was allowed to be crazy, but if I'd got drunk down by the riverside with a bunch of boys, Mother would have packed me off to a nunnery. I envy you."

"I have an idea," Rosaria said to her. "Let's get drunk and you and I will throw the boys in the river." The table dissolved into laughter, and Rosaria found herself quite liking this delicate Venetian girl. She seemed vulnerable and a little tragic, like a Puccini heroine who dies in the last act.

"Cederna sounds like such a lovely place," Cristina commented. "Achille, when the war is over, will you go back there to live?"

She's in love with him, Rosaria suddenly realized, and she's wondering if their futures could mingle. Crissi would adore him forever, and she is beautiful enough to model for Tiepolo. Achille misses his brown-skinned lady, and he is starting to need a wife.

Men always fall in love with nurses, she reflected. And Cristina is precisely the sort of person he ought to marry. But the notion made her sober and unhappy.

"Like Cincinnatus retiring to his farm?" Achille drawled. "I don't know. They say that there will be no more wars after this one, and it might be time to put the army behind me and get back to engineering. How about you, little brother?"

"I'm going to play the piano." Terenzio spoke without hesitation. "I'll take a flat in Rome and study at the Accademia."

Their futurizing was interrupted by a battalion of waiters with sherbet, and Rosaria carefully copied Cristina in the selection of spoons. That's another reason I shouldn't marry Achille, she decided sourly. He would spend the rest of his life teaching me etiquette. Cristina was born knowing what spoon to use.

"What shall we do this afternoon?" Guido inquired.

"A wealth of possible pleasures awaits us," Terenzio announced. "There is a puppet show in the Piazza Vittorio Emanuele, and a motion picture called *Quo Vadis,* with Romans and hungry lions and succulent Christians. Alternatively, there is a piano concert at four in the Palazzo Municipale."

"I've never seen a moving picture," said Rosaria impulsively.

"You aren't missing anything," grumbled Guido. "Who's giving the concert? Can't be anyone good or he'd never come to Udine."

"It isn't anybody good," Terenzio admitted. "I shall be offering patriotic songs for the generals, some Satie for myself, and anything my audience would like to hear. Any requests?"

"Play 'Caro Nome' from *Rigoletto,*" said Rosaria quickly.

Their eyes met for a moment of conspiracy as they simultaneously recalled how Leonida had loved this particular aria. "An excellent choice, madam."

Then there was a bang above them, and the room shivered. Bits of ceiling fell on the carpet, and the serving maids all screamed.

"That was a bomb," observed Terenzio as air raid sirens wailed belatedly. "Damn Austrians will do anything to keep me from playing the piano."

"A raid at midday? What the hell are they doing? Listen!" Achille cupped his hands behind his ears to catch a faint and distant whistling sound. "That's an incoming shell, and we shouldn't be able to hear it from here."

Guido frowned. "It could be an acoustic freak. The wind?"

"Our lads will be all right at Zaga, but I've been worried about the front near Caporetto." Achille pushed away his sherbet. "The troops there are terrible, and half the officers are drunkards."

"Listen, my driver's outside." Terenzio spoke with studied nonchalance, wishing to spare the ladies any alarm. "Sandro and I could run down to

Division Headquarters, check the status of the front, and meet you back here for coffee."

It was quickly agreed. Terenzio and Sandro left as soon as the all-clear had sounded, but the waiters stopped pouring Pinot Grigio and began to close the restaurant's shutters to protect the windows against bomb fragments. An apologetic manager hurriedly brought the check for Achille's signature. In the distance they heard another explosion.

"Look, we'd better get our coffee at the hotel," Guido proposed, taking his sister's arm. "With this cloud cover, the Austrians could send in one Albatross at a time and keep Udine tied in knots for the rest of the afternoon."

"They might need me at the hospital," Cristina protested.

"You're on leave." Guido was firm as he guided his sister toward the door. "And I've already got you an expensive room at the Italia. Come on!"

Guido and Cristina rushed on ahead, but Achille seemed slow to follow, as if he were lost in meditation.

"Is it serious?" Rosaria asked.

"I don't know. I had hoped to forget about the war for one afternoon and concentrate on you."

"Do you want a prediction?" she teased him as they went out into the street. "You're going to marry Cristina."

"Do you think she's decided?" He laughed and slipped his arm around her shoulders. "Good of you to alert me, but I'm going to marry you."

There was another detonation to the east, and they looked up into the clouds. Somewhere above them, an Austrian pilot was flying blind, bombing randomly while Italian anti-aircraft batteries blazed unseeing into the darkening sky. "The ultimate in Russian roulette," muttered Achille. "He can't see us and we can't see him."

The sirens were screaming again now. Rosaria picked up her skirts and ran as Achille pulled her down the avenue toward the Hotel Italia. They approached the rear entrance and ducked behind a sandbag barrier. Frightened, she moved into his arms, and he held her tightly. Above them they could hear the motor of the Albatross as the anonymous Austrian prowled the skies.

"Achille . . ." He had not held her like this since the day of his departure for Libya, and she found herself trembling involuntarily.

"Tommaso is a fine man," he told her firmly. She sensed what was coming, already dreading the decision he was going to demand of her. "And if you want to marry him, I'll give you the biggest dowry in the history of Cederna. But I don't think you love him. Am I being arrogant? I think you love me."

"Don't," she whispered as he leaned forward to kiss her, and she turned away from him to face the rough burlap fabric of the sandbags, holding the text on Giambattista Tiepolo against her breasts. The day went strangely quiet, as if the war had lost interest in them.

"Why not?"

"If you marry me, it will split your family down the middle. I was your father's mistress, and everyone knows it. I am a peasant woman with an illegitimate child, and everyone knows that too. To marry me, you would have to leave the army, and we would become a laughingstock.''

"No, not that it would make any difference, but the war has changed everything,'' he insisted. ''There are nurses in Cristina's hospital who have affairs with married men, and no one minds as long as their lovers are commissioned officers. We've already lost half a million men in this war. When the carnage is finally over, will anyone have the energy to worry about the dignity of my family tree or your poor lost honor?''

"Oh, Achille.'' She was trying not to cry. ''Tommaso has waited for me so long.''

"Not as long as I.'' Almost violently, he spun her around to face him. ''I have always wanted you for my wife, always, since we were children. When I was younger, I accepted the verdict of society that a marriage between us would be impossible, but two long wars have taught me something about the shortness of life. When we win this war, I want you to be my wife and my countess. I wish to make Massimo my adopted son and heir. Have you given yourself to Tommaso? No, it doesn't matter, and I had no right to ask.''

"I have not,'' she told him honestly. ''I wanted to settle things with you.''

"Then let us settle things!'' Sweeping her into his arms, he carried her into the hotel and down a darkened corridor.

"Where are we going?'' she protested angrily as he kicked open the door to his room and deposited her on the bed. The book on Tiepolo fell on the floor, forgotten, and Achille kicked it beneath the mattress. ''I'm not some two-penny harlot you can haul into bed on a whim.''

"This is hardly a whim.'' He held her tightly. ''Look, I know things have been insane between us and I should have organized—''

"Organized,'' she hissed. ''I'm a woman, not a damn regiment. Who told you you could manage my life? Ever since you put me to work in your father's vegetable garden you've been pulling my strings as if I were a marionette.''

There was an explosion so close that the windows rattled, but Achille ignored it, intent upon caressing her breasts. For a moment she lay still on the bed with her arms over her head, letting him do what he liked with her. This needs to be my decision, she told herself fiercely. Either I make love to him or I don't, but I decide.

"Rosi, I want to take your clothes off now.'' He spoke with a strange politeness, his fingers on the buttons of her blouse.

"Do it, then.'' The decision was quickly made. ''Please!''

As from a great distance, she watched him undo the ivory buttons on her silk blouse, one by one, until he had bared her breasts. Her nipples stiffened when he bent to kiss them, and she felt a deep ache in her stomach.

"Now it's my turn.'' Catching him off-guard, she tipped him over on his back. Jumping quickly to her feet, she stepped out of her skirt, and then attacked the buttons on his field jacket. There was a moment of giggling, and then they were both naked.

"Do you love me? Say it! Please say it!"

"What shall I say?" she asked shyly. "I've wanted you for so long."

"Then say 'I love you, Achille!' Please!"

"I love you. I do love you!"

"Be my wife!"

"Oh, if you want me. Oh, my husband, my sweet husband."

Faintly, vaguely, she could hear artillery in the distance, big guns pounding away, but Achille seemed conscious of nothing but her, and after a while she forgot about the bombardment and concentrated on him. Her body was ready, but instead of possessing her immediately he savored her like a feast, to be consumed one course at a time. She had been passive with Leonida, accepting the caresses of the great man but scarcely daring to return them. With Achille, she found her courage, and when he kissed her where she had not been kissed before, she touched him boldly, feeling his hardness.

"Come into me, please." She guided him with her hand. "Please, I can't wait."

They melted together, and at a certain point an unfamiliar spasm of pleasure rippled through her. Rosaria cried out, and cried again when it happened again. In the fleeting moment of sanity that followed each moan, she wondered if the neighbors would guess what was happening and pound on the wall to make them stop.

"Oh, Rosi! Oh, God!" Achille groaned, just as artillery shells began to land just down the street in the Piazza Vittorio Emanuele. The windows shattered and people in the hotel began shrieking, making it less likely that anyone would bother listening through the walls to two lovers.

"What's happening?" she asked. He collapsed by her side. Immediately she curled into his arms, fearful that the war would steal him from her.

"Some people we don't know are shooting at some other people we don't know," said Achille. For a moment the shooting seemed to have stopped and there was quiet all around them. "It has nothing to do with us."

"Then let's sleep. We've never slept together, have we? I want to wake up in your arms."

"Let's sleep." He smiled and she closed her eyes.

9.

. . . .

"Achille!"

His name was being shouted. There was a pounding at the door. Achille sat up in the shadows, awakening in the half-light of early morning, disoriented, an orderly man in a demented world.

"Guido?" Light from the corridor slashed in as the door flew open and Major Rosselli burst into the chamber.

"Christ, Achille, I've just come from Second Army Headquarters. The front has collapsed and the Seventy-seventh could be cut off at any minute. Didn't you hear the cannons? What have you been doing? Oh, I see."

Guido's face darkened with anger. It was only then that Achille realized he was not alone in bed. Shaking the auburn hair out of her eyes, Rosaria sat up beside him, covering her breasts with the blanket.

"I hate to bother you two lovers, but an army of unfriendly people is coming this way."

"There's an Austrian attack?" Achille sprang from the bed, awkward in his nakedness as he searched for his trousers.

"Sod the Austrians!" Guido snarled. "There are seven regular German Army divisions pouring through our lines at Caporetto. I tried to get back to Zaga late last night, but the roads are jammed with deserters. Your socialist friends are throwing down their rifles and running away. The army is dissolving."

"Tell me about the Seventy-seventh. What's our tactical situation?"

"Not good. Marcello Campione got a call through to me this morning. Apparently Giuseppe Papafava was wounded at our forward observation post. Sandro took a squad out to rescue him and got cut off himself. Now it's a stalemate. The Germans can't get by Sandro and he can't retreat."

"I must go." Achille turned to to Rosaria, watching her eyes widen with distress. Her bare shoulders dark against the whiteness of the sheets, she seemed more beautiful than ever and he silently cursed the war, and Guido, and all the miserable Germans. One night, he raged, one short night! Is this all we will ever be permitted?

"Don't be brave," she begged him. "Just save Sandro and get out of there. I need both of you."

"I want him alive to give you away at the wedding." Achille tried to smile as he laced up his boots.

"What shall I do?"

"Stay here," he instructed. "Stay here and by God I'll find some way to get back to you. I swear it."

Cristina Rosselli rang for a servant, and no one came. Nothing of the sort had ever happened before, and she sat on the edge of her bed, perplexed. First a sleepless night, she fretted, with all those guns and bombs, and now no breakfast? It seemed unfair.

She dressed as usual rejecting a soft, fashionable dress in favor of a starchy nurse's outfit, since she craved the self-confidence that came from her white cotton uniform.

I have never done anything as important as being a nurse, she told herself as she fixed her hair in the bathroom mirror and pinned on her cap. Even after the wedding, I want to go on being a nurse. I will care for the poor. Rosaria will be my friend and help me. The people of Cederna will come to love their new countess.

She was still in the bath when a shell detonated some distance from her bedroom window, spraying shards of glass over her bed.

Another shell followed the first. When the whole building swayed, she decided that it would be safer to wait in Achille's room. Feeling romantic, she ran down the corridor and pushed open his door, imaging how he would return victorious from the battlefield and find her, perhaps curled up on his empty bed. The sinfulness of the idea made her shiver.

As her eyes adjusted to the darkness, however, she realized slowly that there was already someone in the colonel's bed. Cristina was the product of a convent school, and in her instinctive innocence she could not, for a moment, think of a reasonable explanation.

"Oh! I'm sorry. Something's wrong."

"I know." Rosaria Lombardi sat up, not bothering to disguise her nakedness. "I've been trying to pretend it isn't happening."

They spent the night together. Cristina tried immediately to reason her way around this dreadful fact. Perhaps it meant nothing. Once, in Venice, she had seen Guido strolling arm and arm with a woman who was distinctly not of their social class. Mother had explained that the rules were different for men, doubly different for soldiers, and triply different for Guido Rosselli.

"Would you hand me my dress?" Rosaria asked quietly. "Someone is coming."

Before Cristina could comply, Terenzio Leone burst in, breathless, his once-smart carabiniere uniform dirty and soaked with sweat.

"Thank God I've found you. There's been a Austro-German breakthrough." He paused and Cristina saw his eyes widen as Rosaria tucked her bare legs beneath the covers. For a moment he seemed stunned. "Oh, Rosaria, you finally did it! Sorry, carissima, but the honeymoon has to be suspended. We've got to evacuate Udine."

"My hospital," Cristina said. "There'll be wounded boys coming in. I've got to go there."

"I like you so much for thinking that," Terenzio said. "They'll be moving the hospital, and Rosaria can ride out with you. But watch out. There are gangs of deserters roaming the streets."

"Leave us a weapon," said Rosaria.

Terenzio tossed a side arm onto the bed, the big 10.35-millimeter service revolver carried by carabinieri, and headed for the door. "See you in Cederna, Rosaria, and I'll play 'Caro nome' on the Blütner for you. Meanwhile, take care of this little girl, okay?"

As the door closed Rosaria jumped from the bed, and the sight of her nudity stunned Cristina. In her polite Venetian society, people were careful in matters of dress, and it was the first time she had ever seen an unclothed adult of either sex. No wonder Achille wanted to sleep with her, she conceded, looking at Rosaria's full hips and heavy breasts and making the inevitable comparison to her own slender, boyish body. She's a woman and I'm just what Terenzio said I was, a little girl.

"Does he love you?" Cristina asked hesitantly.

"Who, Achille?" Rosaria was pulling a slip over her head. The question seemed to amuse her. "Love is such an inadequate word. Let's go!"

It would be the supreme idiocy, thought Sandro, to die for King and Country. How did I get myself into this?

"Sergente, what are we going to do?" one of the corporals called out. Despite the increasing danger the men were behaving with courage, confident that Colonel Leone would rescue them even now. Unfortunately, Sandro had no idea what Achille was doing or even if he had managed to return to Zaga. All day, there had been only desultory fire from the Seventy-seventh, but it was impossible to say whether the regiment was preparing to retreat or attack or just saving ammunition.

"Watch our left flank while I check on Sergeant Papafava," Sandro ordered, deciding not to reveal his pessimism. In fact, their situation was appalling. They were sheltering in a shallow trench just behind a clump of beach trees. The Germans were now only seventy-five meters away, but Sandro's men were using their Breda machine gun to keep them at bay. Half a kilometer behind them, the main body of the Seventy-seventh seemed to be holding its position, but Italian units on either side had given way, and Achille's regiment would soon have to withdraw or face encirclement.

Achille needs to pull the regiment out of there while we cover his retreat, Sandro told himself as he crawled through the beach trees to the machine-gun emplacement. Then we will try heroically to be taken prisoner and get Giuseppe to a German field hospital.

"Sandro, we're nearly out of ammunition." There was pain in Papafava's face as he supported himself behind the Breda, half-buried in brass shell casings. The veteran regimental sergeant major had been hit several times in the legs, but he was still valiantly commanding the machine-gun crew, firing short, lethal bursts whenever the Germans tried to advance on the Italian observation post. Just below Giuseppe's right knee was a tourniquet stanching the flow of blood from a severed artery; without medical attention soon, he would lose that leg to gangrene.

"Let me look." With his field glasses, Sandro studied the terrain between them and the Germans. This had once been a field of wheat, but the ardor of two armies had reduced it to a jumble of crater and shrapnel. Off to the right, Sandro could see shreds of blue canvas from a half-burned carnival tent; the division's recreation office had scheduled a marionette show for that evening. The Eighty-third Infantry Regiment's mess and command huts had once stood to the northeast, but there was nothing there now. The officers and noncoms were all dead, and the men were mostly prisoners of war.

"Get the young ones out of here while there's time," Papafava proposed. "I'll cover you."

Sandro shook his head. "The Germans have covered the field between us and the Seventy-seventh with grazing fire and we'd be cut to ribbons. Do you want to surrender?"

"Do you?"

"Not yet."

"Then get some more ammunition into this gun, you bloody socialist." Papafava grinned at him. "And we'll kill some Germans."

Sandro had just begun to feed another belt of ammo into the Breda when he noticed that the sky was growing rapidly darker. He was wondering how Achille had arranged a total eclipse of the sun when he realized that the Seventy-seventh was firing every smoke canister it had into the German position.

Was the Seventy-seventh covering its retreat? He tried to see, but there was black smoke everywhere now and the volume of fire over the battlefield suddenly seemed to have increased a hundredfold. The noise was painful and bewildering. Sandro found it difficult to think, and even Giuseppe Papafava stopped firing and looked puzzled.

Despite the uproar, he sensed movement behind him and whirled around with his side arm, finding himself face-to-face with Achille Leone and a squad of volunteers from the Seventy-seventh. The colonel looked remarkably cheerful.

"Come on while the smoke lasts!" Achille shouted to make himself heard over the gunfire. "We've cleared a corridor for your people. Once you're safe, we have orders to pull the regiment back behind Zaga and regroup."

"Giuseppe's hurt."

Achille nodded. "We're bringing up a stretcher. Everything's going to be all right. Sandro, I can't tell you how proud I am. If only Father were here to see this. Half the units on this line are headed for Sicily with their hands in the air, but our regiment stood and fought and stopped those German bastards cold. Let's go! You've got to give the bride away at the wedding.''

"What?"

"Come on! I'm going to marry your beautiful sister."

Sandro was on his hands and knees, feeling a strange new joy, when he heard the peculiar whistle of an incoming German trench-mortar shell. The keening of the round cut out suddenly, which meant that the shell was virtually on top of them. Frantically looking for cover, Sandro threw himself face-down into the trench. No, no, he thought, in the last moment of consciousness remaining to him. Not now! Not when we are all going to be happy at last!

"Allah Akbar! Allah Akbar!"

Thinking at first that he was in bed, Sandro Lombardi rubbed his eyes and sat up, perplexed to hear a thousand voices shouting "God is Great" in Arabic. It took him another moment to remember that this had been the battle cry of the old Lupi di Lazio battalion, a verbal souvenir of their famous victory at Sidi Osman.

"Achille?" Abruptly, he remembered the shell and realized that he had been stunned by the blast. He found it difficult to believe that he was not hurt; there were mangled corpses all around him, and as he looked for Achille he found an arm with no body attached to it. The trench was gone, and the little clump of beach trees had been leveled. He was sitting in the middle of the open battlefield.

"Achille!" he screamed. The wind was blowing the smoke away, exposing them, and he scratched frantically through the mud, pushing bodies out of the way, praying desperately to the God in whom he did not normally believe. Let Achille be alive, he demanded. He is the best man we will ever have.

He found Achille beneath parts of another man's body. The colonel's face was covered with dirt and blood, and it was impossible to tell whether he was breathing or not. Sandro tried to find Achille's pulse, but even under the best of circumstances his blunt fingers had never been very good at finding pulses.

"Is this it?" he sobbed. "Are we going to die together?" He got to his hands and knees to pull Achille free of the mud. There was blood everywhere and the colonel's body was inert as Sandro cradled it in his arms.

"Allah Akbar!" The ghostly roar came again, and as the smoke cleared Sandro looked across the battlefield to the west, where the Seventy-seventh Infantry Regiment was coming over the top by the hundreds, charging wildly into the German position.

"Suicide," he grunted, but it was a wonderful sight. Even the Germans held their fire for a moment, watching this strange regiment launch a blistering counterattack when the rest of the Italian Army was in headlong retreat. Sandro could see Guido Rosselli at the head of the regiment, waving his pistol defiantly.

A moment later the Germans opened up with a dozen heavy machine guns, cutting cruelly into the ranks of the Seventy-seventh. Men began to go down with screams, while others scrambled hopelessly for cover.

No one will be left alive, Sandro realized that the attack had served only to provide him with the opportunity to carry Achille to safety. He lifted the silent colonel into his arms, stumbling over corpses as he staggered west toward the Italian front. He ignored the bullets flying past him since there was no way of being cautious now. "Save us," he prayed in desperation. "Bring us home safe to Cederna. Lord, we did not deserve this, whatever we have done."

He was panting and crying, and his whole body hurt. Achille was heavy and felt dead. Sandro looked up at the darkening sky and suddenly wondered what kind of sadistic god would preside over this battlefield.

"You should be ashamed of yourself," he screamed at the empty sky as he trudged through the mud. "I hate you!"

IO.

. . . .

"Why would the Germans bother us?" Cristina hesitated in the doorway, frightened by the anarchy on the street. "Do you think we should stay here?"

"It depends how much you object to being raped," Rosaria snapped, although she fully understood Crissi's reluctance to leave the safety of the Hotel Italia. Above them, Austrian planes still swarmed through the clouds, bombing haphazardly. The piazza in front of the hotel was a scene of hysteria: desperate merchants were boarding up their windows with scraps of wood, while families with sobbing children waited by mounds of suitcases and steamer trunks for taxicabs that were never going to come.

"Madam, we are closing the hotel now." The Italia's manager eased Cristina firmly across the threshold. "You and your maid will have to make other arrangements."

Irritated by the manager's fine eye for social status, Rosaria led Cristina into the riotous piazza. The city's fabric was coming unstitched. Moving their ladders frantically from pole to pole, *telegrafisti* from the Royal Italian Signal Corps were taking down the telephone wires. At the corner, a trio of roughly dressed men pried open the shutters of a closed food store and then smashed the glass to steal tins of meat. As the two women pushed through the panicky mob, air-raid sirens howled endlessly, but the Udinesi had become too fatalistic about the Austrian Air Force to pay much attention.

"Our commanding officer will let you ride out with us," Cristina explained as the two women threaded their way through the crowd toward the Military Hospital. "You could help with the patients, and Colonel Carducci is such a kind man. His father and my grandfather served together during the Crimean War."

When they reached the hospital the door was open and the foyer was empty. There was only one nervous military policeman on duty.

"Signor Carabiniere?" she quavered. "The Nineteenth Medical Group? The doctors and all the nurses?"

"They left for Verona about an hour ago."

"Oh, God, they'll think I've deserted them," Cristina cried in desperation. "Can we get a train to Verona?"

"The train is gone."

"Surely there'll be another?"

The carabiniere looked at them as if they had missed the point. "The Germans just bombed the tracks. There isn't ever going to be another train out of Udine."

Stunned, they walked slowly away from the hospital. It seemed quieter now, since the Udinesi had surrendered their city to army patrols and gangs of looters. There was an acrid odor drifting in from the east, and Rosaria wrinkled her nose. "What's that smell?"

"Mustard gas," Cristina explained. "I wonder what's happened to our men?"

"I don't know, but they have gas masks and we don't. We'd better start walking." Taking Crissi's arm, Rosaria suddenly noticed that the younger woman was crying. "What's wrong?"

"Is he going to marry you?"

Rosaria nodded. "I know it's insane but last night he asked me, and I said yes."

"Over the past year, I got to know your Achille quite well." Cristina tried to smile as the tears ran down her cheeks. "And yesterday at lunch, I organized it all in my mind, how he would marry me after the war, how I would live in Cederna with you as my best friend. I had convinced myself that he was falling in love with me, you see, and all the time he was just being polite to Guido's hysterical little sister."

"You can still be my best friend."

"Are you just being polite too?"

Rosaria laughed, taking Cristina's arm and tugging her down the street toward the city wall. "Crissi, I never bother being polite. Come on, we've got some walking to do."

At the edge of the city they found a flagstone road leading southwest toward Verona. It was filled with a great ribbon of refugees stretching off to the horizon, thousands and thousands of families all jostling one another in their shared desperation to be gone before the enemy arrived. The rain had made the fields sodden and impassable. Bracing herself, Rosaria led Cristina into the melee.

"Out of the way! Make way there!" screamed a man just behind them, and Rosaria observed that the mob had not developed much group solidarity. Red-faced and panting, a fat man pushed belligerently past them with a two-wheeled cart piled high with mattresses and suitcases.

Sensibly, some of the refugees were traveling light, carrying only a shoulder bag or rucksack. But others were trying to rescue everything they owned, and Rosaria saw horse-drawn carriages bearing chairs and tables and brass bed frames. Men strode by in white shirts and ties and good black suits while their wives stumbled along behind in long dresses and feather hats.

"Look, they must be deserters." Cristina pointed at a crowd of forty or fifty young men with short haircuts and black shoes. Most of them had traded their military clothing for badly fitting civilian trousers and shirts, but some were so desperate to be out of their uniforms that they straggled along in their underpants with blankets across their shoulders.

"What happens if they're caught?" Rosaria asked.

"They get shot." Delicately, Cristina averted her gaze as they passed a soldier who had dropped his pants to defecate by the side of the road.

Rosaria wondered if they themselves would be reduced to the same indignity before the day was out, since the barren, water-soaked fields offered little privacy. "How long will it take us to walk to Verona?" she wondered, worrying about practicalities. She was carrying a small leather bag with some toiletries and underwear, but her skirt and blouse would have to do until she reached Cederna. If they found shelter, she could sleep rolled up in her cape, but the sky was still ominous and it was getting cold.

Cristina winced. "Maybe a week. It's been several centuries since a member of my family was this uncomfortable."

"You need some peasant blood in you."

Joking to keep their spirits up, the two women made their way through a herd of dairy cattle who were methodically covering the road with manure as their owner stolidly drove them toward the safety of the south. The banality of all these cows reminded her of home, of Cederna and the Castello Leone, and she wondered how long it would take to get back to Massimo. I had no business leaving him, she thought guiltily. If something happens to me, he will be an orphan, and if Achille is also killed, who will look after him?

After an hour's walk they encountered a column of Italian Army ambulance cars turning off a mud road onto the main highway, trying to make their way back toward Udine. There must be a lot of casualties at the front and Rosaria wondered for the hundredth time if Achille and Sandro were safe.

Trying to break through, the ambulance drivers were sounding their Klaxons frantically, but the crowd refused to give way.

Cristina rushed up to the officer in charge. "Captain, I'm trying to find the Nineteenth Medical Group. They left Udine early this morning."

"We passed them a kilometer back that way." The officer pointed up the secondary road. "Some of their trucks broke down and they made camp in a woods off to the left."

"What's happening at the front?" Rosaria demanded.

"We're losing the war." The ambulance column commander shrugged, and he pushed past them with pistol in hand, threatening to shoot anyone who stood in his way.

They heard the singing long before they saw the deserters coming down the road toward them, and Rosaria recognized the strains of an old socialist hymn her father used to sing. There was a strangely convivial atmosphere about the mob, as if they were on their way to a picnic or a party. Many of the men were swigging from their canteens, and there was a powerful odor of cheap army cognac in the air.

"There must be a thousand of them, and they're drunk." Cristina seemed apprehensive about walking through the mob. "Should we hide?"

"They won't hurt us." Rosaria reached into her leather bag to touch the butt of Terenzio's pistol. Boldly, she walked directly into the throng of fleeing soldiers, ignoring lewd comments tossed in their direction.

"Rosaria, hey, wait a minute!" Suddenly there was a tenor voice from behind and Rosaria felt a hand on her shoulder. Startled, she pulled the pistol from her bag and pointed it at the soldier who had accosted her. It took her another moment to recognize Emilio Lodi, wearing a shepherd's wool jacket over his uniform. He looked feverishly drunk and maniacal.

"It's me!" Slurring his words, the young man from Cederna raised his hands in mock surrender. "Listen, we're getting away, Rosaria. No more war."

"Oh, it's you!" She was not at all pleased to see him. "What's happened to the Seventy-seventh? Colonel Leone and Sandro and Major Rosselli?"

"Who cares?" Lodi was wild with alcohol. "For us the war is over. We're going home to get on with the revolution."

"The war isn't over. You can't just declare a war over and walk away from it."

"We just did," Lodi proclaimed jubilantly as other deserters collected around them. "Boys, this is Rosaria the Red, the woman I was telling you about. If we can get back to Cederna, she can hide us."

"No, look, I think you should go back to your units," Rosaria began, but her words were lost as the men sent up a raucous cheer. Before she could challenge the feasibility of sheltering a thousand Royal Army deserters on the Leone estate, Emilio's friends hoisted her triumphantly onto their shoulders.

"Put me down! The orders of the Party were to act within the law," she cried, but the moment had gone mad, and no one paid any attention to her. White-faced with dismay, Cristina Rosselli edged away while the deserters burst into another revolutionary marching song.

In that same demented instant, a carabiniere *autocarro* pulled up the road. The vehicle's canvas top was down, and Rosaria saw that it was a puzzled-looking Terenzio. There were only two carabinieri against an ocean of deserters, but the fleeing soldiers reacted hysterically, some dashing back up the road toward Udine and others retreating into the marshy fields. Out of one corner of her eye Rosaria saw Cristina knocked to her hands and knees in the confusion.

"Rosaria," Terenzio shouted, standing on the seat to see what was going on. "Rosaria, what the hell? Emilio, is that you? Listen, there are Austrian aircraft—"

"You bastard!" Rosaria heard Emilio mutter under his breath as he snatched the revolver from her hand. "You're not going to put me up against a wall!"

"No, it's Terenzio! Stop!" Rosaria screamed desperately, but she was still a prisoner atop the shoulders of two other men, powerless to intervene.

The weapon jumped in Emilio's hand. At first Rosaria thought that the shot had gone wide, because Terenzio merely looked more puzzled than before. Then she saw the red stain spreading over his tan uniform; without changing his expression of deep perplexity, he fell into the back of his vehicle.

"Terenzio," she screamed. The quick-thinking carabiniere driver slammed the *autocarro* into reverse and accelerated backward down the road.

From the north there came the whine of aircraft engines approaching at low altitude and Rosaria spun around in time to see a pair of Austrian biplanes diving at them. Both pilots leveled out side by side a hundred meters above the road and began a strafing run with their machine guns.

"Crissi!" The nurse had disappeared and panic swept through the crowd. The two soldiers who had been carrying Rosaria dumped her onto the road and dived for cover. She fell, hitting her head against a rock, but horror of the approaching aircraft gave her the strength to hurl herself into the roadside ditch.

It was filled with ice-cold water, and she felt her body go numb with the shock. I'm going to faint, she feared. I'll drown.

There were bullets flying all around her now, but the battle seemed to ebb in importance as she rallied her last strength for the task of crawling out of the ditch and into the stubble of a wheat field. Then she passed out, thinking, Massimo, Massimo . . .

"Lucky for you I came along," said Emilio Lodi affably. The shock of the Austrian air raid had cleared most of the cognac from his brain and he was beginning to think carefully about his future.

"I am Staff Nurse Cristina Rosselli from the Nineteenth Medical Group." The Venetian woman spoke with the natural authority of an upper-class gentlewoman, even though she was soaking wet. Like Emilio, she had jumped into a water-filled ditch during the Austrian strafing run. "I've got to find my unit."

You might be my ticket out of this mess, Lodi calculated. If they catch up with me, it might look better if I am found caring for wounded Italian soldiers. And Major Rosselli's beautiful little sister could testify that I shielded her with my body during the air raid. They'd never court-martial me, even if someone from the Seventy-seventh did survive to say I'd deserted. Once the revolution begins, it won't make any difference, but in the meantime I need protection.

"Do you know what happened to Rosaria Lombardi?" the nurse demanded.

"She went on to Verona with some mates of mine." Emilio had last seen

Rosaria's crumpled body lying face-down in a field. I was supposed to marry her, he reflected sadly. Sandro had it all worked out. But I couldn't marry a woman with a bastard child, and she knew that I shot Terenzio, so maybe it's just as well she's dead.

"Who are you?"

"Name's Emilio," Lodi told her as they walked down the road. He kept taking her arm solicitously and she kept shaking him off. "Look, the important thing is getting you back to your patients. How can I help? Maybe I could serve as an orderly or stand guard duty?"

"I'll be all right," said Cristina. She seemed anxious to get away from him. "Shouldn't you try to find your unit?"

He followed her up the road, inventing a fabulous story about being the last survivor of a valiant unit, but she did not pay much attention.

"We're here," she cried suddenly, pointing at three tents pitched in the middle of a little woods. It was nearly dark, but the Nineteenth Medical Group pennant was flying over the largest tent and a light burned inside. Nervously Emilio tagged along as Cristina rushed to the entrance and pulled back the canvas flap.

"Dr. Carducci! Oh, sir, I'm so glad I found you."

It was an awful scene. Lodi lingered at the doorway, appalled at the smell of infection and disinfectant. In the surgical tent were two dozen seriously wounded patients on field cots. Some of them lay utterly still, dead or dying or drugged with morphine. The less fortunate were conscious, groaning or crying in pain. His face gray with fatigue, Dr. Carducci moved from cot to cot, administering medicine to some and verbal comfort to others. He looked up at the sound of Cristina's voice.

"Signorina Rosselli, thank God you're here!" The doctor's voice was warm. "I sent all the others ahead with the patients who were in reasonable shape. There should be ambulances coming in the morning to collect us. Who is this young man?"

"Private Lodi, Signor Colonnello." Emilio snapped to attention. "I got separated from my unit while we were holding a position on the Isonzo. We fought like tigers, sir, and I was nearly captured. Well, perhaps I could give you a hand here."

"Bravo!" Dr. Carducci smiled, although Cristina looked doubtful. "Look, there's soap and water in the next tent. Signorina, try to find a scrub suit for this good lad, and we'll get some work out of him."

Obediently Emilio followed the blond nurse as she picked up an oil lantern and led the way into an adjacent tent. In the shadows he could see stacks of medicines and blankets and bedpans and mattresses. Cristina quickly located a white cotton orderly's uniform, a bar of yellow laundry soap and a jerrican of water.

"Make sure your hands are clean," she told him briskly as she led him outside. "Then report to Colonel Carducci."

The revolution should begin any time now, Emilio decided as he gave his hands a token wash and climbed happily into his new white uniform. Once the general insurrection begins I can leave here, but in the meanwhile I should be safe. Nobody shoots an orderly. He tucked the pistol he had confiscated from Rosaria into his trousers and wandered off into the woods for a pee.

On the way back he detoured around the supply tent, discovering a rear entrance covered with mosquito netting. Through the mesh he could see into the tent, where Cristina was standing by an oil lamp, slowly removing her water-stained uniform.

"Oh, Christ! Look at that! Look at that body," he whispered almost angrily as Cristina methodically stripped. She was a slender, almost frail woman, but her breasts were firm and high, and Lodi hoped she would turn more into the light so that he could see her nipples and loins. Oh, God, he thought, feeling his penis getting hard, God, if I could have a woman like that, just once! That's what the upper classes get in their beds every night, the bastards; they get to sleep with dreams.

There was a pistol shot.

Cristina had just turned to face the lamp, putting one foot on the table to wash between her legs with a white flannel cloth. Lodi was so stunned by the sight of her inner thighs that it took a moment for the sound to register on his consciousness.

"Oh!" Inside the tent, Cristina reacted to the noise, putting her hands on her breasts.

What should I do? Lodi crouched in the bushes, fearful and yet unable to take his eyes off Cristina's nakedness. It should have been safe here, he told himself resentfully. An instant later he saw huge blond men in strange brown uniforms push their way into the supply tent. Cristina froze. Hidden in the bushes, Emilio got out the revolver, but his body was shaking.

"What do you want? Who are you?" he heard Cristina shout at the three German soldiers, switching to German to proclaim that she was a nurse. "Bitte, ich bin eine Krankenschwester!"

Unimpressed, the first soldier slapped her hard across the face, sending her toppling backward onto the floor. The three men gave each other casual instructions in deep guttural voices, as if this were a routine military operation, something to be done and gotten over with. One soldier held Cristina by the hair while another took off his boots and trousers. The third man fastidiously covered a mattress with a clean sheet.

I could shoot them, Lodi quavered. Afterward, the army would give me a medal. That nurse would be grateful and take me into her bed.

He pointed the gun, but the possibility of missing obsessed him. While he was killing the first two, the third might fire back, or there could be other enemy soldiers nearby. He lowered the gun, uncertain and afraid. Then he raised it for a second time, but his finger would not tighten against the trigger.

Inside the tent, Cristina Rosselli tried to wriggle away, but the soldier who had taken off his trousers caught her by one ankle and yanked her onto the mattress.

"Nein, nein, ich bin eine Krankenschwester!" she cried again, trying to cover her breasts with a towel. Methodically the Germans pinned her to the mattress, one man holding her arms above her head while the other two pulled her legs apart.

"Zitta, zitta!" In badly pronounced Italian, they told Cristina to be silent, but she continued to shriek until the man who was holding her head punched her hard on the thorax, knocking the wind out of her. When she stopped shouting and turned her head to one side, the man with no pants raised himself over her. From where Lodi crouched in the shadows, his penis looked enormous.

"Per favore, per favore!" Cristina twisted and writhed in agony as the man tried to force himself into her. "Sono vergine!"

The three were like a team of athletes patiently trying to overcome a common obstacle. The soldier who had struck Cristina a moment before was now stroking her forehead, coaxing her to relax, while his colleague patted the struggling rapist encouragingly on the shoulder.

Now! I've got to do it now, Emilio resolved, his hands sweating as he held up the revolver. This is the last possible moment to save her honor. And mine. He selected the order in which he would shoot the three, and then aimed carefully at the nearest. I will be a hero, he predicted. Later, I shall be praised.

He still could not fire. The fear was too great for him, and he lowered the gun. With a grunt, the soldier lying between Cristina's legs thrust forward with his hips and the woman screamed.

I must kill myself, Emilio decided. I am not a good socialist or a good soldier, and I can't even defend an Italian woman. He picked up the revolver again and put it to his forehead. When she sees my body later, he fantasized, she will understand why I was driven to this. For a long time he squatted in the bushes with the muzzle of the revolver against his brain, his eyes closed, listening to the Germans murmuring and Cristina panting and crying as the men violated her one after another.

Even for this, the courage never came. When he put the gun down and opened his eyes the Germans had finished, and the last man to have raped Cristina was doing up the buttons on his trousers. The nurse had rolled onto her side, sobbing relentlessly, her legs drawn up against her stomach, her hands covering her face.

"Auf Wiedersehen." For a moment, Lodi feared that they might silence her with a bullet, but instead they merely shouldered their rifles and disappeared.

He listened to their footsteps until he heard the sound of motorcycle engines. We're behind enemy lines, he realized suddenly. That must have been an advance patrol.

Cristina will be hysterical, he guessed as he darted around to the front of the supply tent. I will help her through the crisis. He paused, seeing Dr. Carducci's body lying a few feet from the entrance to his surgical tent. There was a pistol in the physician's hand, and he had been shot in the face. From inside the surgical tent, there were cries and groans from the patients.

Lodi entered the supply tent just as Cristina was sitting up. She was wiping her eyes on a towel, and she looked at him blankly.

"Are you all right?" he asked.

"Something is broken inside." She was pressing her hand against her belly. There was blood on her thighs.

"That doctor is dead."

"Get me my dress. Go away while I wash," she ordered. There was a strange harshness in her voice. "Leave me that gun. You don't seem to be very good with guns."

"We're going to be taken prisoner," Lodi blurted out, as he fetched her damp uniform and put the gun at her feet. He tried not to look at her body but there were dark red marks forming on her breasts and they fascinated him. "You speak German. If you tell them I'm an orderly, they won't put me in a camp. I'm sorry about what happened to you."

"Nothing happened to me, do you understand?" She pointed the pistol at him, holding it with both hands. "If you ever tell anyone, my brother will deal with you."

"Yes, yes, signorina," Lodi murmured as he backed away. In the distance he could hear the wounded men crying.

"Tell the patients I'm coming." Still naked, Cristina got to her feet and then dropped down to one knee as pain rippled across her midriff. She choked back a cry and then rose again, waving the gun at Emilio. She looked tiny, he thought, with those thin, bare arms and legs, and that enormous service revolver.

"Go," she said softly. "Go, you pathetic little bastard, or I'll kill you."

I must get back to my Massimo, Rosaria told herself as consciousness gradually returned. It seemed to her that only a minute or so had passed, and she expected to see Emilio and Cristina and the soldiers. But the road was deserted except for a long row of corpses, the people killed in the Austrian air attack, and she understood that she had been unconscious for some time.

Terenzio! It suddenly came back to her, the nightmare of poor Terenzio being shot with his own revolver. But the carabiniere jeep had long since disappeared.

She climbed stiffly to her feet. Miraculously, she found her black wool cape by the side of the ditch, but her leather bag had disappeared.

Poor Cristina, she worried as she stumbled south along the road. I hope no one hurts her. She looked at each corpse as she passed, hoping that one of them would be Emilio, but they were all strangers.

11.

....

"You can't sleep here. Hey, Sergeant, wake up!"

"Where am I?" Sprawled on the floor in the corridor, Sandro Lombardi opened one eye and looked up at a medical officer poking his shoulder. He got to his feet feeling wretched.

"You're at the Treviso Royal Army Hospital," said the physician. "And you're blocking the passage with those long legs. Go sleep somewhere else and let us worry about your colonel."

"How is he?" Sandro prepared himself for bad news. After escaping from the battlefield at Zaga he had carried Achille on his shoulders over the foothills of the Julian Alps. At a town named Cividale, a first-aid specialist had stopped the bleeding from a deep wound in Achille's skull. He also found that Achille's back and shoulders had been ravaged by shrapnel and his left arm had been fractured in two separate places, above and below the elbow. Surgery would be required to remove a jagged piece of steel in his side, and the femur in his right leg was utterly smashed.

The army doctor shrugged eloquently. "He's still alive. Don't ask me why. Where was he wounded?"

"On the Isonzo just north of Caporetto about two weeks ago."

"Two weeks ago? How the hell did you get him here?"

"It was complicated." There was no point in trying to explain how he had brought a half-dead senior officer across one hundred twenty-five kilometers of battlefield. When the army had pulled out of Cividale Achille was still unconscious, so Sandro had commandeered a donkey and wheelbarrow from an inattentive farmer and carted the silent nobleman a further fifty kilometers southwest to the Tagliamento River, staying just ahead of the advancing Austrians and Germans.

At Pordenone, a field medical unit had given the wounded colonel a bed but nothing else, because there were no doctors to treat him. With Achille now semiconscious and in atrocious pain, Sandro had demanded *morfina;* when his request was denied, he had stolen it from the pharmacy at gun point. Near despair, he had then hijacked an ambulance and raced over the Piave River, reaching the safety of the far shore a few minutes before Italian Army sappers detonated the bridge in a desperate effort to stop the enemy avalanche.

The physician nodded sympathetically. "You're a brave man, Sergeant. Come back tonight and we may be able to let you see him for a few minutes."

"If the Krauts don't get here first." The two men exchanged a wry smile, since they were only ten kilometers behind the Italian front and could hear the artillery quite clearly. If the army failed to hold the Piave River, then the war was lost.

At the front door to the hospital, a carabiniere lieutenant was checking the identity cards of those coming and going. Exhausted, Sandro produced his tattered identity card and waited while the military policeman searched a long list.

"What's your name?" asked the lieutenant.

"Sergeant Sandro Lombardi, Seventy-Seventh Infantry Regiment," he said promptly. The carabinieri had been executing deserters wholesale to stop the hemorrhage of troops fleeing from the front and Sandro suddenly became anxious that no mistake be made about his status. "My colonel was badly hurt on the Isonzo, and I was assigned to bring him here. What's this all about, sir?"

"Security check." The carabiniere officer shrugged, his eyes still focused on his list. "We've got enough troubles without that Russian business spreading down here."

"What Russian business?"

"You haven't heard?" The lieutenant gazed at him suspiciously. His eyes were blue and cold. "The Bolsheviks seized Moscow, arrested the Provisional Government, took Russia out of the war, and proclaimed a Marxist government. Naturally, everyone is worried about the safety of the Russian royal family."

"Naturally." Sandro pretended to agree, although he favored the summary execution of every monarch in the world. He suddenly wondered if Amadeo Bordiga was right. If the backward Russians could bring off a coup d'état in the middle of a war, then why should revolution be impossible in Italy? And if not now, then when?

"Wait a minute! Is this you? Sandro Lombardi?" Disconcertingly, the lieutenant seemed to have located his name. Frowning, he dug through a huge stack of pink folders until he found one with "Lombardi" written across the front.

"There must be a thousand men in the army with that name," Sandro snorted, now anxious to locate the PSI Headquarters in Treviso and find out how the Central Committee intended to react. If the Party decides upon an immediate insurrection, he resolved, then so be it. At least this way, I will not be faced with the dilemma of having to rebel directly against Achille. And the Italian Government has never been this weak.

"Are you the brother of a certain Rosaria Lombardi?"

Sandro's blood ran cold for a moment. Could Rosaria have been killed or captured? "Yes, I last saw my sister in Udine on October 24."

"All right, then, you're the one. Emilio Lodi? Does that name mean anything to you?"

Sandro was frankly mystified. "Lodi was a good friend of mine, and a private with the Seventy-seventh, but I don't know where he is now."

"Don't you?" As he spoke, the lieutenant beckoned to a pair of carabiniere enlisted men standing guard at the hospital entrance and the two men approached. "According to this report, your sister Rosaria and your good friend Emilio led a mass insurrection of several thousand deserters during which a carabiniere officer was shot and seriously wounded. You're under arrest!"

"Look, I've been at the front for two and a half years," Sandro shouted. "What crime did I commit?"

"Conspiracy to overthrow the King's Government," snapped the lieutenant, gesturing to his subordinates. "Lock him up, boys. Another job for the firing squad."

The officer's jaw cracked as Sandro hit him and the man slumped over his table, knocking his pink file folders onto the floor. The two enlisted men both reached for their revolvers, but Sandro ran right over them and raced out of the hospital into the Treviso city center.

As he spun down the first side alley to his right, there was a shot over his head, but Sandro ignored it and kept on running, heading for the working-class section of Treviso where he could find safety among poor people who hated the war and the police.

Revolution now, he thought. Let it be now!

The point of the dream was that he had died and gone to hell, which looked remarkably like an Italian Army barracks. Guido was already there, organizing things, and so were the men from the Seventy-Seventh Infantry Regiment, sitting around polishing boots and rifles.

"Dante had it all wrong," Guido was assuring him briskly. "Cultural conditioning led us to expect harsher conditions, but it's actually much more pleasant than the trenches."

"Everyone is Italian." Achille was puzzled. "Where are all those Germans we killed?"

"They all went to heaven," Guido explained. "The theory seems to be that the Germans have always been crazy and are therefore without sin. We Italians, on the other hand, have always known precisely what we were doing. Wake up, okay?"

"What? Guido?"

"Achille, wake up."

"No, please, don't shout. I'll wake him for you." There was a soft, insistent, feminine voice in his ear. His back hurt and there was a pain in his head so massive that he tried not to move as he opened his eyes. The room seemed very dark, and all he could see was a figure in starched white cotton. "General? Are you awake, sir?"

"Cristina?" he asked. "I dreamed I was in hell. Where is Rosaria?"

"My name is Margherita, Signor Generale. I don't know any Rosaria."

"I'm not a general." Achille was confused, but his vision cleared slightly, and he saw a hospital room and a chubby, dark-haired nurse. I have been here for a long time, he remembered. Sandro brought me here. Where is Sandro?

"Don't you remember when the Supreme Commander came to see you? They made you a general for being so brave. Now we're going to let Colonel Rosselli talk to you for just a few minutes, if you're feeling strong enough."

When did Guido become a colonel? Achille closed his eyes again. He was tired, trying to orient himself. There had been an operation, and he remembered coming out of the ether. Afterward they gave him pills to put him asleep, and several times a day this Margherita would come with a stainless-steel syringe to inject him with *morfina*. It took the pain away, but made it hard to remember things.

"Comandante? Can you hear me?" Guido's Venetian accent was unmistakable, but the music had gone out of his voice.

"I've been sleeping. They give me shots and it's hard to concentrate. I took that nurse for Cristina."

"We don't know where Crissi is," said Guido. "She stayed behind to care for some wounded and she was still north of the Piave when we blew the bridges."

"Where is Rosaria?"

"Nobody knows. Listen, there are some policemen here who want to interview you about her, but I am going to send them away until your head is clearer. When they come back, don't say anything about your relationship with her."

"Police? What's wrong?" Achille tried to sit up but his spinal column telegraphed a warning spasm of pain to his skull and he settled back down against the pillow.

"Achille, there was an incident of some kind during the retreat. Rosaria and Emilio Lodi apparently led a mass breakout of deserters. I've told the police that Sandro couldn't possibly have been involved because he was with us at the front, but when they tried to question him here in Treviso, he assaulted a lieutenant and fled."

"There must be some mistake," Achille protested, although some of it made sense. Rosaria had been vehement in her insistence that the working class had no vested interest in the Great War. That day in the Hotel Italia, she had been whispering to Emilio, saying something about obeying orders. What orders? Of course the only orders that had ever meant anything to her, the orders of the Italian Socialist Party.

That night when I held her in my arms and made her gasp and cry out, he asked himself, was she thinking about revolution even then? Is everything politics?

"The mistake was getting into bed with her. Look, have they told you about Terenzio?" Guido seemed impatient. "Your brother intercepted this huge crowd of deserters carrying Rosaria on their shoulders and singing Marxist songs. He was only trying to warn them that Austrian aircraft were coming, but Lodi opened fire and put a bullet through his right hand and into his chest. We've moved him to a hospital in Venice."

"He's all right? Teri's not going to die?"

"He's going to be fine," Guido insisted. "Do you remember Lodi? He worked for your father in Cederna."

Achille nodded. Years ago, Sandro had talked about arranging a marriage between Rosaria and Emilio Lodi. He wondered if they could have been closer than anyone realized. Could the story about Rosi be true? He closed his eyes, thinking for the first time in his life that it might be just as well if he died. It's time for my morphine, he remembered. I want to go back to sleep.

"Listen, Achille, I'm going out to Palestine. They're putting together an Italian Expeditionary Force to help the British. Since I speak Hebrew and a little Arabic, the General Staff figured I might make myself useful." There was a strange, angry tone in Guido's voice. Achille opened his eyes and looked up sharply.

"You can't go. Who's going to look after the regiment?"

"The regiment? Oh, Achille, don't you remember anything? They've had you on too many painkillers. At Zaga we attacked to rescue you and Sandro."

A half-memory returned, something Sandro had said about the regiment going over the top. "You had no business attacking under those circumstances. You must have taken heavy casualties, and I didn't want my life redeemed at that price. You should stay and rebuild the Seventy-seventh instead of chasing off to Palestine."

"Achille, the regiment is gone."

"What do you mean, gone? They haven't disbanded my regiment? Not after everything! Where is Giuseppe Papafava?"

"I don't know. Some of the men are wounded," Guido whispered. "But most of them are dead. The regiment is gone."

There was a long silence. After a while Guido got up and left without saying good-bye. Achille lay looking at the ceiling, feeling the hurt in his body contend with the pain in his mind. I could die now, he decided. There is nothing left. We have lost the war. I have lost my regiment and my two best friends. And my woman has betrayed my love.

"There, there, General." When the nurse came in she found tears on his cheeks. She gave him his morphine, and he went back to sleep.

12.

. . . .

This is silly. She stepped down from the coach, realizing that she had been worrying obsessively about her son ever since Udine. He will be fine, she assured herself. He's had Benita to look after him, and Valeria to feed him, and Girolamo to tell him stories and spoil him with chocolates. It's poor Terenzio I ought to be worrying about, and Sandro, and my darling Achille. Oh, I hope there is some news from the front!

It was cold and there was a light rain falling. Shivering, Rosaria pulled the cloak more tightly around her shoulders. It had taken three exhausting weeks to come from the Austrian border to Cederna, moving from one cheap hotel to another and standing in endless queues for seats on trains that never seemed to arrive. For one entire week, she had been stranded in Venice while the Italian Army fought to defend the city, and there had been no transportation of any kind to the south. Finally, a lorry driver had taken her to Florence along with a load of pigs, and she had found local buses for the rest of the journey to Rome.

The coach pulled away, leaving her a few meters from the Mayor's new palazzo in the Piazza Bixio. The Mosconi residence was now nearly finished, after thirty months of expensive construction. With a private smile, Rosaria remembered how Terenzio and Girolamo had burned down the Mayor's previous home on the night that Massimo was born. As usual, the police had blamed everything on the poor anarchists, but no arrests had ever been made.

She gazed at the new brick building and found it rather vulgar. The mist was too heavy to see clearly, but just as she turned away a child's face appeared briefly in a second-story window, and for one awful instant, she imagined it was Massimo.

The apparition disappeared. I'm too tired to see straight, she told herself as she trudged across the piazza. If I'd telephoned from the coach depot in Rome, Girolamo could have met me with the car and I would be home with my little Massimo by now. I wonder if there is any news from Russia. If the Bolsheviks can consolidate themselves in Russia, they might take Germany as well. Then the war would have to stop and Achille could come home.

When she saw the tower of the Castello she quickened her pace, thinking about the day when she would live there with Count Achille Leone. Perhaps it would be better to wait until he is safe in Cederna before saying anything about the engagement. The announcement should come from him, and I will simply add that my belief in democratic socialism does not permit me to accept the title of Contessa, and that I wish to be known simply as Signora Rosaria. Signora Rosaria Leone.

Signora Leone. She tried it out on her tongue as the road turned into the formal gardens. Before anything else, she decided, the future Signora Leone would like a glass of red wine and a hot bath. She sighed, imagining the pleasure of stripping off her filthy clothing and climbing into a tub with Massimo for a long, luxurious soak. Girolamo would have saved all the back issues of *Il Messaggero* for her, and later there would be dinner while she caught up on all the news.

Then the front door of the Castello opened, and Sergeant Virgilio Cirillo came out with the two enlisted policemen who went everywhere with him. "It's her," he said nonchalantly, and the two younger policemen took Rosaria by the arms.

"What is this nonsense?" she sputtered as they twisted her wrists behind her and the handcuffs clicked shut. "What have I done?"

Reaching into the breast pocket of his field jacket, Sergeant Cirillo extracted a piece of legal paper and waved it under her nose. "It's a long list, but incitement to riot, sedition, treason, and conspiracy to murder Terenzio Leone are at the top."

"There's been a misunderstanding. Please, I need to see my son."

Cirillo snorted as he glanced again at the legal document.

"That's all been taken care of. Given the probability that you will be executed or sentenced to life imprisonment, the Lazio District Court awarded custody of your illegitimate child to his natural father."

"His natural father is dead."

"According to court records, the natural father is one Junio Mosconi. Accordingly, the child has been moved to the Mosconi residence."

Rosaria felt her body go cold. From somewhere inside the Castello she could hear Giorgina's raucous laugh and the tinkle of glasses. The mistress of Cederna has come home, Rosaria thought dully. She's already hit the gin bottle. "When Achille returns . . ."

"General Leone is dying in a hospital in Treviso," said Cirillo, shutting the Castello door behind him. "I wouldn't count on him to rescue you."

"My brother will kill you for this."

Cirillo leaned forward and spat very carefully in her face. "You Marxist cunt," he said. "I'll see you in hell first."

Book

Five

. . . .

1918 – 1920

I.

. . . .

The *rapido* from Rome was only thirty-seven minutes late, which was a miracle because the Austrians were still bombing the tracks whenever they could. Venice was the end of the line and everybody was getting off. Terenzio scanned the disembarking passengers until he spotted his guest, a short, robust man with thick spectacles and a weather-worn leather suitcase.

The lawyer seemed irritable as he lumbered down the platform, and Terenzio prepared himself to deliver a barrage of relentless good humor. The Leone family had enough problems without making this indomitable attorney into an enemy.

"Welcome to Venice, Tommaso. How was your journey?"

"Long." The lawyer slung his suitcase over one shoulder and followed the carabiniere captain down the platform toward the Scalzi Bridge. Outside, it was chilly and overcast. A brisk wind off the lagoon was whipping up the dark waters of the Grand Canal.

"Been in Venice before?"

Tommaso nodded, shivering with the cold. There were sandbags piled around the entrance to the train station, and scaffolding where workmen were repairing damage done by a recent enemy bomb. "I've seen it looking better. I'd forgotten how cold it gets this time of year."

"Well, it's February. My father always said that Venice only revealed her soul in winter." Terenzio realized with a twinge of sadness that he quoted Leonida about once a day.

"I miss your father." At the water's edge the stocky lawyer turned, sincerity in his voice. "If the old man were still alive and in charge, he'd have won this damn war by now. Is there going to be an air raid today?"

Terenzio shook his head, moving to the quayside and signaling for a boat-taxi. A gondoliere expertly propelled his craft into position. "It's been a while since the Austrians have been able to get this far south," he explained as they boarded. "Maybe 1918 will be the year we win. Meanwhile, we've got to get Rosaria's situation sorted out and Achille back on his feet."

He murmured an address to the boatsman. The gondola moved smoothly into the canal, heading northeast past Saint Geremia's Church.

"I hope you're right." Sea spray fogging his glasses, Tommaso settled awkwardly on his seat. "Have you recovered fully? Have they got you back to work?"

"I'm fine," Terenzio lied, carefully shielding his damaged thorax. In fact, he was still amazed that one little bullet could have done so much damage. The hole in his rib cage had healed, leaving a ridiculously small scar, but on cold days there was a deep ache in his chest, and a persistent soreness in his right hand. "They've asked me to organize a small field orchestra to perform in the field for the troops, and I've never felt better. Tell me, how is poor Rosaria?"

"Naturally, she's very bitter."

"And little Massimo?"

"Helen Higgens was allowed to move into the Mosconi place to look after him, and she reports that he is healthy although he keeps crying for his mother. Junio has not permitted me to visit Massimo, although the child and I were very close. The next time you and Girolamo burn Junio's house down, make sure the bastard stays inside!"

Terenzio grinned sheepishly. For the record, he denied any involvement in the regrettable destruction of the Mayor's villa, but the incident had already passed into Cederna legend. "Tommaso, what the hell is Junio playing at?"

"It's an ugly sexual obsession. You were too young to notice, but when we were boys, Junio was always mesmerized by Rosaria . . . well, I suppose we all were, but he was fixated by the notion that she is destined to be his mistress. I think he's trying to use his status as Massimo's legal guardian to force Rosaria into a sexual accommodation."

"He doesn't know Rosaria very well."

"It's me he doesn't know very well," said Tommaso. There was an angry strength in the lawyer's voice.

"Look, there's so much we need to talk about. I've booked us both into the Hotel Fantin downtown. By the way, they're doing *Rigoletto* at the theater tonight, my father's favorite opera. We might have a drink in his memory and then take in the performance. Do you like Verdi?"

"I suppose so." Tommaso was still testy. "But I'm a socialist lawyer, and with my clients being slung into jail for offending the upper classes, I don't have a lot of time these days to listen to *musica lirica*."

Terenzio felt his patience slipping. "Fine, but when you and Sandro have your revolution, don't shoot the piano player, okay?"

"Is that a piano player's uniform? You're a *sbirro*, Terenzio, a cop!"

There was a long, uncomfortable silence. The gondala turned left into the Canale di Cannaregio and passed beneath a bridge where a few scrawny seagulls huddled. They looked hungry, and Terenzio was sorry that he had nothing to feed them. Everybody was having a tough winter. The Germans were still up in the mountains killing Italians, and out in the lagoon, poor Venetians were assassinating seagulls for meat.

"A long time ago, I applied for a commission in the carabiniere because of a boyish ambition to go to Libya with my brother," he explained soberly. "It had nothing to do with wanting to hurt poor people. You know that."

"Sorry, Teri." The lawyer relented a little. "Rosaria and I both realize that this latest misery is not your fault. Speaking of pianists, are you going to be able to play again?"

Terenzio winced at the question. The knuckle in his right index finger was utterly gone, thanks to Emilio's bullet, and the surgeons had fused bone fragments into a straight, unbendable digit. "I'm going to be the best damn left-handed pianist in Italy," he said wistfully.

"Teri, I'm sorry." Tommaso reached forward and put his hand on Terenzio's knee. "Look, let's finish our business and then go see that opera. What was that aria from *Rigoletto* that Leonida always made you play? Was it 'Dear Name'?"

"Yes, 'Caro Nome,' " Terenzio said sadly. "I think it reminded him of Rosaria."

For a moment the two men fell silent, each lost in separate memory. Then the lawyer unbuckled his briefcase and took out a folder of legal papers.

"Given his weakened condition, this is not something I want to raise in front of Achille, but I have been looking at some old Cederna tax records in connection with another case. I stumbled across some documents that suggest that Bruno Benelli may have been systematically defrauding your father. It will take some digging to find positive proof, but . . . well, take a look at the figures. A lot of money is missing."

"Are you sure? We seem quite rich." Terenzio gazed blankly at page after page of large numbers, realizing that he had never spent a moment of his life thinking about his family's finances. Leonida had left him a generous trust fund that paid him a princely stipend every month, and Achille had once commented that Bruno's investment strategy had improved their financial position substantially.

"You are moderately rich but you'd be disgustingly rich if Bruno weren't siphoning money out of the estate. Do you want me to look into it? It may mean some embarrassment to your sister."

"Let's investigate. Although I sometimes I feel guilty about hating my own sister."

"Why should you feel guilty?" Tommaso smiled comfortingly. "Everybody hates your sister."

A few minutes later the gondoliere steered toward the *fondamenta,* a walkway of granite blocks that ran along the edge of the canal. Set a few meters back from the left bank of the Cannaregio, the Rosselli home was an expensive-looking four-story palazzo, originally built of red brick and then covered with bluff-colored stucco. There were elegant white marble balconies on each of the upper floors, with huge terra-cotta flowerpots and green wooden shutters on the windows.

Terenzio gave the boatsman thirty lire, plus a few centesimi for a tip, and then clambered ashore, where Signora Rosselli waited at the door.

"How is my brother?" He kissed her on the cheek, thinking how devoted the old lady had become to Achille Leone, and how hard she was working to coax him back to health. The matriarch of the Rosselli clan looked frail. With Cristina missing somewhere behind enemy lines, Guido in Palestine with the Italian Expeditionary Force, and a convalescent general in her guest room, the old woman had more than her share of worries.

"He's not having a good day." Guido's mother shook hands with Tommaso. "If only my sweet Cristina were here to take care of him."

The interior of the Palazzo Rosselli was luxurious, and there were maids on every landing as the two visitors climbed the stairs. On the top floor, Achille had been given the largest room in the house for his recovery. A nurse was preparing his medication tray and the shutters were tightly drawn, as if the wounded general wished to exclude the world.

"Achille, are you awake? Tommaso Savarino is here."

General Leone raised his head slowly from the pillow. Terenzio noticed that Achille had lost even more weight, but he tried to convince himself that his brother was getting better. After all, when Sandro had carried him into that hospital in Treviso, Achille had been very close to death. After three separate operations on his head, back, and right leg, followed by endless weeks in an army surgical ward, the patient had caught a nasty hospital infection, spending Christmas in a feverish delirium. It had been February before Achille had been well enough to move to the Rosselli residence for his convalescence, and then only with a nursing staff provided by the army.

Are his wounds still bothering him that much, Terenzio wondered bleakly, or is it the business with Rosaria? If only she were here! One way or the other, we've got to get him off morphine and out of bed, even if it hurts.

"Sandro? Is that Sandro?" Achille seemed to have difficulty focusing his eyes.

"No, it's me," Terenzio told him. Achille often called for Sandro Lombardi. "And Tommaso's come to see you."

"Where is Sandro?" There was peevishness in Achille's voice.

"I've told you before." Terenzio sat on the edge of the bed and took his brother's hand. "Remember? Sandro hit a lieutenant and fled to Moscow."

There was a long silence. Achille blinked his eyes and tried to sit up as his nurse, Margherita, adjusted the pillow. "Teri, I get so confused. How does the front look?"

"Nothing's changed since we stopped the Austrians on the Piave," Terenzio said patiently. "There's no immediate danger of them advancing any further south, but pushing them back is going to take some time, and more luck than we've been having. How are you? Are you sleeping well?"

"They give me morphine and then I can sleep. Margherita keeps trying to make me do without, but there's too much pain in my thigh and I have nightmares. Sometimes I dream that I'm buried in corpses, arms and legs and heads, all the men from the regiment. It's horrible.''

"Achille, it's me.'' Tommaso stepped forward and put his hand on Achille's shoulder, wondering if this shattered man was mentally competent to sign legal papers. Achille looked up, recovering a little as he recognized his old friend.

"Ciao, Tommaso,'' he said. "How are things in Cederna?''

"Terrible! I don't know how much you remember, but when Rosaria came home after Caporetto, she was arrested. She's been confined to a woman's prison in Rome for almost three months now and we need to get her out.''

Achille seemed vaguely perplexed. "In prison?''

"I told you about it last night, but you kept falling asleep,'' Terenzio explained quickly. "When I found Emilio Lodi and Rosaria together on that road south of Udine, Lodi shot me to avoid being arrested for desertion, but Rosaria was clearly not involved.''

"Okay, but what was she doing with five thousand deserters?'' Achille's voice was hoarse, and Terenzio watched as the bitterness roused him from his stupor. "There are too many coincidences here. Just before Caporetto, two carabinieri at the Udine train station saw her talking with Emilio Lodi and heard him saying how the men should throw down their rifles. And during the insurrection, she was observed leading—''

"She wasn't leading anything. It was happenstance,'' Tommaso snarled, but Achille was wide awake now, and angry.

"Was it? Just before the Austrian attack, she and Emilio had another quick conversation, this time in the lobby of the Hotel Italia. They didn't realize I heard. Then, the very next day, she handed Terenzio's own gun over to Emilio and he used it to shoot my brother. Okay, Tommaso, get her out of jail because she is the mother of my half-brother, but don't ask me to believe that she is totally innocent.''

"On behalf of my client . . .'' Tommaso retreated within his lawyerly voice, but Terenzio could tell that he was furious. Poor Rosaria, he thought. Our father seduces her, our lawyer worships her, Achille alternates between loving and hating her, and Junio Mosconi entertains sadistic obsessions about her. She'd have been better off with a crooked nose and a flat chest.

"She was marching around with Emilio Lodi singing revolutionary songs while the rest of us were fighting and dying to defend Italy,'' Achille whispered, approaching exhaustion. "Even Sandro did his duty. If only she could have given the revolution a rest for a little while. Oh, God, what a disaster! Who is looking after little Massimo?''

"In its wisdom, the Lazio District Court has accepted Junio Mosconi's contention that he was the child's natural father, and awarded custody to him. Massimo has spent the last three months as a prisoner in the Mayor's mansion.''

There was a long, harsh silence. In the distance they could hear the horn of a freighter making its way through a channel in the lagoon. "Massimo is a separate issue," Achille announced quietly. "Our father's honor is at stake. Get the child away from Junio."

"I'll challenge Mosconi to a duel," Terenzio proposed. I am a good shot, he reasoned, and fighting a duel will get me kicked honorably out of the carabinieri.

"No, Junio is not a gentleman." Achille shook his head.

"This is the twentieth century." Tommaso took a stack of legal documents from his briefcase. "If you can stop talking like a pair of Sicilians long enough to sign these papers, I will fight your duels for you. We start with a judicial deposition and some menacing letters. This is an affidavit in which you, Achille, as head of the Leone household, demand custody of your half-brother."

"Rosaria is the child's natural mother."

"I know, but the court is far more likely to award custody to a wounded war hero than an imprisoned subversive," Tommaso explained. "Furthermore, I've drafted a letter to the Benelli tribe in which you threaten them with catastrophic financial penalties unless they cooperate. Here's another, for Terenzio to sign, in which he stipulates that Rosaria had nothing to do with his wounding and asks the authorities to grant her bail and provisional liberty."

It was the juridical equivalent of a frontal assault, formal letters and sworn statements and court orders. It took a long time for the two brothers to sign everything, and Terenzio found that his finger hurt with every signature. Achille seemed to lose his concentration, and Tommaso had to put an X at the bottom of every sheet to keep him from signing in the wrong place. When they were finished and the lawyer had put all his ammunition back in his briefcase, he walked to the foot of the bed and looked at Achille.

"I'll be seeing Rosaria in a few days. Is there any message?"

Send her a message, Terenzio pleaded mentally with his older brother. You took her into your bed. You've loved her all your life.

Achille shook his head, sinking exhausted against his pillow. "Oh, I don't know. Look, just say hello for me. Where is my nurse? I need my medicine."

2.

. . . .

"And the nuns hit her. I sit here in prison thinking about my little Chiara locked up in that orphanage, not getting enough to eat, and I just can't bear the idea. Someday she'll wind up on the streets like me."

Anna Maria collapsed in tears in the corner of the cell. The other four prisoners looked away in embarrassment, but Rosaria put her arms around her friend's shoulders and hugged her.

It was a quick and careful hug. After three long months in the Mantellate Women's Prison, she had learned the dangers of touching. Some of her sister prisoners were lice-infested street women, and others suffered from the pox. Furthermore, the nuns who staffed the Mantellate were unable to distinguish between sisterly hugs and lesbian embraces and punished both with solitary confinement.

"Couldn't Chiara's father help?" Anna Maria's pimp had beaten her savagely for years, but when he had laid violent hands upon her child, the woman had killed him with a kitchen knife. It was a tragic, sordid affair, but there was no reason why Chiara should suffer.

"I never did work out who her father was." The woman relapsed into anguished sobs. The others in the cell played a game with centesimo coins and matches, since the scene of a woman having hysterics was too familiar to merit much attention. They all broke down from time to time and it never did any good.

Oh, Christ, what's the point? Rosaria's own morale slipped as she closed her eyes and fought off the tears. For the first weeks of prison she had assumed that her arrest was one more foolish, brutal gambit from Giorgina's side of the board, a juridical blunder to be corrected at the earliest opportunity.

But now the awfulness of her dilemma descended upon her. Massimo had been legally kidnapped. Junio's lustful intoxication with her grew more sinister with every passing year. Sandro was a wanted criminal, living in exile in Moscow and probably unaware of her predicament. Lingering at death's door, Achille was utterly convinced that she had somehow been involved in the soldiers' revolt at Caporetto. Terenzio was still loyal, but his duties kept him far from Rome, and the Italian judicial system was in too much turmoil to bring her to a speedy trial.

"Signora Rosaria?" She tore herself away from her own thoughts. With painful concentration, the prostitute was writing something in clumsy block letters on the back of a photograph. "Chiara is at Santa Caterina's Orphanage in Frascati."

"Anna Maria, we're both twenty-five years old, and we've shared the same cell for three months. You don't have to call me 'Signora,'" Rosaria protested. A few years living with aristocrats, and something has rubbed off on me, she realized. When I look in the mirror I still see the girl who dug potatoes in His Excellency's kitchen garden, but other people sense the difference. I'm not quite a peasant anymore, even if my invitation to join the nobility has been firmly canceled.

"They'll let you out someday, and you'll be rich and successful. I'm going to die in prison." Anna Maria handed her the photograph. "Every morning I cough up blood, and a few years in these damp cells will kill me."

There was no point in making reassuring noises. Anna Maria was no fool, and prostitutes knew their bodies. You could survive tuberculosis for a while in a Swiss clinic, but not in a Roman prison. The picture showed an alert-looking little girl of about four, snub-nosed and tan, wearing a simple muslin shift. For the occasion of this photograph, Chiara had worn wildflowers in her long dark hair.

"She's beautiful."

"She is, and I'm not fit to be her mother." Anna Maria spoke with a strange calmness. "I'm a bad person. I took money from men and did whatever they asked of me."

"You've been a victim of a male capitalism," Rosaria asserted quickly, knowing how Sandro would respond. "In a world where everything is a commodity, you sold the only merchandise you had. It doesn't make you a bad person. Marx says . . ."

Anna Maria shook her head violently. "I'm a bad person, and I'm going to die. Ti prego, get my Chiara from Santa Caterina's. You have a little boy almost the same age, and one more won't be too much for you. Wealthy men will fall in love with you, Rosaria, and you'll have servants. Oh, please!"

Violently, Anna Maria threw herself against Rosaria's breast, clinging to her desperately. We've shared the same corner of the same wretched cell for twelve awful weeks, Rosaria reflected. We've told each other all our secrets and sworn to be best friends forever, but what can I do? I can't even get myself out of here. "I don't know how I can help," she said. "I'm sorry."

"You have to. There isn't anyone else." Anna Maria had a terrible spasm of coughing. "I'll make you!"

"How can you make me do anything?" Rosaria questioned, but Anna Maria closed her eyes and fell silent. Sitting on the stone floor with her back against the cold cement of the cell wall, Rosaria held the woman's head on her lap and stroked her hair.

At one stratum of consciousness, she was fantasizing that a miraculously healed General Achille Leone would appear at the door of the cell, beg her forgiveness, and sweep her off to eternal happiness in Cederna. At another level, she was checking Anna Maria's scalp for parasites. In prison, she thought, fleas and fantasies are both hard to avoid.

Just then a custodial sister came by for a routine inspection. Finding two female prisoners touching one another, the nun sentenced them to forty-eight hours of solitary confinement as a penalty for violating the Mantellate's rule against excessive or unnatural displays of affection between prisoners.

The guards took Rosaria away first, leading her to a punishment cell barely a meter wide and deep, with no heat or ventilation. Just before they closed the iron door and cut out the light, Rosaria realized that she was still holding the photograph of Chiara. On the back was written, "When I am dead, give my Chiara to this lady."

Some of the words were spelled wrong. It was signed "Anna Maria."

"Are you my father?" asked the child, his brown, intelligent eyes brimming with tears. Tommaso inhaled sharply, searching for an answer as he led Massimo into the waiting room of the Mantellate Women's prison. The lawyer handed his court order to the custodial magistrate at the desk, and then sat on a hard wooden bench with Massimo on his lap.

"Masi, sometimes God takes our fathers away too soon, and you only had your real father for a day. He was a great man named Leonida Leone, and I'll tell you all about him when you're older."

In Tommaso's personal cosmology, God was an unpredictable old circuit judge who found everybody guilty, but sometimes suspended the death penalty. But a three-year-old mind demanded a rational universe and Tommaso wondered how he could explain why good fathers like Leonida went abruptly to heaven, leaving little boys in the hands of spurious, wicked fathers like Junio, and how good mothers like Rosaria could sometimes be sent to prison without having actually done anything wrong.

"Don't cry, Massimo." He brushed the child's tears away and cuddled him gently. "This is going to be a happy day for a boy like you. Momma will be here soon."

It had definitely been a good day to be a lawyer. That morning, Tommaso had persuaded a Lazio District Court that Rosaria Lombardi should be released on bail. After lunch, he had appeared before a Rome Family Court judge, winning a revocation of Junio Mosconi's authority over Massimo Lombardi and securing the appointment of General Achille Leone as the child's legal guardian.

The lawyer had rushed to the Mosconi residence with the Family Court order, fortunately finding the elder Mosconi at home and his violent son away on business. The Mayor had quickly surrendered Massimo, perhaps remembering how somebody had burned his house down the last time his feckless son had irritated the Leone family.

"Signor Junio told me to call him Papa," the boy explained tearfully. "When I wouldn't, he hit me with his belt. Couldn't you be my father?"

For the first time in his life, Tommaso understand how it felt to be angry enough to kill. I'm going to take Cederna away from Junio Mosconi, he resolved. And then I'm going to put the bastard in jail.

He swallowed hard. "Massimo, your mother will chose a substitute father for you someday and I hope it will be me, but until then, I could be your secret father."

"My secret father?"

"I love you more than anyone else, Masi, and when no one else is around, you could call me Papa."

"Papa?"

"Yes, Papa. You say that Junio man hit you with a belt?"

"Almost every day." There was a note of pride in the child's voice, and Tommaso could hear Leonida talking. "But I never called him Papa."

Tommaso held the boy tightly, his eyes watering. "No one will ever hit you again, son," he promised. "As long as I am alive, no one will ever . . . hit you again."

She always lost track of the hours in solitary confinement. A day seemed a fortnight. When the door of the tiny cell opened, they said nothing, but she was puzzled when the guards took her upstairs rather than down. She felt weak, and as she stumbled into the bright lights of the waiting room, she was thinking about food, wondering whether she had missed lunch or dinner or both, and if she would have to wait until morning for nourishment.

"Momma!" A child's ecstatic shriek split the air, but the guard refused to allow her to greet her son until he had removed the manacles and handed her a cheap cloth bag with her belongings. Then they made her stand before a junior custodial magistrate sitting at a desk in the corner. He was a sallow young man who took forever to find the file with her name on it. Cheerlessly he demanded her signature at the bottom of a legal document, and she signed without reading.

Then she turned, and little Massimo was in her arms. Tommaso was hugging both of them. Rosaria sank to her knees, uncomprehending and exhausted.

"It's all over," the lawyer said. He kissed her hair passionately, and in a tiny corner of her mind she wondered if any Mantellate fleas were riding out to freedom on her scalp. "We've got you out on bail, and Terenzio will testify that you are innocent of insurrection, so the charges should eventually be dropped. As a temporary expedient, we got Achille established as Massimo's legal guardian."

"Oh, that was good of him."

"It wasn't his idea." Tommaso seemed irritated as he lifted her to her feet.

"He's too ill to think very clearly and he's still convinced that you had something to do with the soldiers' insurrection after Caporetto. Bruno and Giorgina are back in total charge of the Leone estate, and you have been very firmly fired from your position there. I'm sorry."

Rosaria shook her head, feeling nothing but relief. "I'm glad. I was tired of the endless tug-of-war on my loyalties, trying to generate a profit for the Leone family and still do the right thing for the poor people in Cederna. Now I can be a real socialist at last. Is there going to be a revolution?"

Tommaso shook his head impatiently. "Rosaria, this country is becoming a democracy. When the war is over, we socialists can take power legally."

"The rich will never give up power," she said. "I met a lot of people inside that prison. Some were innocent and some were guilty, but they were all poor."

"And you're free because the system finally worked."

"I'm free because a rich man decided I should be given conditional liberty. The best we can ever hope for in Italy is a kind of eternal parole. And now Masi and I don't even have a place to live."

"Yes, you do," the lawyer assured her quickly, and Rosaria sensed a new strength in him. "I bought that little house on the Via Calatafimi, just behind the Casa del Popolo. It was going cheap, and I had your things moved there from the Castello."

Had the cash come from Terenzio Leone? She decided to let Tommaso keep his secrets. He is my best friend, she told herself.

"The one with red shutters and the garden in back?" she murmured, leaning weakly against him. "I've got a little money saved . . ."

"You don't need to worry about money. After Massimo was born, Achille established a generous trust fund for the two of you."

"I don't want Achille's money." Suddenly she was furious again. "Not a lira! Not a centesimo!"

"You need to rest." the lawyer tried to soothe her, but she collapsed into tears and Massimo began to sob sympathetically. It was a few minutes before Tommaso could get everyone's eyes dry enough to move toward the door. They had reached the hallway before she suddenly remembered why she had been thrown into solitary confinement.

"Oh, Tommaso, wait just a moment." Rosaria turned and approached the custodial magistrate. "Signor Giudice, before I leave, would it be possible for me to say good-bye to a sister prisoner? Her name is Anna Maria Caselli, and we shared a cell."

"Caselli?" The expression on the magistrate's face evolved from irritation to embarrassment. He checked an entry in his ledger, and then stood behind his desk clearing his throat for a judicial pronouncement. "While in solitary confinement last night, the prisoner Caselli hanged herself. You may be assured that we are investigating . . ."

"She's dead?" For a moment Rosaria thought she would faint, but then she was strengthened by a slow, unexpected anger. "Oh, Anna Maria, that was the ultimate blackmail!"

"Was she a friend?" Tommaso took her arm and led her to the exit. Behind them the custodial magistrate was explaining that the suicide had not been the responsibility of the prison service, and self-destruction was against the regulations of the Mantellate.

A moment later her face was bathed in sunlight, and she found herself in downtown Rome. Tommaso located a bench in a nearby park, and they all sat down. She tried to feel happy.

Instead she relapsed into tears as a symphony of sadness played in her brain. There was poor, dead Anna Maria to mourn, and Achille's shattered body and hate-filled mind, and sweet Terenzio with his broken hand, and Sandro in awful exile, and that beautiful library in the Castello where she would never sit again in the alcove near the window, her hands upon the keyboard of a gleaming black Olivetti.

"There are things to grieve about," the lawyer reasoned. "But maybe there are also reasons to rejoice. You're out of jail and you have your son. Back in Cederna, there are thousands of poor people who will be cheering when you come home because things are worse there than ever, and they need you badly. And for what it's worth, there is at least one man who still loves you."

"I'm being self-indulgent," she admitted, digging through her cloth bag to find the tattered photograph of a little girl.

"Who is that?"

"Her name is Chiara Caselli, and I have to go to Santa Caterina's Orphanage in Frascati and bring her home with us because her mother died last night."

"Why should you be responsible?"

"Somebody has to be responsible." Rosaria shrugged. "Isn't that what socialism is all about?"

"You can't just waltz into an orphanage and demand to be given someone else's child." Tommaso took her hand gently and held it between both of his. Massimo climbed down from the cement bench to play with some fascinating sticks he found in the grass.

"I know." Getting her emotions under control, she wiped her eyes and tried to smile. "Perhaps I could find a lawyer who specializes in getting people out of tight places."

"Together we can rescue your little Chiara," he promised, putting one arm around her shoulders and holding her close. She rested against him, feeling his pocket watch against her breast. He's like a big old oak tree, she thought. He never goes away or even sways. He gives me such calmness.

"That's good . . ."

"And it would make a better impression on the orphanage authorities if I could present you as my fiancée."

"Yes, we could say that, if it would help." In the confusion of the moment she did not quite catch his meaning.

"Before you went away, we talked about my running for Mayor with your support." He spoke as if arguing a case before a tough but reasonable judge. "If we were to announce our engagement in Cederna, we could work together openly without a continual scandal. The election is coming, and if we won, the municipality could employ you to handle its social and medical services and to deal with the housing problem."

It was a dazzling idea. If I am ever going to forget Achille, I will need a real job, a genuine mission in life. There are a million things in Cederna that need doing. I'm free now and I could make things happen!

"And someday, when you're ready, we could actually be married." The lawyer rested his case.

For a long time, she stared at him, fantasy and memory pirouetting through the minefield of her emotions. She closed her eyes and remembered lying naked in Achille's bed in that hotel in Udine. Will I ever feel that way again? Would marriage be fair to Tommaso? Doesn't he want a virgin?

"It would have to be a long engagement," she said hesitantly. "I've got some forgetting to do."

"I can wait forever," he said. Then Tommaso put Massimo on his shoulders for the walk to the coach station. Rosaria put her cloth bag over her shoulder and took Tommaso's hand as they crossed the street. We could be a family, she thought.

3.

....

"The old man's dozed off again," said Tullio. Achille was already drowsy from his shot, but he was awake enough to hear his orderly whispering to his nurse.

"The wind will rouse him once we clear the port," Margherita said.

Thirty-one is hardly an old man, Achille Leone thought, but he pretended to be asleep to avoid embarrassing his staff. I must be kinder, he resolved, feeling guilty about the way he sometimes lost his temper and abused them. Tullio is a good orderly, and Margherita a splendid nurse. It's June, and the weather is magnificent. If this pain would only go away.

"What's the point of sailing around the Adriatic if he's asleep?"

"Shhhh! It's his yacht," Margherita hushed the enlisted man. "The doctor says he needs the sea air."

The only good thing about life at the moment was this boat, and Achille congratulated himself on the purchase as he sat in his wheelchair, listening to the rrrrrhh of hemp running through chocks as the crew released the hawsers. During a trip to the seaside resort of Treporti one bright day in May he had discovered the *Veneziana* riding at anchor with a For Sale sign on its sixteen-meter hull. The boat came with a three-man crew, quarters for servants, a galley, and a spacious, well-lighted stateroom.

Achille even liked the name, since *Veneziana* meant "Venetian Girl," which reminded him of Guido's little sister, still tragically missing after the disaster at Caporetto. His physician had ordered him to spend more time outdoors, so, on an impulse, Achille had signed a check and bought himself a new home. I needed somewhere to live here in Venice, he told himself. I could hardly have imposed much longer on Signora Rosselli's hospitality. And the money was there in the bank, more than he realized, thanks to Bruno's skill with investments.

Another of life's little ironies! While the woman he loved was betraying him, his loathsome brother-in-law was quadrupling his income.

At a command from the helmsman, the yacht swung from the quayside into the quiet waters of the Arsenale Harbor where the Doges of the Most Serene Republic of Venice had built the ships that once dominated the Mediterranean. Achille opened his eyes, finding himself alone, tucked up with blankets even though it was a warm day in June. His staff had parked his wheelchair in a sheltered companionway just aft of the jib and left him to snooze in the afternoon sun.

Men who are unsuccessful with women always fall in love with sailboats, he thought as depression began to creep over him. Am I becoming a caricature? The crippled rich man and his yacht? Should I begin throwing gala parties for actresses and politicians? Only a few hundred kilometers away, men are dying in the mud, while I sit here in luxury.

He could almost feel Sandro sneering Marxistically all the way from Moscow. And what would Rosi think of my millionaire's yacht? *Merda,* he thought, what difference does it make? We couldn't hate each other any more than we already do.

They cleared the Arsenale Harbor and turned to starboard down the Canale di Navi toward the Lido and the open waters of the Venetian Adriatic. The wind was freshening from the northwest, and the crew let out the mainsail to catch the following breeze.

The two most beautiful things in the world, Achille decided, are a woman's breast and a sail filling with wind. A memory of Rosi's body swept over him, but he dismissed it angrily.

"Ready about!" the helmsman called softly. The *Veneziana* jibed, turning gently southeast into the ocean channel, passing a bulk freighter and an American Navy cruiser assigned to help the Italians patrol the Adriatic.

I should resign from the army and take a cruise around the world to recover, he thought. The war will be over before I am well enough to do any more fighting. And there is no one in Italy for me any longer. Guido is in Palestine, and Sandro is in Moscow. Of the three women who might have loved me, Anfi chose Arab nationalism over marriage, and Rosaria preferred revolutionary socialism to my bed. And Crissi is either a prisoner or dead. Why should I stay here? I could go to America. Italy will be ruined when this war is over.

That's what I'll do, he told himself as a sad sleepiness claimed him. When I'm better I'll sail to America.

The *Veneziana* bumped gently against the pier. Achille opened his eyes in confusion. It was nearly sunset, which meant somehow that he had slept away the entire afternoon. There was pain in his right thigh where the bone had been crushed. The surgeons had put a great stainless steel rod down the middle of the femur to hold it together, but his leg still hurt. There were times when he wondered if it might not be better to have the wretched limb sawed off, and be done with it.

"Have I been sleeping? Someone should have woke me," he grumbled as his crew made the *Veneziana* secure in its slip. Margherita began to justify her decision to let him slumber, but they were interrupted by a familiar voice from the dock.

"Comandante!"

After eight months in Palestine, Guido Rosselli looked as brown as an Arab. Bounding across the quay, he helped secure the *Veneziana* and then jumped down onto the afterdeck.

"It's good to see you!" Achille said warmly. "What's happening in Palestine?"

"The place always had too many Arabs," Guido complained. "Now that the British have invaded, it also has too many Englishmen."

"What's the news from the front?"

"While I was at headquarters for my reassignment orders, the Austrians launched their final offensive. They hit us with fifty-eight divisions, but we pushed them back and inflicted twice as many casualties as we took. It was a victory, Achille."

"Where are they sending you now? You should get a regimental command at least."

"That's what I need to talk to you about. I came back from Palestine because the Comando Supremo got some detailed intelligence on Italian prisoners of war. Crissi and Giuseppe Papafava are alive, although poor Giuseppe has lost both his legs. Crissi is apparently unharmed, and the damn Austrians have her working as a prisoner-nurse in a field hospital near Udine."

Achille found it difficult to concentrate because the pain in his leg was getting worse. It always did at this time of the day. "I'm glad. When the war is over, she will surely be released."

"We can't wait!" Guido said aggressively. "Look, as the fighting moves back toward Udine, Crissi could be maltreated by the Austrians, or hurt when we launch our final offensive. Achille, I know precisely where she is. Let's go and get her."

"Sure." Achille tried to joke. "I'll hold the gun and you push my wheelchair. And the two of us will fight our way through a thousand kilometers of enemy territory."

Guido ignored the sarcasm. "The new Supreme Commander is General Armando Díaz, who was a friend of your father's. We could get Crissi out if we had an airplane and a crew and a commando team, all of which the hero of Caporetto could get from the Comando Supremo if he asked. And we're going to need you on your feet again to lead us."

"Guido, I can barely move."

"I've just talked to your doctor. He says you would make quicker progress with more exercise and less morphine. Since you're a famous general and a peer of the realm and everybody's fair-haired boy, he's going to prescribe dope for you as long as you demand it, but he thinks you're becoming an addict."

Achille bridled at the word. Margherita was standing by with his medication tray, his assortment of pills, and the sterilized needle lying on a white towel. The morphine came twice a day, although there were times he wanted it more frequently. Two minutes after the hypodermic pierced his skin, he would feel strong enough to rescue a Venetian princess single-handedly. The sensation would last for a while and then there would be beautiful sleep. He could forget about the war, and his lost regiment, and Rosaria Lombardi, and all the missing little sisters in the world.

"Look, we can talk later." In the back of his head there was a voice saying that Guido was speaking the truth. Am I becoming an addict? He gestured to Margherita, who approached with his medicine.

Abruptly furious, Guido Rosselli snatched the tray away from the frightened nurse. "Concentrate on Crissi for a moment! We encouraged her to become an army nurse, remember? We brought her into a war zone with the promise that we would protect her."

"I want my medication."

"I want my sister!" Guido shouted, and he threw the morphine tray into the murky waters of the Arsenale. "And I want you to want my sister!"

"You bastard!" As anger caused adrenalin to race through his system, Achille found the strength to get to his feet. The crutches he used for climbing up and down the hatchways were leaning against the gunwales and he hobbled toward them furiously. But Guido got there first, and the crutches followed the medicine into the water.

Tullio and Margherita backed away. If these two high-ranking lunatics wanted to murder each other, nurses and corporals needed to stay clear of the carnage.

"Are we going to fight?" Guido shouted. "Fine with me, but we'll do it without crutches and without *morfina*."

Furious but unsteady, Achille lurched forward. Guido retreated up the companionway toward the *Veneziana*'s prow. From behind, Achille could hear Margherita entreating him not to hurt himself. In the one corner of his brain that never went crazy, he realized that he was actually walking unaided for the first time since Caporetto. His thigh hurt massively, but bone and muscle were working together again. I'm going to break his stupid neck, he swore silently. If the bastard would only stand still! Clinging to the bulkhead, Achille finally cornered his old friend against the jib, and swung mightily with his fist.

Guido ducked skillfully and then caught him in a clinch, pinning his arms to his sides. "You missed, Comandante," he laughed. "But not a bad punch for a hopeless cripple."

"Wait till I'm stronger," Achille panted. "Where is Crissi exactly?"

"There's an old manor house twelve kilometers southwest of Udine that the Austrians are using for a hospital. Terenzio is ready to go as soon as you are. I wish Sandro could be with us."

Achille nodded, backing away as Guido released him. The moment his arms were free, he braced himself against a shroud, spun Guido around quickly, and tossed him over the gunwales into the water. It cost him a spasm of pain in his back, but he grinned for the first time in months.

"Get the crutches while you're down there," he shouted. I'm back, he thought. The recovery starts today. I'm me again.

"You don't seem to need them," Guido sputtered and laughed as he swam toward the ladder.

"I know, but you might. Come on, we'll haul you up."

"Wait, I'll get your hypodermic." The needle and medicine bottle were floating toward Albania, and Guido paddled after them.

"Don't bother." Achille limped aft to haul his friend out of the water. The pain in his leg was coming back, but it seemed containable now, something he could isolate and control. "I don't need it anymore."

4.

....

I could almost like my life, Tommaso Savarino decided as he listened to the bell in the tower of Santa Teresa's church. Almost.

The sixth gong meant that his working day was over. Glancing at his pocket watch to verify Saint Teresa's divine punctuality, he capped his fountain pen and closed the folder before him on the desk.

Tommaso liked a day with a schedule, and he mentally checked off items on his agenda. From eight o'clock to noon, he dealt with paying customers; that morning, in fact, he had assisted one of Cederna's wealthiest men in the preparation of a perfectly senseless legal vendetta against the Mayor's Cederna Flour and Baking Company. The case would bring joy to the heart of any socialist lawyer, since it involved a huge fee, hinged entirely upon an obscure point of Roman law, and made no practical difference to anyone except for the two millionaires who were suing one another.

At ten the mail had come, including a report from an investigator hired with some of Terenzio's money to probe the delicate question of Bruno Benelli's finances. There were still missing pieces to the puzzle, but the day was fast approaching when he could prove to the Leone family that their accountant had been defrauding them for a decade.

After lunch at his father's trattoria at the poor people's end of the Piazza Bixio, Tommaso had then returned to the Casa del Popolo, where he spent the afternoon cheerfully working free in his capacity as Secretary of the Cederna PSI and legal adviser to the Farm Workers' Union.

It had been a good afternoon. After filing a brief to prevent the Municipal Government from seizing certain peasant-owned properties for nonpayment of taxes, Tommaso had submitted an electoral affidavit announcing the PSI's intention to contest all eleven of the seats on the Cederna Town Council. Enrico Mosconi was a popular politician who had been Mayor of Cederna for a long time, but the next election would be held as soon as the war ended, and this time Mosconi was going to have some competition.

And tonight, he promised himself, to conclude a perfect day, I shall dine with Rosaria Lombardi. Life will become perfect on the day we are married.

Rosaria now lived in her little house on the Via Calatafimi with Massimo and Chiara, the orphan they had rescued. Tommaso continued to sleep alone in his apartment over the trattoria. Since her release from prison, Rosaria had seemed quiet, and tight, and angry, unwilling to share her feelings.

Something happened in Udine between her and Achille, the lawyer surmised. It was never meant to happen, and it is clearly never going to happen again. I need to give her time to recover.

If this evening went as usual, they would sit talking at the kitchen table after the children had been put to bed. Since her release from prison, Rosaria had become a one-woman welfare agency in Cederna. At the moment she was using Achille's trust fund to purchase derelict dwellings for restoration as low-cost housing for homeless peasants. The two of them would spread their papers out on the table and plot strategy until midnight. Sometimes they would hold hands, and there were nights when he wondered if he might not be asked to stay over, but the invitation never came. When they said good night, she always kissed him on the cheek.

Someday, perhaps, he thought with a twinge of sadness. Someday . . .

He walked to the window. There were storm clouds gathering in the west and he wondered if it would be prudent to take his umbrella. Summer was over and the September rains could start any day now.

Then an iron-gray Lancia pulled into the piazza and halted in front of the Casa del Popolo. It was the new Mosconi luxury car, paid for by the Cederna Municipal Treasury, and in the back sat Junio Mosconi himself, wearing his aviator's hat. In front, there were two thugs from Simbruino, one driving while the other held the kind of shotgun that country people called a *lupara*.

Junio's appearance with armed men frightened him enough to think of the pistol his father had once given him. Tommaso disliked guns and kept it locked in the file cabinet with his confidential papers.

He left the weapon where it was, reasoning that Junio was not crazy enough to murder him in broad daylight. With his umbrella beneath his arm, he marched out into the piazza. The Lancia was waiting immediately outside, making an encounter impossible to avoid.

"What do you want, Mosconi?"

"To impart the merest admonishment." Posturing and play-acting as usual, Junio sprawled languidly in the back seat. "Has my old classmate forgotten how quickly the weather in Cederna can turn bad?"

"I am prepared for bad weather." Tommaso raised his umbrella, snorting at the suggestion that he and Junio had been classmates. It was true that they had both enrolled at Rome University's School of Jurisprudence, but the Mayor's son had scarcely attended a class and failed all of his examinations while Tommaso had taken his law degree with honors.

"I hope so, my dear attorney, because certain powerful people are becoming very impatient with you," Junio drawled. "My father and his ten loyal associates on the Cederna Municipal Council have just discovered that they will face socialist opponents in the next election. I have to tell you that these patriotic community leaders are very distressed."

"This town has seven thousand registered voters, and your coalition of rich landowners cannot expect to run it forever. Read the fine print in the 1911 Voting Rights Bill," Tommaso countered. Under Italian law, mayors were elected by a majority vote of the municipal council. In Cederna, old Enrico Mosconi would lose his position the instant the PSI could elect at least six councilors, one of whom would replace Mosconi as Mayor.

"Be careful!" Junio's temper began to fray. "There are brave men at the front fighting and dying, while the *patria* is betrayed by the subversive scum you represent. When the war is over and our heroes come home, there will be a settling of accounts. There will be retribution. Tommaso, there will even be revenge. Penalties will be imposed. Even now lists are being prepared and punishments ordained."

Tommaso noticed that the man with the *lupara* was pointing it in his direction. He tried not to look at the shotgun, and swallowed before speaking to ensure that his voice was steady.

"Junio, those brave soldiers are going to march home and vote for me and my colleagues in the Socialist Party. And none of us is afraid of you."

"You should be." In a fury, Junio jumped down from the Lancia. "Savarino, your mere existence offends me. If you replace my father as Mayor, I will kill you. Do you understand that? You are a silly little solicitor with thick glasses, and the sight of you disgusts me."

"You can't threaten me," the lawyer sputtered, but he retreated as the Mayor's demonic son advanced upon him. Junio's famous limp had disappeared, and he wielded his malacca cane like a sword, using it to drive Tommaso back into the Casa del Popolo.

"There's no one to protect you now," he screamed. "Achille is a cripple and Sandro has gone to Russia, which is where he belongs. Cederna is only big enough for one strong man, and now it's me. I'm going to be Mayor, not you. I'm going to fuck Rosaria Lombardi, not you!"

Desperate, Tommaso got the door closed and bolted while Junio pounded it insanely with his cane. Then he stumbled into his office, breathless with anxiety, and unlocked the drawer where he kept the pistol. His hands were trembling.

If Rosaria saw me now, he thought, she would never marry me. I can be brave enough playing the bold defender of the proletariat in court, but the sight of a lupara turns my knees to jelly.

The pistol in the safe was a miniature automatic designed for a woman to carry in a handbag. Tommaso took it out and looked at it, thinking that it betrayed everything he represented. A lawyer's function was to protect the weak from the strong. The moment you started to carry a pistol, you admitted that the law was designed by the strong to protect themselves from the weak. This was a secret attorneys were supposed to keep to themselves.

He put the gun in his pocket and stepped outside again, but the Mosconi Lancia had disappeared.

Tommaso breathed deeply for a few minutes to restore his inner balance. In the center of the Piazza Bixio the women were drawing water from the communal well. At the north end of the town square stood what Rosaria called the Kingdom of the Wicked: City Hall, Father Maurizio's church, the carabiniere station, the grand new Mosconi residence, and the Mosconi family *panificio* where the women bought their increasingly expensive bread. The five buildings stood shoulder to shoulder, sneering architecturally down at the Casa del Popolo, which huddled at the poor end of the piazza along with Savarino's Trattoria and a bar and a tobacco shop.

Touching the automatic in his jacket for reassurance, Tommaso addressed himself mentally to the Kingdom of the Wicked. I have always been frightened of you, but I am good at living with fear. If she will have me, I shall someday take Rosaria Lombardi as my wife. And I am going to win the election. To stop me from becoming Mayor of Cederna, you will have to kill me.

He closed his eyes for a moment and prayed, although it was unfashionable for a socialist to believe in God. It started to rain, so he put up his umbrella and set off across the Piazza Bixio for Rosaria's house on the Via Calatafimi.

5.

· ·

"We're going to win the war!" General Achille Leone had never, until this moment, been entirely sure. He followed his brother onto the Ciprioni's flight deck and the two of them peered through the window at the battlefield below.

To the west they could see the Alps, rising toward Switzerland. The nearest peak was Mount Grappa where Italian troops were nailing down the Austrian left flank and threatening the whole Austrian defensive line. To the right, all along the plain between the Piave and the Adriatic Sea, other Italian units were surging toward Trieste.

Four years ago, it had seemed quixotic to think that little Italy, all arias and ice cream, could prevail against the stern might of the Austrian Empire. When the Austro-Germans had smashed through Italian lines at Caporetto a year ago, victory had seemed more than ever an idle dream; for most of that awful winter, the war had become a matter of avoiding total defeat.

"Maybe by the end of the year." Terenzio's voice was uncharacteristically flat and tired. They had taken off at dawn from the military aerodrome at Treviso, flying north over the Piave River. For a year, this had been enemy territory. Below them were the seven field armies General Armando Díaz had marshaled to punch through Austrian lines. The attack had been launched at dawn on the twenty-fourth of October, six days ago, precisely one year after Caporetto.

"No, we're going to do it today," Achille assured him. "What's the date? We'll be telling our grandchildren about our triumph on the thirtieth of October 1918."

"If we live to have grandchildren."

"What's wrong with you? Are you nervous about today?"

"Sorry, Achille, it's just that I lost a friend yesterday. It seems unfair to get killed in the last battle of the war, doesn't it?"

"Was he someone I knew?"

Terenzio shook his head and turned away. "He was only a corporal. You wouldn't have known him."

There is a part of Terenzio that no one understands, Achille suddenly realized. This is my brother, and I hardly know him. Father never quite focused on him either. After the war we'll spend a lot of time together and he'll be my best friend.

"Sir, that should be Vittorio Veneto just ahead," the pilot announced.

"Good! Lieutenant, fly due north and take the squadron down to five hundred meters." Achille consulted his map to get his bearings. After flanking the enemy on both wings of the battlefield, General Díaz had sent his main force splashing across the Piave against the lynchpin of the Austrian defensive network, an obscure town named Vittorio Veneto. The redoubtable General Enrico Caviglia had been assigned the task of breaking the Austrian line at this point with the Italian Eighth Army.

"Five hundred, sir?" The officer at the controls was hesitant. A low-altitude reconnaissance run into the foothills of the Alps with artillery fire and poor visibility was not his idea of a good time.

"This is what we came to see." As a brigadier general, Achille hardly needed to explain his orders to a lieutenant, but he disliked asking men to risk their lives without knowing why. Each of the squadron's ten Ciprioni troop carriers contained a twenty-man team of *arditi,* assault troops especially trained to fly anywhere and fight anyone. Achille's mission was to conduct a reconnaissance of the battle for Vittorio Veneto, and land the *arditi* if they were needed to tip the balance of the battle.

As the aircraft lost altitude, Achille massaged his thigh, trying to keep the blood moving. Since that famous day when Guido had boarded the *Veneziana* and brought him by force back to the land of the living, he had been exercising with fanatic intensity to get his mind and body working together again. The army doctors had pronounced him fit for active duty, and General Díaz had assigned him a key role in planning this battle.

"Five hundred meters, sir," reported the pilot, glancing at his barograph. "That should be the road from Conegliano."

Even in the fading light the sight was incredible. From the window of the Ciprioni, Achille saw tens of thousands of Italian troops racing along the road toward Vittorio Veneto. None of them could have had more than a few hours' sleep in the six days since the offensive began, but they were pounding up the road at a dead run.

I've never seen Italians running into combat before, Achille realized, gazing to the north where there were flashes of cannon and howitzer fire. The shells were all flying toward the Austrian position and nothing was coming back, suggesting that the enemy's artillery had been put out of action.

"There's Vittorio Veneto," Achille cried as the squadron came in low over the ravaged town. "Good God, Teri, look at the place!" The community had been destroyed by Italian artillery, but the Italian tricolor was flying over what remained of the town hall. The center of Vittorio Veneto was thronged with tens of thousands of troops, and even from five hundred meters they could see that their uniforms were gray-green.

They were General Caviglia's troopers. The Austrians were gone, except for the few who had surrendered, and the many who had died.

As they sailed past Vittorio Veneto, the pilot led Achille's squadron into a long slow turn to the east. The roads out of Vittorio Veneto were mobbed with the remnants of a retreating, defeated army, thousands upon thousands of men trudging north. This was no tactical withdrawal or strategic feint; the Austrians were going home. The war was over.

"So we've won," commented Terenzio. Achille eased himself out of the copilot's seat, favoring his damaged thigh. His legs cramped quickly in the close quarters of the tiny flight deck, and he led Terenzio back to their seats.

"You don't seem enthusiastic."

"Oh, I don't know." The carabiniere captain shrugged. "Was Father right? When the shouting dies down, will it all have been worth it?"

"It has to have been worth it, Teri." Achille curbed his impatience. Terenzio had stood loyally by his side through his surgical operations, his brush with morphine addiction, and his own bleak depression after Caporetto. He was entitled to a bad day. "We have a shattered country to re-create. The economy is in terrible shape."

"And so are we! I wanted to play the piano, and now I have this broken hand. You wanted to marry Rosaria, and she's engaged to Tommaso. I had a friend, and now he's dead. What exactly did we gain?"

"Who was your friend?"

"It's just somebody I'll remember." Terenzio dodged the question. "How about you? Think you can get Rosi back? Are you going to try?"

"Of course not! The woman is marrying Tommaso, someone I respect," Achille snapped, feeling his mood shift. No one was allowed to talk to General Leone about Rosaria Lombardi, and Terenzio had just broken the rule. "It took a war to make me see the extent of her faithlessness."

"She was never faithless. I'm sure of that."

"I suppose you wanted to go to bed with her."

The younger man raised his eyebrows, as if the notion had never occurred to him. "No, I only wanted her for my sister."

"I never understood her behavior after Caporetto," Achille objected. "Why did she do what she did?"

"Why don't you ask her?"

For a long moment the two brothers stared at one another, listening to the whine of the aircraft's engines and the whistle of wind. "If she's marrying Tommaso, then it doesn't make a lot difference, does it?" Achille said finally, and went back to work on his map.

After another reconnaissance of the battlefield, Achille made the decision he had been authorized to make: there was no point in committing his *arditi* to combat. Caviglia's troops were doing splendidly without them, and landing ten aircraft in the gathering darkness would constitute an unnecessary risk.

The choice saddened him a little, since it meant missing the last great engagement of the Great War, but there was a more personal battle they had left to fight.

In the Ciprioni's passenger bay, the *arditi* were checking their pistols and oiling the daggers that served as the symbols of their unit. Despite the fact that he was temporarily their commanding officer, Achille was appalled by their insolence, their fondness for gratuitous violence, and their morbid fascination with death. Many of the *arditi* were habitual drunkards who had volunteered for this duty to avoid prison for vicious crimes, and he found it difficult to accept Guido's enthusiasm for them.

Homicidal psychopaths are perfect for missions like this, he decided. But what will we do with them after the war?

"I've sent the other nine aircraft back to Treviso," he told Guido, who had been briefing the *arditi*. "General Caviglia doesn't need any help from us, and it leaves us free for our secondary mission. Twenty men should be plenty."

Guido nodded confidently. "Wasn't Vittorio Veneto a wonderful sight?"

"A generation that can go from Caporetto to Vittorio Veneto in a year can accomplish anything. We'll build a new Italy on this battle."

"You're absolutely right," Guido enthused. "This war has been a triumph of the will. We need to build a nation based on self-sacrifice, and martial courage, and loyalty, and discipline. If it hadn't been for those goddamn socialists, we'd have had our Vittorio Veneto a year ago."

"That's not fair. Caporetto happened because the men in charge of the army a year ago were incompetent. For every cowardly deserter like Emilio Lodi, there was a courageous soldier like Sandro Lombardi. How can you make a blanket condemnation of the entire PSI? We're going to have to work with them after the war."

"Work with them?" Suddenly, Guido turned to the squad of *arditi* who awaited his orders. "Boys, let's tell General Leone what we're going to do to all the fucking socialists."

"Morte!" With an automatic, ritualistic chant, the men raised their daggers. "Death to socialists! Death to traitors!"

Shaking his head with irritation, Achille turned and made his way up the passageway to the flight deck. Guido seemed to believe that Italian society should be organized like a basic training regiment. The war had changed them all in a variety of ways. The experience of battle and being close to death had made Achille a more cautious man, anxious for peace, ready to rebuild. Fighting seemed to fill Guido with the desire to find new enemies and fight some more.

"Where are we?" he asked the pilot. "What are those lights in the distance?"

"Udine, sir."

"Do you see the field I've marked on the map?"

The pilot nodded. "I can't guarantee a safe landing."

"There never were any guarantees," General Leone told him as he strapped himself into the copilot's seat. "Take us in."

I used to be pretty. Perhaps even beautiful. At least that's what people said.

Cristina gazed at her pocket mirror, seeing the lines in her face and wondering if her hair might turn blond again when the war was over. The hospital's chief physician had denied that stress could cause a sudden loss of cortex pigment. Hereditary factors must have been responsible for her premature graying. She might have explained how her blondness had faded just after she had been raped by three German soldiers, but this was something Cristina had decided to keep to herself.

Tiredly she ran a comb through her silver hair and washed her hands. It would soon be time to serve dinner to the wounded Italian prisoners who were her patients, update her medication charts, and get everyone settled for the night. Dr. Fischer would make his evening rounds, and if there were no nocturnal emergencies she might even catch a few hours of sleep before dawn. Cristina had been continually on duty for one solid year now, seven days a week, and sleep was the only luxury left in life.

She tried to find something cheerful to think about. Nothing came to mind beyond the fact that it was Wednesday. There was a cook named Franz who prepared Viennese strudel for desert on Wednesdays, and she liked strudel.

She was standing in the nurses' station thinking about strudel, when she heard an aircraft coming in low over the old manor house that the Austrians had converted into a field hospital. She had waited twelve months for this sound, and she walked quickly across the ward. Terenzio's revolver was still in her handbag, since the Austrians had never bothered to search her. It was already dark and the evening was overcast. The aircraft was audible but invisible, which meant it was flying without lights.

The plane came very close before it went abruptly silent. There was no airfield nearby, and she wondered if any of the guards realized that an airplane had just landed in the sports field behind the trees at the foot of the formal gardens. Perhaps not. The smart young men were all off fighting at the front and the Austrians soldiers guarding the hospital were elderly and often drunk.

"Giuseppe?"

The sergeant major was lying perfectly still with his eyes open. Cristina had never known him with his legs, but now he seemed very tiny and very old. "Did you hear?"

"If it's the commander, give him my compliments," he whispered.

"I don't want to leave you." Dr. Fischer had just performed an operation to repair the arteries in Giuseppe's stumps, and he could not be moved in his present condition.

"Get going," the old sergeant major ordered. "Watch out for Lodi."

Cristina nodded, aware that the deserter still constituted a danger, although at the moment he was nowhere to be seen.

The Germans had assumed that Emilio Lodi was an authentic medical orderly. Under Cristina's direction, he had even learned something about hospital procedure. But there were dark undercurrents of hysteria and violence in his personality. Sometimes he ranted about the coming Marxist revolution, criticizing her for her family's wealth and social prestige. There had even been frightening occasions when he taunted her with the loss of her virginity, arguing that since her honor had been tarnished, she should grant him access to her bed. When she refused indignantly, he reacted with infantile tantrums.

It was a strange relationship. That he had watched her being raped, and done nothing, she found impossible to forgive, and yet he seemed to feel that she owed him something. Cristina had every intention of denouncing him to the military authorities as soon as they were rescued. Yet in the meanwhile they worked together, caring for their patients.

She stepped out onto the terrace. The night was overcast and there was a light rain falling. Earlier, there had been thunder off to the north.

"What's happening?" Emilio Lodi had a sinister way of materializing when he was least expected, and Cristina turned to find him leaning against the side of the building smoking a cigarette.

"Keep your voice down." She hushed him with a finger to her lips.

"There's a guard on duty right around the corner." Emilio followed her to the little brick wall that edged the terrace.

Clutching her handbag, Cristina peered into the darkness at the foot of the formal garden, seeing men moving in the shadows. Their faces were still indistinct, but one of them walked with a certain unmistakable lightness. "It's Guido," she whispered jubilantly. "My brother has come for us."

"I'm a deserter," Emilio hissed back. "If he catches me, I'll be executed."

Cristina put one leg over the wall. "Better stay here."

"You'll tell them where I am." Roughly Lodi threw her to the tiled floor of the terrace before turning in the direction of the Austrian guard post, out of sight around the corner. "Achtung!" he screamed in his primitive German. "Italienische Soldaten!"

"Crissi!" She heard Guido's hoarse voice and saw him run toward the terrace. Desperate, she got to her hands and knees, groping in her handbag for the revolver. Emilio Lodi backed away, gibbering.

"Was?" An Austrian with a machine gun sauntered around the corner in casual response to Emilio's cry. The cooks from the hospital's kitchen pulled guard duty when the regulars were too drunk, and this was Franz, the gentle old man from Linz whose specialty was strudel. Franz always made sure the gray-haired Italian nurse had an extra slice because he thought she was too thin.

"Nein, Franz, nein!" she pleaded as the cook pointed his machine gun at Guido. "Er ist mein Bruder," she explained. "He is my brother." For a long and peculiar moment Franz and Guido looked at one another in perplexity.

"Guido, don't shoot him!" she gasped.

"Why?"

"He always gave me extra strudel." Guido was famous for his ruthlessness in combat and Franz was an elderly pastry cook. It never occurred to Cristina that the Austrian would fire first, but he did. Cristina screamed as Franz methodically shot her brother in the chest with a six-round burst, and then began blazing away at the advancing *arditi*.

"God help us! Guido!" Suddenly Achille Leone appeared behind the terrace wall. Taking in the situation in a glance, he quickly shot Franz in the head. The pastry cook collapsed on the terrace, his brains spilling out on the tiles.

For Cristina, things became confused. Guido was whimpering and she crawled to his side, calling for Achille to help her.

Just as Achille began to mount the wall, Emilio Lodi snatched the machine gun from Franz's dead hands and fired point-blank at Achille. Just in time the general ducked behind the wall, but Emilio desperately began raking the advancing comando team with automatic fire.

Out on the garden lawn the *arditi* took cover. It was an impossible situation. Inside the hospital, a ringing alarm would bring reinforcements within seconds. There was blood pouring out of Guido's right shoulder, and he seemed unconscious. In another minute, a real firefight was going to take place, and Achille would be forced either to attack and take heavy casualties, or to retreat and leave the Rosselli family behind.

I should have done this a long time ago, she resolved, taking Terenzio's revolver out of her handbag. Her hands were slippery with Guido's blood. Does this thing actually work?

The pistol jumped in her hand when she shot Emilio the first time, hitting him in the back. He looked at her in amazement, unable to believe that this was actually happening to him. He was trying to aim the machine gun at her when she shot him a second time, hitting him in the face.

It all became a blur after that. She was crying and trying to stop the bleeding from Guido's upper right chest as men poured over the parapet. There was more shooting when other Austrian guards blundered guilelessly out of the ward and Achille's men killed them. At a certain point, Terenzio Leone patted her shoulder and said that everything would be all right. He reminded her that the pistol was his and took it back. Men came with a stretcher and carted Guido away.

She was sitting on the tiles crying when Achille gathered her into his arms. He walked with a limp now, but he seemed as strong as a king as he carried her off into the darkness at the foot of the garden.

The Ciprioni lumbered into the air and fought for altitude, the engines groaning. It banked over the hospital with bullets punching through the fuselage as the Austrians tried furiously to blow them out of the sky.

On the flight deck, Cristina Rosselli knelt over her wounded brother, using a borrowed *arditi* dagger to cut away clothing and loose flesh. She sutured a spurting artery and dressed the wound, but in the poor light it was hard to see how extensively Guido was hurt. He was semiconscious and in atrocious pain, but she feared that *morfina* would block his respiratory system.

"Damn it, Guido!" Achille crouched beside her, holding one of Guido's hands. "We've beaten Arabs and Turks and Austrians and Germans and you get yourself potted on the last day of the war by a hospital guard. It's not fair."

"I'm dying." There was phlegm and blood in Guido's throat, and Cristina helped him turn his head to one side so that he could cough it up.

"Don't talk!" Guido's face was utterly white, and his skin had gone cold, meaning that shock had set in. He had lost liters and liters of blood.

"Don't die!" Achille seemed to think that Guido could be ordered to stay alive. "Guido, it doesn't end this way. We won the war and slew the dragon and rescued the beautiful princess. Now we live happily ever after."

The plane ran into turbulence and dropped through the darkness like a stone. It was so awful even the *arditi* began screaming, and Cristina whimpered, trying not to wet herself with fright. As the pilot fought for control, the cabin lights went out and the starboard engine began making a strange *ping-ping-ping* sound.

"I am going to die." Guido spoke in a singsong voice as Cristina caressed his face with her fingers. "Achille, I have the right . . . my sister is frail. Achille?"

"I'm here."

"Marry Crissi and give her a son. It would be like a son for me. Crissi, keep him away from morphine and take care of him." Guido's voice was weak. "Do you promise?"

"Guido, rest," Cristina began to make the soothing noises nurses make when their patients are dying.

That's precisely what I should do, Achille told himself suddenly. The notion of marrying Cristina had been lingering in the back of his head ever since he had heard the news of Rosaria's engagement to Tommaso, but now he considered it seriously for the first time. The war has kept me from being lonely, he realized. War has that function. Will I be able to tolerate peace? Cristina loves me. We have shared so much. And now, if Guido dies . . .

"Achille? Please . . ." Guido was begging. "I'm frightened."

"Guido, we promise," Achille told him fiercely. "We will do everything you ask, but just try not to die, please."

The wounded officer fell silent as they crossed the Piave and the Ciprioni finally leveled out at a thousand meters over the river's dark waters. The starboard engine was on fire and had to be feathered. When Achille managed to get the cabin lights on again, they found that Guido's eyes were closed. There was more blood trickling out of his mouth, but it was difficult to tell if he was still breathing. Crissi's expert fingers could not find a pulse, and it was impossible to hear a heartbeat with the engine throbbing.

She rose and Achille put his arm around her shoulders. Guido was taking up all the room on the flight-deck floor, so they wedged themselves behind the pilot's seat. They had never before been physically this close, and Cristina was shivering. The pilot switched off the lights for better visibility, and the only illumination now came from the burning engine. The aircraft kept sliding to starboard.

"Is he dead?"

"I don't know." The plane lurched through more unsteady air. "I can't even tell if I got the bleeding stopped or if he just ran out of blood. How soon before we land?"

"A few more minutes." Achille glanced out the window. "I know a good doctor in Treviso. If we make it that far."

"Achille, whatever happens, don't pay any attention to what he said about us."

"I want to marry you," he said slowly. "Don't say no, please, I have no one . . . I mean, there is no one I care about as much as you."

"Oh, Achille." She began to cry. "I would be your lady, but you must know something. I swore I would never tell anyone, but just before I was taken prisoner, bad things happened to me."

"Your hair has turned to silver."

"I was raped."

There was a long silence. The lieutenant at the controls was sobbing with terror as the plane slewed wildly around in the sky. The Treviso aerodrome was just ahead of them, but the Ciprioni was losing altitude fast and tilting crazily to the right.

"We have all been raped." Achille Leone wrapped his arms around her as he braced himself for the crash landing. "If we live through this, I'll take care of you, Crissi. We'll stay together and take care of each other."

"Yes," she said. The shivering came back to her as the airplane collapsed onto the runway and shambled to a halt. "Yes . . ."

6.

....

On the morning the revolution came to Cederna the newspapers arrived late, because early-morning riots in Rome had blocked traffic.

Tommaso Savarino went down to the kiosk in the Piazza Bixio to fetch the Rome *Messaggero* and the *Corriere della Sera* from Milan, and on his way back to the Casa del Popolo he saw a few women collecting in front of the shuttered doors of the bakery. They were angry, understandably, and he made a mental note to ask Rosaria to calm them down. The ballotting was scheduled to begin at one, and this was no time for foolishness. Sergeant Cirillo needed only the slightest excuse to arrest every socialist voter in town.

Rosaria was waiting in the office on the second floor of the Casa del Popolo, and the two of them eagerly devoured the news. It was so good he forgot, for a moment, the problem of the bakery.

"It's happening," Tommaso said excitedly as he scanned the *Corriere*. There was scarcely room on the page for all the correspondents' reports. Throughout the peninsula, even in the stolid, conservative south, groups of peasants were seizing unused agricultural real estate from landowners. In most cases, they were even managing to stay within the law, since the new government of Prime Minister Francesco Nitti had enacted legislation sanctioning land sequestrations.

"Look here! There are going to be socialist town councils in half the municipalities in the north," Rosaria sang out excitedly. "Oh, if only Sandro were here to see us elect a socialist Mayor in Cederna."

Tommaso nodded, feeling a hodgepodge of emotions. On one hand, he hated the idea of an old friend languishing in a Russian exile. On the other hand, Sandro believed in violent revolution rather than peaceful evolution, and this would always make him an uncomfortable ally.

He was phrasing a noncommittal reply when the women in the piazza began to chant. "Pane! Pane! Pane!" they demanded their daily bread. "Death to Mosconi!"

"I don't like the sound of that." Tommaso went to the window and saw at least a hundred women and adolescent girls had now gathered in front of Mayor Mosconi's Cederna Flour and Baking Company.

"I'll go and talk to them," Rosaria promised, but she lingered over the newspaper, savoring the good news and looking for more election results. "Look, if we win here today, the Party will have made a clean sweep in all the towns in our district. That will mean—" She stopped talking suddenly, and grunted, as if she had been struck in the stomach.

Tommaso moved quickly to look over her shoulder. On the bottom of page 3, there was a picture of Achille in full uniform. The article explained that General Leone, the hero of Caporetto, would be going to France as military adviser to the Italian delegation at Versailles, helping to negotiate a peace settlement to the Great War.

"Well, he's become a celebrity," Tommaso said lightly. As a matter of habit, Achille's name was seldom mentioned between them. "His father achieved fame as a soldier before going on to diplomacy, so perhaps . . .''

"Yes, of course," she murmured in a broken voice. Tommaso needed to read the rest of the article to find out what was really bothering her. It seemed that the valiant general was engaged to marry Signorina Cristina Rosselli, the heroic Italian nurse who had remained behind enemy lines to care for wounded Italian soldiers and spent a year in Austrian hands as a prisoner of war.

So, he wanted to scream, we are back at the beginning! When will she understand that it is pointless? Achille is going to be an important man. With his war record, he could be Prime Minister some day. Even if he still loved her, which he does not, he could hardly afford to have a peasant mistress with a police record for subversion.

"Is Guido Rosselli still alive?"

"He's giving the bride away at the wedding," Rosaria whispered. He wondered if she was going to cry. Rosaria seldom surrendered to tears, but there were times when she became silent and sullen. Then she turned and threw the newspaper violently to the floor. "Damn them!"

"Rosaria, let's talk about Achille's marriage. In a way, it offers you and me the chance to . . ." Tommaso moved to her side, wondering why he was so good with judges and juries and so bad with women. As he tried to comfort her, the noise from the Piazza Bixio became more insistent. There was now an angry mob of several hundred people in front of the Mosconi bakery.

"I don't want to have this conversation." She shook her head vehemently and rushed toward the door. He was about to follow her when the phone on his desk rang, and Tommaso paused to take an urgent call from the Lazio District Chairman of the Socialist Party.

"Tommaso, things are getting rough. Some of the landowners in your area have hired gangs of storm troopers to intimidate our candidates," the PSI official warned. "They've already put a dozen of our people in the hospital and a few in the cemetery. There are demonstrations and shootings going up and down the peninsula. What's your situation?"

Tommaso quickly explained the problem. Most of Cederna's poor were forced to survive on a cheap, coarse bread called *pagnotta,* normally produced in great quantities by the Mosconi bakery. In a crude pre-election maneuver,

Mayor Mosconi had closed his bakery the previous evening, threatening to keep the *panificio* shut permanently if his Conservative Nationalist Coalition lost the election. The women needed that bread to feed their families, and they were angry.

"Stay off the streets, Tommaso! We need you alive to be the next Mayor of Cederna," the headquarters official advised as Tommaso put down the phone. If there is a riot in the Piazza Bixio, I'm not going to be Mayor of anything, he realized as he rushed down the stairs to the street level. Rosaria Lombardi had already crossed the hundred meters of paving stones to the *panificio*, but instead of calming the crowd, she was delivering a speech.

"Make your husbands vote for the Socialist ticket. If Tommaso Savarino is elected Mayor, we will confiscate this bakery and produce our own bread. It's time we smashed capitalism in Cederna."

"Death to Mosconi!" someone shouted in the crowd.

"Death to Mosconi," Rosaria echoed passionately, raising a clenched fist, her face flushed and her body trembling with violent energy.

Christ, she's gone mad, Tommaso concluded as he reached the edge of the crowd and tried to force his way through to the front of the bakery. Suddenly, a young women scooped up a loose paving stone and sent it crashing through the front window of the *panificio*. With a shout, a dozen women dashed forward and began looting the few remaining loaves of yesterday's bread from the display window.

Tommaso was appalled. "Stop," he shouted, shouldering his way through the mob until he reached Rosaria. She had just thrown a stone at the bakery. Her face was flushed and wild. "Why don't you make them stop?"

Before Rosaria could reply, the front door of the bakery opened and Mayor Mosconi burst out brandishing a shotgun.

"*Puttane!*" the old man shouted, firing the *lupara* into the ground at their feet and stinging several of them with birdshot. It was a tactical error. The women responded with a fusillade of jagged rocks.

The Mayor retreated into the panificio, blood on his forehead, but a trio of reckless girls raced in after him. Tommaso tried to force his way through, shouting about legal consequences, but no one yielded and he felt the hot hysteria around him. There were flames inside the *panificio*.

"They've set fire to the place!" He was worried. Mosconi's bakers heated their ovens with methane stored in steel tanks.

He started into the building, but Rosaria caught him, dragging him back by his coattails. The girls who had started the fire dashed free of the flames, but the Mayor was nowhere to be seen. "Stay out of it," Rosaria said steadily.

"What they're doing is illegal."

"Mosconi sat in his office and let his son kidnap me and then Massimo. Don't tell me about legality!"

"Do we have to have a bloodbath in Cederna because Achille is marrying someone else?" he said, his lawyer's mind cutting to the heart of the problem.

Was courting Rosaria a complete waste of time? Always hating Achille is not the same as ever loving me.

Furious, she slapped him hard across the face. "Don't ever say his name to me again!"

A real man would hit her back, Tommaso thought, but he turned away bitterly and tried again to push his way into the burning *panificio*. He had just reached the front door when the canisters of natural gas exploded. The building disintegrated, searing Tommaso's eyebrows and throwing sparks and soot and burning splinters over the crowd.

He stumbled backward, momentarily blinded by the blast and jostled by the women in their haste to leave the scene of what had just become homicide. Sirens split the morning air, and Tommaso knew that Sergeant Cirillo would open fire as soon as he saw the mob and the burning building. For a moment he nearly surrendered to the common panic, stumbling over the broken surface of the piazza.

"I can't see!"

"Let me help you." It was Rosaria's voice. She took his hand and led him quickly away from the scene of the disaster. He could feel the heat on his back, and the wood beams of the *panificio* crackled loudly as the building burned. Everyone was screaming, and the crowd evaporated as women dashed down side streets, anxious to avoid an encounter with the police.

They paused at the door to the Casa del Popolo, turning to watch flames consume the bakery. Tommaso's head ached, but his sight was slowly returning.

"I'm sorry that I hit you." There was a strange, flat quality to Rosaria's voice.

"The Mayor must be dead."

"Good," she said quietly. "I'm glad."

"That's not how I want to do politics. Now people will be too frightened of Junio to come out and vote. This could cost us the election."

Abruptly, Rosaria seized him by the lapels of his suit coat and pulled him inside the Casa del Popolo. Shutting the door with her foot, she leaned forward and kissed him hard on the lips. This had never happened before, and he was stunned.

"We are going to win," she told him succinctly. "You and I will visit every house in the district and make them come out to vote."

"But if Junio attacks . . ."

"Then we'll kill him too." She turned and raced up the stairs. "Let's get that gun."

"The Fatherland! The Fatherland!" Junio strutted around the council chamber, stamping the marble floor with his cavalry boots and slapping his thigh with a riding crop. He looked silly.

It's the Motherland, Rosaria said to herself. Italy is a mother, not a father.

"Our revenge! Our destiny!"

He might at least pretend to be sad, thought Rosaria angrily. Or has the prospect of taking the old man's place as Mayor himself softened the blow of his father's death?

All afternoon she had carried Tommaso's little automatic in her handbag, ready to shoot Junio the moment he interfered with the campaign. But their paths had not crossed, and the election had proceeded without incident, despite a heavy voter turn-out.

But there was trouble brewing in the hall. At the north end of the chamber was a raised dais with an elaborately carved wooden throne where the newly elected Mayor of Cederna would take his place. At the moment the throne was occupied by a stern Interior Ministry official who had been sent by Rome to supervise the election. Before him, in the middle of the council chamber, there was a row of tables where election volunteers were counting stacks of paper ballots.

Sergeant Cirillo was standing by the door with a carbine. Rosaria knew he was trying to decide whom to shoot first when the rioting started. I bet it will be me, she thought.

There were too many enemies in the hall for comfort. Giorgina sat alone and aloof in a far corner of the chamber while Bruno bustled around patting rich people on the back. The landowners and merchants of Cederna were all supporters of the Conservative Nationalist Coalition, and they all clustered to the right of the Mayor's throne, well-dressed men who moved with a certain self-confidence. Cederna's ruling classes had been shocked by the Mayor's violent death, but they had quickly arranged for Junio to take his father's place on the ticket.

"I wonder how many of them are carrying guns," she whispered to Tommaso. In his precise handwriting, the lawyer was annotating the speech he intended to give if the socialists won a majority of the eleven council seats.

"How many of our people have guns?" The lawyer glanced to the left of the mayor's throne, where the socialist candidates and their supporters had all collected. The spectators' benches were filled with former Leone estate employees who had been discharged by Bruno. They were now being harangued by Mercuzio Mercatelli, who was telling them why they should hate the Benelli family even more than they already did.

"The results are ready." The Interior Ministry official did his sums one last time and then called for their attention. A hushed murmur crossed over the room.

"For Cederna Ward One, I declare Signor Bruno Benelli elected."

There was a grumble from the farm workers, but the result had been a foregone conclusion. Ward One was mostly the Leone estate. Bruno had threatened his remaining employees with abrupt unemployment if he lost the election.

"For Cederna Ward One, I declare Signor Junio Mosconi elected."

Damn! Rosaria shook her head in irritation as the Conservative Nationalists cheered. The Socialist Party had recruited the only Marxist dentist in the world to run against Mosconi in that ward. But sympathy for the dear departed Mayor had clearly carried the day. If the Conservative Nationalist coalition won a majority, it would now be possible for Junio to inherit his father's job as Mayor.

"For Cederna Ward Three, I declare Mercuzio Mercatelli elected." The farm workers all cheered wildly, although Mercuzio had run in impoverished East Cederna. A socialist who can't win in a slum, reasoned Rosaria, needs to get out of politics.

She gritted her teeth while Ward Four voted loyally for the wealthy *medico* Dr. Beniolo, but relaxed a little when wards five, six, seven, and eight were all nailed down with healthy majorities for PSI candidates.

Then the wave of victories stopped as the Conservative Nationalist Coalition unexpectedly captured wards nine and ten, evening the distribution of seats on the council at five to five, with one seat yet to be decided.

As the Interior Ministry inspector shuffled papers, Rosaria moved down the bench to sit next to Tommaso, ready to offer comfort in his moment of disappointment.

"For Cederna Ward Eleven," said the Interior Ministry official with the merest hint of a smile, "I declare Tommaso Savarino elected."

"My God, we've won," Rosaria cried. The chamber exploded into a medley of rage and jubilation. Ever since the Middle Ages, the landowners in Cederna had been selecting one of their own to handle the municipality's paperwork, but the Mayor's violent death seemed to have liberated people from five centuries of fear. For the first time a socialist was settling himself upon the throne, and the landowners were stunned and dismayed.

"The PSI majority desires an emergency session of the Cederna Municipal Council." Tommaso spoke firmly. "Will councilors please take their seats for a quorum count?"

"Assassino!" Junio screamed, waving his cane. "Murderer! Murderer!"

Tommaso turned calmly to the carabiniere noncommissioned officer. "Sergeant Cirillo, will you help Councilor Mosconi find his seat?" He gently reminded everyone that he was now the law in Cederna. The councilors reluctantly took their seats, except for a defiant Junio, who had to be pulled into his place by Dr. Beniolo.

"Let me come directly to the point." Tommaso turned to the five wealthy men on the opposition bench. "Capitalist forces in this community have traditionally manipulated rents, food prices, and salaries without regard to the welfare of the people. During the Great War, this wanton profiteering created a new class of poor and unemployed here, and the PSI has prepared a legislative program designed to remedy what has gone so tragically wrong in our beloved Cederna. We will be voting tonight . . ."

He's taking charge, Rosaria realized, wondering how the relationship between them would change way now that Tommaso was the Mayor. When he completed the paperwork to hire her as Director of Social Services for Cederna, she would become effectively his employee, just as she had been Leonida's employee and Achille's employee.

When do I get to be in charge of me? Tommaso nodded at her as he spoke, and she obediently rose to distribute copies of the PSI's legislative agenda for Cederna.

"What are you talking about?" Junio was on his feet again, shouting as Rosaria tried to hand him a copy of the draft bill. He refused to accept it from her hands, so she quickly passed the stack to Bruno Benelli, before scurrying back to the socialist side of the room. "My father is murdered and you talk about land reform?"

Junio seemed convinced that he could reverse the election by thundering abuse at the new Mayor, but his colleagues all began to study the document, knowing that Tommaso had the votes to turn it into enforceable law. Rosaria watched their faces as they digested its implications. Tommaso had worked for weeks on this bill, checking and double-checking to ensure that it would resist any challenge in court.

"In summary, this draft ordinance has the legal effect of sequestering all unused agricultural land within the municipality and making it available for redistribution to landless farmers," the new Mayor explained. "It also requires the establishment of workers' councils for any agrarian entity having more than twenty workers, and empowers these councils to make binding decisions on wages, working hours, and conditions of employment. It also sets out a mandatory regime of price and rent controls."

Bruno Benelli was the brightest man on the Conservative Nationalist bench, and he was on his feet before the others had finished reading. "This is Bolshevism, Mr. Mayor, and the elimination of private enterprise. Effectively, you are confiscating my property."

"It isn't your property," Rosaria hissed. Tommaso shot her a dirty look, but she was unable to restrain herself. "That land belongs to Count Leone."

"Who has left me in full control," Bruno retorted easily.

"Only until midnight tonight, Benelli," roared Mercuzio Mercatelli, who was already savoring his revenge. Having been humiliated and dismissed by Bruno, Mercuzio was now prepared to return as leader of the Leone Estate Workers' Council.

"This clever little legislation affects only those agrarian establishments with more than twenty employees, as of midnight tonight." Bruno ostentatiously produced his pocket watch. "Let the record show that it was eleven P.M. when I discharged all currently employed workers on the Leone estate. Good evening, gentlemen."

There was an uproar. There were still some four hundred families dependent upon the Leone estate for their entire income. Mercuzio was on his feet, fists balled, ready to fight, while Tommaso pounded his gavel trying to restore order. Junio Mosconi was jumping up and down, unable to make himself heard.

"Bruno, you can't do that." Outraged, Rosaria threw down her notebook. "Achille would never consent."

"Since when do women speak at council meetings?" Junio Mosconi advanced on Rosaria threateningly. Bruno Benelli prudently retreated toward the door, dragging a furious Giorgina out of the council chamber.

"It's time we women had our say," Rosaria shouted back at him.

"Shut up, you little whore," Junio sneered. "Shouldn't you be on your back in some rich man's bed?"

"Impotent pervert!" she screamed. Tommaso repeatedly pounded the desk with his gavel, but the moment had already toppled into madness. Losing control completely, Junio lurched across the center of the room and struck Rosaria solidly across the face with his cane.

It hurt, more than she expected, and she dropped involuntarily to her knees before him, her head spinning.

Behind her the room erupted in pandemonium, since Rosaria was Joan of Arc to most of the farm workers. Momentarily frightened by the pain, Rosaria crawled backward on her hands and knees trying to get away from Junio while Tommaso jumped down from the dais to protect her. Simultaneously the peasants from the Leone farm surged forward, knocking over chairs and tables in their haste to take revenge. One of the Conservative Nationalists fired a pistol shot into the ceiling, but Mercuzio Mercatelli's men swarmed over Junio, pounding him with their fists.

"Don't kill him," Tommaso screamed, aghast at the legal implications of murdering two Mosconis on the same day. Oh, go ahead and exterminate him, Rosaria thought, her mind raging out of control. Let's have him dead before he murders one of us. Kill him, kill him, kill him . . .

Her jaw aching, she crawled behind an overturned bench, watching as the farm workers kicked Junio to the floor. Several landowners had drawn pistols in self-defense, but they backed away in fear as the peasants punished Junio with their fists and feet.

When Tommaso and Sergeant Cirillo managed to stop the beating a moment later, Junio was sprawled on the floor. His face was covered with blood and one leg was bent awkwardly beneath him. He groaned in agony as Dr. Beniolo quickly assessed the damage.

"This is the leg that kept you out of the army," Rosaria heard the physician mutter. "Congratulations!"

"Why?" There was pain in Junio's voice.

"This time it's really broken."

Rosaria's head was still spinning as Tommaso helped her to her feet, after ascertaining that she was not seriously hurt. "We've got to stop Bruno," she mumbled. It hurt to speak.

Tommaso nodded. He seemed amazingly calm as he climbed back to his Mayor's chair. "All in favor of the 1918 Cederna Land Reform Bill will signify their consent by raising their right hands." The Conservative Nationalist councilors were all rushing away and ignored him, but Tommaso paused to count six raised socialist hands, his own included.

"The measure is passed."

The conservative councilors carried Junio from the room. He was shouting about death all the way to the street.

"This meeting," said Tommaso quietly, "is now adjourned."

Outside, the insurrection was already brewing.

Rosaria and Tommaso had been arguing all the way down the corridor, and she looked up in amazement as they reached the steps of the Municipal Building, stunned to see that there were already a thousand peasants in the Piazza Bixio. To celebrate the socialist triumph, Benita had even brought the children, her own Sergio, Massimo, and Chiara, the little waif they had saved from that orphanage. Mercuzio Mercatelli was making an inflamatory victory speech. Sergeant Cirillo and his carabinieri had disappeared, along with Junio and the Conservative Nationalist mob.

"I'll be in court the first thing in the morning," Tommaso vowed. "We will have Junio arrested for assault and battery as soon as he's out of the hospital, and I should be able to win a revocation of Bruno's dismissal of those workers."

Rosaria pressed her hand to her jaw to ease the pain. Then she bent down to pick up a sleepy Massimo, who was confused by all the excitement.

"Oh, congratulations," enthused Benita, hugging both of them in turn. "You're so clever! This feels like the French Revolution."

"If Bruno can find a lawyer half as good as you are," Rosaria said to Tommaso, "he will tie us in knots for six months. And if Bruno stalls successfully, the other landowners will do the same. Unless we control that land, we've only won a paper victory."

"We need to stay strictly within the law."

"Let's make them stay strictly within the law we just passed," she hissed at him. "Listen, this is Bruno's golden opportunity. When I administered the estate, I got Leonida to pay the highest salaries in the district. If Bruno can fire the remainder of Leonida's old people, he can bring in scabs at the bottom of the pay scale and save a fortune."

Then the crowd discovered them at the top of the steps. There was a big round of enthusiastic applause, marred by only a few angry jeers.

"We're going to starve," a woman shouted at Tommaso. Virtually every working-class man and woman in Cederna was standing before them in Piazza Bixio, and most of the mothers had brought their children. "What good does a socialist Mayor do us if we don't have jobs?" asked a woman.

"Signora, we will take steps . . ." Tommaso gave a short speech, telling the people that socialist administrations had taken power legally in thousands of towns and municipalities, which demonstrated the superiority of legality to violence.

"Kill Benelli! We should kill all the bastards," someone shouted.

Tommaso frowned. "We can't have that kind of talk. How many rich men do you think we can murder in one day before the government sends in the army?"

"All right, Mr. Mayor," sang out a sarcastic voice. "What are you going to do?"

Tommaso hesitated, and Rosaria quickly stepped forward. Her jaw still hurt, but the adrenaline began to pump as she began to speak. "The municipal administration must remain strictly within the law," she told them, to let Tommaso off the hook. She spoke slowly, trying to project her voice across the huge piazza. "But those of you who have been employees of the Leone estate need to take direct action to secure your rights. The dismissal was not legal. We need to go now to the Castello Leone and occupy that land."

There was an answering roar, and Rosaria felt an exciting rush of power. It was a little like sex. Not precisely the same, but the sensation was kindred.

"We want to avoid violence," she shouted. Tommaso was pulling on her elbow, trying to get her to stop, but she shook him off and danced down the steps. "The women will march in front with the children. The men will stay behind!"

She plunged into the crowd, feeling a sense of invulnerability. Tommaso clung to her like a headache. "Since when did you become an expert in guerrilla warfare?" he demanded.

"Garibaldi taught Leonida, and Leonida taught me." This is what he would have done, she decided. I am reclaiming my son's birthright.

"We must leave the children behind."

"No, this is their fight too."

"Rosaria, you're an unnatural woman," said Tommaso tiredly. He took the pistol out of his pocket and switched off the safety.

"I have lived among unnatural men," she told him in an undertone, and then turned to the crowd. "The land belongs to us," she screamed.

"To us! To us!" chanted the crowd, and the peasants followed her out of the Piazza Bixio toward the Castello. The women began a *ninnananna*, a nursery song, bouncing their children gaily on their hips as if this were a picnic and not a riot. Bringing up the rear, the men were chanting the socialist "Bandiera Rossa," the "Red Flag," and many of them were carrying farming implements like axes and scythes with long wooden handles. It was past midnight, but the moon was so full that it almost felt like day.

After a kilometer of gravel the road dissolved into the great sweep of manicured grass before the front gates of the Castello Leone. The scene was surreal. Cirillo had found reinforcements, and a ten-man squad of policemen blocked the end of the road. In the distance the Castello was shuttered and dark, except for lights around the front door. Behind the row of armed carabinieri stood Bruno's automobile with Giorgina sitting in the passenger seat. Dressed in a suit with waistcoat and awkwardly holding a shotgun, Bruno was barricaded behind the door of the vehicle.

Suddenly Rosaria felt an overpowering sense of déjà vu. The last time I was here, she remembered, I was coming home after Caporetto, thinking I would soon be Achille's wife. Instead, Sergeant Cirillo spat in my face and threw me into prison.

Now I have returned, leading a mob of peasants to seize control of what might have been mine on my wedding day . . .

"Halt!" Sergeant Cirillo stepped out in front of his men, waving a revolver at them. "Don't come any closer."

The crowd shambled to a halt. Cirillo had chosen the location of his blockade well, since there were bushes on both side of the road, and no room for the mob to outflank him. Rosaria stopped a meter away from Cirillo, suffering a moment of apprehension. The policemen were all down on one knee, pointing their rifles directly into the crowd.

If they open fire, those of us in the front rank will be killed, she realized. Would they dare shoot? Oh, God, if they hit Massimo! Perhaps they would aim carefully and hit just us and not our babies. If they kill me, Tommaso will be a good father for Massimo. Poor little boy, she thought suddenly. You were born for trouble, child. Please don't start crying now.

"Turn these people around and lead them home," Cirillo ordered.

"These are employees of the Leone estate," Rosaria replied. "They are proceeding legally to their place of work."

Cirillo stepped forward so the two of them could whisper. "They were discharged by their employer, and you are trespassing."

"Their discharge was not legal. Your action in stopping them contravenes Article 32 of the Italian Constitution."

"Who are you to tell me what the law is?" Cirillo snapped, but his voice quavered for just an instant and Rosaria knew that he was frightened. It was ten men with rifles against a thousand with knives and the police had not anticipated so large a challenge quite so soon.

Without thinking, Rosaria hissed at him. "Your address is Via Bonifacio, number eighteen. You live there with your wife, Angelina, and your two daughters, Marina and Rebecca."

"What are you saying? Are you threatening me?"

"Reality is threatening you," she said. "We are going to occupy those fields and bring in that harvest. You can stop us by opening fire, but you can only kill some of us and the survivors will go to the Via Bonifacio and cut the throats of your wife and children."

There was a long pause. "Let's go," said someone in the crowd behind her. Rosaria kept her eyes on Cirillo's face, ready to cover Massimo with her body if the policemen ordered his troops to open fire.

"Kill them!" Giorgina Benelli advised at the top of her lungs, leaning out of the open window of the car. Anger rippled through the crowd, and people began to push forward on either side of Rosaria. Cirillo seemed transfixed.

Lacking an order to fire, the police line began to yield, backing away as the peasants surged onto the lawn and raced toward the Castello.

Prudently Bruno Benelli climbed into the driver's seat and started the engine of his automobile, accelerating across the lawn toward them. The crowd divided to let the big car pass, but they smashed the glass on both sides with rocks as it hurtled by and then chased it down the road with taunts and jeers.

Hugging Massimo to her breast, Rosaria walked up to Sergeant Cirillo as the peasants poured past them by the hundreds. The policeman was silent. Rosaria leaned forward and spat in his face.

Cirillo might have reacted violently, but a gang of adolescent boys swooped down on him from behind at that precise moment and seized his pistol. Then they kicked him off the road into the ditch. One of the boys covered Cirillo with his own pistol while the others took turns undoing their trousers and pissing on him.

Rosaria turned away, laughing hard for the first time in a year and watching as the peasants fanned out to occupy the fields and the outbuildings. Mercuzio was organizing his forces, dispatching squads to take control of every parcel of Leone land.

Massimo had fallen asleep in Rosaria's arms. As she stood on the lawn, Tommaso came up and stood beside her. He was angry, and she realized how much he hated spontaneous politics.

"Do you intend to take control of the Castello itself?" he said in his lawyer voice. "Legally it would be hard to justify."

Rosaria shook her head. "There's nothing in there I want." It would be different if this were ever going to be my home again, she reflected. If I were living here with Achille . . .

"Then let's get back to Cederna." Tommaso tried to take her arm, but she pulled away. "I wish you hadn't spat in Cirillo's face."

"I hate him," she explained simply. "I needed to prove that I wasn't afraid of him anymore. Why are you so upset?"

There was a long silence. She had been on her feet for twenty straight hours and exhaustion was threatening to overwhelm her. There was a painful bruise on her face where Junio had struck her, and carrying the sleeping Massimo was getting to be hard work. Tommaso moved a few steps away. A cloud had crossed between them and the moon, and the night had grown suddenly dark. She could no longer see his face, and they were alone in the empty field.

"When you spit in the face of a policeman and threaten to kill his family," Tommaso said quietly, "you move us to a dimension where lawyers are not very useful. Maybe you'd better bring Sandro home and have his kind of revolution, not mine."

"They're afraid of us now," she lashed at him. "Did you see the terror on Bruno's face?"

The lawyer shook his head. "We are terrifying ruthless, powerful people who do not enjoy being frightened. Unless we can impose socialism on them the way they have imposed capitalism upon us for so long, they will make us pay for their fear.''

"Tommaso . . .'' she called. His voice grew faint as he moved away in the darkness.

"They will extract payment in our blood.'' His voice had become a hoarse whisper. ''And we will pay and pay and pay . . .''

And then he was gone.

She touched her cheek where Junio had struck her, and it was still painful. With a sigh of fatigue she shifted Massimo to the other shoulder, wondering if Benita had taken Chiara back to the Via Calatafimi.

It's time to go home, she thought, lingering on the lawn before the Castello as memory washed over her.

All right, Achille, she wanted to shout. Go ahead and marry your little Venetian princess. You may talk to kings and prime ministers in Paris and Rome, but here in Cederna you'll need my permission to pick a turnip in your own damn garden.

Where is the triumph? She searched her soul for that exaltation she had felt during her speech in the Piazza Bixio, but the wildness had disappeared, leaving only a hollow feeling.

I've won, she tried to tell herself. Sandro would be proud of me, but Sandro is far away. Tommaso is disappointed because he wanted to win with pieces of paper. Achille will be devastated when he hears that I have confiscated his inheritance. And sweet Cristina, who once asked me to be her best friend, will think I did it out of spite.

Did I?

She shrugged, too tired to examine her motives. We won, she told herself, turning toward Cederna as she stumbled through the darkness. Behind her in the fields she could still hear the peasants singing about their Red Flag. It is enough that we won. Motives are secondary to economics, and our people will eat this winter.

Ahead of her on the road she saw Tommaso's silhouette. I need him, she realized, and she hastened her step until she caught up with him.

"I'm sorry,'' she confessed. ''I've always wanted your kind of revolution, not Sandro's.''

He nodded. ''I'll carry Massimo. You must be tired.''

Silently she surrendered the sleeping child. You would make such a wonderful father, she said to herself, feeling an intense guilt. If I were a good woman, I would take him into my bed tonight and give him a child.

Instead, she kissed him on the cheek. He took her hand, and together they walked down the road to Cederna.

7.

. . . .

It was an arrangement. Angelica liked him and he admired her. Although the Russian woman was several decades older, they slept together at night and made love whenever he asked. In the morning, she brewed tea and brought in the mail. Neither the tea nor the lovemaking was quite warm enough.

That's the trouble with arrangements, Sandro mused as he opened his eyes. Nothing is ever as hot as you like it.

"Mail from Italy!" After being exiled by Czar Nicholas II for subversive activities, Angelica had lived in Italy for decades, but she had not lost her Russian accent; in fact, the Slavic intonation in her voice seemed to have deepened since her return to her native land with the delegation of Italian socialists. She tossed two envelopes onto the bed before padding off in her bathrobe to make breakfast. Sandro thirsted for real coffee, but none had been available in the Soviet Union since the revolution, at least not for low-ranking foreign revolutionaries. "Comrade Trotsky is addressing the Comintern Foreign Group at nine, remember?" she called from the tiny kitchen.

Nodding, he quickly opened Rosaria's letter, hungry for news about home. Ever since the beginning of his Moscow exile and Rosaria's release from prison they had been in regular contact, although the mail was painfully slow. It was now a bleak Moscow January in 1920, and this letter had been mailed from Cederna in late September of 1919.

Some of Rosaria's news was old. Through Socialist Party channels, Sandro had already heard about Tommaso's victory over the landowners in Cederna. Privately he was pleased, although most of the Italian socialists in the Moscow delegation regarded electioneering as marginal to the revolutionary process. A small-town bourgeoisie might stupidly surrender to a respectable reformist like Savarino, but real political change was only going to happen when capitalism was destroyed root and branch.

Rosaria's seizure of the Leone estate, on the other hand, was interesting news. This is precisely the kind of thing the proletariat needs to do, he told himself. We need dress rehearsals for the revolution. Those people worship Rosaria. She could be a real revolutionary yet, if I were there to help. Otherwise people like Tommaso will redirect the whole movement toward timid reformism. If I could only go home!

The second envelope bore a mysterious return address on the Boulevard de Clichy in the Montmartre section of Paris, and it took him a moment to realize that as part of the Italian Armistice Commission, Achille would have found a house in Paris. After a warm "Carissimo Sandro," the letter came straight to the point. "Although my relationship with Rosaria has ended," the letter said, "my affection for you remains as strong as ever and I have investigated the question of your legal status."

The details were set forth concisely. If Sandro would file a deposition explaining the circumstances under which he had struck that carabiniere officer in Treviso, the assault-and-battery charge could be tried in absentia before a friendly judge. The offended lieutenant had accepted a financial settlement and would testify that the incident had been a banal misunderstanding. Desertion was a more serious matter, but the Nitti Government was granting amnesty to certain categories of those who had gone absent without leave, and Tommaso Savarino was working on Sandro's case.

The legal documentation could best be accomplished in Paris, and Achille had enclosed both a check drawn on a Helsinki bank to cover the cost of Sandro's travel, and directions to the new Leone apartment in Paris where he could stay while the Italian Embassy there completed the paperwork.

Sandro's mind was made up before Angelica returned with the tea. "I want to go home," he said. "They're going to drop charges."

"You are still in the middle of your training here," she objected.

"Maybe, but I'm going to die if I don't get a cup of real coffee soon."

Angelica nodded. There was a little tear in one eye as she slipped off her housecoat and came back into bed. "I'll get you a passport," she promised.

"We'll miss Comrade Trotsky's conference."

"Trotsky can wait," she said, and came into his arms.

8.

When so much else was lost, how did this survive?

Aboard the *Veneziana,* mail had been accumulating during Achille's stay in Paris, and at the bottom of the pile he found the little book on Giambattista Tiepolo, together with an apologetic note from the manager of the Hotel Italia in Udine.

Rosaria must have brought it with her to his room, leaving it under the bed while they shared that fragment of love. Then the Germans had crashed through the line at Caporetto and distorted all their lives forever.

I now know that the Italia Hotel dusts beneath its beds at least every second year, he reflected. I also know that it takes more than thirty months to forget the best thirty minutes of your life.

It was time to go. Achille looked around at the stateroom of his yacht, wondering if he should have his honeymoon aboard his beloved *Veneziana* or take Cristina immediately back to his Boulevard de Clichy residence, where there were servants and shops nearby in Montmartre.

It was too late to start reorganizing his honeymoon. Cristina had always been nervous aboard the *Veneziana,* but they could spend their first few days of wedded bliss safely secured to the dock if she preferred.

Then he put the Tiepolo guide into the pocket of his *giubba* next to his whiskey flask, and climbed up the hatchway. With adequate supplies of culture and alcohol, a man ought to be able to survive his own wedding. He locked the empty *Veneziana* behind him and walked down to the Riva degli Schiavoni dock, where he caught the north-bound Grand Canal vaporetto.

Tourists were beginning to filter back to Venice and the ferryboat was crowded. Achille ignored the now-familiar sights and distracted himself with his book, planning a day when he could hike around Venice looking at all the Tiepolo frescoes in the city. When they finally returned from Paris with a definitive peace treaty, there would be time, if Cristina was interested. He disembarked at the Ponte degli Scalzi and found that Guido had not yet arrived, leaving him time for a visit to the nearby Scalzi Church and the first Tiepolo on his list.

"We're closed to the public." An elderly priest accosted him from the shadows as he entered.

"Padre, could I look at the Tiepolo fresco?"

"It was destroyed during the war," the cleric said dourly. "The Austrians kept trying to bomb that big ugly train station next door and kept hitting my beautiful little church instead."

Was there anything the war had not destroyed? As the priest vanished, Achille sat down at the back of the church, watching women in black dresses scrubbing the floor beneath the altar.

You must concentrate on all that has gone well, he reprimanded himself. Father once said that luck was transmitted through a family with the same genetic inevitability as syphilis. And we have been a lucky tribe. In five hundred years of soldiering, no Leone ever went through a bloodbath like that one.

And so few of my friends survived! There is me with a steel girder in my thigh and Guido minus an arm and poor Giuseppe Papafava without his legs. Sandro, the biggest target of them all, walked away without a scratch, but most of the others are in the cemetery. So I was lucky.

They made you a general because you were good at making decisions, he told himself. And you've decided. Save what there is left to save, and leave the rest behind. That means Rosi. He sat for a little while longer and then walked out of the ruined church, leaving the Tiepolo book behind on a pew.

"Let me help you." Achille extended a hand as Guido tottered briefly on the vaporetto gangplank, still off-balance without his right arm.

"My legs still work," Guido snapped as he stumbled ashore. "Don't treat me like a cripple."

"Sorry, old friend, I was afraid we would lose you to the fish." Achille realized that Guido was still resentful. After Cristina's rescue, the popular press had gone into raptures over the romantic engagement between the heroic nurse and the brilliant general, forgetting about the badly wounded brother who had done, as usual, most of the fighting. The army had promoted Guido to full colonel, covered him with medals, and—despite Achille's protests— put him firmly on the retired list. Like many veterans, he continued to wear his uniform as a symbolic gesture, but his military career was over.

"The fish can wait," Guido grumbled as they walked down the Grand Canal. "Well, is everything ready? When do the two of you leave for Versailles?"

"The end of the week, and I'm afraid we'll be there for a year or more," Achille explained. "There are still a thousand border questions to be arbitrated, and I seem to be the only member of the Italian delegation who can read a map."

"Well, try to put some backbone into our politicians! They're giving away everything we fought for."

Achille nodded, searching for a way to avoid the argument they had been having since the Armistice. Achille and his fellow liberals had always seen the war as the successful defense of democracy, but rabid nationalists like Guido wanted concrete territorial rewards for their suffering: the acquisition of great hunks of North Africa, a colony in central Turkey, and most of the Yugoslav coast.

"It's tough explaining European geography to Americans, but we're doing our best," Achille joked. "Listen, how was your trip to Milan?"

"It started badly." Guido lit a cigarette, a habit he had acquired during his recovery. "I got off the train in uniform and ran into a crowd of Marxist bullies who kicked my legs out from under me and spat on me while I rolled on the ground."

"Christ! They still haven't forgiven us for the war. Had you provoked them in any way?"

"No, unless you consider the sight of a one-armed colonel to be unreasonably provoking. Milan looks like a civil war could break out any moment. There are socialist mobs roaming the streets, screaming about revolution, sacking shops, and beating up veterans. In fact, Mussolini told me—"

"Mussolini?" Achille wondered if Guido had lost his sanity along with his arm. Benito Mussolini had begun his erratic career as a socialist journalist with revolutionary tendencies. Sandro had once been enthusiastic about him. In 1914, Benito had caught a bad case of patriotism, and spent most of the war as an enlisted man. Given a medical discharge after a serious training accident, Mussolini was now staging a political comeback as the leader of a veterans group in Milan. Nobody knew what he stood for now. "Why did you see Mussolini? What's the name of his latest lunacy? The Fascio di Combattimento?"

"Yes, the Combat Group," Guido said tersely. "We call ourselves fascisti."

"We? Oh, Guido, for Christ's sake!" Achille came close to exploding but controlled his temper. This is my wedding day, he reminded himself. I don't want a fight with the man who will be giving the bride away. "Look, I know the country is in turmoil and the socialists have gone a little crazy, but what kind of Italy would this ex-corporal give us?"

"An Italy where no stinking socialist coward could spit on a one-armed colonel," said Guido quietly, and they went into the church.

"Darling, we could have dyed your hair," said the Signora Rosselli. The ceremonial gondola turned in the dark water, its prow festooned with flowers.

"The gray is part of me now, Momma." Cristina felt a quivering in the pit of her stomach. "What worries me is how little I know about being a wife."

"How can you say that?" Signora Rosselli reacted with irritation. "You can manage servants, and a nurse ought to know something about children."

"No, I mean . . ." Cristina lowered her voice to avoid sharing her distress with the gondoliere. "In bed."

"You lie still and let your husband do what he wishes, and afterward you praise him. Not too much or he'll think you're vulgar, but a little because men are vain. Say it was sweet. That's what I always said to your father."

"Momma?"

"If it hurts, you should do the rosary in your head. Say your Ave Marias."

"Momma, sometimes Ave Marias don't work for me. When you were little, did Grandma teach you any Hebrew prayers?"

"What a thing to say!" With an angry hiss Signora Rosselli pointed to the Ghetto Vecchio district on the opposite bank of the Cannaregio, where Venetian Jews had once been compelled to live. "For four hundred years we were prisoners over there, flogged or jailed or sent off into exile or executed whenever the Venetians needed a scapegoat. When Napoleon conquered Venice and allowed us to leave, your father's father bought the Palazzo Rosselli on the other side of the Cannaregio. And just in case Venice should change its mind about Jews, we became Christians."

"Achille says that Italy's a liberal democracy now," Cristina protested. "The persecution of the Jews is part of history."

"You can't take history back for a refund if it doesn't work, girl, and it doesn't ever seem to work for Jews. So forget the past, and teach your children to pray in Latin. God doesn't understand Hebrew anymore."

Cristina closed her eyes. Oh, Lord, help me, she tried to pray. I love him so much, but I'm afraid, after what happened, I'm afraid I can't be a wife. She listened within her head for a response. The nuns had described a kind of glow as grace flowed to one's soul, but she felt nothing but a kind of cosmic emptiness inside. God isn't listening, she told herself. He is angry because we are neither one thing nor another.

"Dry your eyes," Signora Rosselli commanded. "When he meets you at the altar, Count Leone will see that his bride has been crying on her wedding day."

Obediently Cristina raised her hankerchief. Poor Achille, she thought. When he meets his bride, he will see a terrified Jewish girl clutching her rosary beads.

Having quarreled and made up, the two men stood by the door of Santa Geremia's Church, taking nips from Achille's whiskey flask to keep from quarreling again.

"Will you stop in Rome before you go back to Paris?"

Achille shook his head firmly. He had not set foot in his family home for five long years. Girolamo and Valeria were looking after the Castello on his behalf, but Rosaria and Mercuzio Mercatelli controlled the surrounding fields. "The Foreign Minister wants me back at Versailles immediately. Besides, if I went back to Cederna, I would inevitably be drawn into a conflict with the local PSI. I represent the Italian Government in Paris, and the Prime Minister wants the Socialists to back him, so we are avoiding a confrontation. It's all politics.''

"Or is it a desire to avoid a conflict with Rosaria? Forgive me for asking, Comandante, but before I present you with my sister, may I be assured that you've got the Lombardi woman out of your system?''

"Guido, your attitude toward the Sixth Commandment could be described as relaxed,'' Achille protested. "Are you being fair? On one occasion, you found me in bed with Rosaria. You, on the other hand, have shared a mattress with several hundred dubious personalities over the years. If you wanted to marry my sister, my only concern would be whether you currently had the pox.''

"I don't, if your sister is interested.'' Guido tried to keep the conversation light. "No, this is about politics, not sex. Rosaria has seized the land you inherited from your father and you seem to have no interest in getting it back.''

Achille took another drink of whiskey and tucked the flask back in the pocket of his *giubba* as he saw gondolas in the distance. "What happened in Cederna has also gone on in five thousand other communities in Italy where socialist administrations have taken control. Prime Minister Nitti . . .''

"That traitor!''

"Guido, he's the smartest Prime Minister we've ever had. And he believes that an attempt to use force against the Socialists at this juncture could trigger a civil war. Look, we had a democratic election in November, and more than half of the people voted for parties of the left. We can't just carry on business as usual.''

"But it's your house and your land.''

"The Castello is still under my control, and Girolamo is in charge of it. It is true that Rosaria is refusing to take orders from Bruno Benelli, but she and Mercuzio are taking good care of the land and equipment. They brought in the harvest, sold it, and sent us our legal share of the profits. We can't even be sure that Rosaria has broken the law until the whole land confiscation issue is tested in the courts, and the socialists in Cederna have the best lawyer.''

"Lawyers don't count anymore. Listen, Mussolini is organizing squads to support landowners like you.''

"Why should Mussolini care about us? Isn't he supposed to be some kind of socialist?''

"Mussolini has cast off his antiquated Marxism like a suit of old clothing,'' Guido assured him. "He now believes that Italy's future lies with capitalism. We're all for legality, but until we get a government capable of enforcing its laws, we're going to have to play rough. I've been helping to organize some of our *arditi* veterans into action squads. While you're off in France being terribly liberal and law-abiding, I could go to Cederna with some anonymous gentlemen in black shirts and bang a few heads together.''

Achille shook his head emphatically. "No, if this turbulence does escalate into a real revolution, the Nitti Government will do whatever is necessary. Otherwise, landowners like me will get our property back in the courts, probably with some compromises on both sides. Sandro and I agreed in Paris that we would both do what we could to avoid any further violence in Cederna."

"And where is my favorite Bolshevik? Was he invited to the wedding?"

"Sandro's still in France. The PSI has appointed him to act as their liaison with the French Socialist Party until we can get the paperwork completed for his return to Italy."

"Comandante, the world no longer belongs to idealistic liberals like you." With a sigh Guido put his remaining hand on Achille's shoulder. "My man Mussolini is a thug and your friend Sandro is another thug, and the future will belong to the thugs."

"Guido, here comes the wedding party." There was a sparkle on the water as the bridal party began to gather. "Perhaps we could continue this discussion later?"

Guido took his arm as the two men walked into the church. "Choose yourself a thug and get on somebody's side, Achille," he whispered. "The nice folks in the middle are going to get hurt."

"When are we going to marry you off, little brother?" Giorgina inquired as the Leone gondola drew up before Santa Geremia's Church. There was gin on her breath, and Terenzio hoped she would refrain from disrupting the wedding. As best man, he himself was dressed in his carabiniere ceremonial uniform, sword, cape, and Napoleonic hat. He felt silly about the sword, but it was still cool enough to be comfortable in the cape.

"I'm in no hurry," he said nonchalantly. "Guess I haven't met the right girl."

"You could seduce Rosaria Lombardi," Giorgina rasped. "It seems to be a family tradition."

Angry, Terenzio kept his silence, thinking that poor Rosaria needed at least one man in her life who loved her but did not want to take her to bed. I stood by her when she needed me the most, he reminded himself, and when I could still manage a piano, I played my most beautiful music for her. That will have to do.

"Well, perhaps you will think of our family's reputation when you choose a bride," Giorgina remarked. "Thus far, your noble brother's mistresses have included an Arab widow and a Marxist whore. And now he is going to marry a hysterical Jewess with gray hair."

"The finances of the Rosselli family are in very good order," Bruno Benelli said as he assisted his wife onto the *fondamenta* before the church. "Guido has been kind enough to introduce me to some of his new political friends, and people from Mussolini's inner circle have been calling for investment advice. Plus I was given to understand that the Rosselli family is no longer precisely Jewish."

"Jews are Jews," said Giorgina, and she swept into the church.

"Let it go for tonight," Achille said gently. "You're tired, darling, and we have our whole lives before us."

"I'm sorry! Oh, God, I'm sorry!" Sobbing, Cristina clung to him, and the sight of her nakedness inflamed him again. With such flawless skin, the silver hair made her seem exotic rather than old. She has such a splendid little body, he thought, with that slender waist and those high, elegant breasts. For a moment he was tempted to try yet again to exercise the marital rights he had so recently acquired, even though his efforts over the past two hours had been unsuccessful.

"Don't be sorry." There was no law that marriages had to be consummated on the very first night. And she had been raped. That would take some getting over.

"I wanted to be perfect for you." She wiped her eyes on a linen pillow case, and shyly covered her nipples with the sheet. Then she ran her hand over the scar on his thigh where shell fragments had seared his flesh. "You've suffered so much. It must have been different with Rosaria."

Achille was stunned that she could have read his mind with such precision. Until now, there had been a tacit agreement between them never to discuss her. "Actually, I seldom think of Rosaria," he lied. "And I do not ever expect to see her again."

"I'm sorry." Cristina looked crestfallen. "Even though we were rivals for your love, I always felt that she and I could become best friends. She's such a brave woman, and so strong."

"Strong, perhaps, but terribly disloyal," Achille replied with feeling. "Her betrayal after Caporetto, her conspiracy with Emilio Lodi, these are things I could never forgive."

Cristina looked at him strangely and edged away from him on the bed. "Is that what they told you? There was no conspiracy. We met the deserters by accident, and Rosaria was trying to persuade them to return to their units and do their duty when Emilio snatched the revolver and shot poor Terenzio. None of it was Rosaria's fault."

"The carabinieri reported that she was sitting on their shoulders, leading them, singing revolutionary songs."

"The men were all drunk and they picked her up against her will. Rosaria was trying to talk some sense into them when that Austrian plane attacked."

"After Caporetto, the authorities sent her to prison," Achille stammered. "I find it hard to believe that she was totally innocent."

"Achille, I was there." Cristina's voice grew very small. "She betrayed no one."

Achille conquered his face with an artificial smile. Extinguishing the candle smoldering by the side of their bed, he methodically corked the bottle of Venetian Medoc he had opened to help Cristina relax. "Well, it is all part of the past now, contessa mia," he said lightly. "Rest and we'll talk tomorrow."

"Where are you going?" she asked in alarm as he rose from their bed and slipped into a robe.

"I need some air." He climbed the hatchway to the deck of the *Veneziana*. "Sleep, my darling."

The ship was silent. "Oh, my God," he whispered as he walked barefoot across the darkened deck, "what have I done? What have I done?"

Book
Six

1921 — 1922

1.

································

The fighting began in various places at various times.

In Cederna, the civil war started properly on New Year's Day of 1921, when Junio Mosconi led a gang of men wearing black shirts into Piazza Bixio and began clearing away the charred rubble where his father's bakery had once stood.

Rosaria objected immediately, but she was overruled by the Honorable Tommaso Savarino, Mayor of the Municipality of Cederna. "It's his rubble. He can do what he wants with it."

By the end of that second week, Junio's Blackshirts had constructed a crude one-story wooden building that stood a defiant hundred meters from the Casa del Popolo. On Saturday afternoon, the fascists celebrated their efforts with a drunken party. Tommaso and Rosaria watched from the window of the Casa del Popolo as the Blackshirts raised a huge, crudely lettered sign over their front door. It said, "Fascio di Combattimento—Viva Mussolini!"

"We control this town," Rosaria argued fiercely. "Let's close them down!"

"A democracy is a marketplace for ideologies, and fascism is a hodgepodge of mankind's worst ideas," replied Tommaso. "The Socialist Party is selling housing and low-priced food and guaranteed employment for the young people. What has fascism got to offer?"

"I don't know," said Rosaria. "Theater?"

Tommaso shook his head impatiently, and went back to work on the plans for the new elementary school. "Nobody needs theater," he said.

That night, the Municipal Councilor for East Cederna, Mercuzio Mercatelli, was beaten half to death.

When Rosaria got to Mercuzio's house the following morning, she found him stretched out upon a bare mattress and covered with a soiled sheet. His aged mother was bent over him, wailing softly. The room smelled of excrement and Rosaria froze in the doorway, wondering if she had come too late, or ought not to have come at all.

"Signora?"

The old woman looked up, her face was a mask of fury. "They beat him with clubs and made him drink a liter of castor oil."

"Have you called the doctor?"

The old woman shook her head. "Beniolo doesn't treat socialists."

"Oh, Mercuzio, I'm so sorry." Rosaria knelt by the man's bed and took his hand, thinking guiltily that this might have been anticipated. After a slow start in Milan, the Blackshirt movement had expanded southward toward Rome, with gangs of fascists beating up labor leaders and PSI politicians, or sometimes making them consume a powerful laxative. Poor Mercuzio had gotten the double treatment.

"Rosaria, is that you?" He turned his head toward her and opened one swollen eye. "They made me sign a paper resigning my council seat."

"It's completely illegal," she said quickly, but his words triggered a sudden alarm. Without Mercuzio, there would no longer be enough votes on the Municipal Council to sustain Tommaso in office as Mayor.

"I'm taking him to my brother's farm in the mountains where he'll be safe," Signora Mercatelli rasped. "If he hadn't got involved with you and your radical friends, this wouldn't have happened."

"Oh, don't run away, Mercuzio!" Rosaria tried desperately to rally the man's courage. "We'll protect you."

Mercuzio wasn't listening. The stricken man groaned and turned on his side as a savage cramp overtook him. "Oh God, it's coming again!"

With a curse, the old woman tried to maneuver a bucket into position beneath her son, but the diarrhea spurted out onto the mattress, an endless brown stream, and the smell grew worse.

"The fascisti just wanted to humiliate you, but you'll be better in a few days, and then we can make plans," Rosaria pleaded as Mercuzio covered his shame with the sheet. "We need to go to the police. Did Junio lead the men who hurt you?"

"What difference does it make?" Mercuzio gasped. "Go away, Rosaria!"

"We need to bring charges."

"No, I didn't see any of their faces. Please go away!"

"I'll find a doctor." Rosaria backed toward the door. "Rest until I come back."

"Don't come back!" Signora Mercatelli ordered. "You bring danger with you!"

"Signora . . ."

"Don't come back!" the old woman shouted, and she slammed the door.

Oh, Christ, is it my turn?

Filled with unaccustomed fear, she halted at the edge of the Piazza Bixio. It was noon and the sky was clear. At this hour the fountain would normally be surrounded by women, drawing water and gossiping. Instead, the piazza was vacant, except for a twelve-man squad of Junio's Blackshirts who were drilling in military fashion in front of their new Fascio. They were all dressed like corporals in some comic-opera army, with gleaming leather boots and daggers and those famous black shirts.

She slipped into a doorway, watching as Junio led his fascisti into a ragged right turn and then marched them south toward the Casa del Popolo. They were singing a bit of doggerel from the trenches.

To be young, young,
In the beauty of spring,
A lifetime of drunkenness,
Of thee I sing!

Tommaso's alone in his office, she realized as they approached the Casa del Popolo. Oh, God, suppose they hurt him!

Ever since I was a little girl, Tommaso's always been there for me, she reminded herself, drying my eyes and bandaging my knees and bailing me out of prison. If they hurt him, what will become of Massimo and me?

It was a selfish notion and she was ashamed of it a second later. Then she began to panic as she watched the squad come to a clumsy parade rest. Ceremonially, Junio stepped forward to deposit an envelope in the Casa del Popolo letter box. After pounding on the door with his stick, he ordered an about-face and marched his squad back toward the Fascio.

When it seemed safe, she scampered around the margins of the piazza, avoiding the Kingdom of the Wicked and hoping that no one would see her.

"Puttana!" someone screamed, and Rosaria looked over her shoulder to see Junio's squad galloping boisterously in her direction. "Whore!"

"Puttana!" they chanted each syllable in unison as their feet struck the ground.

It's broad daylight and this is a public place, she tried to reassure herself, but it was still terrifying and she picked up her skirts and ran.

"Put-ta-na! Put-ta-na!" The cry came closer as she dashed the last twenty meters to the Casa del Popolo, seeing that Tommaso was holding the door open for her. Breathless, she flung herself inside as the attorney slammed the door and dropped their new reinforced steel bars into place. She collapsed into his arms, almost faint with relief, listening to the Blackshirts taunting her from outside. After a while they grew bored and drifted away.

"Are you all right?" Tommaso took her arm and helped her upstairs to the couch in his office.

"My God, I was afraid they were going to kill both of us." Her heart was still pounding fiercely. She felt dirty and humiliated. "I saw them delivering a letter. Since when does Junio send you letters?"

With a shrug, Tommaso pointed to a letter on his desk. "It was just a lot of silliness. Listen, how is Mercuzio?"

"They broke his ribs and made him drink castor oil. He's resigned from the Municipal Council."

Tommaso reached for the telephone. "I'll call Sergeant Cirillo. They can't get away with this."

"Do you think for one moment that Cirillo doesn't know? He goes in and out of Junio's headquarters a dozen times a day."

"As Mayor, I represent law and order in Cederna."

"How long can you stay Mayor? Without Mercuzio, you won't have a majority on the council. We need to ask Sandro to come home and run for that empty seat."

"Sandro's in France."

"The army is going to drop charges against him," Rosaria argued. "You said so yourself. And Junio is afraid of him. Tommaso, we need Sandro."

Tommaso shook his head firmly. His face was white, but he seemed determined to manage the situation his way. "If Sandro comes back, there will be violence."

"There is already violence. Tommaso, what was in that letter?"

With an irritable shrug, the lawyer picked up Junio's note and read it aloud. "Dear Mr. Mayor, your term of office has been foreshortened by a decision of the Cederna Fascio di Combattimento. We will accept your resignation at the next Municipal Council meeting. The penalty for disobedience is death."

"I'm calling Sandro," Rosaria stormed. "Don't you understand? This time Junio means business. He's going to kill you."

"No."

Rosaria turned and caressed his face quickly. "I care about you," she said. "If we're going to get married someday, then you have to stay alive."

Tommaso shrugged, gazing out the window at the Piazza Bixio. Rosaria came to his side and took his arm, but he seemed unresponsive. Outside, the women had returned to the well to draw water. The Blackshirts had retreated within the Fascio to drink and polish their daggers and plot darkly against the forces of socialism.

"Poor little Italy," Tommaso said softly. "Once we were a love song. Now we're a dirty joke."

"God help us, the civil war could start right here," Rosaria fretted as Sandro's welcoming committee began to assemble in front of the Casa del Popolo.

"Is Uncle Sandro coming home?" Massimo was innocently excited by the crowd. "Will everyone be glad to see him?"

"Almost everyone." Tommaso Savarino glanced nervously at the Fascio, where the Blackshirts were gathering as well. "Rosaria, he hasn't been home in six years. We'll need to explain to him how things have changed."

Rosaria looked around apprehensively. A hundred young socialists had turned up to greet Sandro, mostly hotheads who were bored with Tommaso.

Sandro, on the other hand, was a mythic figure for them, an authentic hero in the Great War who had learned about revolution from Lenin and Trotsky. And on his way back from France, Sandro had stopped in Livorno to attend the annual PSI Congress and rub shoulders with the giants of Italian socialism.

At ten A.M., the coach from Rome lumbered into the Piazza Bixio. Instantly the young radicals in the party unfurled a sheet on which the words "Welcome Home Comrade Sandro Lombardi!" had been painted. It was a nice gesture, but Rosaria guessed that somebody's mother would soon discover that one of her sheets was missing.

The driver stopped his vehicle in front of the Casa del Popolo and Sandro bounced down, the triumphant hero returning to his people. He had grown heavier on French cooking, and looked older. "Sandro!" Rosario cried with tears on her cheeks. "Welcome home, my brother!"

"Rosaria!" He gathered her into a colossal hug, lifting her off the ground and swinging her around, but she sensed he was playing to the crowd. When he shook hands with Tommaso Savarino, he frowned and kept his distance, as if to express socialist solidarity mixed with a hint of disapproval. He's become a politician, she realized, listening to impassioned cheers from the crowd. He will soon be too important for us here.

"Speech! Speech!" The crowd took up the chant. They found a box for him to stand on and he climbed up, smiling and running his hands through his long hair, a tall man suddenly made taller. Rosaria wondered where he had got his suit. Did Achille buy it for him? It looked tailor-made and French, although he was wearing a proletarian turtle-necked sweater rather than a bourgeois shirt and tie.

"Comrades, I have just come from the General Congress of the Socialist Party, and I bring you news that will change all our lives."

"Viva! Viva il socialismo!" someone shouted, but Sandro shook his head.

"Within what was once the PSI, there were many of us who realized that Italian socialism needed to align itself fully with the aims and objectives of the Soviets, since the Russians have given us the only realistic model for revolution. My colleagues in this group have argued that we need to acquire arms to prepare ourselves seriously for an insurrection in the near future. Comrades, the time for rhetoric is past."

"Va fa'n culo, Lombardi!" came a shout from the Kingdom of the Wicked. "Fuck you!" Sandro looked coldly toward the Fascio, seeing it for the first time. When he had left home, there had been a bakery on that spot.

But he ignored the interruption. "Unfortunately, the cowardly reformists who lead the PSI are frightened of revolution and their Central Committee has rejected the fraternal advice of the Soviet Union. As a consequence, my group has withdrawn from the Italian Socialist Party. Under the guidance of Antonio Gramsci and Amadeo Bordiga, we have constituted a new political party containing the best men and women from the old. My friends, I bring you greetings from the Italian Communist Party."

Oh, God, no! Rosaria was devastated. Not a split in the Party, not now!

For a moment the crowd reacted with stunned silence. Rosaria glanced quickly at Tommaso, who had edged away from Sandro after his insulting reference to "cowardly reformists." The lawyer's face was ashen.

"You choose this moment when we are besieged on all sides to break up the Party?" Incredulously, Tommaso pointed to Junio's Blackshirts. "Do you want to hand Italy over to them?"

Sandro shook his head fiercely. "There is no need for disunity. The Socialist Party belongs on the refuse heap of history. All of you should join the Communist Party and prepare for an insurrection soon. This is 1921. It could happen this year."

"You've been gone since 1915, Sandro," Tommaso snapped. "During that time, the Italian Socialist Party has defended the proletariat in this community. You need to understand—"

"There are many things I need to understand, Mr. Mayor," Sandro shouted back violently. "Even in Russia we have heard of Cederna's shame. Why was nothing done when Compagno Mercuzio Mercatelli was beaten half to death by a Blackshirts mob? And when my sister was chased through this piazza by those common criminals, why did no one avenge this insult?"

"You clown! Go back to Moscow, you bastard, and take your streetwalker sister with you!" one of the Blackshirts screamed, and a rock sailed toward Sandro's impromptu meeting.

"This is getting out of hand," Tommaso warned. "We have a lot to talk to Comrade Sandro about, but there will be violence here unless we get inside."

"There is more I need to understand," Sandro continued, his voice growing so soft that the young men in the crowd pushed forward to hear him. Slowly he took an enormous military pistol out of his coat pocket and held it aloft. For a moment it reminded Rosaria of the way Father Maurizio had raised the crucifix during Mass when they were children and still went to church. "In Moscow, everyone talked about the brave women of Cederna fighting capitalism by burning down the bakery. How could the men of Cederna permit the existence of a fascist flophouse on that same site? Does no one in Cederna have a match? Is there no gasoline? Or has His Excellency the Mayor confiscated your balls?"

Rosaria moved away, half-fascinated and half-horrified by Sandro's power and charisma. Suddenly Tommaso pushed past her, screaming furiously. "No, no, you madman, you'll ruin everything we've accomplished here!"

"Tommaso, I've come back to show you how a man defends his honor." Deliberately, he pointed the automatic pistol in the direction of the Fascio. "Viva il communismo!" he shouted, and pulled the trigger.

The retort was terrible. The Blackshirts retreated a few steps as a window shattered behind them.

Sandro seemed to have mastered the art of speaking softly and yet being heard by a multitude. He opened his arms like a father gathering together his children. "My brothers, my friends, that building should never have been built, and today we must unbuild it." Almost without pausing in his speech, he fired a second time and began to walk down the street, shooting occasionally at the Blackshirts and talking to the young men who ran along beside him.

"Viva il communismo! Viva!" Some of the women and older men backed away, perplexed and worried, but all the young men and a lot of the girls went with Sandro, walking boldly into the Kingdom of the Wicked and cheering every time he discharged his automatic pistol.

Junio appeared briefly at the door of the Fascio, carrying a shotgun, but when he saw the size of the crowd he ducked back inside, escaping out the back door.

"Viva! Viva!" Little Massimo shouted as Rosaria came to stand beside Tommaso. They were alone now, since the older people had fled. Everybody else was with Sandro.

When the crowd reached the far end of the Piazza Bixio, someone found a match and gasoline was made available. Junio had saved money on his Fascio by building it out of wood, and the structure caught fire easily.

"He's gone mad," Tommaso remarked as they walked back toward the Casa del Popolo. The flames soared skyward, almost as high as the steeple of Santa Teresa's Church.

"I suppose so." Rosaria watched Sandro's comrades pursuing the hapless fascisti around Piazza Bixio. Whenever they caught a Blackshirt, they beat him savagely. "On the other hand . . ."

"On what other hand?" Tommaso demanded furiously. "What other hand is there?"

"I was terrified when the Blackshirts chased me through the streets and called me a *puttana*," she said quietly. "And I've been afraid of Junio Mosconi since I was a child."

"What are you saying? Politically, this is a disaster!"

"I know, I know, I'm sure you're right, but . . ."

"But what?"

There was a sudden roar as the roof of the Fascio collapsed and the whole structure caved in upon itself. Rosaria gazed at the inferno with a smile on her lips. "But it's a lovely fire," she said.

2.

. . . .

"Yes, Prime Minister," Achille replied in English. "I've just been appointed military adviser to the Interior Ministry and we must return to Rome immediately, but my wife and I could perhaps get away in the spring for a visit to England, if . . . yes? Well, thank you, sir, and good-bye."

"Who was that, my darling?" Cristina entered their bedroom as Achille replaced the receiver.

"David Lloyd George," he murmured absently, running through a list of friends to whom he needed to bid farewell. There was Robert Seton-Watson and Count Brockdorff-Rantzau and several of Clemenceau's assistants.

"David Lloyd George is a wicked Welshman." Cristina giggled. "He always winked at me in the most peculiar fashion."

Achille closed his notebook and smiled. Cristina had become very dear to him during their year together in Paris. With her natural charm and ease with foreign languages, Crissi was the toast of the Italian delegation. And in their life together she had become a real friend and companion. If only . . .

"Father knew him when he was the Italian Ambassador to Britain. Even then Lloyd George always winked at pretty women." Achille patted his knee, and she sat on his lap and put her arms around his neck. "He wants me to think about taking a position with the League of Nations."

"It would be fine with me."

"Perhaps someday, but we both want to go home. We'll always have this house in Paris if things in Cederna are too stressful. How is the packing coming? You're not tiring yourself, are you?"

"I'm fine." She kissed his cheek. "What did you mean about Cederna? Has our dear Sandro been breaking the law again?"

"It's hard to know what the law is anymore." Achille was anxious to conceal his concern, because he wanted Cristina to be happy in Cederna. But the situation was not promising. Tommaso was still reluctantly serving as Mayor, but to stay in office he now depended upon the votes of Sandro Lombardi and two other municipal councilors who had joined the Italian Communist Party.

Having burned their headquarters to the ground and driven the Blackshirts out of Cederna, Sandro had created a paramilitary organization called the

Forza Proletaria to keep order. But in virtually every other district fascism was getting stronger every day, and Mussolini's men were not going to put up with Sandro Lombardi forever. Violence in Cederna was inevitable.

"Achille, once we're settled in our own home, things between us will be better," Cristina said shyly. "I'll be more relaxed."

"We're all right, Crissi." There were times when her inner torment became almost visible. "I'm not unhappy with you."

"But you're not happy. And I want to be a proper wife to you, in every way. It's just . . . whenever we try, I see those men in my mind and feel their hands on my body and everything inside of me gets tight."

"I know, I know," he soothed her as she burst into tears. "Crissi, war has its victims. Nobody blames Giuseppe Papafava for having no legs, or Guido for losing an arm. They got shot. You were raped. None of it is your fault. Once we're back in Italy . . . carissima, don't cry."

A few hours later Achille was still upstairs supervising the servants who were folding blankets and turning over the mattresses to air. Cristina appeared at the bedroom door. Her eyes were still red, but she was composed.

"There's a young black woman downstairs. She's speaking a language I can't identify, and she has a beautiful little boy with her."

"Give her some money." Ever since the French had conquered Morocco, Algeria, and Tunisia, Paris had been filling up with North Africans going from door to door to beg or sell native art.

Cristina shook her head. "She has a piece of paper with your name and this address. I offered her some francs, but she won't go away."

Perplexed, Achille went down to the vestibule. It took him a moment to recognize Meeya, because the Sudanese girl had been barely a teenager when he last saw her, skinny and wearing native garments. Now she was a splendidly buxom young woman, self-possessed and dressed in European clothing.

Although he had never seen him before, or even suspected his existence, Achille identified the child instantly.

He turned to Meeya and kissed the ex-slave girl on the cheek. "Where is your mistress?" he asked in Arabic. He had already guessed the answer. In the aftermath of the Great War, influenza had raced through Europe and North Africa, claiming hundreds of thousands of victims.

In rapid-fire Arabic, Meeya described an overpowering fever that had swept over Anfi in September, leaving her fatally weak. Fearing death, she had produced money, instructions, and an address in Paris. The funeral had been in early October.

A sadness assailed him. Anfi, Anfi, he mourned, if we had only been able to love each other a little more, and our countries a little less . . .

"Achille? Who are they? What does it mean?" Cristina demanded. Counting backward through the years, Achille dropped to his knees before the boy, who seemed to be about five. Yes, he would have been conceived in 1915.

The child gazed at him with dark, solemn eyes. He was a handsome lad, with European features and soft brown skin.

"Eineh Hosni," said the boy. "My name is Hosni."

"Hosni." Achille repeated the child's name, taking him in his arms and turning to face Cristina.

She backed away. "Who is he?"

"His name is Hosni al-Sharif." Achille felt a sudden happiness surge through him. "This is my son. I have a son."

After Cristina had run upstairs to their bedroom, sobbing, Achille sat down and held Hosni on his lap. Reviving his rusty Arabic, he explained that they would be going to a big house in Italy where they would live and hunt rabbits together. This seemed to make the boy happy, especially the news that Meeya could come as well.

When Meeya and Hosni were comfortable, Achille climbed the stairs, dreading the encounter with Cristina.

I'm not going to apologize for this, he decided. But it must have been a shock for her.

The bedroom was cold, and Cristina was lying on the bare mattress beneath a pile of blankets. Her face was covered, but her little feet were sticking out. He tugged at a toe to get her attention.

"Crissi? I'm sorry if this hurts you, but I don't regret that Hosni has come into our lives. His mother is dead now, but she was a wonderful, brilliant woman, and many years ago I asked her to marry me. She said no, but gave me this boy instead. He's mine, and I want him to live with us."

"Come to bed," Cristina said suddenly.

"To bed? I had the impression you were feeling unhappy."

"I feel fine. Come to bed."

"I don't know where the sheets are," he fretted, kicking off his shoes and crawling onto the mattress. When she lifted the blankets, he saw that she was naked.

"I'm going to give you a son," she said, and took him in her arms.

Afterward, she cried a little, although not in the furious way she had wept in the past when they had tried and failed. Achille lay by her side, gently stroking her breasts. We made a start, he thought. It was awful, but at least we have finally begun our marriage.

"Did I hurt you?"

"It was sweet." She raised her face for a kiss, but her eyes were closed. "It was sweet."

3.

. . . .

In her house on the Via Calatafimi, Rosaria Lombardi was giving the bathtub its pre-Christmas scrub when the knock came at the door.

At first she worried that it might be the fascists. 1921 had been a difficult year, and there had been several angry Blackshirt raids, although each time Sandro's Forza Proletaria fought furiously to defend Cederna. Sandro himself had moved into the Calatafimi house to protect his sister and nephew, but today the leader of the Cederna Communist Party was at a meeting in Rome.

"Massimo, stay in your room!" Having come to accept that the adult world was inexplicably dangerous, the child scampered into his bedroom and closed the door.

Carefully she looked through the window and saw an expensively dressed gray-haired woman on the doorstep. "Rosaria? It's me," the visitor called.

"I never imagined you'd come here." Rosaria swung opened the door and stepped back in astonishment as Contessa Cristina Rosselli Leone entered. Instinctively the two women hugged.

"Why not? Oh, Rosaria, after everything that's happened, you're still more beautiful than me. It's not fair!"

There was a moment of embarrassment. To Rosaria, her home suddenly looked cheap. Massimo's toys were scattered across a threadbare rug, and there were still coffee cups left over from last night's meeting of the League of Socialist Women.

"Massimo, come out, it's your Aunt Crissi," she called, and the boy tumbled out to be kissed and petted.

"Oh, Rosaria, he's so handsome." Cristina seemed reluctant to let him go.

Massimo had inherited Leonida's utter sense of self; even at six he was never shy with strangers, and when he had absorbed enough of Cristina's praise he dashed off to play with some wooden trucks Uncle Sandro had built for him.

"Crissi, I'm so glad to see you," Rosaria said sincerely as the two women went into the kitchen and drew up chairs around the table. It's all right for me to like her, Rosaria decided. Being born rich was hardly her fault, and she never meant to harm me. We both got locked up after Caporetto, and afterward, when Achille's loneliness reached the point where he had to marry someone, she was standing in the right place.

"Rosaria, I've missed you."

"And I've missed you," she admitted. "What is Paris like?"

"It rains all winter and the coffee is terrible, but otherwise it's lovely," Cristina said. "Achille has a comfortable house in a neighborhood called Montmartre. When your terribly Marxist brother came to stay with us on his way home from Russia, he absolutely fell in love with the place, even though he got all my maids to join the Communist Party. Have you become a communist too?"

"No, I'm still a boring old socialist." Rosaria spoke lightly, but her refusal to join her brother's new revolutionary party had caused a substantial rift between them. "I'll make us some good Italian coffee while you tell me about your trip. Did you come down on the train?"

"As far as Venice. Achille wanted to pick up his old sergeant, Giuseppe Papafava, who was in an army hospital there. My mother has been seriously ill, and after we visited her we got aboard Achille's awful boat and sailed down around Calabria and up past Napoli to Rome. I'm not a very good sailor. I threw up every day. We're keeping the boat at Fiumicino Harbor just outside of Rome, and Achille says we're going to take a world cruise someday, so I can throw up in all the Seven Seas."

The two women laughed merrily, although Rosaria privately observed that the Leone family seemed to have pots of money: a giant country estate in Cederna, a house in Montmartre, and a yacht at the port of Fiumicino. According to Tommaso, a lot of Leone risk capital had gone into munitions stocks at the beginning of the war, and Bruno's skill with investments had made them all extremely wealthy.

When the time comes to negotiate over the status of Achille's land, she reflected, we will have to liberate him from a little of that cash.

"Well, how do you like being married?" Rosaria spooned ground espresso into the *caffettiera* and lit her new gas stove with a sulfur match. She was not sure she wanted to know the answer.

Cristina wrinkled her nose. "I was shy at first, but now I think I'm going to have a baby."

For a moment Rosaria felt her mind spin out of control. That could have been my baby, her mind was raging, my baby, my baby, it could have been ... my baby. She turned away quickly and busied herself with the coffee. There were tears on her cheeks, and she wiped them away quickly with the back of her hand. "How wonderful," she stammered.

"Yes, but until the baby comes, I want to help you down here in Cederna." Unaware of the emotion she had just provoked, Cristina excitedly unveiled her idea. "During that year in the Austrian military hospital, I learned a lot of medicine. Besides the prisoners, we took care of the women and children who lived nearby, and I once even helped perform a cesarean section."

"Yes, there were . . . wonderful newspaper articles about you."

"You don't have a nurse in Cederna, and that awful Dr. Beniolo won't see poor people unless they can pay. I think we should set up a clinic."

Rosaria shook her head and turned to explain the facts of life to Cederna's new contessa. "Crissi, it would be lovely if we could work together, but Tommaso and Sandro and I are leading an occupation of Achille's agricultural property. There's a sort of war going on between our families."

Cristina looked crestfallen. "This isn't fair. The last time we were together, up in Udine, we both thought Achille was going to marry you. I was miserable, but I still wanted to be your friend. Why can't you be my friend now?"

"This has nothing to do with personalities." Rosaria felt the tears starting to come back and she turned to the sink to hide her emotion. "It's a question of politics."

"Is it? Oh, I know you're still in love with him, but—"

"I am not in love with anybody," Rosaria snapped. "After Caporetto, I was treated like a criminal, thrown into prison, accused—"

"I know. We all . . . suffered after Caporetto. And Achille never properly understood what happened that day until I explained that you did nothing to encourage that gang of deserters. He feels bad about the misunderstanding."

"Wonderful!" Rosaria raged. "First he asks me to marry him and then he accuses me of being a traitor. Then he sends his pregnant wife down to apologize on his behalf. Perhaps our terribly brave brigadier could come in person if he has an apology to make. No, don't tell him that! I don't want to see him."

"Come and see him tomorrow," Cristina urged. "Achille wants to have you and Sandro and Tommaso come for luncheon to talk about this problem with the farm. And it would be nice if you brought Massimo so he could meet Hosni. Have you heard about Hosni?"

Everybody in Cederna had heard about Hosni. Rosaria hit the kitchen table with her fist. "When I had a baby out of wedlock, everybody here said I was a *puttana*. Now we learn that Achille was off in Africa producing an illegitimate child, and everybody says he's virile."

Cristina ignored her fury. "It would be lovely if Massimo and Hosni became friends, the way Achille and Sandro and Tommaso were all friends when they were boys. Please come for lunch?"

Rosaria shook her head. "If Tommaso accepts your invitation, then Massimo can go up with him," she conceded.

"Then you don't want to be my friend?"

"Crissi, I want to be your best friend." Rosaria reached forward and took her hand and squeezed it with genuine warmth. "I just don't see how I could ever set foot in the Castello again."

The Venetian woman nodded, heading for the door. "I can understand that. Shall I come back Monday so we can make plans for our clinic?"

"Yes, of course, and God knows we need a clinic, but I don't know where we'll put it.'' Rosaria's mind turned quickly to the practical questions involved. "I suppose we could use this living room."

"Oh, that's no problem.'' Cristina laughed. "We'll just buy a house."

"Why didn't I think of that?'' Rich people are so innocent, she reflected. Rosaria kissed her friend good-bye and went back to scrubbing the bathtub.

"Sandro, have some wine?"

Shaking his head, the leader of the Cederna Communist Party poured himself another glass of Appia *acqua minerale*. I need to stay angry until after dessert, he resolved, and alcohol will lighten my mood.

He glared up and down the great Sicilian refectory table, watching as Tommaso Savarino accepted a second goblet of wine. In all the years I worked as a peasant on this estate, he remembered, I never once ate in this room. When we were children, Achille and I had picnics, and when we were adolescents, he bought me lunch at Tommaso's father's place, since I could never afford to pay my share.

But the Castello dining room had always been an inner sanctum for the Cederna gentry. What a great irony! To sit here and eat lunch with Count Achille Leone, I had to become a revolutionary.

At the far end of the table, Achille was performing his role as host, passing the wine, orchestrating the arrival of courses, and keeping the conversation flowing politely. Sandro watched him with mixed emotions. If we had a man like Achille Leone on our side, he sighed, there could be a successful revolution tomorrow. But he's not on our side, and never will be. Achille still manages to believe in a nice, well-mannered, caring capitalism, administered by socially conscious engineers like himself.

In fact, it had been the kind of luncheon only a triumphant capitalism could provide. Valeria had started them off on homemade fettuccine covered with sauce from the Castello's own tomatoes and washed down with bottle after bottle of Leonida's prize-winning 1897 Cederna bianco secco. On his very first hunting expedition, young Hosni had brought down a brace of pheasants for the game pie that came as the second course, with pecorino cheese and sorbet and Sicilian melon and pastries from Brescia and buckets of expensive cognac to follow.

The table conversation had been polite but artificial, since everyone was determined to keep politics off the agenda until the men could retire to the study for cigars and class warfare. Cristina was charming, and Achille was the model of geniality, but it had not escaped anyone's attention that the socialist Mayor and the communist militant were forcibly occupying several thousand hectares of prime agricultural land and refusing to obey their host's orders.

When the *pranzo* was finished, Achille remained below for a moment's conversation with Cristina while Sandro and Tommaso climbed the stairs to the study.

"Be civil," Tommaso pleaded. "We need a face-saving deal."

"Do we?" Sandro stood in the great study looking at the familiar book-shelves and the great oak desk where Leonida had once worked. The Olivetti was still sitting under the window; would Achille recruit another peasant girl to use the machine?

"Cederna is creating too high a profile," the attorney went on. "In every other community in the district, the kind of land sequestrations we achieved in 1919 have all disappeared, some through renegotiation with the landlord and some when the Blackshirts beat the workers into submission."

"And in Cederna we beat the Blackshirts into submission," Sandro observed acidly. "Pardon me, but I like our system better."

"Look, Achille was our childhood friend. I've been his lawyer, and the two of you saved each other's necks once a week during the war. He doesn't want violence, and his financial position is so enviable that he doesn't have to screw us for every centesimo his land can produce. If we let him, Achille will give us a deal that will still make us the envy of every other socialist municipal administration in central Italy."

Sandro turned on him sharply. "Listen, you and Rosaria passed legislation in 1919 taking control of the land away from the owners and vesting it in workers' councils."

"But we were against Bruno back then. This is Achille!"

"Landowners are landowners, and politics is about social classes, not personalities," Sandro lectured. "You put the 1919 Cederna Act on the statute books, Tommaso, and if you try to retreat one centimeter from that position, I and the other two Communist Party councilors will bring down your administration."

"And hand Cederna over to Junio Mosconi on a plate?"

"The Forza Proletaria will deal with Junio."

There was a polite cough at the door. Achille was smiling, but Sandro knew from experience that he always smiled, even when he was furious. "Well, perhaps you two great tribunes of the people will explain what you propose to do with my property?"

Let's go for a frontal assault, Sandro decided. "First of all, a gang of fascists roared into the Piazza Bixio this morning on a truck and fired several shots at the Casa del Popolo before my people chased them away. I want an army checkpoint established between Cederna and the Via Salaria to protect us."

"Protect you?" Achille laughed. "You communists are doing your incompetent best to overthrow my government. Do you seriously expect us to defend you from Mussolini's goons so that you can get on with our destruction? Face it! Your communist insurrection went off half-cocked, and now it's stalled. My father once said there were two things in life you couldn't have just half of. One was an orgasm. The other was a revolution."

"Your father had no end of pithy epigrams," Sandro snorted. He walked to the window, looking out at the telephone pole in the garden and remembering the day he and Achille had installed Leonida's telephone. Those were days of great innocence, he reminisced. I wish my enemy were not also my best friend.

"Sandro, let's put our cards on the table. With Mercuzio gone and Rosaria busy with the social services in Cederna, the management of this estate has gone downhill. The harvest this year was mediocre, and the equipment is in terrible shape. You've seen how well Giuseppe Papafava gets around on his wheelchair. Let's put him in charge of the farm as general manager, and he can report jointly to the worker's council and to me as the owner."

"No! I admire Giuseppe tremendously, but he's your old sergeant major, and he's not one of us. Nor is he a Marxist."

"Sandro, what ultimately do you want?"

"Ultimately, I want all of the agricultural land in Italy, including yours, confiscated by communist-controlled local governments and transformed into peasant cooperatives."

Sandro was certain that they were on the verge of a revolution. The government was being held together by competent technicians like Achille, but the political leadership was hopeless. The fascists were energetic but stupid. If the communists could just gather themselves for one serious push, the whole house of cards would collapse.

"Look, this is my land," Achille retorted. "I want to use it to give high-quality employment to as many people as possible, but in the final analysis the land belongs to me. You communists cannot go around arbitrarily confiscating people's property."

"There's nothing arbitrary about it," Sandro said. "This land was given to one of your ancestors five hundred years ago as a sordid bribe from some medieval Pope. Your father told me all about it. My people have worked it for five centuries, making your family rich while we have stayed poor. Every so often in history, the cards need to be shuffled and redealt, so new players can get into the game. We call this revolution, and we're going to have one in Italy."

"My family kept this land for five hundred years because we fought for it." Achille had stopped smiling.

"Well, you're going to have to fight for it again, Achille," snapped Sandro, and he walked out of the study and down the stairs.

Outside, it was cold but clear. Rambling through the fields toward the chestnut grove, Achille and Tommaso smoked cigars while the boys chased rabbits. No able-bodied Italian rabbit in history had ever been caught by a little boy, but Massimo and Hosni kept on trying.

Achille watched them with a simple gladness that took away his worries for a moment. Hosni was beginning to recover from the loss of his mother, and Massimo seemed incredibly bright. Cristina was pregnant and happy, and the household staff had quickly come to treasure her, although Valeria and Girolamo had been stiff at first, still disappointed that their new contessa was not Rosaria.

And Rosaria? Achille was stung but unsurprised by her rejection of a truce-making lunch. I've treated her so badly, he recognized. I should go and talk to her, but well, what the hell would I say?

"Achille, what do your people at the Interior Ministry think is going to happen?" The ever-practical Tommaso intruded on his meditation.

"We're sliding toward a full-fledged civil war," Achille replied. "I can see only one way to avoid a catastrophe. You socialists have got to join us democratic liberals to create a moderate coalition large enough to defeat both communism and fascism."

Tommaso shook his head sadly. "Personally I agree, but my socialists are terrified of cooperating with capitalists, even to save their own necks. And besides, your democratic liberals are paralyzed. Sandro and his communists think they can engineer a revolution in the middle of a civil war. Only Mussolini seems to know what he's doing."

"Is it time for you and Rosaria to leave the Socialist Party?"

"We could never leave the Socialist Party. It's like a church for us."

"Then let's make some practical arrangements," Achille said. "If we do have a full-scale civil war, I want you to bring Massimo here to the Castello for safety. Obviously, you and Rosaria and little Chiara are welcome as well, but where my half-brother is concerned, I have the right to insist."

Tommaso consented immediately. "When the fighting starts, he will not be safe in the Via Calatafimi house. And the two boys do seem to get along well."

"They're going to be great friends." Achille remembered how Leonida Leone used to march off on wonderful expeditions into the fields with a flock of adoring boys.

"We were all friends once. Now all those old alliances are coming apart."

"Disagreements among friends can be settled without violence." Achille hauled himself back to the political reality around him. "The death of poor old Enrico Mosconi was unnecessary, and the assault on Mercuzio Mercatelli was intolerable. I am seeing Bruno Benelli and Junio Mosconi this evening, and what I'm saying to you leftists I shall be saying to the right-wingers: I want no more fighting in Cederna."

"How can you put us on a par with them?" Tommaso was insulted. "There is no moral equivalence between the socialist movement and those criminals. The Blackshirts are becoming more vicious every day, and your government does nothing to control them."

Achille shrugged helplessly. As military adviser to the Interior Ministry, he rubbed elbows with Italy's senior policemen, many of whom wanted to tolerate fascism as a useful counterweight to communism. And the army was badly contaminated; many senior officers had become secret adherents to

Mussolini's cause and military supply depots were handing out weapons and ammunition to Blackshirt gangs.

"What you say is perfectly true," he admitted. "You understand that I have no policy-making role in my present position. I can't give orders to anyone. I merely advise Interior Minister Taddei on military matters."

"Well, advise him to arrest Junio Mosconi," Tommaso suggested. "He keeps sending me death threats."

"I will speak to Mosconi very seriously." Achille was instantly worried, since other public officials had been lynched by Blackshirt gangs. "And I'll ask the Minister to assign some policemen to protect you."

"No, Cederna is my home. If I walked around with bodyguards, the fascists would think I was afraid of them. Besides, I've got this pistol."

The attorney produced a tiny antique weapon from his suit-coat pocket. Achille looked at it dubiously for a moment, and then the military technician in him took over. "I bet you've never fired it. We'd better make sure it works. See if you can hit that flowerpot."

"I'm a lawyer, not a gunfighter," Tommaso grumbled, but he took aim at a cracked terra-cotta vase sitting beneath a stone wall. The miniature pistol fired, but the pot remained untouched.

"You even missed the wall."

"Fascists are bigger than flowerpots, even if they aren't much smarter. I'll manage to hit Junio if the moment arrives."

"Let me try!" Massimo rushed up, with Hosni bouncing behind him.

"Why not?" Achille smiled. I've seen too little of this lad, he told himself, kneeling down and placing the weapon carefully in Massimo's hands. Father always taught his sons to shoot and I need to start functioning as a father figure to this boy.

"No, I don't want him to grow up using guns," Tommaso intervened quickly. "There are already too many violent men storming around this country waving weapons and I don't want my . . . my boy becoming one of them."

"Since when is he your boy?" Irritated, the two men stared at one another. Achille wondered if he was about to lose another friend.

"I've earned the right to be this boy's father," Tommaso began, but Massimo casually aimed and fired. The terra-cotta vase exploded into a thousand fragments.

"Got it on the first shot!" Achille was delighted; it occurred to him that Leonida would have been pleased as well.

"I'm sorry." The child turned to the lawyer, aware that he had disappointed him. "I just wanted to see what it felt like to shoot a gun."

"Child, your ancestors have been gunslingers for five hundred years." Tommaso turned away sadly. "Why should you be different?"

4.

....

The year 1922 began with a funeral.

"You've put the Star of David on Mother's gravestone." Cristina seemed surprised but pleased. She pulled her fur coat more tightly around her, shivering as a cold wind swept off the lagoon and swirled dead leaves into the air. The island cemetery of San Michele was normally well tended, but nothing had ever been quite the same since the war, and nobody raked the leaves any more. With gang fighting all over the country as Marxists and fascists battled for supremacy, Achille found it amazing that anything still functioned, even a cemetery.

"I would even have buried her under our real name if I had known it," Guido said. "It's time for us to start being what we are."

"What do you mean?" Cristina paled and Achille wondered if she was going to faint. The new Contessa Leone had been frequently ill since the start of her pregnancy and her mother's death had been a shattering blow.

But Cristina was tougher than she looked. Sick or well, she staggered down to Cederna's new Mothers' Clinic every day, treating sick children, pregnant women, and tottering old ladies. She and Rosaria had delivered several babies successfully, and the two of them had even performed one emergency cesarean section, managing to save both mother and child.

"When Napoleon let the Venetian Jews out of the ghetto, a few decided to adopt the family names of Christian protectors," Guido explained. "Father once told me what our original family name was, but I was just a little boy at the time and I don't remember."

Guido took his sister's arm as they walked from the grave site to the ferryboat station. There were tall, melancholy cypress trees at their back, and an expanse of cold, empty water before them. Guido intended to take the vaporetto to the Fascist Party Headquarters in central Venice. For Achille and Cristina, a covered motor launch stood by to take them to the train station for the long journey to Rome.

"So the name Rosselli . . ."

"Our name is like everything else in our lives, a lie." Resplendent in his black fascist uniform, Guido was staring at the ground, pulling on a cigarette.

"My life isn't a lie," Cristina said. "Whatever Grandfather's name was, I am a nurse and a wife and now I'm going to have a baby. And for a long time I was the only one in our family who could accept our Jewishness. So let's bury the lie with Mother!''

"I had to wait until she had died before I could be Jewish." Guido's voice was hoarse and tormented. "She hated anyone knowing."

For Cristina's sake, Achille wanted to avoid an argument over politics, but he could no longer bite his tongue. "Mussolini and his backers are anti-Semites. I can understand wanting to find your roots, but why become a Jewish fascist?"

"You're wrong! A handful of bigots have made their way into our movement, and Mussolini has rightly attacked several Marxist intellectuals who happen to be Jewish, but the man himself is free from racial bias. I've talked to him on this specific issue."

"Guido, listen to me!"

"No, you listen to me!" The one-armed man whirled, speaking with great intensity. "Had it not been for stubborn people like you, Mussolini would already be in Rome straightening out the mess that liberalism has created. Subversives like Sandro and Rosaria may have created minor local obstacles, but you have made yourself a major enemy."

"Are you threatening me?"

"Absolutely not. In fact, Mussolini asked me to send you his warmest personal regards. He regards you as Italy's foremost soldier."

"I regard him as Italy's foremost scoundrel."

"That's because you've never understood what fascism has to offer." There was passion in Guido's voice. "There has been too much violence, Red violence and black violence, and the Duce is the only man who can make it stop."

Achille shook his head furiously. "Guido, we had the beginnings of a real democracy here. My father and I were both committed to seeing that it survived, with elections, and political parties, and a constitution, and freedom."

"Freedom? Freedom to conduct class warfare, to strike, to sabotage the nation? Freedom is for later. Right now, we need national unity, with everybody working behind a single leader. We need order and discipline."

"Then win an election!" Achille shouted at him. "In the 1921 vote, you fascists managed to elect thirty-five deputies out of five hundred and thirty-five available seats. A catastrophe like that entitles you to instant political oblivion."

"Elections are frauds," Guido yelled back. "The Duce has said that under fascism, men will be counted qualitatively rather than quantitatively."

"That's intellectual garbage!" Achille howled. At one level of consciousness, he tried to remember all that he and Guido had meant to each other. But the brave and jovial Rosselli seemed to have been replaced by this white-faced one-armed martinet capable of nothing but mouthing slogans. "Mussolini has stupefied you. You strut around in those ridiculous comic-opera costumes!''

''I wear this uniform with pride,'' Guido thundered. He was dressed in the uniform of an officer in the Fascist Militia, black boots and tan riding breeches and black shirt, covered by a black field jacket and black leather belt and shoulder band. On his head he wore the standard modified felt fez, ornamented with a little black tassel.

''You look like a clown. All of you belong in a circus!''

The two men were standing toe-to-toe on the *fondamenta* now, shrieking at one another. ''We will take power,'' Guido screamed. ''We will march on Rome!''

''March and be damned! We'll shoot you down in the streets!''

''Stop it! Stop it!'' Cristina suddenly gasped. Achille turned in time to catch her as she fainted. Sweeping her into his arms, he carried her to the waiting motor launch and gave the order to depart. There was no word from Guido on the *fondamenta,* and Achille did not look back.

5.

· ·

While carpenters put bars on the windows of the Casa del Popolo, a squad of men from the Forza Proletaria tore up the floorboards in the downstairs meeting room. It was hard work on the warmest day of August, and the men kept sending out for beer.

There isn't much *forza* left in the *proletaria,* thought Rosaria. The revolution has gone out of them. When Sandro had come home to organize Cederna's Communist Party, he had comandeered the entire ground floor of the Casa del Popolo, banishing the Socialist Party to the second floor.

Then, drawing upon his military experience, Sandro had recruited a hundred young men into a popular defense force, effectively taking law enforcement in Cederna away from the carabinieri. In a handful of other municipalities similar vanguard companies had been created, but the Communist Party had hoped for a nationwide revolutionary militia, and it had never emerged.

Today in Cederna, no more than a dozen Forza Proletaria volunteers had responded to Sandro's summons, and they worked lethargically, taking rifles out of their hiding places under the floorboards, covering them with a thick coat of grease, and wrapping them in canvas.

"How long have these things been here?" Rosaria was furious at the discovery. The Casa del Popolo was meant to be a place where children could be safe and people could meet and talk. And Sandro had turned it into an arsenal.

Sandro looked up from the window where he was helping the carpenters bar the windows. The fascist attack could come at any time, and Sandro was thinking defensively.

"In August of last year."

"Why didn't you tell me?"

"I founded the Casa del Popolo, not you," he said bluntly. "These weapons are the property of the Communist Party, and we kept them here to be available when the popular insurrection began."

"Why are you taking them away now?"

"It no longer seems that the objective conditions for a revolution exist, and there could be a police raid. We're going to bury them in the hills."

"Why bother?"

"Because the revolution will come someday. And then we'll dig them up."

"Good for you. I'm going home." Rosaria shrugged, envying Sandro's total faith in the dialectic of history, the inevitability of things. Rosaria now doubted that anything was inevitable, except that the Blackshirts would destroy Red Cederna. The fascisti had already become the dominant force in northern Italy, and they were moving inexorably south. The new Prime Minister was a dull, colorless man named Luigi Facta who seemed mesmerized by Mussolini.

Sandro followed her to the door, putting an arm around her shoulders and lowering his voice. "Sorellina, we've established an encampment in the hills just above Cederna," he whispered. "You follow that little stream that runs by the Castello through the forest about five kilometers. Remember that cave where we used to play? Tommaso will remember. We're putting sleeping bags and supplies there in case things fall apart down here."

"I remember." She was not much interested in playing Cowboys and Red Indians with a gang of failed revolutionaries.

"You need to start taking this seriously. The telephone has been out all day, which could mean trouble is coming tonight. Leave the children at the Castello and come up into the mountains with us."

Shaking her head, she walked to the door. At the front entrance to the Casa del Popolo was a Forza Proletaria guard, keeping Piazza Bixio under surveillance and drinking Perrone beer from a bottle. Ignoring him, Rosaria stepped out onto the cobblestones.

The heat struck her like a club. It was the hour after lunch, and there was no sound in the piazza except the hum of cicadas. They had been heavy that year, and a swarm of locusts always played hell with a harvest.

Prime Minister Facta should issue a decree proclaiming the locust our national bird, she was thinking when she heard the sound of an approaching motorcar. Fearfully she ducked back into the doorway of the Casa del Popolo while the militiaman put down his beer and raised his gun.

"It's all right," she reassured him, seeing that the vehicle was Achille's new Daimler. Girolamo was at the controls, and he stamped on the brakes to bring the vehicle to a halt.

"Rosaria, we've got problems!" Girolamo threw open the door. "Cristina went into labor last night and it's not going well. Dr. Beniolo's in Rome, and so is Achille."

"Why haven't you taken her to a hospital?"

"We can't! There was fighting out on the Via Salaria this morning, and a huge truck was burned just at the turnoff to Cederna. I can't get the car through, and it might be too late anyway."

"Does Achille know?" Quickly she slid into the front seat, mentally counting the months. Cristina was not due for another two weeks.

"We can't get in touch with his office and Cristina's asking for you."

"What can I do?"

"I don't know," said the old man in despair. "I don't know."

I used to sleep here with Leonida, she reflected as she hurried through the little sewing room. It seems like such a long time ago.

There was a scream from the master bedchamber, and Rosaria rushed into the same room where she had given birth to Massimo, remembering how frightened she had been before, and how happy afterward.

In the same bed lay Cristina Rosselli Leone. In her anguish she had lost any modesty, and she was naked except for a bloodstained sheet drawn carelessly across her middle. Despite the open window the room was like a furnace, and Crissi was bathed in sweat. Valeria, who was sponging her face, caught Rosaria's eye and shook her head firmly. Meeya stood in a corner, wringing her hands in despair.

"Crissi, it's me." Rosaria hurried forward, noticing that Cristina had gained almost no weight during her pregnancy, which made her stomach seem unnaturally distended. Her legs were spread wide apart, and there were spots of blood on the mattress between her thighs. Her face was very pale. "How close are the pains?"

"A few seconds. God, Rosaria, I'm so scared," Cristina cried as another contraction swept over her. "I'm running out of strength. Oh, here's another one!"

As Cristina's body heaved with the convulsion, Rosaria quickly inspected her birth canal, finding that she was hardly dilated at all. The opening was no bigger than a hundred-lira coin. The baby seemed to be a healthy size, and Cristina's pelvis was too small. It was hopeless.

"Crissi, how long has it been like this?"

"Since just after midnight," the woman gasped, pointing to her black medical bag on a side table. "Rosaria, we have to do a cesarean section. Everything is there."

Rosaria was stunned by the proposal. Instinctively she backed away from the bed, remembering from her childhood how Sandro and the other men had once performed a cesarean on a horse. There had been blood and torn flesh everywhere, and in the end the poor mare had died in agony, although the foal had survived. "I can't do it without you," she stammered. "I can't!"

Cristina screamed with another contraction. "You have to. If not, the baby and I both die."

"But I don't know what to do," Rosaria quailed as Cristina rode out another useless, horrible labor pain.

"You've seen me do it." Cristina seized her hand, panting desperately. "There's a bottle of ether and you saw how I applied it when we delivered Tiziana's baby. Use a lot and make sure I'm completely unconscious before you start. I'm not afraid to die, but I don't want to wake up until it's all over."

"Crissi, I can't."

The pregnant woman began to sob wildly as another spasm battered her frail body. "Are you going to sit there and watch me die? This is torture."

"No, I . . ."

"Once I'm completely unconscious, you cut me from here to here." Cristina threw the sheet aside and ran her finger down her abdomen from just below her naval to a few centimeters above her pubic hair. "There are some blood vessels there, and you need to clamp them. Then cut the uterus, very gently because my baby is right there. After the baby is free, scoop out the placenta. Wait! Ahhhhh! Oh, Christ, they're getting worse. Am I dilating at all?"

Rosaria looked quickly and shook her head. There was no change. A baby is never going to come through there, she realized. Oh, God, I've really got to do it!

"Get the ether." Cristina's voice grew weak, but she issued instructions methodically. "When it's over, suture off the blood vessels and sew me up as best you can. Remember how I did it with Tiziana. Keep me warm, and have the morphine ready when I wake up."

"I'll try," Rosaria whispered, she washed her hands carefully and then spilled out the contents of the medicine bag. "Valeria, mind her pulse for me."

Administering the ether was the easy part, because Rosaria had watched Cristina do it on several occasions. She picked up the wire cup designed to fit over the patient's face, and put a quantity of white gauze into it. Uncorking the bottle of diethyl ether, Rosaria splashed the gauze with the colorless liquid, smelling its powerful, sickly-sweet aroma.

"Rosaria, listen." Cristina took her hand and squeezed it. "Do your best, okay? If it doesn't work, don't blame yourself, but save my baby, please."

Rosaria saw that she was on the edge of panic. "I'll try," she agreed, slipping the wire cup over her friend's mouth and nose. "Relax, Crissi, don't try to talk."

The terror in Cristina's eyes was so awful that Rosaria had to look away until her eyelids dropped. When she glanced back at her patient, the new Countess Leone seemed to be sleeping peacefully, although the contractions continued to rack her poor body.

Rosaria discovered that she was weeping. "I can't do this," she moaned. "I'll make a mistake and kill her. I don't want to."

"You have to," Valeria said quietly. "There's a child in there. Do it for Achille."

"I'll do it for Crissi," she said, and picked up the scalpel.

"He's a beautiful child." Achille Leone stood in the study, brushing away a tear with the sleeve of his uniform jacket. "I know that I will love him in time, Giro, I know that I shall, but just at the moment, I find it difficult . . ."

"Hold him." Girolamo peremptorially handed over the newborn babe. The old majordomo seemed exhausted. They had all been on their feet for days.

Achille looked at the child Cristina had died to give him. "He's mine," he said. "I'd better start taking care of him. We'll need to get a wet nurse."

"Rosaria knows a nursing mother who might help." Girolamo headed for the door. "After the delivery she felt shaky, so I let her rest in the sewing room where she used to sleep. I'll take her home now and come back with the wet nurse."

The child was small but healthy. His eyes were still tightly closed, but he was sucking voraciously on one tiny pink fist. Oh, little man, Achille thought sadly as he cradled his new son. Will I ever be able to look at you without remembering your mother?

It never gets any easier, he reflected, walking up and down the Persian carpet and rocking Cristina's baby to keep himself from crying. Years and years of war, watching friends being killed in combat, and you never get used to it. And now this! God, poor Crissi, the awfulness, the awfulness . . . oh, God, the awfulness!

Achille leaned against a bookshelf, fighting despair and exhaustion. For the previous forty-eight hours, he had been trapped in his office at the Interior Ministry, the servant of a powerless government, watching the Italian state implode. Every day now there was savage fighting in the north as huge military formations of fascist troops attacked socialist and communist strongholds. To protest the government's inability to deal with the fascist threat, the Socialist Party had staged a fatuous general strike. The Blackshirts had promptly broken the walkout with violence, even forcing train conductors to move their rolling stock at gun point.

The civilian politicians were too frightened to respond. The army and police were divided in their loyalties. As military adviser to the Interior Ministry, he had been urging the government to respond firmly, but Prime Minister Facta seemed paralyzed. Achille longed to be once more in command of troops, but he was now an adviser, albeit an important one, and advisers could only advise.

Then, after two days of grappling with utter chaos, Achille had headed for Cederna and his pregnant wife, only to find that the road from the Via Salaria was blocked by the huge carcass of a burned-out truck. After hiking twenty kilometers uphill, he had arrived home to find that his wife had been dead for several hours.

Suddenly there was a soft, tired voice from the door. "Signor Conte, I'm so sorry about everything."

He turned to find Rosaria Lombardi at the door. Her hair was disordered and her eyes were red from crying. There were bloodstains on her blouse.

His first thought was that she was still the most exquisite woman he had ever seen. Then he felt ashamed for having focused on Rosaria's beauty while his wife lay lifeless in the next room.

"Did she suffer?"

Her voice quivered as she spoke, but Rosaria seemed disinclined to let him off lightly. "It was painful. As a nurse, she knew how it was all likely to turn out. After we gave her the ether and took the child out, she just stopped breathing. I'm sorry, but if we hadn't done something, we would have lost both of them. This way, there seemed at least to be a chance. At least Crissi believed it was the only way."

"Was it absolutely necessary to carve her up like that?"

"It was her decision," Rosaria flared quickly, only a centimeter from hysterics. "Was it absolutely necessary to leave a sickly woman alone in the last month of her pregnancy?"

"I'm sorry," he mumbled, his anger subsiding. Rosaria's face was pale and her body was trembling. For an instant he moved forward, intending to take her in his arms. He stopped himself just in time. "I didn't mean to criticize what you did. I don't know . . ."

Rosaria stood before him, her fist clenched, the tears streaming down her face "You don't know anything! I had to take that scalpel and cut my best friend open. The blood poured out everywhere. I knew I was killing her! Once we'd started, there was no way to stop, but I knew I'd never get her sewn up in time and my hands turned to jelly and I kept shaking and I failed. The first time she ever asked me for anything, and I let her down and now she's dead. If I'd only . . . if I'd only . . ."

"No, Rosi, look . . ." Appalled at the violence of her agony, Achille lurched forward, holding the baby in one arm and trying to put the other one around her quaking shoulders.

"Don't touch me!" She slapped at him wildly, and when he tried to seize her wrist, she raked his cheek with her nails, drawing blood. "You've ruined everyone's life! First mine, and now Crissi's! You should have been here! You had no business leaving her. She needed to be at the Policlinico in Rome, and only you had the resources to get her there. Instead you were off serving your stupid King. It's your fault!"

"The phones . . . the phone lines were down," he argued, but she had turned away, sobbing.

Outside, a Klaxon sounded. Achille put his hand to his cheek and felt the blood where she had scratched him. The horn blared again, signaling that Girolamo was waiting with the Daimler to take Rosaria in search of that wet nurse. Rosaria whirled and rushed down the stairs.

Achille stood alone in the study, fighting his way back to being the bold infantry commander who had helped win the World War. I love her, he thought. Perhaps she will hate me forever, but there it is. With my wife lying dead in the next room and her child in my arms, I need to face this central fact about my life. I love Rosaria Lombardi. Am I a scoundrel? Or am I just being honest with myself at last?

The baby was becoming restless. He wondered how soon they could find the wet nurse. Racing down the stairs to the front door, he found Rosaria wiping her tear-stained face with a hankerchief.

The baby began to cry, and Rosaria looked up quickly. "He's getting hungry," she said, taking the infant into her arms and calming him with quick expertise. She avoid Achille's eyes. "I'm sorry I scratched you. I didn't mean . . ."

"It's all right." He tried to smile, but his facial muscles refused to cooperate. "After you find the wet nurse, come back so we can talk. There is so much . . ."

Rosaria shook her head violently. "There's nothing to talk about. As soon as things settle down in Cederna, I'm going to marry Tommaso. Under the circumstances it would be unwise politically and socially for us to meet again."

"I just wanted to explain—"

"There's nothing to explain. You've got your grieving to do, and so do I. You've lost a wife and I've lost my best friend. You knew, didn't you, that we had become very close?"

"Yes, I know. It's strange, but there were times when I thought you might know her better than I."

"There were at least two things you didn't know about her." Rosaria turned her back on him, her hand upon the door handle. "She loved you passionately. One day she even asked me how to make you happy in bed."

"The poor child" Achille was astonished and shamed. "She came to my bed like a brave little conscript reporting for duty. I was always afraid of hurting her. We loved each other as well as we could. What else was there I didn't know?"

"Every Wednesday the two of us took the coach to Rome. I had meetings at PSI headquarters and Cristina went to the ghetto to see a rabbi."

"What for?"

"She was taking instructions in Judaism. She wanted this child to be raised as a Jew, and she found she could only pray in Hebrew."

"I didn't know," Achille admitted. She went out the door and got into the back seat of the Daimler.

"Husbands are always strangers," she said, and Girolamo drove her away.

6.

. . . .

Cowards to the last, they came in the dead of the night, the day before Cristina's funeral.

Sleeping on the floor at the foot of Tommaso's desk, Rosaria heard the trucks roll into Piazza Bixio and circle the fountain. As the motors died, her ears detected the famous Blackshirt chant, "Eia Eia Alala! Eia Eia Alala!"

A meaningless concatenation of syllables, she thought. How appropriate for them. Getting stiffly to her hands and knees, she hunted for her shoes. Fearing a Blackshirt raid, they had taken to sleeping at night in Tommaso's office on the second floor of the Casa del Popolo, reassured by the steel bars on the windows and the presence of a contingent of armed Forza Proletaria volunteers in the Communist Party Headquarters downstairs. Benita and little Sergio had joined them for the evening.

"What is it?" Tommaso, who had been snoring, sat up next to her. What a strange relationship, she reflected. We have never made love, and yet we sleep each night side by side, surrounded by children, like an old married couple.

"We have visitors," she told him as he climbed into his trousers. She had never seen him in his underpants before. He put his tie on, and then his suit coat.

" 'Giovinezza, Giovinezza!' " Outside, the fascists began singing their marching song about the virtues of a drunken youth, and the noise woke the children. Benita sat up on the couch with a cry of alarm, hugging Sergio with one arm and little Chiara with the other. Awake and excited, Massimo ran to the window and looked out.

"Bad men," he reported.

"We don't need to panic," Tommaso instructed them all. "Rosaria, you call the police while I will check the guards downstairs."

"I can just see Sergeant Cirillo breaking his neck to get here and rescue us." Moving to the desk to use the telephone, she saw from the window that the situation was horribly serious. There were six big trucks in the piazza, and even in the dim light she could see dozens and dozens of men in black shirts in a skirmish line.

Quickly putting the phone to her ear, she asked the operator for the carabiniere station. It was a moment before she realized that the phone line was dead.

"It's not working," she told Tommaso as he dodged back into the room. "They've cut the wires again."

"And the volunteers are gone," he said quietly. "Our brave Forza Proletaria has disappeared."

"But Sandro left them here to guard us," she objected. Guilt began to overpower her as she realized how perilous their situation was. On the previous day Achille had dispatched a message from his office at the Interior Ministry saying that there could be trouble in Cederna and insisting that Massimo be sent up to the Castello for safety. Rosaria had agreed in principle, but had delayed surrendering her child. Now he was in deadly danger and it was her fault. "How about the back door?"

"There are already men out there."

Rosaria peered out into the piazza. "Look, behind the Blackshirts on the other side of the piazza? That's Bruno's Lancia. I think Bruno has come for those papers."

Tommaso dug into his files, producing a packet of legal documents, enough evidence to send Bruno to jail for embezzlement if the Leone family chose to press charges. "I should never have kept this file here." Tommaso looked around quickly. "Where can we hide it?"

"Give it to me." Rosaria took the packet and stuffed it quickly down the front of her skirt into her panties and then pulled her blouse down to hide it completely.

Outside, there was a roar, and Rosaria saw one of the trucks move steadily toward the entrance to the Casa del Popolo. There was something mounted on the front, a thick steel girder meant to be used as a battering ram.

"They're coming in." Suddenly the driver accelerated and they heard the splintering of thick pine boards as the front door came down.

They froze into a tableau. Tommaso stood behind his desk, as if to receive an important client. The tiny automatic was in his pocket, but Rosaria guessed he would try to talk his way out of the situation. Massimo seemed strangely calm, and Rosaria knelt and hugged him, not sure who was supposed to be comforting whom. A sensible child of the streets, Chiara hid under the desk. White-faced with terror, Benita crawled beneath a mattress, covering Sergio with her body.

Downstairs, there were shouts as the Blackshirt squad wrenched the shattered door off its hinges. Riding boots resounded on the wooden staircase and Junio appeared in the doorway, carrying a huge pistol. He was flanked by two Blackshirts with rifles.

"Retribution," Junio declared. "Punishment!"

He's completely mad, Rosaria realized. We should have killed him a long time ago.

Tommaso Savarino said nothing. He glanced quickly at Rosaria and then at Massimo, smiled, and returned his attention to the Blackshirt commander. Junio stalked to the Mayor's desk and placed the enormous revolver against Tommaso's forehead.

"The file on Bruno?"

"No." Tommaso seemed calm.

"We'll find it ourselves, Signor Mayor," said Junio. "Now tell Rosaria to take her clothes off."

"No."

Rosaria was paralyzed. All she could think of was getting Massimo out of the room before Junio committed whatever horror he intended. Should I undress? Junio would find the papers and rape me, but if it would distract him long enough to let my boy escape . . .

"I have issued an order, Savarino," Junio said. "Tell her to strip, or I'll kill you."

"Good-bye, Rosi," said Tommaso. It was the only time Tommaso had ever called her "Rosi." That was always Achille's name for me, she realized, trying to speak but finding no words. She got to her feet, and one of the Blackshirts pointed his rifle at her.

"Then you refuse?" Junio demanded.

"I refuse." Tommaso's voice was steady.

"You did well to save your honor, Tommaso." Junio smiled, still holding the muzzle of the pistol to the lawyer's forehead. "I was going to shoot you anyway."

He squeezed the trigger.

Rosaria screamed so hard that she never actually heard the revolver's retort, but Tommaso fell over backward with blood spraying out of the top of his head and she knew he was dead. Massimo struggled to escape from her arms, and she released him, thinking, run, child, run, please, run, run away from this terrible country. Go to America, and never come back.

"And now, Rosirosalina, wipe away your tears. You have been disobedient to your lord, and there are penalties." She opened her eyes and saw Junio standing over her with the gun.

"Leave me alone." She got to her feet and backed away, wishing she could be brave like Tommaso.

"Dominion has come unto me," Junio raved. "Take off your clothes and kneel before your sovereign lord."

I'm going to die, she thought. I can't undress. My fingers won't work. This is how Crissi must have felt when I gave her the ether, knowing that she was going to die. Out of the corner of her eye she saw that Massimo had darted to Tommaso's side. Run, Masi, she pleaded with him silently.

"You killed my papa." A child's voice came from behind Tommaso's desk.

The perspiration was running down her forehead so heavily that it was hard to see. Don't talk, piccolino, she wanted to tell Massimo. Children survive by being small and silent. Crawl under something and wait until it's over.

"He was my secret papa!" Massimo was talking about Tommaso, but Rosaria could hear Leonida in him. There was a pistol shot, and at first she believed that Junio had pulled the trigger. The room went a little dark, and she could see nothing. This is what it feels like to die, she found herself thinking. There is no pain. Where am I shot?

"Mascalzone," said Junio. "You brat!" His tone was peevish. Rosaria opened her eyes in time to see the Blackshirt leader drop his gun on the floor. With an expression of deep irritation, he was looking at the red stain spreading down the front of his black shirt, as if contemplating the expense of having it laundered. "Destiny!" said Junio, turning to face the child.

Dry-eyed and confident, Massimo held Tommaso's little pistol in both hands and shot him again in the chest. "Mascalzone," Junio muttered a second time, and fell over backward.

The two Blackshirts at the door swung their rifles toward Massimo but hesitated, unable to believe what had happened.

"That's Leonida Leone's son!" Rosaria screamed, crawling toward the boy. The two fascists exchanged a quick, uncertain glance, and reached a consensus.

"Our orders are to torch the place," one of them said. "Let's do it and get out of here."

There was a clatter on the staircase and the Blackshirts were gone. Rosaria stood up, discovering that she had wet herself. The electricity went out but there was enough light for her to see Massimo clinging to Tommaso's body, and weeping for another lost father.

Leading the three children, they got out just as the Casa del Popolo went up in flames. In the confusion Rosaria and Benita slipped down the back alley, dodging Blackshirts who were busy throwing jerricans of gasoline onto the fire. Operating on pure terrorized instinct, they ran first to the Via Calatafimi, but men were already there, ransacking the Lombardi house and carrying out papers to Bruno's car. In the darkness, they quickly reversed direction without being seen. Circling through the town, they made their way along the road to the Castello.

Tommaso is dead, she thought. Tonight I will sleep in a field somewhere, and tomorrow I will wake up and realize that my Tommaso is gone forever.

"We've made it," gasped Benita. "I wonder if Count Achille will let me stay the night too. In the morning I can go to my cousin's place in the mountains."

"Of course he will. Ask him to take care of Massimo and Chiara until I can organize something," Rosaria said. "Achille loves Masi."

"Why should I ask him anything?" Benita was perplexed. "Where are you going to be?"

"They'll come looking for me, and the rest of you will be safer if I am somewhere else." Rosaria thought of the documents she still carried beneath her dress. She knelt and kissed the children good-bye. "Be a good boy," she said to Massimo, "and do what Uncle Achille tells you."

"Why can't you stay with us?" demanded the child. "Don't leave us."

"I'll come back when I can," she promised as she turned into the shadows. She paused to take her bearings, trying to remember precisely where it was in the hills that they had all once played Cowboys and Red Indians in a cave.

7.

· ·

It was one of those brittle conversations that could snap at any moment.

"So sad! What are you going to call the baby?" Giorgina dabbed at one dry eye with a jasmine-scented hankerchief. Achille watched suspiciously as his sister circled the salotto, a gin in hand, praising the flowers and looking morbidly at Cristina's closed coffin.

Bruno Benelli sat stolidly on the divan, smoking a cigarette and thumbing through the morning papers.

"Crissi and I believed there would be time for us to decide." He was trying to be polite. From the kitchen he could hear children's voices, all the little ones for whom he was suddenly responsible. Helen Higgens was spoiling them all with English toffee and stories about Irish fairies, and he wanted to be there with the children. If Giorgina and Bruno would leave him in peace, he could cuddle his new son, and tease little Chiara, teach Hosni a few more words of Italian, and try, somehow, to ease the pain in Massimo's heart.

"Babies need names," Giorgina insisted.

"I am considering calling him Ludovico after our great-grandfather."

"Is that a politically opportune name?" Bruno looked up from the financial pages of the morning *Messaggero*. "As I recall, Ludovico Leone was famous primarily for helping Napoleon fight the Vatican. Why burden the child with an anti-religious name?"

"No one in my family has ever been anti-religious," Achille protested. "We merely objected to the popes' running Italy."

"My banking friends tell me that the Vatican and the Italian Government will enjoy much closer relations in the future. Perhaps my new nephew would be happier with a less controversial name. Particularly since people will remember that his mother was Jewish."

"I will have to consider the matter." Achille cut off the debate, realizing that Bruno was delivering a quiet warning. The Pope had intervened in the struggle for Italy's soul by throwing Vatican support discreetly behind Benito Mussolini. Bruno believed that sensible people should make their peace with both Pope and Duce.

Father would have seen it coming, Achille reflected, resolving that he would raise little Ludovico to fight fascists, mistrust accountants, and regard popes with extreme circumspection. And Bruno could go to hell.

"You have so many responsibilities, my poor fratellino," Giorgina sympathized, and probed for information at the same time. "Do you mean to say that the wretched Rosaria simply dumped her child on you and vanished? You never actually saw her after the killings?"

"No, she was on the run. The fascists were after her for revenge and the police have issued a warrant for her arrest. She clearly did not want to create an embarrassment by asking for my protection."

But she could have, he told himself. After all that we have meant to each other, she could have asked.

"We will never know what happened that tragic night," said Bruno. "As I understand it, Junio went to see Tommaso about bringing an end to the fighting in Cederna, but Rosaria opened fire the moment they entered the Casa del Popolo. In the confusion poor Tommaso seems to have been killed, and the police surmise that Rosaria set fire to the building to destroy the evidence against her."

So that's the authorized version? Achille held his tongue. Hiding beneath a mattress, Benita had seen nothing, but little Massimo had described the violence with stunning precision. Would anyone ever believe that a seven-year-old-boy had killed Junio Mosconi?

"Poor Achille." Giorgina stood before him and put her arms around his neck. He could smell gin and tobacco on her breath. "Bruno and I have decided to move back here with our Teresa and help you with all these children. Now that those awful socialists are gone, Bruno can run the farm for you, and I will look after the house."

"No!" Achille realized that Giorgina had always taken him for a fool. "I am appointing Giuseppe Papafava to run the farm," he said. "Our peasants will never again work for Bruno, and I don't want you living here."

"Why?" There was a genuine tremor in Giorgina's voice, but Achille said nothing as he walked to the French windows and looked off toward the hills.

Because my Rosi is up there somewhere, he thought, and someday she might come back. When that happens, I don't want you here to drive her away.

"He's suspicious," she said as her husband helped her into the black Lancia. "Are the watchers posted?"

"There are men in the trees." Bruno pointed into the darkness. "If she comes back, we'll know."

Giorgina touched a fresh cigarette to her lips as Bruno put the car in motion. "If Achille ever sees those papers, we're finished."

"I'll deal with it," said Bruno. "Mussolini has taught me a lot about taking what I want and using the right kind of force to get it."

"I'll tell you what I think . . ." Giorgina began.

"Shut up and let me concentrate," said Bruno Benelli, and he began to hum as he drove down the road to Cederna. Putting her hand gently on her husband's knee, Giorgina fell obediently silent. Becoming a fascist has made him so masterful, she thought. He's even becoming adequate in bed.

8.

....

At the end of October, after weeks of suspense and uncertainty, Mussolini's Blackshirt rebellion burst into fullness.

Achille had been working nonstop for a week, spending his days on the road, organizing the defense of Rome and briefing policemen and army commanders in a desperate effort to stiffen their spines. Every night he slept in his office at the Interior Ministry, getting reports from the provinces as city after city fell to Mussolini's men.

Just before midnight on the twenty-eighth, Achille was standing before a large map of the Italian peninsula, using little black drawing pins to mark cities and towns and municipalities all over the north. Outside, a furious autumn storm was raging. The children were all safe and cozy in the Castello, but nothing had been heard from Sandro and Rosaria since the night of Tommaso's death. He wondered if she was somewhere in the woods, wet and cold. There were times when he wanted to resign from the army and go looking for her, but he knew she would never be safe unless he stopped fascism, and to do that he had to stay where he was.

His office door swung open and Interior Minister Paolino Taddei entered, fresh from a meeting of the Italian Cabinet. A career policeman who had made a successful transition into political leadership, Taddei had been one of Leonida's many friends. As a child, Achille remembered him coming out to the Castello for garden parties.

"Achille, I have some good news for you," said Taddei. "First you'd better update me on the tactical situation. What's the latest?"

"It's confused, sir."

"Let me look at the map," muttered Taddei. The black thumbtacks represented army posts and government buildings taken over by Mussolini's fascisti. Achille had just put a large black tack through the center of Venice, where Guido Rosselli had organized the takeover of the prefecture and police headquarters. A half dozen red thumbtacks stood for working-class districts in northern industrial cities where communist fighting forces, like Sandro's Forza Proletaria, were still offering savage resistance.

In central and southern Italy, the map was reasonably blue, reflecting areas believed to be loyal to the government. As an afterthought, Achille marked

Cederna with a blue thumbtack, since Sergeant Cirillo was once again in control. Sandro's Forza Proletaria had retreated into the hills, and Junio's death had temporarily deprived the local fascists of a leader.

"Ah, dear little Cederna," reminisced Paolino Taddei. "I haven't been there since—well, you were in Libya at the time and I went out during the interventionist crisis for a meeting your father had organized. In fact, Leonida asked me to get some boyhood chum of yours out of jail."

"That would have been Sandro Lombardi."

"The communist? Was that the Lombardi I set free?" Taddei chuckled. "Ah well, I could never say no to Leonida Leone. Now, how bad is it? It seems that my first major accomplishment as Minister of the Interior has been to lose half the country."

"Signor Ministro, it's gloomy, but not catastrophic." Achille groped for the proper adjective. "The crucial thing is to keep the fascisti out of Rome. As long as the central government still functions, then there is always the hope of bringing the rest of Italy back under our control."

"There aren't enough policemen in Rome to defend it. That means the army is our only hope. Tell me the truth, Achille. Will the army still obey my orders? Or yours?"

The Interior Minister was looking for a simple, encouraging answer, and Brigadier General Achille Leone wished heartily that he could provide one. Taddei was an honest, intelligent man, one of the few senior politicians who had stoutly opposed fascism from the start, but the situation was anything but simple.

"Ninety percent of the officers in the army would respond to a precise, clear-cut order from the King," Achille said bluntly. "In the north, there are some commanding officers who will sit on the fence, and a few who have become complete traitors. The men in the Rome garrison will do their duty if we can give them explicit written instructions authorizing the use of deadly force. I need orders tonight."

"It's time for my good news." With a smile, Paolino Taddei spread a document on Achille's desk. "This is what we've been waiting for."

It was a draft for a state-of-siege decree for the King's signature, written during the late-night emergency session of the Cabinet under the direction of Prime Minister Facta. The language was typically ornate, but it covered the main points. Law-enforcement power was to go to the armed forces, acting under the general authority of Interior Minister Taddei. The Blackshirt militia was to disband, and the police were to arrest the leaders of the insurrection. And the army had the right to shoot anyone who disobeyed.

"When can I take it to the War Ministry?" Achille felt his spirits rise.

"When it has been signed," shrugged Taddei. "Facta has an appointment with His Majesty at two-thirty this morning to show him the text. Then we can move."

"Two-thirty in the morning?" Achille groaned with impatience. They had all been on their feet for days without any serious sleep. The sooner the Italian political system faced up to the necessity of shooting a few fascists, the better.

Taddei paused at the door. "Assuming we get the King's backing, Achille, do you think the army can stop them?"

"We beat the Austrians and Germans," Achille told him. "Bring me a royal signature on that paper, sir, and I'll bring you Mussolini's head on a platter."

On the tray there were two gins, one cognac, two glasses of red wine, and a black coffee for Bruno.

I hate this tiny apartment, Giorgina thought irritably. At the Castello, one rang for servants whenever one needed them, but here I must carry drinks around in the middle of the night like a skullery maid.

Then she heard a car come to a halt on the street below. She frowned and moved to the window. The senior Blackshirt leaders from North Lazio had all arrived just after twelve for a late-night strategy session, and casual visitors did not turn up on the Via Depretis at one o'clock in the morning.

In the glare of the gaslight she saw a tall military officer getting out of a staff car. He moved with a slight limp. With a gasp, Giorgina left the drinks where they were and fled into the living room. The men were standing around the table looking at a survey chart of central Italy, and Bruno was drawing a red arrow down the Via Salaria from the north.

"Achille is on his way up," she announced.

The Blackshirts looked startled, but the unflappable Bruno merely pointed to the bedroom. "Wait quietly in there," he told the six men. Then he picked up a deck of playing cards and shuffled them. "Giorgina, put some noise on that contraption."

The Blackshirts retreated. Giorgina quickly opened the burnished mahogany doors of her precious Victor Talking Machine, purchased for two hundred American dollars from a company in Camden, New Jersey. Ever since the war, society people had been ordering phonographs of Dixieland music, and she selected a Victor Red Label phonograph entitled "Le Jazz Hot." A few turns of the crank filled the room with African-American music from New Orleans.

"Achille? What a surprise," she said a moment later, leading her brother into the living room where Bruno was placidly playing *solitario*. "The rain kept us awake, and we decided to have a drink."

"I hope I didn't disturb you," Achille apologized. "I had to make a quick trip over to the War Ministry and saw the lights."

Bruno looked up from his cards with a sneer. "Really? One o'clock on a rainy morning in the middle of a civil war, and you detour a kilometer out of your way to see if our lights might still be on? Achille, I regard that as a great favor."

Be careful, husband, Giorgina wanted to say. Tomorrow it should all be different, but as of tonight, people like Achille still administer the universe.

Achille frowned, no longer bothering to be polite. "In fact, I did come to do you a favor. Despite everything that's happened, you're family and I wanted to warn you against any further involvement with this fascist foolishness. At two-thirty, Prime Minister Facta will be taking a state-of-siege decree to the Quirinale Palace for the King's signature. Once it goes into effect, we will be sending some of your Blackshirt colleagues to prison and others to the cemetery. I suggest that you stay home and concentrate on solitaire until it's all over."

Giorgina stammered a reply. "Achille, we've had our disagreements over the years, but this a lovely gesture. Well, we're certainly not going anywhere, are we, husband?"

"Home by the fire," grunted Bruno.

When Achille left, they both watched from the window as an aide-de-camp jumped out of the waiting staff car and saluted briskly. Achille's driver pulled into the empty street, and two vigilant motorcycle policemen kick-started their machines and followed the general toward the War Ministry.

"And thus the hero departs." Bruno spoke with a tight, controlled anger. "Tall and graceful and ineffably noble, generous even toward short, fat bookkeepers whom he privately despises because we need to grub for the money and power he has had since birth."

"Bruno, don't," Giorgina pleaded. There were times when he frightened her. She went to the bedroom door and released their six Blackshirt guests.

"Nothing has changed," Bruno said to them. "We know Sandro and Rosaria are somewhere in the hills near Cederna. Get your men together and move out at daybreak. Think, Giorgina! Where would they be hiding?"

"When we were children, Achille and Tommaso and Sandro all played in a cave," she remembered. "They never let me come and I don't know exactly where it is."

"That's a start. Find them! There is a reward of ten thousand lire for the man who locates them, and double ten thousand for the squad leader who neutralizes them."

The six men looked stunned. Ten thousand lire was a lifetime's salary for most of them. "Are there warrants?" one of them asked. "Do we arrest them?"

Bruno snorted. "Signor Mussolini used the word 'neutralized.' The Duce expects us to do what needs to be done without having to draw us pictures. Do you understand?"

They understood. The Blackshirts departed, and Bruno moved to the phone, asking the operator for a number in Milan.

"If the King signs that decree?" Giorgina fretted.

"If Vittorio Emanuele wants to remain monarch of this country, he needs to think very carefully about what he signs."

"How can you stop him?"

"Mussolini will send someone to the palace who can explain certain political realities to the King." Bruno Benelli silenced her with a finger to his lips. "Duce," he said into the telephone. "Good Evening, Duce."

The waiting was hard. Arriving back in his Interior Ministry office, Achille called his brother at carabiniere headquarters in Rome. Terenzio disliked fascism primarily for its terrible music, but his colleagues in the Corps of Carabinieri were sitting on the fence, waiting to see if the Facta Government could enforce its will on the restless nation.

He exchanged the latest news with Terenzio and then telephoned the Castello, getting a grumpy Girolamo out of bed. It was reassuring to know that the lines were still up.

"It's quiet here," the old man reported. "All the kids are asleep. So was I until you rang."

"Have you had any visitors?"

"If you mean Rosaria, no." Girolamo read his mind perfectly. "But Bruno was in Cederna this afternoon with a couple of Blackshirts. They picked through the wreckage of the Casa del Popolo. Everybody wondered why."

"So do I, and it makes me nervous. Make sure the gates are closed and the windows are sealed. Will you and Giuseppe Papafava get out some rifles and take turns mounting guard?"

"I'm eighty and Giuseppe's got no legs," retorted Girolamo. "But if Mussolini comes by, we'll turn Massimo loose on him."

Achille made another call, to Army Headquarters, briefing a uneasy major general there on the contents of the prospective royal decree, but he was running out of things he could usefully do until they were given their marching orders. At three, he heard cheering in the Interior Ministry foyer, and rushed down the corridor in time to see Luigi Facta returning from his appointment with King Vittorio Emanuele. It was still pouring outside, and all the politicians were wet.

Feeling optimistic, Achille stood at the top of the stairs, cheering with the others and watching the procession of aides and ministers and secretaries and bodyguards file through the lobby. The Ministry was filled with people; it was hard to remember that it was the middle of the night.

As part of Facta's entourage, Paolino Taddei followed the Prime Minister to the top of the stairs, chatting with him quietly, but he took his leave at the first landing and joined Achille Leone. The Interior Minister looked less than ecstatic.

"I don't know what to say," Facta whispered quickly. "In concept, His Majesty approved the text of the state-of-siege decree, but he didn't actually sign it. He told the Prime Minister he will put his signature to it as soon as it is properly printed and ready for distribution."

"We're in the midst of a revolution!" Achille burst out. "Why couldn't our bureaucratic sovereign just put his name at the bottom of the paper and let us get on with it?''

"Perhaps he's being cautious.''

"He's stalling for some reason. What's going to happen between now and dawn that could possibly make a difference to him?''

"You can't hurry a King,'' Paolino Taddei reminded him.

"He's not going to be King much longer unless he starts taking this seriously! It's three in the morning, and Mussolini can do a lot of damage with a few extra hours.''

"We're getting the presses working now. Facta has another appointment with His Majesty at nine-thirty in the morning,'' the Interior Minister assured him. "Listen, we know the proclamation is coming, so we need to review our emergency plans. Achille, get out on the streets and check the status of the Rome Garrison. Tell those commanders on the periphery that they should need to stand fast until morning. Then go to the War Ministry, brief the General Staff, and tell the key people I want them here for a conference at dawn.''

"I'm on my way, sir,'' Achille replied, but Taddei held his arm, walking down the corridor with him, calm, but talking with obvious emotion.

"This delay is just a tiny setback, Achille. We're going to win today. And your father would have been proud of you.''

"I sat in an office, made a lot of phone calls, and moved pins around on a map,'' said Achille wryly. "Father would have shot Mussolini and then gone to bed with a woman and a bottle of champagne.''

"When are you going to stop comparing yourself with Leonida Leone?'' the Interior Minister demanded. "Your father was good at bold, romantic swoops, but here we've been managing a complicated twentieth-century political-military crisis. Leonida would surely have done it differently; I'm not sure he would have handled your end of it better than you did. When this is all over, I'm going to send you home with a bottle of champagne. You can find your own woman.''

Achille shrugged to hide his emotion. "Thank you, sir,'' he managed to say. "I just hope we can clean up the mess without too much bloodshed.''

"We can. Listen, once we have this crisis behind us, you and I and the other democratic liberals need to sit down and decide what kind of Italy we really want,'' said Taddei warmly. "We need to bring in the more open-minded Catholics and the reformist socialists and build a new coalition that can get something done. Fascism has cost us a year's worth of progress.''

"We'll need a new Prime Minister,'' Achille put in. "For what it's worth, sir, you're my candidate.''

Taddei was visibly touched. "If that should ever happen, I would need a young deputy with a good war record and a famous name.'' He smiled. "Meanwhile, we've got a war conference in my office at sunrise. Bring me my generals!''

• • •

"Driver, the Via Nomentana is next," said Achille, using a flashlight to consult a map of Rome. Outside the staff car the rain was slashing down furiously, making it difficult to navigate, but thus far his tour of inspection had been successful. The Rome garrison commanders were nervous, since loyalties were shifting beneath their feet, but all of them would obey a direct command from the King. Soldiers like precise orders; everybody was encouraged by the news that they would have directions in the morning.

"Yes, sir. I think the garrison's at Porta Pia." The chauffeur maneuvered the staff car through the darkened streets on Rome's eastern periphery. A moment later they pulled up to an army checkpoint and stopped. Achille jumped out, seeing that the troops had constructed a barricade across the Via Nomentana with barbed wire at either end and a movable barrier in the middle. There was a major in command of the detachment, and he rushed up to salute, visibly frightened.

"Signor Generale, they'll be back any minute now . . . they say we have to let them through."

"Who? Steady on, man. What the hell are you talking about?" Feeling the rain trickling down the back of his neck, Achille followed the officer to the barrier and looked out east along the Nomentana. In the flickering light from the gas-fired street lamps he could see a huge mob, perhaps five hundred men, wearing water-soaked black shirts and sheltering beneath the trees, obviously waiting for someone to tell them what to do.

"How many men do you have?" Achille asked quietly.

"A platoon, sir," replied the major. "It was all quiet until a few minutes ago, when that crowd arrived. Their leader came up to the barrier and said his men had permission to march into Rome. When I said my orders were to keep them out, he went back to call his headquarters. He was really polite and said that his people were all veterans who didn't want to fight with the army. But if they decide to push by us, we can't stop them with forty men."

"You can and you will." Achille told him. "Your orders—"

"Signor Generale, I don't know what my orders are!" the major exploded. "They keep telling me to keep the fascisti out of the city center but to avoid bloodshed. When I called my headquarters, they told me to use good judgment and act in my country's best interest. I want to know whether to open fire or not!"

"We'll have a royal edict in the morning."

"Sir, we could all be dead in the morning. They're Italian citizens. This is an Italian street. What authority do I have to tell them they can't walk down it?"

"Damn, listen . . ." Achille began hotly, but he was interrupted by a ghostly chant. "Eia Eia Alala! Eia Eia Alala!" sounded a chorus of several hundred voices. The two officers rushed to the barricade and peered out into the rain. Achille was soaked and his hands were slippery as he unsnapped his holster and took out his side arm.

There was a series of popping sound as the Blackshirts shot out the street lights, plunging the Via Nomentana into darkness. "Eia Eia Alala! Eia Eia Alala!"

We keep fighting the same battles in the same places, Achille thought as he watched the raucous mob lurch toward him. Great-grandfather Ludovico fought the Papal Army here when Napoleon took Rome away from His Holiness, and Grandfather Massimo scrapped with the French here when Garibaldi retreated from the city in 1849. Father marched right down the Nomentana in 1870 and shot his way into Rome, just like those Blackshirts are trying to do.

And I'm as good a man as any of my ancestors. So we're going to stop the bastards right here!

"We're going to warn them once," he told the major quietly. "Have your trumpeter sound the riot alarm. If they fail to halt, give the order to open fire."

A trumpet call echoed thrice along the Nomentana. Every subversive in Italy knew this to be the universal warning: stop or we open fire.

The insurgents seemed to hesitate for a moment and then stumbled forward as their leaders drove them on. Most of them seemed to be armed with military rifles, stolen from army arsenals. "Eia Eia Alala!" they shouted defiantly. "Eia Eia Alala!"

"You scum! You shall not have my country!" Achille shouted at them. "Turn around and go home or I'll send you to hell!"

"Cornuto!" someone shouted back. "Cuckold!" Knowing they outnumbered the soldiers ten to one, the Blackshirt mob marched closer and Achille knew that he was going to have to open fire. It was the first time in his career he had looked forward with pleasure to bloodshed.

"Major, tell your men to lock and load," he said levelly. "You will fire on my command."

"They'll kill us all! I don't have any legal authority to open fire!"

"I'm giving you the order."

"Sir, who gave you the authority?" the major challenged him, more frightened of five hundred surly fascists than he was of one brigadier general with a pistol. Briskly Achille pushed the major aside and climbed on top of an ammunition box.

"Boys, this is General Achille Leone!" He raised his voice loud enough to be heard by both the platoon of Italian infantry men and the front rank of approaching fascists. "On my command, one well-aimed fusillade to our front! Ready, aim, fire!"

There was a murmur of dismay from the Blackshirt rabble, who had not expected this. With his own side arm, Achille began firing in the direction of the advancing mob, and there was a ragged volley as the army platoon blasted the front rank of the advancing Blackshirts. Then the platoon got into the spirit of things and blazed away for five full minutes before the noncoms could get them stopped.

Achille jumped down behind the barricade, expecting a countervolley, but instead there were screams of pain and injury as the fusillade took effect. Leaving a lot of dead Blackshirts behind on the cobblestones, the Blackshirts scampered east along the Nomentana.

"Now that wasn't hard, was it?" Achille turned to the major, prepared to forget the man's insubordination if he seemed prepared to obey orders from this point forward. But the barricade commander was gone.

Worried, Achille put a lieutenant in charge and told him to shoot anything that moved. Then he went back to the Interior Ministry.

"We need to confiscate every truck in the northeast, and start working the back roads." Guido Rosselli knew that he was irritating the leader of the fascist movement in Venice, but he was too tired to care. "Interior Minister Taddei will have every north-south railroad line blocked by dawn."

"How do you know?" The Venetian Blackshirt chieftain was charismatically stupid. Each of the regional fascist potentates was called a ras, and to Guido's disappointment most of them had turned out to be intellectual lightweights, except for the ones who were clever criminals. The ras of Venice was one of the stupid ones.

I know because Taddei is being advised by Achille Leone, Guido thought. I've been sitting here in the Venetian Fascio di Combattimento all night trying to slip Blackshirts past his roadblocks, and Achille has been sitting in the Interior Ministry devising ways to stop me. This is trans-peninsular chess, and I can't get some of my pawns to go out in the rain.

"Look, our problem is logistics," he began the complicated explanation again, as the transportation committee gathered around the table and pondered the maps he had spread out before them. "By now we should have five hundred men past Porta Pia on the Via Nomentana, but we need ten times that many men to take the city."

"But it's pouring out there," the ras observed. Guido felt his patience slipping. It rained a lot during the Great War, he complained mentally, but we still managed to win. Where are all those heroes now?

Guido particularly resented the fact that Mussolini was still hunkered down in his office in Milan, figuring the odds and covering his ass. Why isn't our magnificent Duce out there in the rain, being brave?

"Rosselli, phone for you," someone called from down the corridor, and Guido wearily left the ras and his transportation committee to puzzle over railway schedules. Alone in a private office, he picked up the phone and heard Bruno Benelli's tenor voice.

"Guido, we've had a massacre here," said the bookkeeper. "That unit you sent us got stopped on the Via Nomentana. Achille turned up and got the army to open fire. He killed a couple of dozen and chased the others away. We now have no fascist forces in the city. Where is everyone?''

''Up here; we've been told that the King has authorized the army to use force,'' Guido countered. ''When my less heroic Blackshirts hear about the Via Nomentana they're going to hide in the cellar until this is all over.''

''Listen, the King hasn't signed anything yet, and Achille's action was illegal,'' Bruno assured him. ''Get me twenty or thirty thousand Blackshirts marching on the capital looking suitably fierce, and we will triumph. Achille is good at war, but this is only opera, and all we need are some spear carriers on the stage.''

''I'll do my best. There's a group on the Via Salaria that should be at the north gates of the city before dawn.''

''Good. When the Via Salaria group passes Cederna, your column commander should send fifty good men up the road to help me deal with Sandro and Rosaria Lombardi,'' Bruno added. ''Lombardi is still up in the hills with a force of maybe twenty men and some machine guns, and the situation needs to be rectified.''

''Rectified? What's going to happen to Sandro and Rosaria?''

''In this kind of contest there are winners and losers,'' Bruno drawled carelessly. ''What would have happened to us if the Communist Party had marched on Rome?''

The Lombardi family would have spared my life, Guido told himself uncomfortably as he muttered an assent and put down the phone. Sandro had been a good man in combat, and Rosaria had been Crissi's best friend.

Guido was strangely upset at the idea of Achille fighting battles without him. It seemed fundamentally wrong, the two of them being on opposite sides. Reluctant to tell his colleagues about the Via Nomentana massacre, he leaned against the conference room door instead of barging in.

''I don't care what that one-armed kike says, I'm not moving until it stops raining,'' he heard the Ras saying through the door. There was the clink of glasses as the fascist leaders relaxed over a drink.

The building was empty, except for the transport committee. Outside, the rain was still falling, and it was nearly dawn. Somewhere there was a phone ringing. It doesn't matter what they call me, he told himself. It's the idea that counts, an Italy free of Marxism, a strong and assertive Italy.

''When we take over, we're going to kill every damn communist,'' the drunken conversation continued.

''First we kill all the Masons, and then we kill the communists,'' somebody disagreed. There was a peal of laughter.

''No, first we kill the Jews, then the communists, then we torture the Masons to death.''

''Shut up,'' said the ras, and Guido put his ear to the door. ''We kill the Jews last. We're going to need them a little longer.''

''But eventually?''

"Eventually, yes; of course, eventually."

No, no, he thought, that's just so stupid! Abruptly he found that he was short of breath. The one-armed kike needs some air, he decided, and he moved quickly toward the door.

Outside, black was just turning to gray, and the rain had become drizzle. Wandering without destination, Guido stumbled down a side alley, and found himself at the Fondamenta Nuove station as the north-bound vaporetto splashed up to the dock.

It was empty except for the crew, and he climbed aboard. There was a thick mist rolling in off the lagoon, and the north shore of Venice disappeared behind him as the boat bobbed through the ocean swells. It means nothing, he told himself. The movement is not inherently anti-Semitic. Other Jews support Mussolini, although not many, and it is inevitable that stupid people will say stupid things.

"San Michele," called the conductor. They were at the island cemetery and Guido went ashore to visit his mother's grave. The day we buried her, he remembered, Achille told me that fascists hated Jews, and we ended up cursing each other.

At what precise point did my life turn to shit? When did I stop being happy? He stumbled along a gravel path through the half-light of early morning, with a row of mausoleums on his right. It wasn't losing my arm, not really . . .

There were noises in the mist, the sound of boys laughing. Guido stopped in the part of the cemetery where the poorer Jews of Venice had always buried their dead beneath simple tombstones. His mother's more elegant tomb was farther along, in a part of the cemetery reserved for rich dead people.

Laughter? At this hour, there was no legitimate reason for anyone to be here, not laughing, and Guido flattened himself against a cypress tree, trying to see, thinking that they might be *tombaroli, grave robbers.*

The wind suddenly shifted the mist, and four adolescent boys came into clear view. They were working their way down a row of gravestones, inspecting each one, and kicking over those that bore the Star of David.

Guido got his pistol out and fired into the air.

"What do you want from us?" he screamed as the boys scattered.

"That you should go away," one screamed back. "Go back to your own country!" Guido fired in the direction of the voice, but he never could shoot properly with his left hand. After a while he put his pistol away, sat down on his mother's grave, and wept.

Fatigue was closing in. Achille stumbled back into his office just before five and stretched out on an office couch. His was dizzy with exhaustion and closed his eyes. This is for my children, he told himself. All our children. What kind of Italy would fascism give us?

He thought about them all, little Ludovico, sucking his way through the wet nurses of Cederna, and Hosni, good at sports and bad at Italian, and

Chiara, who liked going to church, and Massimo, the sad, cerebral child who had lived with them since his mother's disappearance in August.

He closed his eyes and experienced a moment of intense melancholy as an image of Cristina swam into his consciousness. The sorrow is always going to be there, he told himself. I loved her as well as I could; she loved me better than I could love her back. She gave me a son, and there is no way of thanking her for him now. It's . . . it's just over.

Exhaustion claimed him, and he slept, lying on his back, one foot on the floor. At some point he slipped into an erotic dream of surprising intensity. There was a naked woman making love to him, kneeling over him, taking the active role, pleasuring him with her hands and deep breasts. He woke up with an erection, breathing heavily, almost at the point of orgasm, realizing in agony that the dream woman had been Rosaria.

It was just before dawn. There was no point in trying to sleep now. The rain seemed heavier than before, and if there were Blackshirts marching on Rome, they were getting wet. And if Rosaria is in the hills with the revolutionaries, he shrugged, then she is getting wet too.

He took his father's whiskey flask and stood at the window of his office, drinking and listening to the thunder and watching the lightning dance across the breast of the sleeping city.

9.

. . . .

She awoke, as always, thinking about her child.

Massimo, Massimo, she spoke in her mind, it's been weeks and weeks since I've seen your little face. Is your brother Achille taking good care of you? However he feels about me these days, he has always loved you. Is Valeria giving you goose eggs and goat's yogurt for breakfast, or is she spoiling you with chocolates from Perugia? Has Girolamo told every moment of the Battle of Calatafimi? Are you happy? Or are crying for your mother?

No, no, you're sound asleep in your bed in Castello Leone, she realized, seeing that it was still a few minutes before dawn. Are you having sweet dreams, or nightmares about how that wicked man killed your Uncle Tommaso? Do you remember how you took Tommaso's gun and shot Junio? Or has your child's mind blocked out that awful moment?

And my poor Tommaso is truly gone, she mourned the gallant lawyer as she crawled out of her sleeping bag. He was my port in every storm. Life would have been so simple if I could have loved him instead of Achille. In all the years he was my friend, I never let him take me to bed and he never insisted. Was that right? Somehow it would have been a betrayal of Tommaso's honor—to lie in his arms, accepting his caresses while I dreamed of Achille.

Will I always dream of Achille? Does he ever dream of me?

It doesn't matter, but life is less complicated if I admit to myself that Achille is the only man I can ever love. Even if I never see him again. Even if he never loves me back.

It was cold and damp in the cave, with condensation flowing off the limestone walls, and she felt a stiffness in her muscles as she pulled a ragged wool sweater over her nightdress. Sandro's big body was curled into a ball. She touched his shoulder, but he was solidly asleep, and she decided to let him slumber until after she had made the morning porridge for the five remaining members of their Forza Proletaria.

At the mouth of the cave, the machine gun sat where they had left it the night before, pointing toward Cederna and covering the valley below them. But the men were gone.

She sighed, feeling a mild irritation, more over the manner of their departure than the desertion itself. "They didn't need to sneak away at night," she grumbled. Sandro would have understood. In a sense, it was a relief. Now that they were finally alone, Sandro would have to accept that the revolution was years away or even decades or maybe would never come. In the meantime, they could begin to make plans.

Lifting the hem of her nightdress to keep it dry from the dew, she tiptoed a few steps from the cave, watching the sun crest the horizon over the Tyrrhenian Sea. We can't go on living like savages, she decided as she squatted to urinate behind a spiky juniper bush. It's the end of October, and when winter comes down over the Alps, we'll . . . suddenly, she heard a stranger's voice.

"It's up there somewhere."

She froze, estimating that the sound was not more than a few dozen meters away. Carefully she made her way on hands and knees back to the mouth of the cave. Sandro was stirring. As she caught his eye, she put a warning finger to her lips and pointed toward the valley. He nodded, crawling out of the cave with his big army pistol in his right hand.

"Blackshirts." He followed her pointed finger with trained eyes.

Together, they crouched on the far side of the cave, watching as the militiamen made their way up the side of the hill. There were a dozen men in the squad, each carrying a rifle. Some of them were fat, and they all seemed to be panting with the exertion of the climb.

"Your Forza Proletaria has decamped." She scooped up her leather bag and her dress. "We've got to run."

"Those Blackshirts aren't professional soldiers," Sandro objected. "I can take them."

"Then Bruno would send a regiment up here to kill us. Let's go before they see us."

Sandro nodded reluctantly. He loaded up as many weapons as he could carry and led her down the opposite side of the hill. "If we can make it to Genova, I have friends in the port who will get us on a boat for Russia."

"Russia?"

"It is the only sanctuary we have left. If the revolution fails there, then it fails everywhere."

"But we need . . . I need to get Massimo," she whispered urgently.

Behind them, there were shouts as the Blackshirts discovered the deserted machine gun. An instant later the early-morning stillness was shattered by a powerful detonation.

"They rolled a grenade into the cave." Sandro swore. "The bastards weren't going to take us alive. Let's go."

They began to run, trying to make as little noise as possible, but desperate to get as far away as possible before the militiamen discovered that there were no bodies in the cave.

After a kilometer Rosaria halted, out of breath and desperate. Her bare legs were lacerated by thorns and prickers. "I've got to go back for Massimo. You don't have to come."

"It's too dangerous. Bruno will be waiting for us to turn up there and ask Achille for protection."

"I can't leave without my son."

"Achille may not be able to keep you safe," Sandro objected. "We have no idea what's happening in Rome, but if Mussolini seizes the government, they may arrest Achille."

"He will find some way to protect me." She took his hand and began to lead him through the trees and down the side of the hill. Cederna was ten kilometers to the west.

"How do you know?"

"Because he loves me," she said. "Let's go."

"I'll get the printed text out to you within the hour," Achille said into the phone, looking at his pocket watch for the tenth time in as many minutes. "And in the meantime, Colonel, I should not have to plead with you to do your duty. It is the wish of your King that the Blackshirts be kept out of the city. Do it!"

He put down the phone impatiently. It was well past ten in the morning, and by now someone should have brought him signed copies of the state-of-siege proclamation for distribution to the troops circling the capital. Militarily, the March on Rome had fizzled. Tens of thousands of fascists were camped in fields on the periphery, but no more than a handful had slipped into Rome itself, and the army had held firm.

Since 9 A.M., however, disturbing reports had been coming in. According to army commanders, Blackshirt leaders had been strolling peacefully up to military blockades, politely challenging the army's legal authority to keep them out of Rome. Achille had been promising his brother officers a definitive piece of paper since dawn, and it was time to deliver.

He sensed that something was wrong the moment he left his office to walk down the long corridor to the suite of rooms occupied by Paolino Taddei and his staff. The Interior Ministry Building had been throbbing with activity for weeks, and now, suddenly, the place had gone quiet.

Taddei's outer office was nearly deserted except for a secretary who was sobbing into a hankerchief. Achille pushed by her and found the Interior Minister sitting behind his desk sorting absently through some papers. The politician looked up, but he seemed distracted.

"Ah? Oh, General Leone, yes, you're still here then." He fell silent for a moment. "What was your grandfather's name?"

"He was called Massimo." Achille was perplexed. "Signor Minister, where's the decree?"

"That's right, Massimo Leone," said Taddei vaguely. "He served under Garibaldi in 1849, didn't he, defending Rome against the French?"

"Grandfather fought valiantly, but we lost that battle."

"We seem to have lost another valiant battle today," said Taddei. "For some reason we are all unable to comprehend, His Majesty has chosen not to sign the state-of-siege decree. This means that we lack the legal authority to use force against Mussolini's people."

Achille felt the room spin. Taddei folded some papers into a briefcase and stood up to don his overcoat. Achille supported himself with his back against the door.

"What went wrong?"

Taddei shrugged helplessly. "The King is not a very brave man. Obviously someone managed to frighten him."

"What's going to happen?"

"Luigi Facta submitted the Cabinet's resignation to the King and went home."

"Who will replace Facta?"

Taddei looked at him sadly for a moment and then walked to the door. "After the usual consultations, I believe that His Majesty will invite Benito Mussolini to form a government. I don't know who else could control the situation."

"Then we've lost? Utterly?"

"My boy, you said last night that Leonida Leone celebrated victories with a woman and a bottle of champagne. I'll tell you something else about your famous father."

"What?"

"He dealt with defeat in precisely the same manner. Go home, Achille. We don't work here anymore."

His first thought was of Rosaria Lombardi. My public life seems to have come to an end, he thought bitterly. But there is an unfinished chapter in my private life. I want that woman in my arms. And there is nothing more to keep me here.

He rushed down the stairs toward the street, wondering if he still had enough authority to commandeer a staff car to take him to Cederna. In the lobby was a solitary attendant pushing a broom across the cold marble floor, sweeping up thousands and thousands of cigarette butts.

There was a squad of carabinieri at the front door, which was unusual because the Interior Ministry had its own police force. The carabinieri troops were led by an unshaven sergeant who was smoking a cigarette, and Achille saw that they were pointing their weapons in his direction. He kept his hand carefully away from his side arm.

"What's the meaning of this?"

"Signor Generale, I have to ask you to return to your office," said the NCO, uncomfortable with his role, but obviously determined to carry out his orders.

"Am I under arrest? Why?"

"Not arrested, but detained. My orders are to confine you to your office until . . ."

"Until what?"

"Until I get new orders." The sergeant gestured toward the staircase and Achille marched back to the second floor. The police steered him directly to his own office and shut him inside.

"What am I accused of?" he shouted through the door.

"I don't know, sir," said the sergeant. "Being on the wrong side or something. The city's filling up with Blackshirts and they don't like you very much, so you'll be safer here. Now be quiet, sir."

Christ! He rushed to his desk and tried to call Terenzio, but the phone was dead. His wounded leg had been hurting all morning and he stretched out on the couch, feeling dizzy from exhaustion. It was comfortable, and the building was very quiet. With surprising ease he fell asleep, and dreamed of nothing.

10.

"Achille!"

There was a shout. In the confusion of solid sleep, he imagined himself once again in that Udine hotel with Rosaria. Who was shouting?

"I'm not coming back," he muttered indistinctly. "I'm staying here."

"Achille?"

He sat up, looking for Rosaria through sleep-crusted eyes, but instead found himself fully dressed on a couch in the Ministry of the Interior. His brother Terenzio was standing over him.

"Teri? God, I've slept around the clock." There was light in the window and he sat up, feeling disoriented and wretched. It took him a minute to remember all that had happened.

"I got rid of that squad guarding you but we need to get out of here before they figure out I'm your brother. The fascists are on their way into the city and Mussolini's people have requested a warrant for your arrest for murder. Guido Rosselli called me this morning, and—"

"What am I supposed to have done?" Achille got to his feet, feeling a stiffness in his back and a sour taste in his mouth.

"Multiple homicide. Did you get a platoon to open fire against a crowd of Blackshirts on the Via Nomentana? You apparently managed to kill seventeen and wound twenty-three."

"Good," said Achille savagely.

"Not good," Terenzio disagreed. "Since that famous state-of-siege degree never got signed, Mussolini's claiming you had no legal authority to shoot anybody. Guido wants you out of town until—

"I'm not asking him for favors," Achille declared hotly. "Tell Guido Rosselli . . ."

"We're meeting him in ten minutes in the Piazza del Popolo." Terenzio dragged his furious brother toward the door. "Tell him yourself."

The sky was still gray, but the weather had lifted, and the streets were thronged. The shops and offices were closed, but there was a great multitude on the sidewalks, men wearing black shirts and giving each other that stiff-elbowed fascist salute. It felt like a national holiday.

376 · · ·

"Mussolini arrived by train this morning. The King has invited him to serve as Prime Minister," Terenzio explained as he maneuvered a huge carabiniere truck past Palazzo Venezia, and leaned on the horn as they spun down the Via del Corso. Traffic was intense in front of the Parliament Building. The Blackshirt victory parade had already begun when they lumbered into the vastness of the Piazza del Popolo and parked in front of Santa Maria's Church.

The fascisti were jubilant, milling around in a great disorganized mob, with everyone shouting orders at everybody else. Some of Mussolini's troopers had clearly spent an uncomfortable night in wet fields outside the city because their uniforms were filthy, and they had not shaved. Others seemed to think the march on Rome was an exercise in tourism because they were carrying cardboard suitcases and gawking at the sights of the capital. There was no discipline anywhere and many of the troopers were already stumbling with drink as bottles of cheap grappa circulated through the crowd.

" 'Giovinezza, giovinezza!' " They were singing in a variety of keys, stamping their feet in time with the beat as they chanted their marching song. Terenzio winced at the music.

I've got to escape and organize a resistance movement, Achille thought, although he still found it difficult to accept the enormity of their defeat and Mussolini's victory. Otherwise the rest of the twentieth century will be men in silly uniforms stamping around in boots. I can't live in the desert they are going to make of my country. What would happen to my children? What would happen to Rosi?

"There's the man of the hour," Terenzio hissed.

Achille followed his brother's outstretched finger and saw Italy's new master striding across the piazza. Mussolini was only a little taller than average, but solidly built, like a peasant. He had the thick, gross features of a man who ate too much, but there was a cunning cruelty about his eyes. He walked with an actor's studied gait, neither looking nor smiling at the adoring crowd. Aides and followers rushed up and talked in his ear, and he nodded to some and frowned at others, but never spoke.

The Duce sported a Borsolino hat and a gray overcoat, but his black business suit was too small for him, and he was wearing patent-leather spats and black shoes with white panels on the tops.

Terenzio delivered the ultimate verdict. "He looks like a waiter in the kind of restaurant where you get diarrhea from the soup."

"Charlatan!" A kind of savagery took hold of Achille and he slid his automatic out of his holster, seeing that Mussolini's path would bring him to within a few meters of the carabiniere truck. Fascism could stop here and now, he was thinking. This is what Father would do.

He raised the pistol. This will mean my own martyrdom, he thought. I will kill Mussolini. His Blackshirts will kill me an instant later. This is my last moment on earth.

Suddenly someone reached in the window and wrenched the pistol from his hand. It happened so quickly, he was stunned. He turned in his seat and barely recognized Guido Rosselli. The Venetian had dark circles under his eyes and his skin was sallow, as if he had not slept in weeks.

"Whoever replaced Mussolini would be worse," Guido explained. "Italy would have a real civil war. You would die painfully. And God knows what would happen to Rosi and the children. Are those enough reasons?"

"What do you care about Rosi?"

"She's in danger."

"From you! If she's in danger, it's your fault!"

"Do you want my help or don't you?"

Reluctantly Achille opened the door and helped his former subordinate into the truck, wondering if he could ever trust a man in a Blackshirt uniform. Terenzio started the engine.

"Bruno Benelli sent a Blackshirt patrol into the hills above Cederna this morning to eliminate Sandro and Rosaria," Guido explained quickly. "The Lombardis slipped into the Castello Leone, but Bruno was waiting for them and the building is surrounded. He's going to kill them, Comandante."

Achille felt his heart wrench as a furious Terenzio took the truck careening out of the Piazza del Popolo. They hit one hundred kilometers an hour as they roared through the Borghese Gardens and onto the Via Salaria. Then they turned toward Cederna and Terenzio put the accelerator to the floor. Achille braced himself against the dashboard. "Thanks for telling me, old friend," he said finally. "I expected to see you marching in triumph with Benito."

Guido glanced at him quickly, and then frowned. "I'm going to march by myself for a while," he said.

"Be careful."

Rosaria watched as her brother pushed the Olivetti to one side and propped his gun on the sill of the study window. It was getting too dark to see clearly, but he got off a single shot at someone lurking in the kitchen garden.

This is where everything began, she thought, fighting off a wave of fear. There is Leonida's desk, and here are his books . . . Achille's books now, I suppose, and there is where I used to sit and type. It seems such a long time ago. If only Achille were here!

"Did you hit him?" The smell of cordite haunted the room, and a brass shell casing bounced across the Persian carpet. There were glass shards underfoot; an incoming fascist round had shattered the east window.

He shook his head. "I don't think so. We can hold them until the sun goes down, but once it gets dark . . ."

"I'm sorry things worked out this way." She was sure she had already uttered the same words nineteen times. "You didn't have to come. I just couldn't leave without Massimo."

"And I couldn't leave without you." Sandro peered out the window. "Listen, did you hear a noise? Back beyond the olive-oil shed?"

She shook her head. "I heard nothing. What are we going to do? Suppose we surrender Tommaso's file? That's what Bruno really wants."

"We're past the point where a quick compromise is possible. He's going to kill us if he can."

"What do you suppose is happening in Rome?"

"Mussolini will have taken power by now." Sandro shrugged. "It wasn't supposed to have happened this way."

"Maybe Marx was wrong."

"Marx couldn't have been wrong." Sandro shook his head impatiently. "Maybe we haven't understood him properly. There is obviously going to be a crisis stage where capitalism evolves temporarily into fascism."

"And then comes the triumph of socialism?"

"And then comes the triumph of communism," Sandro refined the point. "But we are unlikely to be there for the party unless we get very lucky. Look, go see if the others are all right. Keep your head down."

Carrying Sandro's enormous military-issue automatic pistol, Rosaria darted through the study to the sewing room. In the hopes that no stray bullet would find them there, they were keeping the children in the little chamber where she had once taken her siestas with Leonida.

Helen Higgens sat with her back against the wall, white-faced and silent while little Ludovico slept tranquilly through his first battle, nestled against her ancient breast. Hosni and Massimo crouched obediently at Valeria's feet, terrified and excited. Meeya held Chiara on her lap; the two orphans had formed a special bond.

"Don't move," Rosaria warned them. "Stay there, please."

"Momma," Massimo called, but she kissed him quickly and raced away, sick with depression. We can't endanger the children much longer, she reminded herself. If there is shooting inside the house, one of them could be hit. When it gets dark, Sandro and I will have to run for it, Blackshirts or not.

On the front balcony, Girolamo and Giuseppe Papafava were sheltering behind a thick stone balustrade and crewing one of Sandro's machine guns.

"There he is," Papafava shouted, pointing at a stout, slow-moving figure in the formal gardens.

Girolamo fired. "That was Bruno. Did I get him?" he demanded, but they all had to duck behind the balustrade when the Blackshirts sent a furious return volley against the stone facade of the Castello. When the firing subsided, Rosaria chanced a quick look, seeing that Girolamo had already potted two Blackshirts, whose bodies lay among the geraniums. Alas, Bruno Benelli did not seem to be among them.

"Are you two all right?"

"We'll be fine until sunset," said Girolamo quietly. "Listen, get us some mineral water and something to eat, will you? I don't want to die hungry."

Rosaria nodded hesitantly. They had bolted all the doors, but the idea of venturing down to the ground floor still frightened her, since there was always the possibility that one of the Blackshirts had somehow forced an entry.

The automatic in hand, she tiptoed down the main staircase. It was dark. The Castello's defenders had shuttered and barred all the windows, and from outside Bruno's men had disconnected the electrical current.

She was creeping toward the kitchen when the pantry door opened to her right, and a man stepped out of the shadows.

Acting on terrified instinct, she whirled, raising the pistol to fire, but the shadow moved too quickly for her, pinning her wrist to the wall, and yanking the weapon from her hand.

"Rosi, Rosi," the man whispered. Her knees buckled and he swept her up in his arms. "Rosi, it's me, it's Achille!"

She began to cry.

"I love you," he said. "I love you."

"How did you get in?" she managed to ask. Her heart was still pounding with fright. Having carried her upstairs, Achille was now kneeling by her side, holding her hand as she lay weakly on the divan in the study. Sandro had closed the shutters and gone to check their defenses. For the moment, they were alone.

"Did you forget that tunnel from the olive-oil shed? We forced the lock into the cellar to get in, and we can get out the same way. Terenzio is waiting out behind the shed with a carabiniere truck."

She shook her head with vexation. In the panic, the tunnel's existence had evaporated from her mind. Fortunately, Bruno had never known it was there.

"Your nice uniform is all wrinkled," she told him. He leaned forward and kissed her hard on the lips. She tried to kiss him back, but she was still crying. All along, in the back of her mind, she had been waiting for Achille to swoop in like some storybook hero and save her, but the reality was difficult to accept.

"Listen, we stopped in Cederna and kidnapped Father Maurizio," Achille said, and Rosaria stared at him in bewilderment. None of this made any sense.

"Why did you bring Maurizio here? He hates me."

"We need a priest to perform the service. I want to marry you."

"Marry me? Now?"

"Long engagements don't seem to work for us."

At first she assumed he was joking, but his face seemed perfectly serious. For a moment she felt like singing. Is this how the opera ends? she asked herself. The tenor marries the soprano and they live in eternal bliss . . . "This is hardly the right time." She tried to concentrate, but her thoughts were coming in fragments. I can't be married today. I don't have a thing to wear.

In fact, she owned nothing in the world beyond the ragged black cotton shift she was wearing. The fascists had burned her house on the Via Calatafimi, destroying her wardrobe in the process.

"Rosi, there may never be another time. I want to be married in front of witnesses and in our home, because we then have to run for our lives. If we do manage to escape to France, I don't know when we'll be back. Bruno wants to have you killed. Mussolini has ordered my arrest."

"Can't we fight back? Isn't there any way of getting rid of fascism?"

"Yes, but it's not going to be easy," Achille said. "At first I hoped this might only be a parenthesis in our lives, a kind of silly season we would all laugh at some day. But this morning I watched Mussolini march through the Piazza del Popolo, and realized this might be a very long parenthesis."

"You mean Mussolini wins forever?"

"Nobody wins forever, but he wins for now. We need to get married and get the children to Paris. Then we can think about organizing the resistance."

"Oh, Achille, we've been fighting with each other for years."

"Mussolini has settled all our quarrels."

"There are the children to think about."

"I'm thinking about them, Rosi, this little tribe we seem to have accumulated. If something should go wrong on our way to France, it needs to be clear to everyone that you have the right to nurture my orphans and I have the responsibility of caring for yours."

"I suppose, from a practical point of view, it makes sense, but . . ."

"My love, I'm not being practical." Achille suddenly smiled. "I want to marry you because I want you by my side for the rest of my life. I know things have always been insane between us, but . . . well, there is a simple existential choice at last. We don't have a lot of time. I love you. If you want to marry me, say yes, and we'll bring in the priest."

"Oh, Achille." She started crying again. "It seems so sudden."

"Rosi, we have loved each other passionately all our lives. This is the least sudden thing we will ever do. Say yes, please?"

"Yes," she said. "With all my heart, yes, yes, yes . . ."

For a long time, they stood in the center of the study, holding each other tightly. Achille's mind raced back to the day he had summoned her from the kitchen garden to serve as his father's secretary. How I lusted for her, he remembered, then and ever since. And now. I want her as badly now as I did then.

He released her slowly, kissing her hair as they disentangled. This is the most desirable woman in Italy, he thought, feeling the hot flush of sexual excitement. And tonight she will lie in my arms, Mr. Mussolini, and not yours. A small victory, tyrant, but one I shall savor.

"What do we do first?" Rosaria was dazed but in control, and the two of them quickly organized their wedding. Upending the great oak desk, they stacked it in front of the east window to block any incoming bullets, and then propped the couch up to cover the window facing south. When the room was safe, Rosaria ran to summon the bridal party. Helen Higgens was so frightened they practically had to carry her, but brave little Meeya led in the children and lined them all up in front of the fireplace behind Valeria, the bridesmaid.

"Would you fetch the priest?" Achille asked his best man. Sandro departed with a grin while Rosaria stepped before a mirror and arranged her hair.

"How did you get Don Maurizio to come?" she asked.

"Guido offered martyrdom as an alternative," Achille admitted. There was the sound of machine-gun fire from the balcony as Girolamo and Giuseppe Papafava treated Bruno's men to a farewell barrage. Acts of savage violence always rejuvenated Girolamo, and the eighty-year-old looked surprisingly frisky as he rolled in to give the bride away.

The pastor of Santa Teresa's Church, on the other hand, was disgruntled.

"This is insane!" His voice was deep and stentorian. "A marriage is not valid if I am coerced."

"Then do it voluntarily or we'll shoot you," snapped Girolamo. "Come on, priest, get on with it."

There was a long pause while Padre Maurizio consulted his conscience. Achille knew him to be an essentially decent man who felt guilty about participating in Giorgina's schemes. Finally the old cleric sighed and took control of the ceremony.

"Under canon law, when two people agree to share their lives, a priest is merely a necessary witness who ascertains that there is genuine consent on both sides. And so I ask: Do the two of you have the faintest idea what you're doing? There is an army of gangsters outside trying to kill you. Achille, your best man is a Bolshevik, and your bride is being sought by the police for murder. Do you want her as your wife?"

"I do." Achille's voice was firm and quick.

"Rosaria, your husband comes from a long line of violent, impulsive, aristocratic madmen much given to atheism and lechery. Do you take him to be your lawfully wedded spouse?"

"I do, sir." She managed to choke out the words, nodding emphatically. "Thank you, Father."

With a sigh, Don Maurizio made the sign of a very small cross.

"I now pronounce you man and wife," he said tiredly and sank into a chair. "Good luck and forgive me if I have ever wronged either of you. Perhaps you should hold the reception in some other country."

Achille kissed his wife. He could feel her body trembling. "I love you," he whispered. She opened her mouth to reply, but no words came out, so she kissed him instead.

From the balcony, they could hear explosions as Guido threw hand grenades into the geraniums and then helped Sandro wheel Giuseppe Papafava and several light machine guns toward the tunnel. Meeya marshaled the children down the stairs while Valeria helped Helen Higgens.

Achille looked quickly around the room. "We have to say good-bye to all this," he told Rosaria. "There's no time to pack."

"Just this one thing." Rosaria said, darting to the alcove under the east window where she had once typed Leonida's *Memorie*. She scooped up the Olivetti M-I and craddled it on her hip. Then they kissed one last time and made their dash for freedom.

"We should be there by now." Restless, Achille peeked through the canvas sides of the truck as they trundled down yet another dirt road. It was still dark.

"Take it easy." There was a hint of mischievous laughter in Sandro's voice. "You'll never make a successful fugitive unless you learn to relax."

"I'm not accustomed to being a criminal."

"You'll get used to it," chuckled Sandro. "Now stop worrying."

Achille tried to obey, since the worst of their flight was now behind them. Thanks to that tunnel to the olive-oil shed, they had escaped undetected from the Castello and negotiated a series of back roads to leave Cederna without being seen. But how long would Bruno sit outside an empty building before realizing that his quarry had fled? Surely by now the alarm would have been raised.

"It'll be dawn in another few hours," Rosaria observed.

"Terenzio and Guido will get us through," Sandro consoled her, but Achille was still worried. The passage to Fiumicino had taken most of the night because there were roadblocks all over Lazio. Guido and Terenzio were up front in the cab, pretending to be on official business. Several times they had been stopped by police and army patrols, and it had taken the combined authority of a carabiniere captain and a senior Blackshirt official to get them through without being searched. The new Fascist Government was hunting down its enemies, which meant that they could be discovered and arrested at any moment.

It was also difficult to keep the little ones quiet. Dirt roads were bumpy, and often the children had just dozed off when the truck bounced into a rut and woke them all up again. Ludovico had drunk two whole containers of evaporated milk but he was crying inconsolably, already missing his wet nurse.

Suddenly they felt the truck rumble onto cobblestones and then concrete. There was a grinding of gears, and Terenzio put the vehicle into reverse.

"I smell fish," Achille announced. He crawled to the back of the truck and lifted the canvas flap that covered the tailgate. It was still dark, and there was mist over the water, but he could just detect the mast of the *Veneziana*. Terenzio backed the truck up to the edge of the dock and killed the engine.

For a moment they all sat still and listened for danger, but the quayside was deserted. There were fishing boats making their way down the estuary toward the open sea, but no sign of the police.

There was no time to lose. Achille went quickly aboard with his key, finding the boat in good order, with ample fuel and food for an ocean voyage. Not wishing to attract any attention, he lit only one small lamp in the aft cabin so that Rosaria and Meeya could put the children to bed. The powerful diesel engine started without difficulty, and the men all came aboard to help him with the hawsers.

"After we get you launched, I'll take Valeria and Helen and Giuseppe to my apartment in Rome until things settle down." Terenzio drew his brother aside. "Helen would never survive a long sea voyage, and we'll need Giuseppe to run the estate."

Abruptly Achille found himself worrying about his younger brother. "Do you think you ought to stay behind?"

"If you and I both flee the country, Bruno will take over the Castello, and I'll be damned if he's going to live in our father's home," Terenzio said firmly. "There are no charges against me, and I'm still a respectable police officer."

"Are you sure you want to remain a carabiniere? With Mussolini in charge, you might find yourself obeying some peculiar orders."

"Achille, they've asked me to create a carabiniere symphony orchestra," Terenzio explained. "I'm going to pick my own musicians, select the music, and conduct. An orchestra is the one instrument you can still play with a stiff finger, and I'll be fine as long as I don't have to perform "Giovinezza" too often."

It was settled. Sharing a moment of melancholy, the two brothers walked to the gangplank, where Guido Rosselli was preparing to cast off. Terenzio tried to lighten the moment. "Well, you're going to sea with a Jewish baby, an Arab boy, and an illegitimate Italian," he joked. "Maybe you could get a grant from the League of Nations."

Achille chuckled, but Guido Rosselli seemed serious. "And the crew contains a socialist, a communist, and a liberal. Is there room for a lapsed fascist?"

"As long as he's firmly lapsed." Achille turned to his old friend, puzzled but happy. "Do you seriously want to come? Of course there's room, but I would have thought you could write your own ticket now that Mussolini is Prime Minister. What will you do in France?"

"I don't want to go to France. If you can put me ashore at Barcelona, I'll catch a boat to Tel Aviv."

"To Palestine? Why?"

"I'm going to live there."

"But you're Italian, and you love Italy."

"I know. But I'm also Jewish, and I'm not sure that this new Italy is going to love me back. There has to be a place where no one can kick over our gravestones, and it might well be Palestine. My nephew Ludovico is Jewish. Perhaps he can visit me some year in Jerusalem."

It was decided. The moment came when there was nothing left to do and no more time to say any of the million things that still needed to be said. In tears, Valeria went ashore and sat in the back of the truck with Helen Higgens, watching her familiar old world dissolve. Meeya and Rosaria made *panini* for the men, and Sandro took a quick course in helmsmanship.

It was still dark, but just barely. There was a mist over the channel, and Achille wanted to be in open sea before it lifted. It was time for those who were staying in Mussolini's Italy to go ashore. And those who could not, or would not, needed to make their run.

Terenzio herded his people into the truck for the drive into Rome. His eyes wet with tears, Achille waved, and as Guido released the final hawser, he turned the wheel toward the center of the channel.

The tide embraced them and the *Veneziana* fled toward open sea.

For a long time Rosaria sat on the edge of Massimo's bunk, watching him sleep and talking to him in her mind. I'll never leave you again, piccolino, she promised silently. I have a husband now, and he will always protect us.

And what kind of person will you become, my son? On my side of the family we seem destined to be revolutionaries, although not very successful ones. Your father and all his ancestors were warriors, but the world has a sufficiency of warriors. I wouldn't mind if you turned out like Tommaso, your secret papa. He was a gentle man who did nothing all his life but help people. You could be a teacher, or perhaps even the kind of doctor who takes care of children.

She lingered for a moment on her recollection of Tommaso, cherishing his memory. It sometimes seemed that he now lived in a quiet corner of her mind, where she could go to visit him.

Massimo sighed in his sleep and mumbled a fragment of some boyish dream. Rosaria stroked his forehead, wondering if all this trauma would trouble him in the years to come. Will he remember being beaten by Junio? Or suffer nightmares over the day the Blackshirts murdered Tommaso? Or will we be able to love all those sad terrors away?

On the far side of the cabin Meeya was holding little Ludovico to her breast, her eyes closed, rocking back and forth as she crooned a lullaby from some faraway African village. Cristina's baby had been fussy at first, but now he was asleep, his tummy finally adjusting to evaporated milk.

His brown eyes solemn and worried, Hosni was still awake, sitting erect and vigilant on his bunk, his arm thrown protectively around a sleeping Chiara. Kissing them both, Rosaria made Hosni lie down, and covered them with a blanket. The boy obediently closed his eyes, and Rosaria sat with him until he slept. She felt the smoothness of his dark skin and wondered what his mother had been like and whether Achille ever dreamed of her.

All these orphaned children, she thought with a burst of sadness. All those mommies and daddies gone to heaven. And all the complicated explanations we shall someday have to make.

On the deck above her, she heard her new husband sing out an order. His voice sounded cheerful, and it made her feel happy. On Achille's command, the diesel engine was switched off and there was a rapid metallic *click-click-click* from the hand crank as Sandro hoisted the main. The *Veneziana* tilted slightly to starboard as a warm wind from Africa took them reaching to the west.

Rosaria climbed the hatchway into the cockpit where Guido and Sandro were sitting side by side at the wheel, steering and talking quietly, as if they had never been enemies.

"Where are we?" she asked. The mist had faded. There were patches of blue above them and the sun had warmed the teak deck. Girolamo was snoring in a deck chair behind the mast. Passing them to starboard was a gunboat from the Marina Militare Italiana, but it showed no interest in the *Veneziana*.

"Achille thinks we're in international waters," Sandro told her. "Sardinia's down there somewhere to the southwest, and Spain's two days' sailing straight ahead."

"Where is . . ." She hesitated, having concealed her love for so long that it seemed indecent now, after everything, to say "my husband."

"Achille? He's just raised the foresail." Guido pointed. "See if you can get him to go below and rest for a while, will you? He probably hasn't slept for days, and we can manage things here."

She nodded. We are all walking wounded, she told herself, climbing onto the deck and making her way toward the bow. And I haven't kissed my husband since that insane wedding.

Inexplicably, she felt a shy reluctance to face him. I'm a bride on my honeymoon, she reminded herself. I'm supposed to feel shy.

"Are we safe?"

She approached him from behind and put her hands on his shoulders. He had been working hard, raising the Genoa foresail, and his jersey was soaked with sweat. He turned and took her in his arms.

"I think so. There is no one after us now."

"What are we going to do?"

"We're making for Barcelona. We can rest there for a few days, take on provisions and wire Lloyds for funds." He outlined their immediate future. "If the weather holds, we'll then sail through the Straits of Gibraltar into the Atlantic, around Portugal and up the French coast to the Seine River. With any luck, we could have a Parisian Christmas in my . . . in our house in Montmartre."

"Paris . . ." she repeated slowly, realizing that the leaving of Italy was less painful for him than it would be for her. He's spent his whole life going away, she reminded herself. And I've spent my life waiting for him to come home. "And what will we do in Paris?"

"We'll try to find peace. We'll raise all these children we've acquired. We'll start making life difficult for Mussolini. And we'll try to be happy. Do you . : . do you think, after everything, that you can still be happy?"

She nodded. "I think so. I really, really do think so." She paused. "I've made the bed in the forward stateroom. Come down and rest. Sandro can be captain for a while."

"All right," he agreed promptly. "This is our honeymoon, isn't it?"

She blushed, but refused to drop her eyes. "We may begin the honeymooning at your convenience, Signor Conte." I am entitled to this, she assured herself.

"My thanks, Contessa mia. We have some champagne aboard and there is a Leone family tradition about celebrating a victory in bed with a woman and a bottle of bubbly."

"Victory? We're alive and we're getting away, but Mussolini gets to keep Italy. Is that a victory?"

Silently Achille took her hand, and they stood at the *Veneziana*'s prow, watching white water rush by. "This is a victory for us," he said finally. "The morning the fascists took over, there were men and women on the sidewalks of Rome, frozen smiles on their faces, cheering even though they were sick at heart. They lost because they sacrificed their honor for what they hope will be comfortable lives. We never cheered, and we never put on a black shirt. Our last communication with fascism was a burst from the barrel of a machine gun. Father would have approved."

"We're going to be exiles," she reminded him. "The civil war is over and Mussolini won."

"The war will be over when we say it's over, you and I and Sandro," he told her quietly. "Signor Mussolini gets to keep Italy for a time. Maybe a long time. Someday we will come back and take it away from him. And in the meantime we get to possess ourselves. We won."

"I know you're right, but I'm still a little frightened." She peered out across the water. "I've never sailed before. And I've never been outside of Italy."

"I'll take care of you wherever we go," he promised. "But I don't know when we'll see our country again."

"Then we will be a nation of us." Rosaria took his hand and they went down into the cabin. "You are my only country now."

Epilogue.

....

The life of a family is like a long song. The melody changes but certain basic rhythms remain the same. It was thus for Achille and Rosaria Leone.

For the next four years, they lived quietly on Boulevard de Clichy in Montmartre. Achille took a senior position with the League of Nations, arbitrating boundary disputes left over from the Great War, while Rosaria found employment with the Paris office of the Socialist Party. To avoid future legal complications, Achille legally adopted Massimo, Hosni, and Chiara, changing all their last names to Leone.

The years were turbulent, but Rosaria and Achille were happy with their children, and the passionate love they felt for one another became the permanent center of their universe. This never changed.

After the March on Rome, an organization called the Concentrazione was founded in Paris to focus the energies of all of Mussolini's enemies. Both Count and Countess Leone became covert members of the conspiracy, using their Montmartre residence to extend hospitality to some of the most notorious anti-fascists in Europe.

In 1926, the Italian Government issued an amnesty for those accused of violent crimes. The decree was meant to free Blackshirt murderers from the fear of prosecution, but it also applied to certain opponents of the regime, and charges against Count and Countess Leone were quietly dropped.

Since the children were all now settled in French schools and Achille was intensely involved in African relief work for the League of Nations headquarters in Paris, they decided to maintain the Boulevard de Clichy house as their principal residence. In 1927, however, they made their first trip to fascist Italy to bring a seriously ill Girolamo home for the last time. Girolamo had asked to be buried in the cemetery of Santa Teresa's Church, accurately believing that the presence of his corpse would provide an eternal source of irritation to Padre Maurizio Padana.

After Girolamo's funeral, they vacationed for a few weeks in the Castello, finding that Giuseppe Papafava was managing the Cederna estate well, having reemployed Mercuzio Mercatelli as his legman and enlarged the work force to provide well-paid employment to a large number of Cedernesi.

While in Italy, Achille established contacts on behalf of the Concentrazione with the Rome anti-fascist resistance, and made arrangements for the Castello to be used as a refuge for revolutionaries on the run. Achille and Rosaria were tempted to stay, but OVRA, Mussolini's secret police, harassed them unmercifully, and Rosaria found that she could not bear living in a dictatorship.

They returned that autumn to Paris, although they made it a practice to visit Cederna almost every year until the end of the 1930s.

The children, for the most part, remained in France, and Rosaria occasionally worried that they were not growing up to be real Italians. Never progressing beyond the pidgin Italian he used with his brothers, Hosni found friends among the Gallicized Arab students who flocked to the Sorbonne. Massimo, on the other hand, had inherited the Leone family enthusiasm for the English language, and he matriculated at Oxford University in 1933 to study medicine.

Guido Rosselli bought a home in Jerusalem and married a Jewish woman from Leningrad. After a period of restlessness he joined a Zionist self-defense force called the Haganah, teaching his troops the aggressive night-fighting techniques he and Achille Leone had devised during the Great War. The two men were able to visit one another only occasionally, but exchanged letters on a weekly basis.

After Hitler's rise to power in 1933, Guido began to worry obsessively about the anti-Semitic character of the German Government, insisting that Ludovico Leone would be safer in Palestine. When Mussolini imposed a carbon copy of the German racial code in 1938, Achille became concerned enough to send his sixteen-year-old son to live for a time with his Uncle Guido and study at Hebrew University.

In many respects, Terenzio Leone was the happiest member of the family, since the political instability of the 1920s and 1930s never interfered with his desire to fill the world with beautiful music. Despite the common assumption that a policeman's band could never be more than a musical joke, Terenzio progressed from captain to colonel by building the Carabiniere Symphony Orchestra into the finest ensemble of its kind in Europe.

Terenzio explained his confirmed bachelorhood by claiming that he could never find another woman like Rosaria, but he put little effort into the search, and never talked about the mysterious corporal whose death at the end of the Great War had saddened him so profoundly. In 1928, Terenzio became very fond of a carabiniere violinist named Silvio, and the Leone family quickly accepted this young man as Uncle Teri's special friend.

Despite their private happiness, Achille and Rosaria could not escape from the political turmoil around them. Rosaria remained a stalwart member of the Socialist Party, and Achille joined a new left-but-not-quite-Marxist grouping called Giustizia e Libertà. Although he was troubled by Stalin's monstrosities, Sandro never left the Communist Party and terrified the family by making frequent clandestine trips back into Italy to organize the resistance.

At the start of the Spanish Civil War, Sandro joined the Garibaldi Brigade, a group of anti-fascist refugee Italians fighting against Franco in defense of the Spanish Republic. He was captured by the victorious Nationalists in 1939, and sentenced to death. Achille flew to Madrid in a desperate effort to win a reprieve, and would have succeeded had Mussolini's government not insisted that the sentence be carried out. The two men had breakfast in Sandro's cell on the morning of the execution, and Achille found his old friend calm and philosophical, regretting only that he would not live long enough to savor the final victory of Marxism over fascism.

He was executed a few hours later by firing squad. Suffering the worst grief of his life, Achille returned to Paris in the summer of 1939.

The political turmoil of that summer soon convinced him that a general war with fascism was inevitable. First, he fired off a frantic cable ordering Ludovico to stay in Palestine with Guido. Then he put Hosni on a plane for Benghazi, where his half-brother, Mustafa al-Sharif, could look after him. After dispatching Chiara and Meeya to Oxford to shelter with Massimo, Achille and Rosaria took the *Veneziana* from Paris down the Seine to the Atlantic Ocean. Since they were both well-known anti-fascists and certain to be interned by the Nazis, they sailed for Portugal just as the German Army swarmed across northern France.

For nearly three years, Achille and Rosaria lived in a small hotel near the airport in Lisbon, working with the British Special Operations Executive and representatives from the American Office of Strategic Services. Having finished his internship at Oxford's Radcliffe Infirmary, Massimo became their courier, flying relentlessly back and forth from Lisbon to London with false passports and munitions and cash for the Committee for National Liberation, the Italian Resistenza.

In 1943, a British submarine landed all three of them near Venice and, at the age of fifty-six, Achille took command of his last combat unit, leading the Nineteenth Partisan Brigade into the Julian Alps between Udine and the Isonzo River, the same country where he and Guido had fought the Austro-Germans a quarter of a century earlier. Massimo served as their medical officer, and Rosaria learned wireless telegraphy and cipherwork to keep the brigade in contact with Partisan Headquarters. In two years of savage combat, Achille's partisans drove the German Army from the Italian northeast.

For Italy, the war ended in April of 1945, when one of Achille's colleagues captured Benito Mussolini trying to escape over the border into Austria. Contemplating the possibility that Mussolini could be traded to the Americans for some political concession, the political leaders of the Resistance cabled General Leone for his opinion. Achille thought instantly of his friend, Sandro Lombardi, executed at the insistence of the Italian Government. "If we shoot Mussolini today," he telegraphed back, "we'll all sleep better tonight."

Mussolini was executed the next day; everybody slept better for years.

The only family casualty of the war was Bruno Benelli. In 1943, shortly after the German Army occupied Rome, Giorgina had spotted a group of Italian partisans hiding in their garden. A Nazi enthusiast to the end, Bruno went down with a shotgun to chase them away and blundered into a Wehrmacht patrol. The Germans mistook him for a fat partisan and promptly shot him dead.

Witnessing the awful scene from the Benelli garden, the partisan commando team made precisely the same error; they identified the heroically deceased freedom fighter from documents in his wallet, and when Rome was liberated a year later, Giorgina became the honored recipient of a state pension for the widows of those who perished valorously in the patriotic war against Nazism. To Rosaria's fury, Giorgina even served as the Executive National Chairwoman of the Daughters of the Resistenza until years of genteel alcoholism finally killed her. Inheriting several hundred billion lire, Teresa Benelli moved to the French Riviera, where she drank pink gin and lived with a succession of retired boxers.

When peace came to Italy, the Leone family returned to restore a badly damaged Castello. Rosaria was selected as a socialist candidate to the Constituente, the constituent assembly that wrote Italy's new and democratic postwar constitution, and she is remembered primarily as the author of Article 48, which extends voting rights to women. Rosaria remained a socialist deputy in the Italian Chamber of Deputies for years, continuing the fight for women's rights, divorce and abortion.

For his part, Achille became active in a new political organization called the Action Party. He was elected to the Italian Senate, but the Action Party always had more chiefs than Indians, and failed to prosper at the polls. By 1950, Achille had retired from politics and gone to work for the Rome-based Food and Agricultural Organization, an agency of the newly founded United Nations.

As the 1950s dawned, Massimo was the only Leone child who continued to live with Achille and Rosaria in the Castello. With his enormous talent, Massimo could have become almost anything, but he specialized in child psychiatry, setting up the Ospedale Tommaso Savarino, a clinic specializing in the treatment of battered and abused children. Since none of the Leone men ever turned out to be very good at practical matters, the administrative end of the clinic was left in the capable hands of Chiara Leone, who violated five hundred years of Leone family tradition by becoming a fervent Roman Catholic.

Ludovico Leone had always been the apple of his father's eye, but during the Second World War the youngest Leone joined an elite Jewish strike force called the Palmach, fighting to create an Israeli state during the 1948 Arab-Israeli conflict. While Ludovico continued to vacation at the Castello, he could only be happy when he was close to Jerusalem and took Israeli citizenship in 1952.

The restless Hosni Leone had grappled for years with his dual identity, an

Arab soul in a European body. He first tried to adjust to life in Benghazi, but found himself rejected by the Libyans because of his Italian ancestry, and by the Italians because of his dark skin. For a time he lived in Montmartre and was married briefly to a Frenchwoman before discovering that he was no more French than he was Italian. In 1953, Hosni moved to Cairo and worked there as an engineer until he was radicalized by the plight of the Palestinian people. He joined El Fatah the following year and became a senior official within the political wing of the Palestinian Liberation Organization.

By the mid-1950s, Rosaria had taken her pension from the Chamber of Deputies and was writing her memoirs on the old Olivetti M-I, despite Achille's predictable fascination with dictaphones and electric typewriters.

It was a new era for both of them. Italy was a democracy at last, a little chaotic and still struggling with economic problems, but everybody was free and safe. It was not something the young people could always appreciate, but there were Sundays in Cederna after Achille retired from the United Nations when the two of them would walk past the Kingdom of the Wicked and bask in the sensation of being free.

The whole family was reunited for the last time in 1955 to commemorate the fortieth anniversary of Leonida Leone's death and to celebrate the unveiling of a statue of the great warrior in Piazza Bixio.

The children came home from the great world beyond Cederna, bringing wives and flocks of children to the Castello Leone. Chiara invited a congregation of nuns. Terenzio, now going gray, brought his friend Silvio, who was bald.

With a team of bodyguards, Hosni flew in from Damascus, and there was a moment of hostile awkwardness when he first encountered his Zionist little brother, Ludovico. Then the two men hugged each other and wept, manufacturing a moment's hiatus in a millenmium of Middle Eastern awfulness.

After the dedication of Leonida's statue, family and friends piled into limousines for a trip to the Rome Opera House, where Terenzio Leone led the orchestra and chorus of the Rome State Opera in a performance of Giuseppe Verdi's *Requiem*.

As an encore, Terenzio gave them "Caro Nome," from Leonida's favorite opera, *Rigoletto*. When the applause was over, Rosaria took Achille's arm, and they went home to Cederna.